The China Factor

A Novel

Timothy Trainer

Joshua Tree Publishing

• Chicago •

The China Factor
A Novel
Timothy Trainer

Published by
Joshua Tree Publishing
• Chicago •
JoshuaTreePublishing.com

13-Digit ISBN: 978-1-956823-66-0

Cover Image Credit: Public Domain Provided by Author

Disclaimer:
This is a work of fiction. Names, characters, places, and events are the product of the author's imagination or have been used fictitiously. Certain long-standing institutions, agencies and public offices are mentioned, but the characters involved are wholly imaginary. Any resemblance to actual persons, living or dead, events, locales or organizations is entirely coincidental.

Printed in the United States of America

Table of Contents

Chapter Titles and Order of Character Introduction

Encounter
XIONG Zimo
Lucas Moore
Chris Kearns
David Olvera
Baffled
Victoria Walters
Ed Adams
Capitol Hill
Kellie (Kaili) Liang
Norman Quarles
Nathan Burke
Trish
Faces
Vera Jamison
ZHOU Shan
Connie
Rendezvous
MOY Meilin
Obstacles
Douglas Stewart
Search
Drew Foster
Aaron Foster
Harry
Lan
PHAN Nhu Linh
Mai

Chapter Titles and Order of Character Introduction

Contact
Contingencies
Bruce Hoover
Janice Doan
Exposure
YAO Jun
BUI Chau
Vinh
Family
Jenkins
ZHENG Puyi
Connections
Duong
Earnest Layton
Movement
Jolt
Curtis Campbell
Devon Conrad
Delay
Jordan Ueda
Oliver Vega
Office Visits
Ngo
Consul General (CG) McAlister
Termination
Networks
Predictability

Spring 2005

Encounters

Xiong Zimo stood outside the H Street double glass doors of the law school in the fading light of the day. He leaned against the railing on the landing of a set of stairs that led from the glass doors to the street level sidewalk, waiting. He lowered a brown leather satchel onto the concrete surface. It was a warm April evening. His black hair fluttered in the breeze. He left enough space on the concrete landing for others to exit and descend the steps to street level. He took off his wire-rimmed glasses and wiped the lenses with a handkerchief. A junior commercial counselor at the Chinese Embassy, Xiong kept a busy schedule by taking evening law classes in downtown Washington, D.C.

Lucas Moore saw Zimo and the loose hanging suit jacket over his narrow shoulders through the double glass doors as he pushed the door open. He stepped out with a backpack slung over his left shoulder. Lucas, lanky at six feet-two inches, stood half a foot taller than his Chinese classmate. Because of the height difference, Lucas took a step down so that he was closer to eye level with Zimo. He slid the weighty backpack off his shoulder and onto the concrete step. Lucas leaned back against the railing.

"Do you have it?" Zimo asked.

"It's on the laptop."

Zimo reached into his suit jacket pocket.

Lucas thought Zimo was reaching for the envelope he was expecting. Instead, Zimo took out a pack of cigarettes. He didn't offer one to Lucas, knowing that Lucas didn't smoke. While Zimo got his cigarettes and lit up, Lucas ignored Zimo but gazed down the street.

A dark older model Chevy Impala with two men inside was parked four car lengths from the corner of H and 20th Streets. One car was parked in the spot closest to the intersection and there were two vacant spots in front of the Impala. The two men had a clear view of Zimo and Lucas. Using a penlight held under the dashboard, they studied headshots of the two men they were there to question. A second car, similar in make and model with three men in it, was parked in the small parking lot across the street from the exit where Zimo and Lucas stood. They were also looking at the same headshots, resembling the two men standing across the street on the steps and landing. The driver of the car in the parking lot transmitted a clicking signal, and as soon as he received the single-clicking response, the five men in jeans and dark polo shirts exited their cars. As they headed toward the H Street door where Lucas and Zimo stood, Lucas and Zimo couldn't see that the backs of the shirts identified them as being FBI agents.

Lucas saw two men getting out of the car parked along the H Street curb. Out of the corner of his eyes, he saw the car across the street empty. Lucas reached down, grabbed his backpack, shoved it into Zimo's chest and turned. With his height and long legs, he put one foot onto the metal railing, pushed himself over it and landed in the gardened space planted with spring flowers and shrubs, his shoes trampling on newly planted flowers as he hopped down to the street level, then over a short wall and onto the sidewalk. He pumped his legs as he sprinted south along 20th Street in the direction of the National Mall. He glanced over his shoulder and saw a man's arms and legs moving like pistons sprinting in his direction. He needed to gain more distance from his pursuer.

Lucas's shoes pounded the concrete sidewalk and pavement as he crossed G Street. He turned right onto F Street. There were very few people on the sidewalk to skirt around. Lucas kept eyeing things ahead as goals to reach during this sprint. With an intersection ahead, he checked the traffic moving on 21st Street. He kept his speed through the intersection then glanced back. Lucas's pursuer was still back there, but the man had slowed to check on his target, allowing the gap between Lucas and his pursuer to widen.

Lucas wasn't a sprinter. He had been a distance runner in high school, but that was years ago. Spending so much time at a desk, he didn't have the lung capacity for this type of running. He couldn't get enough air into his lungs. But stopping at this point wasn't an option. Staying on F Street, he crossed the intersection at 22nd Street. He needed to get to the Metro subway station.

Before reaching 23rd Street, Lucas took a right turn up an alley that connected F and G Streets. Between buildings, there was little light, making it nearly impossible for his pursuer to see him given the distance between them. His chest hurt. His leg muscles strained. He worried they'd cramp before he could find a place where he could slow and rest them.

The pursuing agent was on F Street, but mid-block between 21st and 22nd streets when he lost sight of Lucas. He pressed a button for a quick dial. "Do we have anyone at the Foggy Bottom Metro?"

"Negative," was the response.

The agent needed to sprint to cover five city blocks while dodging pedestrians and traffic. He wasn't optimistic.

Lucas jogged for a minute staying out of the light as much as possible then, when he needed to be in the open, he pushed himself in a burst of speed to cover the two blocks to the subway station. With the Metro subway sign in view, he tried to look around for any indication that there were agents already there. Seeing no one dressed like the agents he eluded, he rushed down the escalator. His fare card out, he inserted it, retrieved it, and walked to the platform and headed to the far end, never looking back. Sweat rolled down his face. His shirt stuck to his skin, and he was breathing hard. Luck was with him as the lights along the platform edge blinked, signaling an approaching train. As soon as the doors opened, Lucas darted in before anyone else. He took a deep breath when the doors closed, and the train started accelerating towards Virginia.

The pursuing agent reached the top of the steps heading underground. Taking deep breaths and filling his lungs, he stood with hands on hips. If Lucas Moore was headed to this subway station and had kept up his pace, there was no way he wasn't already down on a platform and gone. He waited another minute before jogging back to meet his colleagues a few blocks away.

* * * * *

Zimo's cigarette fell from his lips. His body twisted as he put his arms around the backpack Lucas shoved into his body, but it kept slipping out of his hands. His back was to the agents coming from the car parked along the curb. He watched Lucas climb up and jump over the railing. He saw Lucas disappear around the corner followed a couple of seconds later by a man running at full speed in the same direction. Zimo didn't notice all the pedestrians standing around the intersection and staring at the chase then turning their attention in his direction.

The four agents who hadn't pursued Lucas were on the steps surrounding him, taking Lucas's backpack out of Zimo's arms. Two agents on either side had him by the arm and led him down the steps and into the car parked along H Street. Zimo sat in the backseat while the four agents stood outside, opened and searched the backpack weighted down by two thick casebooks, a binder and laptop. They searched the front zippered pocket, finding pens, pencils, and a memory stick.

Chris Kearns, the senior agent on the scene, stood next to his colleague sifting through the backpack. "Any identification in there? A name, a business card?" Chris asked.

"There's a name written on the inside cover of both books. Lucas Moore," Agent David Olvera read out.

"Let's talk to our guy in the back seat," Agent Kearns suggested. Olvera got into the passenger side front seat as Kearns settled behind the steering wheel.

Xiong Zimo sat slouched slightly as his head rested on the back of the seat. Hearing the doors open, he sat up. He squinted when the car's dome light flipped on. "May I get identification for you?" He asked.

Kearns nodded.

Xiong Zimo reached into the inside breast pocket of his jacket and pulled out his wallet then handed over his 'get out of jail' card to Kearns.

"Mr. Zimo?" Kearns asked hesitantly.

"No. Xiong is my family name," Xiong Zimo corrected.

"This card says you're a diplomat. It means you have immunity," Kearns said as he examined the State Department issued card.

"Why did Mr. Moore shove the backpack into you?" Kearns asked.

"I don't know," Zimo stated calmly.

"Were you meeting so that Mr. Moore could give you something?" Kearns asked.

Xiong Zimo thought about the question. He had to be careful answering the question. "Sometimes, Mr. Moore shares class notes with me because I can't write English so fast, so he'll let me copy his class notes."

Agent Kearns exchanged a look with Agent Olvera. "Has Mr. Moore ever given you anything else? I mean something that isn't related to schoolwork?"

"Probably," Zimo answered, keeping his answers short and vague.

"How long have you known Mr. Moore?"

"We were in classes together last semester. We became friends."

"Does Mr. Moore work during the day? Is that why he's taking evening classes?" Kearns asked.

"Yes, he has a day job."

"Where?"

"Patent Office," Zimo answered.

"Do you know what he does at the Patent Office?"

"I guess he examines patent applications."

Kearns nodded at Olvera. They exited the car and joined the other three agents who had remained standing behind the car. Streetlights and lights spilling from the surrounding buildings were enough for the five men to see each other.

"Patent Office?" Olvera asked. "If there's any possibility that this Chinese Embassy guy is trying to collect intel, I would've expected him to say Moore worked at DoD, the State Department, or some other more military related agency, not the Patent Office."

The other four agents nodded in agreement. After a long silence as they wondered what might be going on, Kearns spoke. "We'll keep the backpack. We saw Moore come out with it and his name is in the books. It doesn't belong to Mr. Xiong, and he hasn't said anything indicating he wants to hang on to it. We'll have to cut him loose. We've got Moore's name, and we'll confirm where he works. Given the tip and what's happened this evening, we need to locate Moore and question him. Something of interest to Mr. Xiong is either on the laptop or the memory stick," Kearns said to his team.

"Olvera, make sure you write down his name. We need to input it into the system. You can tell him he can go on his way," Kearns instructed. The last thing he needed was to get a tongue-lashing from his superiors for detaining and upsetting a diplomat when he couldn't even say what the man had done.

Olvera opened the back door, waving Xiong out of the car. Xiong grabbed his leather satchel and walked one block up 20th Street to Pennsylvania Avenue.

"I'm guessing I'll hear about this at some point tomorrow. But we need to find out if Moore's laptop has anything that could be of value to the Chinese. And we need to figure out if this Patent Office angle is serious. How would Moore's job be of interest to the Chinese?" Kearns thought out loud.

* * * * *

Lucas Moore felt the pressure in his ears as the subway train traveled under the Potomac River to Virginia. He heard the announcement that he was on the Orange Line. That was good news. He didn't need to transfer to a different line. What next? Money? Clothes? Stay somewhere other than his apartment? Lucas got his breathing under control, but his mind was racing. He pulled out his wallet and counted his cash. There were thirty-three dollars in it. He had his credit cards.

Six stops into Virginia, Lucas exited the train. No time to waste, he began marching to his one-bedroom apartment less than two miles away. Without his backpack, he had nothing weighing or slowing him down. He felt the evening's dipping temperature on his damp shirt. His speed walking caused his leg muscles to remind him of his earlier exertion. He wanted to jog but decided against it.

Except for headlights, streetlights and neon signs, Lucas walked in the dark. He was in speed walk mode and his mind assessed what might be going on with Zimo. He convinced himself that Zimo would avoid any trouble because of his diplomatic status. Lucas thought about his backpack. The laptop and memory stick created problems, but he realized that they would have to access them first. How was that going to play out, he wondered. Damn it! He remembered that ripped off piece of paper. As soon as Zimo or anyone else opened the laptop, that piece of paper would have the password to get into the laptop.

Before his mind could explore the possibilities, he found himself entering the first floor of his three-story apartment building. Inside the entry, the common area accessed the doors to the ground floor apartments and the stairs leading to the second and third floors. His one-bedroom apartment was on the ground floor.

In his bedroom, he pulled down a wheeled carry-on size duffel bag. He stuffed it with enough clothes for two nights, grabbed his basic toiletries, and took the small stash of cash he had in the apartment. He took off his shirt, now dry, and put on a thicker flannel shirt then called a cab to take him to a hotel a short distance down the street. He dismissed the idea of calling a friend as soon as it entered his mind. Instead of being pelted by questions from someone, he needed time to think.

Waiting for the cab with his duffel bag, he turned off all the lights in the apartment and waited in the dark. It took another thirty minutes for the cab to arrive and take him to the hotel. Once in a room, he flopped face first onto the bed.

I'm in trouble, Lucas thought. *What would they think of the material they find on the laptop or the memory stick,* Lucas asked himself. He rolled onto his back. He started laughing. He laughed hard enough that tears rolled from the corners of his eyes. If anyone had been with him, he might have seemed to have gone crazy with laughter as the tears dripped onto the bedspread. He put both palms on his stomach and pressed. After a minute of convulsive laughter, he stopped laughing and sat up, using both hands to wipe his eyes.

The documents on his laptop might be incomprehensible to most people. He chuckled. The documents included abstracts of inventions and technical writing about inventions, but nothing in code or anything mysterious. A strange feeling came over him. He inhaled deeply and thought that maybe he wasn't in as much trouble as he thought.

* * * * *

Xiong Zimo spent time in the taxi back to the embassy thinking about how to describe his evening. He reported to several people at the embassy. He had his mundane commercial portfolio and reported to one group of superiors on those tasks, but he also had supervisors who were interested in his Patent Office contacts and the information he got from them.

Walking into the embassy and passing security, he decided he shouldn't wait till morning to report.

"Is the Deputy in and available? I have something urgent that I need to report," he said to the evening receptionist. He stood, watching the receptionist call the Deputy's assistant. There were certain things that the number two man at the embassy wanted to know right away, and Zimo believed this fell into the category of not letting things wait till morning.

"He'll meet you in his office in five minutes."

Zimo took his time taking the elevator and getting to the Deputy's office. In the Deputy's outer office, he saw the head of the embassy's security waiting. A woman came out of the Deputy's office and held the door for Zimo and the security officer.

"Take a seat," the Deputy said, sitting behind his big desk. The Deputy had removed his necktie for the day, his shirt unbuttoned at the collar. His fuller cheeks hinted at too much time spent sitting behind a desk. The Deputy appeared to be a man deprived of sleep with slight bags under his reddened eyes. A cigarette burned in the ashtray next to his elbow. No grey or white shown through his slick black hair that was long enough to comb, but neatly cut short along the sides. His appearance left no doubt that he adhered to the tradition of dying his hair black to hide any change of color due to age.

"Sir, I have to report that I had an encounter with the FBI this evening," Zimo began.

"Where and what is it related to, Mr. Xiong," the Deputy asked.

"At the law school this evening when I was meeting with a contact from the Patent Office. My contact ran away. He tried to force his backpack into my arms, but the FBI took it and will probably find what he was going to give me," Zimo explained.

"Did the FBI keep you very long?"

"No. After I displayed my identification, they let me go after a few minutes."

"When is this school term ending?" the Deputy asked.

"There's only a couple of weeks left before the summer break," Zimo said.

"How many others are involved in similar activity?"

Zimo shrugged. The security officer spoke up. "We have two other staff at different law schools doing what Mr. Xiong is doing. This is fertile territory for us. Until now, we've had no exposure or problems. The Patent Office isn't so obvious because there's no clear connection to defense and security related issues," the embassy security officer answered.

"So, including Mr. Xiong, we have a total of three staff members attending local law schools and gathering information," the Deputy summarized.

"Correct," the security officer said.

"We've almost reached the summer break. Tell the other two to be very careful and let them know what happened to Mr. Xiong so that we can avoid this happening again. Someone found out about Mr. Xiong's contact. Remind our staff to be very careful about where they meet with their contacts and what they discuss in public," the Deputy instructed.

The Deputy looked directly at Xiong Zimo. "Stay away from any other contacts you have for now. No more contact with them until you hear from security," the Deputy ordered.

Zimo left the Deputy's office relieved that he wasn't being asked to pack his bags and return to Beijing.

"Increase your oversight of these three," the Deputy said, eyeing his head of security.

* * * * *

Agent Kearns was typing up a summary of the evening's encounter with a Chinese diplomat, making sure to describe his team's brief interview with Xiong and allowing Xiong to leave. He planned to let a couple of the other agents read his summary so that his team agreed on the night's encounter, but that would be after they looked at what was on the laptop and memory stick. The four other agents worked in pairs as one pair was able to access the memory stick and the other looked at the documents found on the laptop.

The typed description of the evening wasn't long. Kearns printed out the document and went to the door of his office. Leaning against the doorway frame, he saw four agents leaning in and reading intently. They weren't looking at each other or saying anything, just focused on two monitors. They'd been going through the material for half an hour.

"Are you guys okay?" Kearns asked.

All four sat in chairs on wheels. They all sat back, looking relieved to have a reason to divert their eyes from the monitors. "Anything wrong?" Kearns wondered.

"You need to try and read some of this," Olvera suggested. "Let me rephrase that. You need to try and understand this stuff." Olvera got out of his chair and gestured to Kearns to have a seat in front of the monitor.

Kearns did as suggested and stared at the monitor for only a few minutes then got up.

"I get it," Kearns said. "I'll make a call and get someone from Justice to come over. We need to have someone a bit more familiar with the subject matter to tell us what we're reading. Before we expend too much time and energy to hunt down Lucas Moore, I'd like to understand what's here so we can zero in on whatever he intended to do by giving Xiong these documents."

Before calling it a night, Kearns got a thumbs up from his team to send his summary up the chain and left a message asking for help to decipher English language documents filled with legalese, strange descriptions, and detailed drawings. If there was anything related to national security in the documents on the laptop, it wasn't apparent to Agent Kearns or his team. Kearns knew a deeper dive was necessary.

Baffled

"First time here to the D.C. field office?" a young man asked before escorting the Justice Department lawyer to her meeting.

"Yes," Victoria Walters answered. "I've been to the FBI Headquarters building on Pennsylvania Avenue, but never here," Victoria added. She made sure she had everything back in her purse and briefcase after going through metal detectors and the enhanced post 9/11 government building security procedures. An hour into her morning, her section chief had assigned her the job of helping the FBI understand what was in some documents. She taxied to the FBI's D.C. field office.

"How long have you been at Justice?" the escort asked.

"Year and a half," Victoria said. As she walked past some open work areas and down corridors, she concluded that the men's unofficial uniform was a dark suit, white shirt, and boring neckties. Most of the men had military styled haircuts. As that thought went through her mind, she smiled to herself realizing that the male Justice Department lawyers dressed similarly. She realized she, too, dressed in the women's version of that same unofficial outfit.

Agents Kearns and Olvera waited in a conference room that seated eight. The simple square configuration of the tables and chairs allowed for two on each side. The equipment in the room was all connected to a television-sized monitor on the wall and eliminated the need to huddle around one computer.

"Agent Kearns and Olvera are waiting in the conference room. Just knock," Victoria's escort said as he turned and walked away.

Victoria pushed her wire-rim glasses up the bridge of her nose. Her purse dangled from her right shoulder, and she put her small briefcase in her left hand, freeing her right hand to knock on the door and shake hands.

When Kearns opened the door to greet her, she wasn't surprised that he was almost a head taller as she was often one of the shorter people in a room at a mere five-foot-two. She kept to a habit of wearing comfortable shoes that might give her an added inch or two, but nothing more. Agent Kearns was what she expected to see. A man somewhere in his thirties, not yet showing too much of a growing mid-section and close-cut blond hair. He had a firm grip when he shook her hand.

"We're glad you're here," Kearns said smiling. "That's David Olvera."

Victoria walked to the far side of the room, shaking hands with Olvera. Unlike Kearns, Olvera didn't tower over her as much as Kearns. He was broad-shouldered and had a deep tan complexion. His black hair parted in the middle and wasn't kept as short as most of his colleagues. His hand gave Victoria the impression he did a fair amount of manual labor or had in the past.

Kearns settled into his chair as did Olvera and Walters. "We called for some assistance because this doesn't look like the types of documents we usually uncover. We opened the documents on this laptop and found this," Kearns explained and nodded toward the text projected on the screen at one end of the conference room.

"Okay, but before we plunge into reading all of this, could you scroll through it slowly because I'd like to see what, if any, drawings are in the documents," Victoria requested.

Olvera controlled the mouse and clicked through the first few pages.

"May I?" Victoria said, taking control of the mouse and clicking through the pages at her desired pace. Finishing the first document, she opened another document and skimmed through the pages and drawings, repeating this through two more documents before she stopped.

"Are all the documents you went through similar to these?" Victoria asked.

"Pretty much the same," Kearns answered.

"That's what made us wonder what's going on. There's nothing about any weapons systems or something sensitive like that," Olvera said.

"These are all like heavy construction equipment, except that they aren't for work on land. Some of the descriptions sound like things that could be used on land. But it's clear that these documents are about developing better dredging equipment and pumps. The descriptions and drawings are for excavation pumps and collecting sediment and things like that. The documents are patent applications submitted by companies saying that they've invented a machine or equipment or added to existing machines and equipment to improve ways of doing these things in dredging operations," Victoria summarized.

"Why the hell would these documents be given to the Chinese?" Olvera asked.

"There's one person we can ask when we find him," Kearns answered. "You seem to be a bit familiar with this type of stuff. Isn't there a database that makes this stuff public?" Kearns added.

Victoria nodded and affirmed Kearns's last comment. "Yes and no," Victoria said. "Looking at these documents, these patent applications were submitted just a few months ago. They're too recent. They aren't supposed to be shared or made public yet. Given the dates, these would be considered confidential, and your suspect violated the rules relating to keeping these confidential. When you do find your guy, he's going to be facing criminal charges.

"As far as this type of equipment, I've been around construction sites growing up. My father had the biggest minority-owned construction company in western Pennsylvania. Because I don't have any brothers, occasionally, my father would let me tag along with him to work sites during the summer."

"Honestly, I'm less concerned about his breaking these confidentiality rules and more concerned about the 'why'. The mystery is why the Chinese want them," Kearns said.

"Wouldn't dredging operations be important for ports, keeping them deep enough for all these big container ships?" Olvera asked.

"Yeah, but the Chinese have some of the busiest and, presumably, biggest ports in the world. The volume of stuff they're shipping to us means they've already solved this problem. Doesn't it seem logical then that they already have the latest technology?" Kearns added.

The three looked at each other for a moment pondering these questions.

"I don't know if this makes sense to you, but it just occurred to me. What if China wants this information because they want to build a deep-water port someplace other than China and they want to be able to shorten the time needed to do it? What if China wants this info so they can improve the way they build ports for its navy? Doesn't that make this a different kind of security question?" Victoria posed. "Maybe we need to think about security or national defense in a different way."

"What about our guy Moore? Isn't this economic or commercial espionage, something like that?" Olvera thought out loud.

"I don't have it right in front of me, but what Moore tried to provide was in a patent application, so it isn't a 'secret'. I'll double check, but I recall the economic espionage laws refer to secrets so I don't think these documents fall under the law because patent applications are filed knowing that the information will eventually become publicly available," Victoria explained. "If things get that far procedurally, we'll bring in someone who can answer those questions."

Kearns let out a big sigh and leaned forward; his blue eyes zeroed in on Victoria as he listened. "Whatever law you use to prosecute Moore is up to you. I'm more concerned about the point you raised about needing to think about security and national defense differently. It opens up a new world of investigations that, clearly, we don't have the resources for," Kearns said. "I hope our teams are having some luck finding Lucas Moore."

* * * * *

The security guard glanced at the FBI identification held in front of his face. "Not going to find patent examiners here," the security guard said. "The Patent Office is moving. Some of the agency is still here in Crystal City, but the patent people are already over in Alexandria."

"Can you tell us where, exactly," Agent Ed Adams asked. After the previous evening's futile chase, he was still in pursuit of the elusive Lucas Moore.

"Hold on a second," the guard said and opened a binder. He looked at the map of the new campus still in the process of being completed. "It looks like he'd be in one of these two buildings," he pointed to a drawing of five buildings that was the planned home of the agency.

Adams and a fellow agent drove the short distance from Crystal City to Alexandria. As they turned off Duke Street and headed straight toward the five-building campus, the curb parking was filled with vans and pickup trucks belonging to plumbers, electricians, heating, and air conditioning technicians. Adams, driving, slowed so they could identify the two buildings the security guard had pointed to on the map. As they neared the newly constructed buildings, traffic was divided by a wide grassy median. Newly planted trees lined the street.

Adams rolled past two buildings not yet occupied and was forced to follow the street in a U-turn. He braked when he saw the name of one of the two buildings that should be where Moore worked. He continued to the corner and turned, hoping to find a place to park. A hundred feet from the corner, a space appeared and he parallel parked.

Adams and his fellow agent entered the Jefferson Building. The entry lobby smelled of fresh paint. The FBI agents noticed the familiar security set-up that divided employees from everyone else. An x-ray scanner for bags, packages, briefcases, and anything else visitors might carry was positioned next to a walk-through metal detector placed next to a counter where two security guards sat. A hand-held metal detector rested on the x-ray scanner.

"May we help you," one of the guards asked as the other got up and moved toward the x-ray scanner.

"We need to find a patent examiner named Lucas Moore," Adams said as he presented his FBI identification. He watched the security guard type on a keyboard. As Adams and his colleague waited, several casually dressed people presented identification and walked toward a bank of elevators.

The agents stood and waited. They watched the comings and goings of several people who were already known to the security guard who had moved toward the x-ray machine.

"Let me make a call upstairs," the security guard at the counter said.

The two agents took a couple of steps away from the counter. There was no seating in the entry area.

"Gentlemen, the system says Lucas Moore isn't here today. He might've called in sick," the guard said.

"Does he have a supervisor we can talk to?" Adams asked.

"Give me a minute. I'll find out if he can come down and talk to you."

The agents moved away from the counter and toward the large windows fronting the street. They stood with their backs to the window, looking in toward the counter and watching.

Adams turned slightly toward his colleague and spoke so that the security guards wouldn't hear him. "Have you noticed how every government building has increased all this security by checking visitors and non-agency people coming in? But do any of these places full of sensitive and confidential information conduct any random checks of employees when they leave the building? I'm just wondering if there's any effort to keep folks honest and prevent them from taking out confidential information," Adams said.

A tall, hefty, gray bearded man got off an elevator. The security guard who was standing pointed him toward the agents.

"The guard on the phone said you wanted to talk to me. You're from the FBI?"

Adams and his colleague showed their IDs. It was always worth doing just to focus someone's attention. "We need to contact Mr. Lucas Moore immediately. We believe he's sharing information and documents related to his work with a foreign government."

The supervisor's fingers combed his long beard as his eyes went back and forth between the two agents. "Wow. That is serious." The man paused and mentally searched for something to add. "Look, I manage a group of patent examiners. I've never had anything like this happen. We train examiners and remind them that they are responsible for the way they handle applications and the information we access. But having you show up, maybe you should talk to someone in the General Counsel's office."

"Okay. But before we leave and given the urgency to find Mr. Moore, do you have an address, phone numbers and email addresses you can provide?"

"Give me a few minutes, I'll go upstairs and see what I can find for you," the supervisor said. He gave no thought to whether he should or shouldn't be providing the information.

Ten minutes passed before the supervisor returned with a printout of the information Adams requested. "One other thing. Where is this General Counsel's office located?" Adams asked.

"That office is still back in Crystal City," the supervisor answered.

"Of course it is. Thanks for this," Adams said as he took the printed page. He started toward the door. "Before we go back to Crystal City, we'll call and give Kearns the info we got here," he said to his colleague as they exited.

* * * * *

Lucas couldn't concentrate on any one thought. It was after three in the morning when he left a message with his supervisor that he was sick and wouldn't be at work. He had the television on all evening and past four in the morning when he finally fell asleep. Lucas awoke after eleven. He couldn't stop seeing the chase replayed in his mind. He left his room and the hotel long enough to grab a sandwich and something to drink. He left the "Do Not Disturb" on his door.

He scarfed down his sandwich and finished off his soda in a couple of large gulps. The drapes were open. He sat in the lone chair in the room looking out into the sun washed afternoon. He needed to talk to someone, but who? A lawyer. He was going to need one. But that costs money. Lucas closed his eyes and thought. He knew some lawyers, but they were the wrong kind of lawyers. He met with patent lawyers all the time, but that wasn't going to be of much help in this situation. He squeezed his eyes closed. He'd end up with a public defender.

Lucas played out scenarios about what was going to happen to him. His job was gone. He'd be lucky if they let him into the building to get his personal belongings. Without a job, his hope of finishing law school was up in smoke. Jail? How could he minimize the odds of imprisonment? Could he cooperate and face only misdemeanor charges?

Lucas didn't like the idea of spending any amount of time out of his room, but he didn't have his laptop. He went downstairs and found what was deemed a business center. There were two computers connected to a printer off to one side of the lobby area. It was partially walled off from the open social area of the lobby. He thought about all those police dramas he'd watched. His nimble fingers keyed in his search terms, and he found what he was looking for in seconds. He read through several websites about getting a lawyer. After twenty minutes, he shut down the computer. Suspecting that he faced criminal charges, he concluded that the few online legal services available were not going to meet his needs.

Back in his room, the television provided background noise. He paid no attention to the noise or anything on the television screen. He sat and stared out the window. He knew what he needed to do, but he'd put it off for just a while longer. He wanted one more night and, hopefully, some sleep.

* * * * *

The morning shadows cast by the three-story apartment building stretched across the parking area. The early morning sun wasn't visible through the trees. A taxi slowed, not turning into a parking spot.

Agent Adams elbowed his partner in the arm to bring him out of his slumber. "Looks like our man Moore is finally making an appearance," Adams said. "Once he's inside we'll go."

Adams's partner rubbed the sleep from his eyes. The Chevy Impala they'd used a couple of nights earlier was parked in front of the apartment building that faced Lucas's building. They watched Moore walk to the building entrance. Moore didn't look around. He showed no outward signs of nervousness. Moore just pulled keys from his pocket and disappeared behind the closed door.

Adams looked at his watch. He'd give Moore two minutes before heading to the apartment. It was just after six. A few lights were on in several apartments fronting the parking area. No one had come down to their cars and left. The agents exited the Impala, careful to close their doors quietly. At Moore's apartment door, Adams knocked as his partner stood to the side of the door.

When the door opened, Adams saw the tall lanky guy he had chased. Adams was several inches shorter than Moore but was broader and thicker in the chest and shoulders.

"Mr. Moore, we've been looking for you," Adams began, holding his FBI identification for Lucas to see. Adams's partner made himself fully visible stepping behind Adams. "You'll have to come with us. We'll have to cuff you."

Lucas said nothing. He nodded and turned around. He put his wrists together behind his back and felt the cold metal. "My keys are in my pocket. Can you lock the door for me," Lucas asked.

Lucas lowered himself into the backseat of the Impala and slumped down. Life as he knew it was over in every way imaginable. He needed to save himself from the worst possible result and that would only happen if he disclosed everything he'd done and everything he knew about Xiong Zimo. He knew Zimo had immunity. The only thing he had was information and he was willing to trade that for leniency.

The agents were in no hurry. They flowed with traffic. Lucas sat with his knees against the back of the front seat and head leaning back.

"Who else is providing your Chinese contact with information," Adams asked.

"I don't know," Moore answered honestly.

"Do you think any of your co-workers are doing what you did?" In the rearview mirror, Adams saw Moore shrug before hearing him.

"I don't know, but I guess it's possible," Moore said.

"Do you have co-workers who are students at the law school or other law schools in the metro area?" Adams pressed.

"Yeah, several at the various law schools around town."

Hearing the answer, Adams and his colleague looked at each other for a moment. Adams closed his eyes for a second and had that *Oh shit!* look on his face.

The agent in the passenger seat turned slightly to look over his shoulder at Lucas. "Any of your co-workers living way beyond their means? Do you know anybody buying expensive houses, cars or taking vacations that make you wonder how they do it on a government salary?"

"I never thought about that. I'd have to think about it," Lucas answered. "But, just like me, they could be using the money to reduce their school debts, not to live lavishly," he added.

"Start thinking. The more you can tell us, the more you help yourself," Adams said. Adams had never given a thought to what the Patent Office did until now. With Moore in the back seat, he didn't say anything out loud, but he noticed his white knuckles gripping the steering wheel as he thought about the potential gold mine of information flowing through that Office with minimal security measures.

Capitol Hill

Two cars parked at opposite ends of the block were occupied by a lone set of eyes. Each man tasked to ensure the safety of an American who lived on the block. The Chinese security officers were used to protecting their own high-level embassy officials and VIPs who traveled from China, but it was unusual to protect someone who worked on Capitol Hill. The Chinese Embassy was concerned about crime in the city and was taking no chances that the American living on this block became a victim.

The security men stayed in their cars except when following the American from a distance when she left her apartment to go to work. They lingered around the Dupont Circle subway stop late in the afternoons and into the evenings until she got home. The security wasn't around-the-clock but enough for the Chinese to have confidence in her safety.

Kellie Liang sat at a desk in her small one-bedroom apartment on P Street. The desk whose flat surface was barely big enough for a keyboard and monitor was squeezed into a corner space between her love seat and a corner window in the tiny living room. The desk's placement allowed her to work by the light of the day and to glance down onto the street. The level of street activity in the morning would tell her when it was time to get ready for the rest of the day. The apartment's location was convenient to the nearby Dupont Circle subway station and didn't require her to transfer to another line to get to work on the Senate side of Capitol Hill.

A towel was draped around her neck after she finished her pre-dawn session on a stationary bike and shower. She'd change out of her loose sweatshirt and jogging pants and into something more business-like before going into the office. But first, she busied herself in her morning ritual. She read through the results of the overnight search generated based on the search terms she had created. Her shoulder-length black hair was clipped in the back to keep her hair out of her face.

Unconsciously, her head moved in toward the screen. An article from the Washington Post's Metro section had been flagged in her morning search results. Strange, she thought. Usually, her interest in China's international economic and security issues were reported in the main sections of major newspapers or other online sources, not in the local section.

The article informed her that a patent examiner was arraigned in federal court on criminal charges for removing confidential documents and providing them to a Chinese national. The article named Lucas Moore as the examiner arrested in Falls Church, Virginia, after evading authorities in downtown Washington, D.C. FBI agents observed Moore with a Chinese national and leaving the materials with the Chinese individual. Kellie wondered what kind of documents and information a patent examiner would turn over. Her eyes moved back to the beginning of the article to see the byline, Norman Quarles. She sent herself an email reminding her to contact the reporter.

Kellie spent another forty minutes skimming the other articles found in her search results. Out of the corner of her eye, she noticed the stream of pedestrians heading toward the subway station. She closed her laptop, changed into a cream-colored blouse and navy-blue jacket and matching slacks. A quick glimpse into a mirror and she decided to unclip her hair, brush it and do nothing more with her hair. In minutes, she exited her apartment.

The Chinese security officer gave Kellie plenty of space before getting out of his car parked at the corner of 18th and P Streets. He saw her descend on the escalator, waited five minutes, and walked back toward his car. In a change of routine, this morning, he went to her apartment building instead of his car, taking the stairway up to her apartment. He slipped on clear vinyl gloves and pulled out a small toolkit.

Reaching her apartment, the Chinese security officer stared at the door, noticing three different keyholes for locks on the door. He opened his small toolkit.

Across the hall, Kellie's neighbor looked through a peephole in her door, watching a well-dressed black-haired man standing at the door, his head down. The neighbor couldn't see what he was doing.

The neighbor cracked the door open, the chain still latched. "Hey, what're you doing," the neighbor asked.

The Chinese security officer's head snapped around. He hadn't heard the door opening behind him. "Fixing lock."

"Really?" The neighbor was suspicious. The man was too well dressed to be believable. "What's the name of your company," the neighbor pressed.

"I'm finished. I go."

The neighbor watched as the man pocketed whatever was in his hand and head toward the stairway.

Back inside her apartment with her door locked, the neighbor called Kellie, but it went to Kellie's voicemail.

When a train arrived at the station, Kellie moved aside to let people out before stepping into the car. In luck, she found an available seat. Every morning, she took these few minutes on the train to take mental stock of what she knew she had to do for the day, knowing that there was a ninety percent chance that it would all crumble into chaos within fifteen minutes of arrival. Rarely did days on Capitol Hill go according to plan. The unexpected always popped up. As she thought about it, she shook her head. That article about the patent examiner and Chinese national kept creeping up on her.

From Union Station she walked briskly toward the Dirksen Senate Office Building. Spring flowers bloomed and provided a rainbow of colors along the path. She felt her dark colored outfit absorbing the warmth of the morning sun. As she approached the entrance, she flashed her identification to the security guards who smiled and waved her through the employee entrance as they did hundreds of others.

Kellie walked the familiar corridors. In a building approaching its half-century mark, there was always something under repair. It seemed that the amount of repair or updating had increased since the 9/11 attacks with more security technology being installed and other support equipment needing to be mounted or fitted into an aging building.

The sound of footsteps echoed off the hard surfaces of the corridor. She took the wide stairs to the third floor, choosing to walk anytime she was by herself just to get a little exercise during long workdays.

Kellie opened the door to Senator Nathan Burke's suite of offices. "Good morning, Trish," Kellie said as she entered. She walked past Trish, the Senator's gatekeeper, receptionist, and the longest serving person on the senator's staff at the tender age of twenty-eight. Passing Trish's desk, Kellie walked inside the office's main entry. About twelve feet from the entry door, a wall separated the entry and waiting area from desks for staff. Kellie turned left into a larger office where a collection of large office desks and office equipment were used by the staff.

Kellie's desk was just inside the doorway of the large office. Her desk was against the wall, and she had partitions in front and on one side of her desk to provide a little privacy. She sat and switched into a pair of blue pumps. She sifted through documents in a folder prepared for a hearing later in the morning. Nathan Burke, a Pennsylvania senator, sat on the Senate's Judiciary Committee, which included a subcommittee that had jurisdiction over the Patent Office. Kellie took a minute to add notes into the file about the article she had read before coming to the office.

She heard the Senator's familiar voice greeting Trish when he entered. She gave him a few minutes before crossing the entry and waiting area to his office. As one of the senior members of the Senator's staff, Kellie had open access to the Senator while many of the junior staff worked through their more seasoned colleagues.

"Good morning, Senator," Kellie said as Senator Burke read something on his desk while motioning her in. The Senator's large office had a leather sofa and leather chairs around a coffee table. The office space allowed for two leather wingback chairs facing his desk. Kellie took a seat in front of the desk while the Senator took off his suit jacket and draped it over the back of the chair.

"I've added a few notes," Kellie said as she reached out and handed the hearing folder to Senator Burke.

Burke took the folder. Last-minute changes were part of life for him. Being a lawyer before he was elected, he easily adapted to constant change. Scribbled notes, new facts, changed circumstances kept Burke energized in his daily work. He accepted the tedium of drafting and reading legislation as fundamental requirements of the job and why he sought to be a senator. He wanted to contribute to positive changes. The one change he was already thinking about and working to avoid was any possibility of losing his seat in the following year's 2006 election. After his initial election to the senate in 1994, he believed that after eleven years he was finally understanding the institution and how it worked.

He skimmed through the added notes. "I guess we have a few new questions for the director later today at the hearing," the senator said smiling at the new developments. "It's a chance to get a few people to pay more attention to our ongoing China challenges rather than being completely absorbed by the war on terror."

Senator Burke put the folder down on the desk and leaned forward. "We need to keep moving forward on your nomination. It's your eye for things like this that makes you such a valuable asset on my staff and it'll be good to have you at the State Department," Burke said.

"Since the November re-election, Bush's folks have been a bit slow finding people to replace some of the appointees who left at the beginning of the year. Things have bogged down, but I've been working with my colleagues about your nomination as a Deputy Assistant Secretary at the State Department. More of them are finally coming around to the idea of having your skill set at the Department."

"Is my father's past something we need to worry about? Do I need to address it in more detail? Could it torpedo this whole thing?" Kellie asked.

"Honestly, your father's import-export business and the criminal prosecution for his role in the illegal trade are being raised by several colleagues and causes a little hesitation in supporting your nomination. But I keep pointing out to them that the White House is on board with your nomination so there's no reason for us as senators of the same party to oppose it. Of course, you know that there's always political posturing and we need to navigate through this, but this is just a long-winded way of saying that things should move much faster in the next couple of weeks."

Kellie wasn't as optimistic as Senator Burke. Below the surface, she simmered. The constant calls from fellow staffers from other senate offices about China asking for help irritated her now more than ever given that it was those same senators who hesitated in their support for her nomination. Those senators were happy to use her and her knowledge, but felt no obligation to help her move her career forward.

Nothing Senator Burke said surprised Kellie. Her father's involvement with Chinese manufacturers and exporters had landed him in jail. She had cooperated with prosecutors and investigators to keep out of the swirling storm that surrounded his case. Her name appeared in articles related to the case because she had met with her father's Chinese business contacts when she was in Hong Kong on a business trip. Fortunately, the investigation into her father's criminal business dealings with the Chinese uncovered how he used Kellie to financially benefit himself and his business.

Kellie's father insisted that she had nothing to do with his business. Given that she was kidnapped and taken to China by one of her father's contacts, the investigation found that she had uncovered and provided significant information used to prosecute her father. An FBI interview of a retired U.S. Customs attaché re-enforced the conclusion that Kellie was not only innocent of any wrongdoing but helped to collect the evidence used to prosecute her father.

After initiating the effort to get Kellie into the Deputy Assistant Secretary position, Senator Burke cornered colleagues in the hallways, dropped in at offices unannounced, whispered in their ears before and after hearings, and called them to get support for Kellie's nomination. The votes should've been overwhelmingly in her favor. Nearing the end of his second senate term, there were some things that never stopped surprising him, and this nomination effort was one of them. Kellie was on her second stint working on the Hill. When it came to China issues, senators and their staff were always in line to get her advice and insights, demonstrating the value they placed on her knowledge.

Senator Burke fought off the anger that rose within him every time he heard a colleague mentioning the hurdle they had in voting for Kellie. *She's Chinese,* they'd say. Burke corrected them every time without raising his voice saying, *No, she's an American like you with a Chinese name.*

"I want you at the hearing this morning," the Senator said. "There may be more to this little article that you've found than we think. A few answers from the director might give us insight into whether there are threats to data and information theft that we aren't aware of."

The subcommittee hearing was underway when Senator Burke arrived in the hearing room. Despite the many senators assigned to the subcommittee, Senator Burke saw only four other colleagues in their seats. He hadn't missed much. The opening statements from his fellow Republican subcommittee chairman and the ranking Democrat were already finished. The director of the Patent and Trademark Office was reading his initial testimony. Burke sat behind his name plate and Kellie found a chair behind him.

The hearing room had enough seating for a few dozen interested people, but attendance was sparse. There might have been a few representatives from pharmaceutical companies interested in hearing the recently confirmed director address drug patents while a few others might be there to hear about software patents. The topics and subjects that were usually raised and confronted by the director were interesting to a small community of people perceived by outsiders to be nerds and geeks.

A table in the corner of the hearing room held the opening statements and the director's prepared testimony for the press and other interested people.

A few weeks earlier, Senator Burke had voted in support of the director's confirmation. The new director had been a Texas patent lawyer and after decades in the weeds of the law, he allowed his political interests to sprout, including fundraising for the winner of the 2004 presidential election. With an eye toward retiring in a few years, he put out the word that he was interested in the job to head the Patent and Trademark Office.

Now, the director sat behind the witness table on the floor facing the raised seats of the senators. He was a veteran of this experience, having appeared in a similar room during his confirmation process. He leaned toward the microphone. The director read his statement as prepared by his staff. The statement was delivered without emotion or enthusiasm. His fluffy white hair was perfectly coiffed, and his suit and tie fit perfectly with the conservative atmosphere of the institution, but his delivery was robotic at best.

Senator Burke heard the director's voice but didn't absorb all that was being said. If he wanted, he could read the statement later or have one of his staff give him the highlights. When it was his turn to speak and pose questions, Burke started with pleasantries and congratulated the director on his confirmation to the new job.

"Director, as your agency moves to a new location, what are the security arrangements in the buildings your agency occupies?" Senator Burk asked.

The director turned his head slightly as if to put his better ear toward Senator Burke, hoping for more from the Senator. Realizing Senator Burke had sat back in his chair to await a response, the director looked at the pages of his opening statement that did not address the question posed.

"We have security in both the buildings we occupy in Crystal City and at our new Alexandria campus buildings. No one can enter without going through our entry security procedures," the director said. He knew that all the buildings had security guards, scanning equipment and procedures for non-agency people. The director's personal experience was enough to answer the question because of his past visits to the agency and his recent observations while in his new job.

"Do the people at the Patent Office handle confidential information?" Burke asked, knowing the answer.

"We consider all the patent applications as business confidential information," the director answered.

"What about national security and defense related documents?"

The director wasn't quick to respond. He looked over his shoulder at his two legislative staffers sitting behind him. While he got the slightest nod from one of the staff affirming the kind of information that Senator Burke was asking about, he wasn't sure how to express himself. "Senator, we receive patent applications from inventors in all business pursuits," the director answered. He cleared his throat and wondered where this line of questions was going.

"Director, are you aware of any special or different procedures for patent applications related to national security?"

Everyone in the room saw the director's quick over the shoulder glance at his staff. He didn't wait for any reaction from his staff. "Yes, there are procedures for those applications. We can provide you with the specifics after the hearing if you'd like," the director offered.

Senator Burke was now smiling. Because of his time on the subcommittee overseeing patent issues, he knew the answer and he knew where he could find the details if he wanted them. He sat forward, his forearms on the dais.

"Director, the question I have now is whether your agency conducts any security checks as your employees or anyone else leaves your facilities. Because of the highly sensitive and confidential nature of what you are entrusted with, what procedures do you have to prevent the unauthorized sharing of information? Are random checks conducted? What about the possibility of people sending information electronically to those who aren't permitted to have information?"

The director sat motionless listening to the questions being fired at him.

"Are you aware of the arraignment of a patent examiner on criminal charges for giving or trying to give a Chinese diplomat information?" Senator Burke sat back as he watched the director turn in his chair, huddling in whispered conversation with his two legislative staff.

Turning back to face his questioner, the director saw Senator Burke staring down at him. "We're looking into the situation," the director responded.

Senator Burke's eyes studied the hearing room's occupants. Those who had decided to attend this hearing were attentive to the back and forth between Burke and the director. "Your agency needs to step it up when it comes to security. We can't assume that your employees won't be tempted to divulge business confidential or national security related information to our competitors whether they are foreign governments or commercial competitors.

"I'm going to ask that the Subcommittee Chairman calls you back to report on your review of your internal security procedures and steps being taken to tighten oversight of your employees," Senator Burke warned.

Senator Burke had no additional questions or comments to make. He got up to leave the hearing room. "Stick around and let me know what the post-hearing chatter is about," Senator Burke whispered to Kellie, still sitting in the chair behind his.

The hearing concluded twenty minutes after Senator Burke's exit. Kellie stood but didn't make any move to leave. She looked over at two other senate staffers who lingered and helped gather the materials their bosses had brought to the hearing then saw the director standing behind his chair with his back toward Kellie.

The director's right hand in a fist pumped up and down into the palm of his left hand as he talked to his staff who had sat behind him. Kellie couldn't hear him, but the looks on the faces of his staff informed her that he wasn't happy. When he finished and turned around to collect his documents, Kellie saw a red-faced man, his eyes glanced up for a second and caught Kellie's eye. He turned and marched out followed by his staffers.

Several people in the audience were clustered in small groups. Most of the people Kellie observed were in a cheerful mood. Kellie wondered if they were happy to see friends or enjoyed the unexpected exchange that occurred between Senator Burke and the director. Whatever the reason, the security issue raised a lot of questions for Kellie to ponder.

As soon as Kellie returned to her desk, her fingers danced on her cellphone keypad. She waited to be connected to Norman Quarles. She glanced down at the new documents placed on her desk while she was at the hearing.

"Norman Quarles, can I help you?"

Kellie's free hand stopped moving. "Mr. Quarles, I'm calling from Senator Burke's office. My name is Kellie Liang, I . . ."

"Great hearing this morning," Norman said cutting Kellie off. "I guess the Senator read my article. Those questions to the director added some spice to the hearing." Norman stopped to take a breath.

"No, the Senator didn't read the article, but I did, and I briefed him on it before the hearing," Kellie said as soon as she had an opening. She was having second thoughts about meeting and talking to Quarles.

"I don't usually report on anything that's quite this exciting. I was at the courthouse checking in on different courtrooms, you know, looking for a local interest story. I sat down and this case came up and it has a local slant with the Patent Office and a patent examiner. When I heard he was pleading guilty and heard him say that he passed information to a Chinese diplomat, that made me sit up and listen to everything going on."

Norman Quarles talked and talked about the arraignment. Kellie failed at taking good notes as Quarles spoke. "Is there any way you can email me all these details you're describing?" Kellie asked.

The talkative Norman went silent. "Mr. Quarles, are you still there?"

"It's only as background information, right?"

"Of course," Kellie answered. Kellie took special interest in any developments about China and its international economic and commercial pursuits. Now, with the possibility of filling a senior position at the State Department, she absorbed as much information as possible.

Norman Quarles lived up to his promise. Within thirty minutes of ending her call with him, she saw an email from Quarles with an attachment. She printed the document and read it.

Lucas Moore pleaded guilty to a criminal charge of removing patent application documents without authority while the information contained in the patent applications was still considered confidential. Quarles's notes added that Moore evaded the FBI after attempting to provide the confidential information to a Chinese diplomat. Moore's sentence was scheduled to be imposed at a later date.

Kellie searched the document for any information about the prosecuting attorney but saw no names. She was curious about the type of invention that was covered by the documents Moore attempted to give the Chinese diplomat. The Justice Department prosecutor would know, but the notes didn't provide names. She decided she could task someone in the office to track it down.

Kellie placed the emailed and printed document in one of several China folders she kept in a locked drawer in her desk. She put it in a sub-folder labelled "National Economic Security". She worried that this added another layer of China issues to her expected new job at the State Department. She and others knew that China's intelligence gathering activity targeted the military, corporate and university research, but she had never thought much about the Patent Office angle. Kellie wanted to know more but feared that what she learned would only make her job more difficult.

Faces

A few pillowy clouds dotted the bright midday sky. The closed driver's side window magnified the sun's heat in the car, but the fresh air from the open passenger side window kept the car comfortable for Agents Ed Adams and Vera Jamison. A picture of Xiong Zimo was taped and hung at the center of the dashboard. A pair of binoculars lay on the dashboard between them.

"Does this guy ever leave the embassy?" Vera Jamison wondered as she peered through a monocular when she saw two men exiting the Chinese Embassy about a hundred yards away.

"Not as often as we'd like him to," Adams said.

Adams and Jamison were in their second eight-hour day shift sitting in a dark sedan. Adams chose a spot with an unobstructed view of the Chinese Embassy. A stop sign was less than five feet in front of the car making the parking spot illegal, but Adams didn't care. Before the building became the Chinese Embassy, it had been a hotel. The embassy building butted up against an apartment building where many of the embassy staff lived.

"Does he go to his evening classes every evening?" Vera asked.

"We never got that far with him. Once he produced that diplomatic card, we had to let him go," Adams explained and shrugged his shoulders.

Vera Jamison raised the monocular to her right eye again. She shifted, sitting up straighter. "Hey, hey," maybe this is the guy.

Adams leaned forward, grabbed the binoculars, and focused on three people exiting the embassy. Two men and a woman. The woman was tiny. One of the men was older, in his forties or fifties Adams guessed. The other man was younger. Adams took a quick look at the photo taped to the dashboard and put his eyes back to the binoculars.

"Grab the camera," Adams said.

Adams put the binoculars back and took the camera from Vera's hand. He put the camera to his eye. He focused the three into the viewfinder. He played with the telescopic lens magnifying their images and snapped off pictures. He didn't know how many images he had but handed the camera back to Vera when a car pulled up in front of the embassy for the three.

"Let's find out where they're going," Adams said and turned the ignition. The car he wanted to follow turned right onto Connecticut Avenue. Adams, needing to make a left turn, had to wait for a break in traffic, but was able to pull out when the traffic light changed and stopped traffic, giving him an opening. The traffic light had also caused the embassy car to stop. There were two cars between them, but Adams wasn't concerned about losing sight of the embassy car. Traffic was heavy on this part of the main artery running through northwest Washington, D.C.

Whoever drove the embassy car wasn't in any hurry. They traveled just a few blocks when the embassy car turned into the Washington Hilton.

"I'm going to let you out behind them, and I'll park. You can let me know where to meet. Hopefully, they'll be in a public area of the hotel," Adams said.

When the embassy car stopped at the main entrance, Adams steered the car to a stop and Agent Jamison got out then leaned toward the open window as if talking to Adams but was giving the three Chinese time to get out of the car and enter the hotel lobby. Vera felt the pockets of her lightweight navy-blue hiking pants for a small notepad.

"They're in," Adams said, knowing why Vera had ducked her head down toward the open window. Once she turned and stepped away from the car, Adams drove the car down to the garage level.

Vera saw the three Chinese about twenty feet ahead of her. She kept her sunglasses on to combat the sunlight flowing in through the wall of glass. She followed them to a restaurant that was catering to its lunchtime crowd. A few vacant tables dotted the dining room.

"Table for one?" the hostess asked.

"Two," Vera answered as she followed the hostess who started in the opposite direction of where the three Chinese were sitting. The only reason she might attract attention was because she was dressed more casually than most of the business suits worn by both men and women. Her long loose-fitting sweater easily covered her holstered handgun.

"Excuse me, but are there any tables on the other side?"

The young woman stopped, looked at Vera without expression. "Wait here while I check."

Vera wasn't very optimistic. The curvature of the dining room and pillars made it impossible for Vera to see where the hostess had gone, but moments later she saw the young woman give her a nod.

"Thanks," Vera said as she followed the hostess to a two-top table. Once in her chair, she looked around and saw the three from the embassy four tables away. She switched seats so that she had a straight-on view of the table, but the older of the two men had his back to her. She had side angles of Xiong Zimo and the woman. Another occupied table was in her direct line of sight. Her phone buzzed.

"We're in the restaurant. I'm toward the back but have a good view of our trio."

"Be there in a few minutes," Adams said. Before getting out of the car, he decided to leave his weapon locked in the car, convincing himself that nothing would happen in the hotel that required a gun.

Adams never liked the idea of wearing a ballcap or any headgear indoors, but he decided he had to wear one today along with sunglasses. Walking toward Vera, Xiong Zimo's back was to him. He didn't think that Xiong would recognize him but didn't take any chances. Vera had removed her sunglasses. He sat so that he would have to look to his right to see the three Chinese. They had no direct view of him.

During his approach to the table and as he sat down, Vera's eyes never strayed from the Chinese. Her brown eyes concentrated on the side view of the woman. A pencil in her right hand, she sketched what she saw into the small notepad.

Adams's eyes went back and forth between the notepad and the Chinese woman. "That's pretty good, Jamison."

"I found out that my interest in art comes in handy when it's awkward or impossible to pull out a camera and take pictures," she said.

"It'd be better if we had a full-face sketch," Adams chided.

Vera ignored the remark. She got up and walked toward the hostess stand with pencil and notepad in hand. She stood to the side of the hostess stand, having a better view of the Chinese woman's face. While her hand worked on the sketch, she asked the hostess for something and was handed sheets of paper.

"What was that about?" Adams said when Jamison returned to the table.

"You said a full-face view would be better, so I found a way to get a better view of her." She slid the pocket-size note pad toward Adams.

"Damn, that's good." He was looking at the hand drawn sketch of the woman with bangs across her forehead. Her short black hair was about an inch below her ears and above the collar line. She had the gaunt cheeks of someone who suffered from malnourishment. Adams looked over at the table. The sketch was good but couldn't capture how small and petite she was. Adams wondered if she would tip the scales at a hundred pounds.

"Do you speak or understand any Chinese?" Vera asked.

"Nada."

"Me neither. Not worth going by the table," Vera said.

"Wonder if one of them is staying at the hotel. Otherwise, why not go to a restaurant somewhere else," Adams said.

"Let's stick around and see how the check is covered. We'll see if our embassy guy takes care of the check. If it's charged to a room, that'll tell us one of them may not be with the embassy," Vera said. She and Adams sipped their ice teas and water, waited, and watched.

Vera's hunch proved right as she and Adams watched the woman sign the check without offering a card. They noticed that Xiong Zimo did all the talking with the waitress, hinting that either the other two spoke little or no English.

"Any possibility that you can discreetly take a picture of the woman with your phone?" Adams asked.

"Even if I did, you know the quality of these aren't that good. I thought the sketch would do for now," Vera responded.

"It's good, but a photo would be better. Given the distance, I can't guarantee that the pictures I took earlier will be that great," Adams suggested.

Vera Jamison walked up to the hostess stand again.

"May I help you?" the hostess asked.

"No, thanks. Just go about your business." Vera stepped to the side of the young woman, inviting a glare from the hostess. Vera pulled out her FBI identification, let the young woman see it and put it back in her pocket. The glare disappeared and the young woman smiled to greet two people stepping forward.

Vera put the phone to her ear for a few seconds, then lowered it to chest level and clicked off a couple of pictures, hoping she had both the woman and the older man. As she started to walk back to the table, she saw the three getting up. She decided to wait a moment to let them exit the restaurant. She looked down at her phone, not giving them an opportunity to look directly at her.

As the three Chinese walked past, Vera gauged the Chinese woman to be barely five-feet tall and the older Chinese man to be about five feet eight or nine, compared to her own five feet seven height. She guessed that he might be about a hundred eighty-five pounds. The older man passed close enough that she knew he was a smoker. He reeked of cigarette smoke.

As the three walked back toward the lobby, Vera went back to her table and started scribbling notes. Adams watched her write.

"Thanks for not interrupting me. I wanted to jot this down while it's fresh. All that height, weight stuff and anything else that impressed me about them," Vera explained.

"Let's get back to the office. We'll see what we have on the camera and your phone. We'll get the office to ask the State Department to help identify our two unknowns," Adams suggested.

Interagency coordination and cooperation could be tricky and time consuming, but the FBI's request for information had a different twist to it this time. Kearns wanted the identities of the two people seen with Xiong as fast as possible. To justify the need, he got on the phone with his new Justice Department contact, Victoria Walters. She helped Kearns write a description of events and information that didn't sound like the usual Chinese intelligence activity. Walters emphasized China's attempt to access confidential information about new dredging technologies that could be used to create deep water seaports for use by naval vessels and commercial shipping, both have national security implications.

Kearns's landline phone rang as he stacked folders and documents before calling it a day. "Kearns, here."

"I'm calling from the Diplomatic Security Service. We got a request for ID on a couple of possible Chinese Embassy staff and was given your phone number."

"Appreciate the call. What do you have for us? We know about Xiong Zimo," Kearns said.

"Okay, the other man is Shan Zhou. Zhou is his last name. He's listed as a commercial counsellor at the embassy. We've got nothing on the woman."

"Thanks," Kearns responded, writing down everything he received about Shan Zhou or Zhou Shan and hung up. Kearns looked down at his note pad where he'd written the man's name. On the line below Shan Zhou, he scribbled "woman, no immunity". She was worth keeping eyes on. He sent an email to Adams and Jamison instructing them to distribute a picture of the woman to all on the team and informed everyone that she did not have diplomatic immunity.

* * * * *

Kellie's keys clinked as she pulled them out of her purse. She turned, hearing the squeak of Connie's door behind her.

"Long day?" Connie asked as she leaned against the door frame standing in jeans and a loose-fitting red blouse.

"No different than any other," Kellie answered, noticing Connie's glasses sliding down low and mussed short brown hair. "Thanks for the message. I was going to pop over after I dropped my stuff inside," Kellie said, stepping toward Connie.

Kellie didn't know what Connie did but knew that Connie worked from home. Kellie guessed that Connie was in her mid-thirties like herself.

"You didn't call a locksmith, did you?"

Kellie shook her head confirming Connie's suspicion.

"The man was Asian and dressed in a suit except that he didn't have a tie. I don't think locksmiths dress that way for work. I don't know what made me look through the peephole this morning," Connie explained. Connie decided not to say that she often took a glance during the day when she'd get up to get a cup of coffee. Anytime she stepped away from her computer, she stole a look through the peephole. Finding a man at Kellie's door had just been dumb luck.

"When I saw him, I cracked the door and asked what he was doing. Funny how he was quick to leave once I confronted him."

"How was his English," Kellie wondered.

"It was accented. When I asked him, his answers weren't proper sentences, you know, words missing."

"Thanks, Connie. Maybe I need to add some security features inside the apartment," Kellie said. Kellie turned to enter her apartment thinking that she needed cameras inside. Putting down her briefcase and purse, she wondered if she should report this as an incident to those who did her background investigation for her State Department position. She worried that if she did, it might put her nomination in jeopardy.

Rendezvous

Sitting at her desk in the apartment, Kellie Liang's eyes scrolled down the list of new emails. Her eyes stopped when she saw a new email from Meilin Moy. The subject line read, "Tea, Coffee". The body of the message was short, "Staying at Washington Hilton Hotel". This only added to Kellie's already interesting day.

Kellie recalled receiving a message from her distant Chinese cousin several weeks earlier about a possible trip to Washington. It included no specifics and no follow-up communication. Kellie scrolled through her emails to check when she had received the earlier email. Two months had passed. Two months of long, busy days filled with her usual workload and the endless glad-handing she had to do to grease the wheels of her nomination for that State Department position. She felt as if Meilin's note had been many months earlier.

She pressed a key to prepare a response. She stared at the blank space on the screen. The two of them hadn't seen each other since Kellie's trip to Hong Kong seven years earlier in 1998. They communicated by email occasionally.

"Morning coffee/tea at 8:00 if that's convenient," Kellie typed, hoping she'd see a prompt response. "Will be great to see you!" she added. She provided Meilin with a cell phone number and hit send.

Kellie stared out onto P Street without noticing anything. Her laptop chimed, announcing a new message.

"Wonderful! Where to meet?" Meilin asked.

Kellie thought about a location. She wanted flexibility to be indoors or outside. Meilin's English was limited, making indoor conversation difficult if the morning rush created an indoor buzz. Speaking Chinese presented another problem. Kellie's Cantonese was good, but not as good as in the past. She had less occasion to speak to anyone in Chinese. Before her father's legal problems and incarceration, she spoke to her father often and almost exclusively in Cantonese. Her anger toward her father had diminished over the past several years, but there were residual levels of anger toward him for using her and contributing to the breakdown of her relationship with her then boyfriend. And now, it somehow seemed it would come back and sideline her career.

"Coffee shop near the corner of Q and 19th Streets. Will wait outside for you," Kellie wrote. She provided the details hoping that Meilin would be able to find the coffee shop.

With the morning meeting set, Kellie began fretting over it. Why now? She looked for some food, then decided she wasn't hungry. She poured a glass of wine but took only a few sips. She picked up a magazine from her coffee table, reading words, but didn't focus on the content. When she finally went to bed, she tossed and turned, getting twisted in the sheets before finally falling asleep.

* * * * *

The morning parade of commuters didn't notice the guy in the parked car. The Chinese security officer in the car at the corner of P and 18th Streets sat up when he saw Kellie in his rearview mirror exiting her building. He checked his watch. It was a bit later than usual, but within the window of time he'd gotten used to seeing her leave. He'd wait until she crossed the street and approached the traffic circle before exiting the car. When she turned up 18th Street instead of walking straight toward Dupont Circle, the security officer got out, tripping over the curb, but catching himself before hitting the ground. He looked around, embarrassed. He clapped his hands together to remove the dirt and grass from his hands.

Other than a couple of people giving him a quick glance as he straightened up, no one paid attention to the Chinese man in a gray suit and white shirt. He kept his distance, walking twenty feet behind Kellie. Several other pedestrians were headed in the same direction between them. After a few days of shadowing Kellie, the security officer was used to her long strides. She always walked as if she was late for something.

Kellie walked the long block to Q Street then turned left toward the agreed meeting point a little more than a block away. Despite the congestion on the sidewalks, the security officer kept his steady distance behind Kellie. She was easy to follow. Other than checking traffic when crossing streets, she kept her eyes forward, rarely looking over her shoulder. A soft-sided black leather briefcase on a long shoulder strap over her right shoulder made it easy to remain focused on her as he followed.

The security officer slowed when Kellie took a seat at an outdoor table. He walked past her and entered the coffee shop and saw a line of at least ten people waiting to order. Instead of getting in line, he sat at a two-top table by the window placing him behind Kellie sitting outside with her back to him. He hoped the morning rush would buy him time to sit and keep an eye out without being asked to move.

Less than half a mile from where Kellie waited, Agents Kearns and Adams were parked three car lengths from the Hilton hotel's main entrance. They arrived at seven in the morning. Their law enforcement identification ensured that they were left alone. Several photos of the Chinese woman they waited for were in their laps. Forty-five minutes into their shift, a bellman came out followed by the Chinese woman who matched the photographs. She got into a cab.

Agent Kearns and Adams, his partner for the day, expected the cab to turn in the direction of the Chinese Embassy, but it turned in the opposite direction. Connecticut Avenue's morning traffic was backed up. The cab driver took advantage of the few feet between bumpers and forced the driver to let him into the south-bound lane. The trailing FBI agents had to wait for a break in the north-bound traffic to make a left turn. Seeing no break, the agent driving pulled out to a chorus of honking cars he blocked while Kearns stuck out an arm gesturing drivers to stop and let them into the south-bound lane.

The cab was three cars ahead in the left lane in slow-moving traffic.

"Wonder if he's going to take the underpass below the circle," Adams said.

"We'll know in a minute." Kearns responded. The lack of any information about the Chinese woman made Kearns curious so rather than leave the surveillance to his team, he joined. The urge to see for himself who she might be and why she was with Xiong Zimo won out over the pile of paperwork awaiting his attention and sitting around waiting to get more information about the mystery woman.

The cab didn't veer left for the underpass. Instead, a left turn-signal started blinking as the cab approached the traffic signal at Q Street. There was no left turn lane, causing several drivers to swerve into the right lane to avoid the delay. The agents pulled up behind the cab and followed it through the left turn. The cab stopped as soon as it cleared the intersection, forcing the agents to stop and block the sidewalk and part of the roadway behind them.

Kearns got out of the car and stood in the blocked crosswalk. Once the Chinese woman paid the fare, she got out and stood waiting for the cab to drive away. Adams waved her to cross the street.

Kellie's chair was angled toward the direction of the oncoming traffic. She watched a cab stop and Meilin exit. She stood up as pedestrians walked past. Once on her side of the street, Kellie waved until she saw Meilin smile and wave back. When Meilin arrived at the table, Kellie bent down, embracing Meilin. Kellie towered over Meilin.

With the passage of years since they last saw each other in Hong Kong, Kellie's welcome embrace of Meilin told her that Meilin was as bone thin as ever. Settling into their chairs, Kellie noticed the slight tinges of gray hair in Meilin's unchanged boyish short haircut. Meilin, in her mid-forties, made little to no effort to use make-up to hide any lines and wrinkles on her face.

"It's very good to see you, Kaili," Meilin said in Cantonese with a wide smile. Meilin used Kellie's Chinese name. During Kellie's Hong Kong trip in 1998, she was introduced to all the Chinese as Liang Kaili, not Kellie Liang.

"You surprised me with your message," Kellie responded in Cantonese, signaling to Meilin that they would continue speaking in Cantonese.

"You've cut your long hair," Meilin noticed.

Kellie smiled broadly. "Yes, it was too much work. This is much easier in the mornings."

As the two women sat and exchanged initial pleasantries, Agent Kearns walked past their sidewalk table and beyond another occupied table before turning around and heading toward the coffee shop entrance. He pretended to be on his cell phone shaking his head, pursing his lips, and looking disappointed. Once inside, he looked around for a place to sit and watch the two women. A table in the far corner gave him a partial angled view of the two women outside. He wished he had the window table occupied by the Asian man sitting alone who had the best view of the women.

Kearns punched in the number for his partner in the car. "I'm inside a coffee shop. I walked by them. It wasn't helpful. They're speaking Chinese."

"Is there a seat available outside?" Adams asked.

"Why, do you speak Chinese?"

"No, but if they do switch to English maybe I'll be able to overhear something."

"At the moment, I can't see a vacant chair, but with these morning commuters, someone can leave at any time. Do it. I'll keep my eyes on them from inside. Keep the phone open," Kearns advised.

Kearns took a minute to get coffee. He sipped his coffee as his eyes surveyed inside and out. His view settled on the Asian man whose seat he'd like to have and saw that he had no drink or food on the table. Kearns knew that the smaller woman had been seen with Chinese Embassy staff, making him curious about the Asian man. He considered the possibility that the man was security for the unknown Chinese woman. Kearns smiled to himself that it might be good fortune to be sitting in the corner where he had some view of the women outside and a good view of the Asian man sitting alone a few tables away.

Kearns glanced outside and saw his partner take a seat at the table next to the two women, keeping his back to them. In case the women did switch to English, there was a chance of overhearing them.

"You're looking very good," Meilin said.

"Yes, things are going very well for me. How about you? How's your position at ChiTran?" Kellie asked, wanting to avoid any detailed conversation about the possibilities of her future position. She wanted to find out about Meilin and the details of her career. Kellie saw first-hand how Meilin worked within the confines of her world. Despite Meilin's very petite physical size, she was not one to be overlooked or ignored professionally. Underestimating Meilin who might look small and frail to some was a miscalculation. Meilin had other skills and talents that she could put to use to the detriment of anyone who crossed her.

"My father is retired and doesn't travel out of Taiwan anymore. His health is not good. And since I'm not known to his Taiwan family, I don't see him much anymore. He left the China company to me as his mainland daughter as you know," Meilin explained. "The other two ChiTran elders were happy with me after what I did when Liwei disappeared, and I took over his operation. Mine was already successful and I made sure to improve and expand his operations. It made it easier for the other two elders to retire," Meilin continued. "I think the others consider me as the new ChiTran elder. We're growing, expanding, and profiting."

"I'm so happy things worked out," Kellie said. Meilin and Liwei had been competitors within the ChiTran world of manufacturers and exporters in southern China. There was a tense relationship between them that Meilin never explained. Liwei's aggressive business style had led to him drugging and taking Kellie from Hong Kong to Shenzhen, China, then keeping her travel documents that prevented her from leaving Liwei's clutches. Meilin swooped in and got Kellie out of Liwei's facility, forcing him to surrender her travel documents. His disappearance days later and the discovery of his body in the waters between Hong Kong and Macao were never solved other than a short article in the Hong Kong paper speculating that it was an accidental death.

"I'm sorry to hear about your father. He always had confidence in your abilities and now you're being rewarded. So, tell me about your trip here and other ChiTran developments," Kellie prompted.

"China is a growing economy. Our business expenses and labor are becoming more expensive. It's my responsibility to look for opportunities to keep ChiTran moving in the right direction and keep it profitable. Just like American and European companies, we must find more affordable labor. We're exploring the possibility of a southern neighbor as a place to expand," Meilin offered.

"Since you're already located in southern China, does that mean you're looking beyond your border? Where?" Kellie asked.

"Vietnam looks very inviting to ChiTran, but there are issues preventing an immediate expansion. It could be several years before we can take full advantage of that country. Still, it's a growth opportunity."

"That sounds very exciting," Kellie responded. As she listened to everything Meilin said, Kellie made mental notes of several key points Meilin mentioned.

Kearns, looking out the window, saw his colleague's cellphone being raised to his ear. Kearns waited a moment then raised his phone, knowing the line was still live.

"Are you able to get anything from their conversation?" Kearns asked.

"Nothing. Everything behind me is still in Chinese," Adams replied.

"I'm sure that trying to establish operations in Vietnam will keep you busy. I'm surprised you have the time to make a trip to Washington," Kellie said, hoping to elicit more information from Meilin.

Meilin nodded. She wasn't surprised that Kellie made a comment or questioned her about this trip. "I have business stops to make in the United States. I'm exploring American partners to make everything work in Vietnam. A few of the details for my stops need to be finalized. Any commitment to proceed with our Vietnam venture requires a lot of resources and we need partners. It's good to have a familiar contact at our embassy here. Do you remember Shan Zhou?"

Kellie's eyes narrowed as she concentrated on the name. "No, I don't remember. Did I meet him?"

"He came to the hotel in Guangzhou . . ." Meilin let her statement hang for a moment. "He wasn't very polite when he met with us. In fact, he was unhappy about something we had done to get your travel documents."

Kellie's head tilted slowly to one side. "I remember him being angry. He thought you or we should've given him more information or something about my abduction. He corrected me about how I should address him."

"Yes, that's right. He's now posted to the embassy as a commercial counsellor even though he works mostly on customs matters. He rose quickly and is very efficient. Maybe it'll be helpful to you to know he's here."

Kellie's mind churned with competing thoughts. She digested the information, and her mind processed the possibilities of how Meilin meant that last comment. To Kellie, Meilin was dropping lots of tidbits of information for her to consider. Her mind was racing and wondered how any of it might clash with or complement the information Norman Quarles had sent. Kellie felt her cheeks warming and took a deep breath, hoping to calm her accelerating heart rate. She fought to prevent her cheeks from reddening and physically exposing her emotions. Different thoughts in her mind were converging and, although she kept a smile on her face, she hid her slight movements on the chair as she felt less comfortable than minutes ago.

"I have no doubt that there are companies that may be interested in considering Vietnam," Kellie said. "I haven't been there, but there's a lot of interest in Vietnam from many companies looking for cost advantages from an energetic and youthful country."

Suspicion surfaced in Kellie's mind. Was Meilin following the news of her nomination? Would the Chinese be that interested in it? If the Chinese were interested, what was going on that she wasn't aware of? Lots of questions popped into her mind without answers. If Meilin raised the subject of the State Department job, Kellie decided she'd brush off probing questions by feigning ignorance of some of the details or telling her she didn't understand the questions in Chinese. Kellie focused on China, but she tried to stay up to date on the region, knowing that China's influence on the region grew ever larger and not always in a positive way.

Kellie thought it strange that the Vietnamese would welcome the Chinese with open arms. Even if the animosities between them arising from the short 1979 war had been shelved, recent territorial disputes over islands in the South China Sea were fresh in the minds of most Chinese and Vietnamese.

She glanced down at her wrist. "Meilin, I'm sorry to say that I need to go to work. We should have dinner while you are in town," Kellie said.

"I agree. Please send me an email. I'm available in the evenings. Any calls to China can wait until dinner is over," Meilin responded.

The two women stood. Kellie took a couple of steps toward Meilin, giving her a quick hug and headed off toward the Dupont subway station.

The Chinese security officer stood and drifted toward the door when Kellie stood. Kearns saw his partner move his chair, giving Kellie space behind him and able to have a better visual on Meilin, but not the taller woman.

Kearns's eyes moved back and forth between the women outside and the Asian man. Kearns raised the phone to speak to Adams. "An Asian guy is going to come out. Keep an eye on him," Kearns said.

The Chinese security officer stepped toward the door and waited until Kellie had walked away from the coffee shop before exiting and falling in behind her.

Kearns, expecting the Asian man to stay with the Chinese woman, bumped the table as he stood up and dashed to the door and out to the sidewalk as soon as he saw the man begin to follow the taller woman.

Kearns gave his partner outside a hand signal to stay put and followed the Asian man. *What the hell is going on here?* Kearns thought. He was half a block behind the woman and about ten paces behind the Asian man. "What's going on at your end?" Kearns said into the phone.

"Nothing. She's still here, sitting for the moment."

"Let me know what happens when she leaves," Kearns said. He kept his distance behind the Asian man. Farther ahead, he saw Kellie approach the top of the escalator at the subway station and disappear. The Asian man's pace slowed then he stopped. Kearns slowed but kept walking in the direction of the subway station. He saw the Asian man turn around and got a glimpse of the man's face as he passed.

Kearns took a few steps before reversing course and followed the Asian man. Kearns put the phone to his ear and spoke. "What's going on?"

"The woman got into a cab."

"Did you notice anyone following her?" Kearns wondered.

"No one. When the cab pulled away, I didn't notice a car tailing her."

"What the fuck is going on?" Kearns said just above a whisper.

"Why? What's going on?"

"Our tall woman had a tail until she got to the subway station then he just turned around. He didn't call anybody, and I didn't see anyone else take over, but I didn't hang around to watch when he gave up the surveillance. I'm about twenty paces behind. Get to the car and wait. I want to see where he's headed." Kearns disconnected but kept the phone in his hand.

Kearns followed the man around the east side of Dupont Circle. As he walked, he speed-dialed Adams. "I just turned off the circle, heading east on P Street. I'm on the north side of the street." Kearns picked up the pace and closed the distance. He saw his target cross 18th Street and get into a car.

Kearns speed dialed Adams again. "My guy is in a car parked on P Street, just a few feet from where it intersects with 18th. He's illegally parked facing west," Kearns said into the phone. Kearns kept walking. After he passed the black Chevy Malibu, he slowed and looked over his shoulder. The car had diplomatic plates. He stopped about ten feet past the car for a few seconds to look at and memorize the plate number. He kept moving, but slower. "Pick me up on P Street between 17th and 18th," Kearns instructed. The country code on the license plate convinced him that it was Chinese, but he wanted a confirmation.

Kearns stopped mid-block and stepped closer to the curb. The embassy car didn't move. When he turned to look toward 17th Street, he saw Adams steer the car onto P Street. Kearns stepped off the curb, getting into the car when it stopped.

"There's something odd about all of this," Kearns said. "Now, he's just sitting there."

Adams pressed the gas lightly and he drove slowly toward the intersection. Both pairs of eyes taking another look at the license plate.

"What do you think is going on," Kearns posed to his partner.

Adams shook his head slowly as he rolled to a stop at the circle.

"Go up to Q and come back around," Kearns directed.

"He was on foot. He left his car and followed our mystery woman to the coffee shop and after she gets to the subway, he returns to his car and just sits. Do you think she lives on this block?" Adams speculated.

Kearns rubbed his chin then turned his head toward Adams. "That makes sense. What doesn't make sense is why she's being tailed. We need to find out who she is as well as our Chinese lady and find out how they're connected," Kearns stated.

"What do we do when we go back around?" Adams asked.

"When we approach P Street again, just turn onto the street and pull over. I'll call Metro Police and have them send someone to get him to move and we'll see what happens," Kearns said.

Navigating the busy streets in the area took longer than expected. Kearns was worried that his Chinese target might be gone when they returned to P Street. As Adams turned back onto P Street, Kearns's concerns vanished. The Malibu was still there, and he could see a head on the driver's side. He called Metro Police, explaining he was an FBI agent and needed them to check on a Chinese male illegally parked at the corner of 18th and P Streets. Kearns decided he could assume the man was Chinese now that he'd seen the diplomatic plates on the car. At the very least, he asked if they could get him to move.

"How long?" Adams asked.

"They said they'd send a car right away, but who knows."

Within ten minutes, a DC Metro police car appeared with its lights flashing. It stopped and blocked traffic, leaving space for the Chinese driver to pull into the traffic lane. Kearns and Adams tried to see what was going on but didn't have a good view because of all the parked cars between them and the target vehicle.

Adams opened his window and cocked his head toward it to get a better view. "I think the driver's not as cooperative as our officer would like. The officer's head is bobbing a bit and pointing toward the circle. Okay, wait, I see brake lights. The cop is stepping away from the car, giving him room to pull out."

Adams straightened in his seat and turned on the left turn signal. He pulled up slowly behind the DC Metro police car whose flashing lights had been turned off.

"Come on, let's go," Kearns said aloud as if the police officers could hear him. After a half minute that felt like several minutes to Kearns, the car ahead moved. "Did you see where the Malibu went? I think he turned into the circle."

"Yeah, he did, but he has several streets to turn onto from the circle."

"My gut says he needs to get back to the spot where he was parked so he can keep an eye on this street," Kearns guessed.

Adams turned off the circle at the first opportunity and they were back on Q Street and through two signals. "Is that him? The fourth car ahead?" Kearns asked.

"I can't see it through these cars," Adams said.

Kearns rolled down his window and stuck his forehead out to see ahead to the next corner. He felt Adams give the car more gas, staying near the bumper of the car ahead. "Can you make the light?" Kearns asked.

"Depends on the cars in front of me."

"The Malibu is turning right. He's heading back to his spot," Kearns noticed.

None of the three cars between them and the Malibu made a right turn. Adams turned right onto 17th Street. Both saw the Malibu two car lengths ahead. The driver wasn't in any hurry. Adams braked to maintain their distance. As they approached the turn onto P Street, the Malibu pulled over just feet from the corner.

"Damn it!" Kearns wasn't happy. "Go past him and find a spot mid-block and pull over. Hopefully, he hasn't noticed us."

"That makes no sense if she lives on this street. He can't see anything from where he pulled over," Adams added.

Adams kept an eye on the rearview mirror and Kearns focused on the passenger side mirror.

"This is interesting," Adams said.

"What do you see?"

"Another black Malibu just pulled out of a spot right at the corner on P and the guy we were following is taking his place," Adams reported.

Kearns watched the second Malibu pass them. It had diplomatic plates, and the different numbers confirmed Adams's visual that it was a second car.

Adams watched the car and saw it pull over at the far end of the block. "I think this other driver took over the spot that was vacated. Why do they have two guys conducting surveillance on this street? They know she's not here so why are they watching here?" Adams wondered.

"We need to find out why they're watching her. Who the hell is she? Do we have a picture of her?" Kearns asked.

"No, I didn't take one. It would've been a bit awkward," Adams said.

Kearns started writing into a notepad. "How tall would you say she was?"

"Five-nine, five-ten, short straight black hair. Her facial features give me the impression that she's biracial, Asian-American. Given that I heard her speaking Chinese with the other woman, that all fits," Adams added.

"Are you estimating her height with heels," Kearns asked.

"I didn't notice her shoes. Maybe take an inch or two off the height estimate, but let's just say she's five-seven to five-ten in height," Adams corrected.

"If only we could question one of these guys. That would answer a few of the questions I have," Kearns said. Kearns punched in a number on his phone. "Vera, I have a task for you and Olvera this evening. If you need to take some time to get anything done this afternoon, go ahead and tell Olvera the same. I'll give you details when I get into the office." Kearns ended the call.

Adams looked over at Kearns. "You sure about this? Messing with Dip plates?"

Kearns smiled and shrugged.

* * * * *

The dusk's waning light was enough to see the lone head in the Malibu. Agents Vera Jamison and David Olvera parked their car on 17th Street as close to the P Street corner as possible.

"What do you think?" Jamison asked, sitting in the passenger seat.

"I'd say another ten minutes, fifteen at the most," Olvera answered.

Lights from the buildings on both sides of the street made streetlamps unnecessary. Before they exited their vehicle, Olvera took out his FBI identification. Both agents tugged on clear vinyl gloves.

"Ready?'

"Show time," Jamison said.

Olvera rounded the corner onto P Street and stepped out into the street on the driver's side. Jamison stayed on the sidewalk. When she saw Olvera stop to tap the rolled-up window, she darted from the sidewalk to the passenger door, finding it unlocked, she ducked into the seat next to the Chinese driver whose head snapped in her direction. She reached out and grabbed the keys in the ignition before he could react.

The driver turned his head back toward his window when he heard the hard tapping. The FBI identification was eye-level. His eyes went up to Olvera's face then over to Jamison seated next to him.

Olvera pointed to the back door and got in behind the driver.

At the other end of the block, the Chinese security officer didn't see anything going on in the street. He had the rearview mirror and passenger side mirror angled so that he could see the entrance to an apartment building.

"You speak English?" Jamison asked.

"A little."

Knowing the answer, she asked anyway. "You're from the Chinese Embassy?" The driver's nod confirmed what they already knew.

"Where's your embassy identification?" Olvera asked.

The driver moved slowly and pulled it from the inside pocket of his sport coat. He handed it over to Jamison who compared the photo with the man behind the steering wheel. Jamison handed the identification back to the Chinese driver.

"Who are you watching?" Vera asked, speaking slowly and deliberately.

"No one," the driver lied.

"Your embassy keeps a team on this street. We know there's another car at the corner. We watched one of your colleagues follow a woman this morning. Who are you following?" Vera Jamison pressed.

"I cannot say."

"You know, but you refuse to say," Olvera clarified his answer.

"Diplomatic immunity," the driver said.

"Not tonight," Jamison threatened. "If you give us the name of the person you are looking for, we go home, and you stay here. But, if you do not give us a name, you come with us."

The driver shifted in his seat. His eyes went from one agent to the other.

When the driver looked back at Olvera again, Olvera spoke. "No name, no immunity." Olvera raised both hands for the driver to see that he wore gloves. "No fingerprints, no evidence."

Jamison heard the driver's breathing change, and his nose flared slightly as he inhaled more deeply through his nose. He was rattled. "This is very easy. You tell us the name and we go home. You don't have to tell anyone about our meeting."

The driver pushed himself into the corner against the back of his seat and the door. He wanted to see both faces in the little light there was in the street. He didn't trust them. He believed that he'd be taken away if he didn't give them the name. He didn't like the idea of being taken away at night. Seeing both agents wearing gloves meant they didn't care about the rules of diplomatic immunity. If he divulged the name, he knew he'd probably be packing up and going back to China within days if not hours. But he had no idea what would happen if he's taken away at night by the FBI. He knew from the Chinese Press that people were taken to Guantanamo and kept there.

"I tell you the name, you go?"

"That's right. You tell us the name, we go," Jamison confirmed.

"Okay. Kellie Liang. Chinese name Liang Kaili," the driver said.

"She has two names?" Olvera asked.

"Liang Kaili is Chinese name."

"Okay. Which building," Olvera asked.

The driver took out a piece of paper from his jacket pocket with an address.

"One more question. How long has the embassy been watching Kellie Liang," Jamison asked.

The driver shrugged. "Maybe one or two months."

Olvera and Jamison looked at each other. "Why?" Olvera asked.

"Safety," the driver answered.

"We don't understand. What do you mean about safety?" Jamison asked.

"Washington is dangerous, lots of murders, crime. We want her safe."

"China wants Ms. Liang safe?" Jamison said, repeating the answer. She saw the driver nod, confirming that she got it right.

Jamison reached out, offering the car keys in her palm. "Thank you," she said after the driver took the keys.

Both agents walked back to their car.

"We have the building address and name. I think we should pay Ms. Liang a visit," Jamison proposed.

"No, not a good idea. Kearns would want to know more about her before we just barge in like that. We need to know more about our mystery woman before we make contact. I want to know what she does, where she works and get some background before we make any move to contact her," Olvera explained.

Jamison and Olvera settled into their car. "You're right," Jamison conceded.

"If the Chinese Embassy is that concerned about her safety, does it mean she's working for them? How does this make any sense otherwise," Olvera wondered aloud.

"If she is working for them, this detail makes no sense because they're too obvious and in the open. Wouldn't they want to hide the fact that she works for them?" Vera Jamison countered.

"Let's get back to the office and see if we can find anything about Liang. I'm hoping it won't take long," Olvera said.

Twenty minutes after leaving P Street, Jamison and Olvera sat at their desks. Their fingers working their keyboards. "Got something," Jamison said. Olvera walked over and stood behind her.

"Kellie Liang works for Senator Nathan Burke. She's been picked for a political job at the State Department," Jamison said. She read on to herself for a moment. "Maybe this is it. Her job would be focused on China. It says her father was prosecuted for some illegal business transactions with the Chinese. We already know she's fluent in Chinese so that's nothing new."

"If she's up for a job at State and being watched by the Chinese, is it strange for her to meet with people from the Chinese Embassy? Maybe there's a big black hole in her background investigation," Olvera suggested.

"You'd think that given what's in the article, someone would've already done the deep dive investigation," Jamison responded.

"I think we report this up the chain and see how they want to handle it," Olvera suggested.

"One thing's for sure, if she's going to take that spot at State, we want to be sure who she's working for," Jamison said.

Obstacles

Senator Burke sat rigid on a sofa in the living room of his small one-bedroom Capitol Hill apartment. He didn't need a big place since he and his wife had decided that she would spend most of her time in Pennsylvania. A supervisory FBI agent and Agent Kearns from the counterintelligence unit sat opposite the senator and described the previous day's activity. The seven o'clock call from the FBI threw Burke's morning off schedule. The words "counterintelligence" had a way of focusing one's thoughts.

The agent making the early morning call didn't elaborate over the phone and explained that agents would be arriving shortly for an in-person conversation. Senator Burke thought about the different senate committees he served on and all the sensitive and classified information available to him. His mind raced through recent activities with hearings, witnesses, and the statements he'd heard. Nothing about any of that alarmed him. He limited the number of his staff who attended closed hearings and reviewed documents from closed sessions. He limited access to classified information to a few on his staff, knowing that background checks were needed for each person accessing classified documents and hearings where classified information is divulged.

"She's not a risk. If that's what you're trying to tell me, I don't accept it," Senator Burke insisted. "You guys always see someone like Ms. Liang as a risk. Just because she speaks Chinese and, through our American eyes, we see someone who looks Asian or, in this case, Chinese, it doesn't mean she's a threat. Why don't you flip your viewpoint. Consider it all another way, she's among a select few who provide us with the benefit of her language skills, knowledge of the culture and a level of acceptance you and I don't receive.

"No issues have ever arisen because of her access to classified information. No one has ever come to me and told me of any problems. If you don't know, you should know that this is her second stint working on Capitol Hill. There were no issues with her background checks in the past or when I requested one for her when I brought her on board," Burke explained.

"Senator, you understand that we'll have to let a few people know about this," Agent Kearns said. "This is an unusual set of circumstances. Do you realize how strange it is that the Chinese are watching her because they claim they're concerned for her safety? Are you aware of any threats against her? Being on your staff, she fills a sensitive position and as a nominee for a position of greater sensitivity, we'll need to contact a few of your colleagues," Kearns continued.

"I hope you are very careful about the way you communicate your concerns. You have no evidence that Ms. Liang has done anything other than meet with an unknown woman seen leaving the Chinese Embassy. They met and we have no idea what they talked about so do not make any accusations or reach any conclusions until you have something more concrete," Burke warned.

"We understand," Kearns answered.

"How do you plan to proceed," Burke asked.

"We'd rather not get into that for now, but if there's anything more you can provide about Ms. Liang that would help, we'd appreciate it. Any information about the woman she met with would help us," Kearns responded. He looked over at his supervisor who had said nothing after the initial morning greetings and handshake but was along for the ride in case Kearns needed a more senior agent as backup.

As all three men rose, Kearns offered the Senator a couple of business cards. "Call me anytime. We'll want to speak to Ms. Liang directly."

"I'll make sure she contacts you," Burke said and walked the agents to the door. After they were gone, he ran his hand through his combed sandy blond hair and walked back to a closet to grab a necktie and his suit jacket. *This was no way to start a day*, he thought.

As soon as a few of his colleagues get wind of this, it would provide them and the White House with excuses to kill Kellie's nomination. If he fought for her, how would that look to voters? Would it jeopardize his re-election next year? Was there a way to spin this so that people would see her as giving the government an advantage?

Burke looked in a mirror and recombed his hair, knotted his necktie, and folded his suit jacket over his forearm before grabbing his briefcase by the door and exiting. Heading to the office, his thoughts competed between his re-election and supporting Kellie. Could he do both or were they mutually exclusive? He wasn't sure.

* * * * *

"Good morning, Trish. If Kellie's in, tell her I need to see her right away," Burke said as he strode by Trish's desk. He was past her before she could respond. Burke pushed his office door closed. After hanging his jacket on a coat rack, he went and stood behind his desk, wading through a short stack of documents and folders. He looked up at the clock above the door then turned his attention back to the stack reaching back and pulling his chair in to sit.

"Come in," he said, hearing the tapping on his door.

"Trish said you wanted to see me," Kellie said as she took a step into Burke's office.

"Close the door and take a seat," Burke said as he rubbed his forehead as if he had a headache. Burke leaned forward, both elbows on the desk and his chin resting on his intertwined hands. "The FBI called this morning then came to see me," Burke started as he lowered his arms and sat back. He watched Kellie whose expression didn't change. "Is there anything going on that could affect your nomination that I should know about?"

Kellie looked at her boss and shook her head. "Nothing. Why?"

"The FBI's counterintelligence unit stumbled across something a bit out of the ordinary."

"I don't understand," Kellie responded, pressing herself back in the chair.

"Did anything strange or unusual happen yesterday," Burke asked.

"Unusual? No. Unscheduled, yes. I met with a woman named Meilin Moy. Our fathers are cousins. I guess that makes us second or third cousins. She's a successful Chinese businesswoman. Her situation might be hard for Americans to comprehend. Her father is a Taiwan businessman, but when he began his mainland China enterprise, he ended up in a relationship with a woman in the mainland resulting in Meilin being his mainland daughter. She's risen to be the CEO of ChiTran.

"I didn't know she was coming to DC. She sent me an email saying she was in town. I suggested a morning meeting at a coffee shop. It was a short meeting, maybe twenty minutes before I came to work. We agreed to meet for dinner while she's in town," Kellie explained.

"Did you know about her contacts at the Chinese Embassy?"

"She mentioned that someone I was introduced to in China seven years ago is now posted at the embassy. It doesn't surprise me that she knows people at the embassy or that she would go there," Kellie said.

"Why's that?"

"When I was in Hong Kong and China, it was obvious she had connections with some government people at the provincial level, you know, like at the state level in the U.S. Her success in business opened doors and gave her access to people in positions of influence. I'm guessing that with her rise to CEO she has made even higher-level contacts in China during the seven years since I first met her."

"Is there anything about your relationship with her that jeopardizes your nomination?"

"Nothing I can think of," Kellie answered.

"What about surveillance?" Burke asked.

Kellie's raised eyebrows and slight turn of head reflexive reaction signaled to Burke that she didn't know about any surveillance.

"It's the surveillance that concerned the FBI more than your meeting with who we now know is your distant cousin," Burke stated. "They thought she was the one who had a protective detail. It came as a surprise that you are the one they're keeping tabs on. One of the Chinese told the FBI that they wanted to be sure you're safe. They've been watching you for a few weeks. Have you noticed anyone following you recently?"

Kellie shook her head slowly. "I've never given it a thought. I was more aware of my surroundings for a while after I came home from Hong Kong because of the kidnapping, but I guess I reached a comfort level that things were safe and stopped thinking about that. I think I told you before that it was Meilin, the woman I met with for coffee yesterday, who rescued me from that situation. Other people helped, but she was the one who got me away from the guy who drugged me."

"The FBI agents don't think there's any immediate threat, but you need to know about this and I'm instructing you to call the FBI and tell them about your cousin. They want to know who she is," Burke said as he dug out one of the Kearns's cards and offered it to Kellie.

"I'll make sure that gets done right away," Kellie answered. "Is there anything else?" Kellie scooted to the edge of her chair, ready to return to her desk.

"Changing gears. There's a closed hearing with the Chief of Naval Operations this afternoon. I know you weren't working on anything related to this, but I want you to take a look at the documents. If there are any issues I should raise or questions I should pose, jot them down and put them in the folder."

Kellie took the folder in the Senator's outstretched hand, stood, and returned to her desk. A call to Agent Kearns was her priority. She needed to check this off her to-do list and put it behind her, hoping a call and explanation would put an end to this.

Kellie put the folder down onto her desk then picked up the receiver to her landline phone, dialing Agent Kearns's number. Kearns picked up on the second ring, catching her by surprise, expecting a secretary to answer.

"This is Kellie Liang calling from Senator Burke's office."

"Ms. Liang. I appreciate you calling. I guess you know about my meeting with the Senator this morning and why we wanted you to call."

"Yes. I just spoke to the senator," Kellie responded. She spent the next fifteen minutes giving Kearns the background about how she and Meilin Moy met and how often they communicated or in this case how little they had communicated over the past seven years.

"Now that you have the background and know about my Hong Kong and China experience, can I ask you a question," Kellie inquired.

"Ask, but no guarantees that I can provide answers," Kearns answered.

"What prompted you to follow Meilin?"

"We saw her leave the embassy with Mr. Xiong. A patent office employee tried to pass confidential information to Mr. Xiong, and we were watching him and wanted to know who some of the others were at the embassy. We had nothing on her and now we know why. She's not an employee of the embassy. She has no diplomatic immunity like the others."

Kearns's last statement perked her up. Kellie needed to be careful. Was Meilin's visit to DC as innocent as she had described or was there something more sinister involved. Kearns pointing out that Meilin didn't have diplomatic immunity meant the FBI was concerned about what Meilin might be doing on her trip.

"Wait, let's back up. You found Xiong with confidential information given to him by a patent examiner? Would that be the same patent examiner that the Washington Post reported about? He pleaded guilty at his arraignment a few days ago."

"The same," Kearns confirmed.

"You were involved in that?"

"Me and several other agents along with the Justice Department lawyers," Kearns offered.

"What's the security angle to this," Kellie asked.

"We weren't sure of any national security angle until a Justice lawyer reviewed the information attempted to be given to the Chinese. She said that the technology covered by the patent dealt with dredging equipment and improvements on existing ways to do this. It could have security aspects to it if we're thinking about deep-water ports and commercial or naval activities," Kearns explained.

"May I have the name and contact details for the Justice lawyer," Kellie asked. Kearns was accommodating. She wrote down the information. "I hope I've put to rest any concerns you have about my meeting with Ms. Moy," Kellie said.

"I appreciate you calling and explaining so promptly," Kearns said. "I hope you'll understand if I need to call with additional questions."

"Of course," Kellie responded and ended the call.

Kellie added Victoria Walters to a list of people she needed to call or meet. She put the contact information next to her desk phone and stared at the cover on the folder in front of her. "SECRET" was stamped on the folder's cover.

Knowing that she was being watched by the Chinese caused Kellie to hesitate in opening the folder. *What if being watched turned into being abducted again?* Kellie closed her eyes and dismissed the thought. She opened the folder and skimmed the documents. She read portions of several pages with highlighted sentences and phrases about the type of warships being deployed in support of activities in Iraq and Afghanistan, the outlook of the navy's replenishment needs for weapons systems because of the ongoing operations in that part of the world.

Kellie saw nothing in the documents that addressed the navy's requirements in Asia. She picked up the folder and walked across the reception area past Trish's desk and tapped on the Senator's door.

"Come in."

Kellie held the folder up. "I looked through the folder. This closed hearing is all about the war on terror and the navy's plans or needs, but nothing about China or Asia. I don't see any reason for me to be there," Kellie commented.

"We can't have blinders on and focus on one region and exclude or ignore our strategic concerns elsewhere. Prep a couple of questions for me to drop on the Admiral," Senator Burke instructed.

Kellie turned and walked away. When it came to things related to the war on terror, Kellie wasn't the lead on the Senator's staff. She went to see Douglas Stewart. Douglas's desk was separated by dividers like Kellie's and located two desks down from hers. She and Douglas had a cordial working relationship avoiding interference in each other's areas of responsibility.

An army veteran, everyone knew that Douglas oversaw the military related issues in the office. Douglas went through a college ROTC program and spent six years on active duty after graduating. He was in constant contact with civilian staff and uniformed officers at the pentagon. Operations in Afghanistan and Iraq forced Douglas to spend more time in uniform than expected despite being a reserve officer. At thirty-seven, he had resigned himself to accepting that he'd probably never rise above the rank of major, a promotion he had received only months ago but the demands on active-duty troops gave him hope about rising higher in the ranks, spurring him to delve into more issues about military readiness and working with intel agencies.

"Douglas, are you getting ready for the hearing with the Admiral?" Kellie asked, knowing the answer.

"Yeah, but not expecting any surprises," Douglas said as he stood up at his desk. He got out of his chair because he didn't like sitting and talking to anyone who was standing. His five-eight height made him a fraction shorter than Kellie even when standing. Though they didn't compete in the office, Douglas knew that Kellie's language skills and China knowledge made her a valuable person on the staff and allowed her to have a lot of face time with Senator Burke.

Douglas worked long hours to gain information from his military and intel community contacts to maintain his close one-on-one working relationship with the senator.

"Just wanted to let you know that the senator asked me to hand him a few extra questions for the admiral. He thinks that we need to be more expansive with our security concerns."

"You mean China, what they're up to, and how we're responding," Douglas guessed given Kellie's China and Asia oriented experience.

"There have been a couple of developments in recent weeks, and we'd like to get the admiral to think about more than the war on terror," Kellie said. She took a few minutes to explain the Lucas Moore situation.

"It's a good idea to let the brass know that we can't look the other way or allow ourselves to be blinded to what's going on in Asia," Douglas acknowledged.

* * * * *

Kellie and Douglas sat behind Senator Burke in the hearing room. The Chairman of the Senate Armed Services Committee tapped the gavel twice to signal the hearing's start. The Committee Chairman read a short statement before turning to the ranking Democrat on the committee who spoke. The staffers sitting behind the senators seemed preoccupied reviewing documents in their laps.

Behind the witness table, the Chief of Naval Operations sat rigid in his uniform adorned with rows of ribbons representing his many medals. The chairs behind the admiral were mostly empty in the closed hearing room except for his staff officers.

Kellie, Douglas, and Senator Burke listened to the back and forth between the admiral and other senators about what the navy was learning in its use of supposed precision ordnance like its cruise missiles and the use of drones. A few questions delved into how the Navy's aircraft were holding up under constant use, the need for spare parts and other details that the public didn't need to know for now as far as the committee was concerned. Nothing during the first forty minutes deviated from the focus on the navy's activities related to Afghanistan and Iraq.

"Admiral, as the top navy officer, I'm sure you look at the global picture rather than limiting yourself to Afghanistan and Iraq," Senator Burke started when he was recognized to take his turn. Burke saw the slightest nod of acknowledgment from the admiral.

"When it comes to Asia and China specifically, what are your concerns?" Senator Burke asked.

"As you know as a member of this committee, we're active in the Pacific region with a large presence along various trade routes and protecting our economic interests in the region. Commercial shipping routes are important to us, and we must ensure that they remain undisturbed. We have our base in Japan and good allies in the Japanese and South Korea. We have very good relations with many governments and countries in the region to offset China's desire to gain access and increase influence in the region."

"What are your concerns about the possibility of conflict," Senator Burke asked.

"Strategically, we monitor several of the potential flash points caused by China's increased claims on Pacific islands that are also claimed by other countries. Vietnam, the Philippines, Taiwan, and Malaysia are among some of the governments that have claims that are challenged by China. It means we need to maintain a strong presence in the Pacific region by supporting our allies," the admiral responded.

"Out of curiosity, does the Navy plan on any port stops in Vietnam?"

For the first time, the admiral's expression changed with a smile creeping across his face. "We don't see that happening in the near or medium term."

"You realize that we concluded a trade agreement with Vietnam in 2000, five years ago, and bilateral trade and commercial activity are increasing. It seems that our former adversary is ripe for cultivating as an ally in the region," Senator Burke commented.

"We're aware that great progress has been made, but for the navy and, if you ask the business community, what hampers significant progress is Vietnam's lack of deep-water ports for the largest naval vessels and container ships. Until Vietnam has deep-water ports, there will be limits. However, don't interpret my comment as saying that we are limited in our mission capabilities in the region. We have other friends in the region who welcome port visits by the U.S. Navy."

"What do you think Vietnam needs for it to have deep water ports that will accommodate the types of ships that are currently unable to use its ports?" the Senator pressed.

"It requires technology, engineering and time."

"How much time?"

"That depends on Vietnam's access to the latest technology, good engineers and companies able to do the job," the admiral responded.

"If the Vietnamese can't do it by themselves, who could?" Senator Burke probed.

"There are plenty of governments in the region that would have both a military and commercial interest in seeing Vietnam's capabilities improve. As you pointed out, we concluded a trade agreement with Vietnam so our economic interests would benefit if there were deep water ports there. The others that come immediately to mind are Japan, South Korea, and China," the admiral answered.

"Once Vietnam has deep-water ports, what are the chances that China's navy would have a regular presence there?"

The four-star admiral looked from one end of the dais where the senators sat to the other. "I could be wrong, but it isn't likely. There is an adversarial relationship between the two countries because of their competing territorial claims that, at times, comes close to hostilities between them. Having said that, the economic and commercial interests for both suggest that there could be extreme economic and trade interests in working together for mutual monetary gains."

Kellie took notes of the admiral's comments. She couldn't help but recall Meilin's comment about Vietnam during their short meeting. Her thoughts went back to the Post article and the information the patent examiner had tried to give the Chinese Embassy employee. China and Vietnam kept popping up. The admiral's comments merged with her thoughts. She pictured puzzle pieces in her mind. Now, she felt like she'd finally found the four corners of the puzzle but everything else was missing.

Minutes passed while Kellie was lost in her thoughts. The sound of the gavel signaled the end of the hearing. She watched from her chair as the admiral, a tall, fit man probably in his late fifties or early sixties walked toward the dais and shook hands with several senators.

Douglas had already exited the hearing room, but Kellie lingered. The committee chairman gave Senator Burke a head nod prompting Nathan Burke to walk over to the chairman. Kellie watched as the chairman spoke and Senator Burke stood there, both hands in front of him holding a small binder. Burke stood with his back to Kellie. Whatever the conversation, Kellie didn't see the chairman smile, but maintain a stern look as he spoke, looking up at Senator Burke. Though not pointing directly at her, the chairman pointed in the general direction of where she and Douglas had been sitting.

When the chairman was finished, and Burke turned and walked toward Kellie. She saw him roll his eyes.

"That didn't look good," Kellie said.

"Not here," the Senator said. They marched back to Senator Burke's office without speaking.

Senator Burke saw several people waiting to see him as soon as he entered his suite of offices. "Sorry to keep you waiting, but could you give me ten minutes," he said apologetically.

Kellie followed him into his office and sat across from him. "We have a problem," she guessed.

"Yep. It may be a big problem. The chairman informed me that the FBI let him know about your meeting yesterday morning and he knows about the surveillance on you. He thought that I exercised bad judgment letting you sit in on today's hearing. I did let him know that the FBI provided nothing that would indicate that you have done anything wrong and that you had already spoken to them to allay any concerns they might have."

"The lack of evidence won't help me," Kellie suggested. "Anything that might imply or insinuate that I might in the future do something will be enough to undermine the nomination and you know that. Whatever I do for you, the other senators, it'll never be enough, will it?" Her last words spilled out unintended. "I'm sorry, I shouldn't have said that. I know how hard you're working for me, and I do appreciate everything you are doing."

Senator Burke pushed himself back in his chair, causing it to recline as he looked up at the ceiling. "Kellie, I understand your frustration and I wouldn't blame you if you were angry. We'll pursue this to the very end. We're not at a point of withdrawing your name."

The two looked at each other for a moment without speaking.

Kellie took a deep breath then got back to business. "What I see is a complex and blurred picture. There's the recent patent examiner's failure to complete his delivery of information, now the embassy has been exposed as keeping an eye on me and Meilin's trip. The patent information issue has nothing to do with me. The other two are connected.

"If we think about what the admiral said about Vietnam and then what Meilin told me about her hope to expand in Vietnam, I think the files intended to be given to the Chinese about dredging technology all come together. I think that the Chinese are trying to gain the upper hand with Vietnam, and we aren't paying enough attention. Individually, none of this means anything. But if we step back and look for a common element, things become clearer," Kellie explained.

Senator Burke folded his arms. He stared at Kellie for a moment. He stood up and moved behind his chair, gripping it with both hands. "Everything you're saying makes sense. We, meaning you, need to be careful. The Committee Chairman says he supports you, but I think he'd turn on you in a heartbeat, and right now he feels like the slightest thing is enough to do that. This Meilin woman, are you planning to meet with her again?"

"I can't just disappear on her. That would seem strange to her. As I already told you, I agreed to arrange dinner with her. Of course, now that I know I'm being watched, I'll change my routine," Kellie answered.

"You need to think about how much to change your routine. If there's a sudden and drastic change, that won't be good. Change must be gradual, otherwise alarm bells go off. Any plans involving the Chinese need to be implemented with the idea of avoiding being photographed or seen by the wrong people. If it gets out publicly and these senators get wind of anything, I may not be able to save your nomination. I'm sure you realize a few of these people are barely on our side. If they get any inkling that the White House's support is weakening, they'll be quick to withdraw support. I see you as an asset in this office and you would be an asset to the government if you get the position at State, but a lot of people can't get past the fact that your father is Chinese. Unfortunately, every time they see you, their biases surface. That's just the reality, Kellie."

"I knew this wasn't going to be easy. None of this surprises me." Kellie said as she stood.

"You need to have a thick skin and weather the current storm," Burke advised.

"I've dealt with the Chinese background issue all my life and that's not the problem. It's the narrow thinking that's more troubling," Kellie responded. She exited the senator's office.

Back in her cubicle, she sat back, taking a deep breath. She wondered if any job was worth the hassle of going through a process where every move she made was being examined and she was being judged, not on merit but her heritage. This all seemed to confirm that no matter what she did, it would never be enough.

Kellie called Meilin at her hotel, arranging dinner. She wanted to get that out of the way and move on, wondering if that was even possible.

* * * * *

Kellie rode the escalator up to ground level at Dupont Circle. Once she reached the top, she got out of the way of other pedestrians and dug into her purse for her sunglasses. It was a cloudless bright evening sky. As she placed them on her face, she thought wearing them had the added benefit of allowing her eyes to scan the people around her without being too obvious.

It was just after six. The sun wouldn't be setting for at least another hour. Kellie fell into a comfortable pace among the many who were headed home. The diverse crowd of people dressed every way possible. She had no way of knowing if someone was following her. Behind the dark lenses, her eyes scanned left to right and back again.

Once she crossed from the circle onto P Street, there were fewer people heading in the same direction. Waiting for the traffic light to change and the walk sign to illuminate, she saw it. The illegally parked car had diplomatic plates. She made a mental note of the license plate, especially the letter code. The car was empty. She looked toward the entry of her building and saw a couple of people enter, but they weren't Asian. No one else was standing around.

In her apartment, she had time before she needed to leave and meet Meilin. She sat at her desk and opened her laptop, checking the country code of the car she'd spotted. Her search confirmed that it was a Chinese diplomatic plate. Kellie sat back, looking down on the street through a thin curtain. She stood up at the window, parted the curtain trying to see to the end of the block where the car was parked. Her apartment was too far away from the corner to see anything. She wondered if someone had followed her from the subway station and where that person might be right now.

Kellie didn't need to change her clothes for her dinner meeting with Meilin. Before leaving the apartment, she made sure to leave lights on making it appear she was there. She closed and locked her door then headed for the rear staircase used mostly for emergencies. Her footsteps echoed throughout the concrete stairwell, opening out the rear of the building and accessing an alleyway. Outside, Kellie walked toward 18th Street. The paved alleyway gave residents and businesses access to garages and delivery areas. Not as well lit as the main street, splashes of light came from garage lights and apartments facing the alley. Kellie looked around and saw no one following on foot or any cars crawling along behind her.

With all the traffic lights in the Dupont Circle area and up along Connecticut Avenue, Kellie took a circuitous route to 20th

Street where several small restaurants lined the street. She padded the time, knowing she'd be early. She climbed the steps to the entrance to a small Greek restaurant.

"Good evening," a woman said in greeting.

"I have a reservation for two. If possible, is there a table in the back?"

The woman led Kellie past several occupied tables that fronted the street. The hostess gestured to a two-top near a corner in the back and on the opposite side from a waiter's station. Kellie looked around, satisfied that she'd be able to see almost every table between her and the entrance.

Kellie's perusal of the menu was interrupted when she saw Meilin being led to the table. Kellie stood and smiled, giving Meilin an embrace while watching the entrance. Both sat and placed their napkins in their laps. Kellie's eyes moved constantly from eye contact with Meilin then toward the restaurant entrance.

"How are your travel plans," Kellie asked in Cantonese.

"Things are clearer. Plans are developing for me to go to California to meet with a couple of engineering companies. Though, the problem is that my plans can change without warning. One minute, the plans are set then I get an email or fax and I need to change things completely."

"I didn't know that ChiTran was involved in engineering," Kellie said.

"We don't do any engineering ourselves, but we try to identify companies that have a mutual interest in a country and work with them. ChiTran can put up some financing if we also receive some preferences when a project is completed."

"The last time we spoke you said something about Vietnam. I don't see how ChiTran can benefit much by operating in a country where you can't ship large quantities out by sea," Kellie said, baiting Meilin.

"It's only a matter of time before the capabilities are there for us to exploit commercially," Meilin began. "It's important to explore all opportunities for ChiTran and China for future growth and expansion of our interests."

Meilin's mention of "expansion" caught Kellie's ear. Whose expansion was Meilin referring to?

A waiter strolled to the table. The two women ordered large salads and regained their privacy.

"Your rise to become the most important person in ChiTran and its success seems to reflect ChiTran's growth. Do you have broader expansion plans beyond Vietnam?" Kellie probed.

"China has many big companies. ChiTran isn't as big as the top tier companies. We need to be strategic in our growth. If we want to grow, we must be smart about our profit margins. Just like American and European companies, we need to look abroad for our advantages in our existing industries and in areas where we might want to grow," Meilin explained.

The more she heard, the more curious Kellie became. Something about Meilin's explanation didn't fit the picture forming in Kellie's head.

"You mean ChiTran is now in the position to invest the kind of money needed for Vietnam to get the capabilities needed to become a major exporter? I'm surprised that those in Beijing would let you divert that kind of money to activities outside of the mainland," Kellie commented.

Meilin took a moment to dab the corners of her mouth with the napkin. She wanted time to react. She needed an off ramp from this detailed discussion about ChiTran, but if she was too abrupt in changing subjects, she knew that Kellie would notice.

"Business in China is not like business here. Of course, you know that. The more success we have, the more attention we attract from the government. I must oversee ChiTran as a business, making money, keeping people employed and all the things you are familiar with, but I must also do some things to keep people in certain positions happy. They might ask for business-related favors and I cannot refuse. At times, some of the business favors are related to current or future commercial activities beyond our borders," Meilin said.

Kellie was leaning forward listening, wondering what type of commercial favors Meilin might be referring to, but couldn't come up with specifics. She was doubtful that Meilin was referring to paying bribes to well-placed people but wouldn't rule it out.

"You're right, it's different for American businesses. We have specific laws that allow or forbid certain business conduct," Kellie said, hoping to prompt Meilin to say more.

Meilin chuckled in reaction to Kellie's statement. "We also have laws, but we have unwritten rules or expectations that we have to be aware of in business," Meilin responded. "Sometimes, heads of companies are asked to do things that might commercially benefit the company but are intended to benefit the government's policies more so."

"I don't know if I can understand it without an example," Kellie pressed.

Meilin stopped herself for an instant. The embassy meeting with Xiong, Zhou and others was about information sharing. She needed the Chinese Embassy to provide her Vietnam business office with anything that might be remotely useful for expanding business and providing long-term benefits for China. She couldn't say that to Kellie without being asked more questions.

"If we find partners to work with in Vietnam, we can offer the Vietnamese government loans to get the work started. If that benefits Vietnam's economy and Chinese companies are already there, the benefits come to both, and everyone wins."

"Would China give Vietnam large loans? I didn't think that relations between the two were that good," Kellie said.

"It's true that we have problems. We have some territorial disputes in the seas, and we remember the short conflict in 1979, but both economies are in growth modes and helping each other is important. The commercial atmosphere is good now for investment and growth. I want ChiTran to be there when Vietnam takes off. Personally, I want ChiTran to be a player in this," Meilin said. What she didn't say was that delivering success to her political contacts might be rewarded with the political prize of a Red Phone, a phone that meant the person was connected to the highest levels of China's government and industry. It was a symbol of success but came with conditions.

The conversation paused as their food arrived and they began eating.

It was an interruption in the flow of conversation that Meilin welcomed. "How is Aaron?" Meilin asked.

Kellie put her fork down and leaned back. Her cheeks warmed and her pulse quickened as she surveyed the tables, realizing that their conversation had distracted her from monitoring who had entered the restaurant. She took a breath to relax.

"After we returned from Hong Kong, we lived together for several months before we separated. My father's prosecution caused some difficulties between us, and my mother was interfering," Kellie explained.

"American mothers are just like Chinese mothers," Meilin commented smiling.

"In my case, my mother kept insisting that Aaron get more involved in helping my father defend himself. Just because Aaron was a lawyer at Customs, she thought he could and should help my father who got himself into all that trouble with the illegal importing business. She didn't think about how it might negatively impact his career," Kellie continued.

"You never see or talk to him anymore?"

"We talk to each other regularly on the phone or through email. It's not every week, but we're on good terms. I think my parents' problems and their interference were the issue,"

"Then there's hope for you."

Kellie laughed. "Maybe."

The two women retreated from their questioning of each other during the rest of their dinner. After paying the check, Kellie went out to the sidewalk with Meilin and waited with her until a taxi came by for Meilin's ride back to her hotel. Neither woman noticed a car parked a few spaces up the street and too far away for them to hear the sound of a camera's shutter pressed repeatedly, taking pictures of them coming out and onto the street lit sidewalk.

Once Meilin was in the cab and it began to move, headlights from a car parked along the curb flashed on and pulled out. As it passed where Kellie stood, neither the man nor the woman in the car looked Kellie's way.

Kellie looked around, now more conscious about who was near her or standing around. She retraced the path back to her apartment. As she turned onto 18th Street, she debated whether to enter the building from the front or through the back. She turned down the alley. She didn't want anyone to know that she'd evaded their eyes.

In her apartment, Kellie kicked off her shoes and sank into a soft leather chair. She put her feet up on a coffee table, letting her head rest on the back of the chair. Kellie replayed a lot of the conversation with Meilin in her head. Kellie was too tired to decode some of the vague and ambiguous references Meilin made during the evening. It had been a long time since she spent a couple of hours speaking exclusively in Chinese. She rubbed her forehead, feeling the pulsing and hoping to stave off a headache.

Kellie laughed at the thought of Meilin bringing up Aaron and asking about him. Their work got in the way of their relationship. She didn't want to tell Meilin that they were still good friends, but it wasn't one where they saw each other every week or talked frequently. She turned her thoughts to the two of them, Meilin and Aaron, each in their own ways helping her get back to Hong Kong all those years ago.

Kellie pushed herself forward, reaching down into her purse on the floor and retrieving her cell phone. She saw the time on the phone. It didn't deter her. It was later in the evening, but not that late. She pressed the button for one of her saved numbers.

"You've reached Aaron Foster. I'm not available, leave your name and number. I'll get back to you."

"Aaron, please give me a call. You'll probably find this interesting. Meilin Moy is in town, and I had dinner with her this evening." Kellie disconnected. She got up and went to her corner desk to send Aaron an email. He'd probably see the email before listening to his voicemail. Her email was short and nearly identical to the voice message she had left but added that the past twenty-four to forty-eight hours had been stressful and she wanted some friendly reassurance. Within seconds of sending the message, she received an autoreply. She read, "I'm out of the office for an extended period. Due to my foreign destination, I cannot guarantee a timely response. I'll respond as soon as possible."

Kellie's shoulders slumped, disappointed by the autoreply. She felt like her opportunity to have a more positive impact was being undermined and she didn't know how to save herself.

* * * * *

Meilin left a short voice mail message for Shan Zhou at the Chinese Embassy. "Dinner with Kaili. Nothing to report. I may have said too much about ChiTran's activities in Vietnam."

Shan Zhou, living in an apartment in the building adjoining the embassy, listened to the message an hour after he received it. There was nothing he could do about what Meilin divulged to Kaili. Shan Zhou's primary job had nothing to do with security or intel collection, but to maintain an open line of communication with American agencies, especially Customs and Border Protection, to keep Chinese goods flowing into the U.S. market.

Shan Zhou, knowing that Xiong Zimo had been detained by the FBI then interrogated by the embassy's security detail, wanted to keep himself clear of any problems that would cause him to be questioned by his own security officers. He emailed the embassy's security office about the dinner and suggested that they follow up with Meilin.

The embassy's security supervisor listened to Shan Zhou's message in the morning. He looked at the previous evening's surveillance reports for Kellie Liang. The assigned security officers failed to note Kellie's time out of the apartment. Why?

The supervisor summoned both security officers responsible for the late afternoon and evening hours. Confronted with information that Kellie Liang had been at dinner with Meilin Moy, both security officers insisted that Kellie Liang never left her apartment.

"If you didn't see her leave, how did she meet Ms. Moy without being seen," the supervisor asked.

Both security officers remained silent.

"Has anything unusual occurred during your surveillance that has not been reported?"

One of the security officers asked to be able to speak one on one with the supervisor. When the two men were alone, the remaining security officer admitted that two FBI agents had discovered him, and the agents knew about the two-car surveillance on Ms. Liang.

"If they know, then she now knows," the supervisor remarked. "She must've left a different way. You told the FBI but didn't report this to us. You've compromised the task. I'll let you know what's next for you. You can go," the supervisor said.

The supervisor decided to remove the surveillance teams on Kellie Liang for the time being. He'd figure out another way to keep tabs on the American.

* * * * *

"Put those in the file," Kearns said after looking through the pile of photographs taken the night before of Kellie Liang and Meilin Moy standing outside of the restaurant. "We have no idea what they talked about. If the situation calls for it, I can use them to pressure Ms. Liang about their dinner conversation. In the meantime, I'll let the folks up the chain know that they had dinner together and let the powers that be decide what happens next."

Search

A cell phone vibrated in Drew Foster's jean pocket. He rolled onto his back. It roused him from a deep sleep. His eyes closed, he dug it out of his pocket, flipped the phone open and let his thumb and fingers navigate the face of the phone and its buttons, stopping the vibration and buzzing. When his eyes opened, he saw nothing but darkness. He was looking up at the ceiling in his darkened hotel room. After a couple of deep breaths, he swung his legs around and sat up on the side of the bed. He had fallen asleep in his jeans and tee shirt.

Looking toward the window, he remembered pulling the drapes closed before going to sleep. On the bedside table, the clock told him what he wanted to know. 10:32 p.m. His phone had been set to wake him at 10:30. He pushed himself up off the bed and walked slowly toward the door to the adjoining room and listened. He heard nothing from the other side of the door. He assumed his nephew, his traveling companion, was as dead asleep as he was just a few minutes ago.

Drew went into the bathroom and splashed cold water on his face. He rubbed his eyelids as if that would revive him to a more alert state of mind. He used his wet fingers like a comb and smoothed his thinning short blondish hair. Drew walked toward the closet using the light from the bathroom to see what he had unpacked earlier. He pulled a black polo shirt over his tee shirt, grabbed a black Yankees ball cap, and slipped on his sneakers. Checking his pockets, he felt his bulging wallet in his right front pocket. He had made sure to get local currency when he checked in. A million Vietnamese dong amounted to much less than a hundred dollars. He didn't feel a room key then recalled that the key card rested in its cradle by the room door to provide power to the lights, the television and air conditioning.

Standing by the door, he removed the room's key card. The bathroom light went out, leaving him in the dark. Before exiting his room, he stopped to listen for a second and felt assured that his nephew next door was still sound asleep. He gripped the doorknob and turned it slowly as if the slightest sound might be heard in the adjoining room and cause Aaron, his nephew, to be stirred awake.

The corridor was deserted as Drew walked to the elevator bank and headed to the lobby. The hotel lobby was quiet at this hour. No one was at the reception counter except the young man who appeared to Drew as a young teenager. "May I have a street map," Drew asked.

The young man nodded, reached down, and placed a detailed street map on the counter.

"I don't read Vietnamese. Can you show me where we are," Drew asked.

"Ho Chi Minh City," the young man answered.

"No, no. I mean where on this map is the hotel," Drew clarified. Drew watched the young man place an X on the corner where the hotel was located.

"Where is Tu Do Street?"

The young man shrugged. "No Tu Do Street."

For a moment, Drew stared down at a map he couldn't read. He then scanned the lobby to see if there was anyone who might be able to help but saw no one. "Is there a manager here? Someone older?"

The young man disappeared from the counter and returned a minute later with the night-time manager. Drew wasn't encouraged. He was bad at guessing ages of Americans. Both Vietnamese men looked like they could be high school or college age at best. Instead of a specific street, he needed landmarks to get his bearings. "Can you show me on the map where the Opera House is?" The Opera House was memorable, not because he ever went into it, but because it was out of place amid a lot of bars in the area.

The younger man placed another X on the map.

"Thank you," said Drew. He folded the map in half and walked away. As soon as he stepped outside, the humidity enveloped him. Despite the late hour, it was still hot and the air damp. He closed his eyes for a few seconds as if that would prevent him from seeing the dozens, hundreds of images racing around in his head. He remembered this city as Saigon, not Ho Chi Minh City. He had joyfully left Vietnam in 1970 and had never planned to return. That was thirty-five years ago. He stood at the corner and looked up and down the wide boulevard then studied the map.

Drew checked his watch and strode as if he was late for something. He ignored the occasional scooters and motorcycles whizzing by and beeping. Two blocks from the hotel, the boulevard intersected with another wide boulevard. Looking to his right, he saw lights illuminating the Opera House. He marched the one block to the Opera House. Once across the street from his landmark, he looked up and down the street. He swore that he was on what he remembered as Tu Do Street. Whatever used to be here was gone, replaced, rebuilt.

Drew continued marching on past the Opera House. He paused at every alleyway and street to study the signs although he couldn't read them. A neon sign got his attention. A bar. He entered and surveyed the small establishment for its late-night patrons. He settled onto a bar stool. A lean Vietnamese man in a tank top and shorts with a very thin moustache looked at Drew from behind the bar.

"Beer, please," Drew said hoping that the man would understand. A nod from the bartender indicated he did.

Drew turned on the stool to look at the few others who were out late on a Monday night. The lighting allowed him to see that he was the only foreigner in the place. The bartender's leisure attire contrasted with the bar's clean and tidy appearance. It was a far cry from the old days where simply breathing was like smoking a pack of cigarettes. This place seemed to be completely smoke-free. At the far end of the bar, about fifteen feet from his stool, two young women nicely dressed stood chatting.

"Glass?" the bartender said, interrupting Drew's survey of the establishment.

"No," Drew said. "Bottle's fine." Drew knew he wouldn't be in this place very long. The bartender walked toward the two young women. After saying something, one of the women wearing a traditional satin red ao dai checked on customers sitting at the tables in the bar. Drew's head turned as his eyes followed the thin young woman. To him, the traditional long tunic with slits on the sides over her black pants made her seem tall. He turned back toward the bar, took a couple of sips from his bottle then waved the bartender over.

Drew pulled out 40,000 dong, just over three dollars, and held it out. "How much?"

The bartender took 20,000.

Drew smiled, nodded, and left the bar. Out on the street, he glanced at his map and started walking, looking for another drinking establishment. His only goal was to be back at the hotel before his nephew woke up and expected him to be there. At the next two bars, he found them much like the first except that as the hour got later, the bartenders were doing all the work without any helping hands around.

Entering the fourth bar of the night, it was different. Instead of fronting onto a main street like the three previous establishments, Drew had drifted about fifty feet down an alley after seeing the glow of a sign reflecting off the dampened pavement. It was 12:40 a.m. Stepping inside, Drew saw that this place could use a little sweeping and the smell of beer and cigarettes hung in the air.

An older man tended to the bar. Drew's slow deliberate steps toward a bar stool were like those of someone expecting trouble. He looked around and noticed there were about half a dozen other late-night patrons, all men and in pairs at tables. Lighting was limited. Whether it was the late hour or maybe it was always this way, the only light provided came from the bar area itself. There were no lamps or ceiling bulbs providing additional illumination. As he looked at each of the occupied tables, he noticed that he and the others were not locals. One of the guys had given him the slightest nod when he looked over.

As he settled onto a bar stool, the lighting on the man tending the bar showed him to be the oldest person Drew had seen working during the evening. The man had bags under his tired eyes, long stringy salt and pepper hair and a thin beard. Drew guessed the man could be anywhere between fifty and eighty years old. The man's tank top exposed bone-thin shoulders and arms. Finally, he might be in the kind of place he was looking for.

"Beer, please," Drew said.

"American beer," the old man asked.

"Vietnamese beer," Drew answered.

The bartender smiled and shook his head.

Drew watched the old man reach into a cooler, grabbing a local beer and placing it on the bar.

"Why do you laugh?" Drew asked.

"Americans come here. Order cheap beer," the man answered. His English good enough to do business with English speaking foreigners.

"Many Americans come in here?" Drew asked.

The bartender stood behind the bar with his arms folded. "All Americans tonight."

Drew felt encouraged by the answer. He slid forward on the bar stool so he could straighten his leg. Reaching into his pocket, he pulled out a folded envelope. In it, he withdrew two fading black and white photos. One photo was of a young Vietnamese woman and the other was him with her. He paused to look at them before placing them on the counter and sliding them toward the bartender.

The bartender placed his hands wide apart on the bar and leaned in to look at the pictures.

"You like them," the bartender said, nodding toward the other men at the tables. "They come back now. For what? What you want? Find her? She looks like all bar girls from war time. Pretty. Long black hair. So what?"

Drew nodded in the affirmative.

"Where did you meet her? Tu Do Street bar? There were many bars, thousands of bar girls." The bartender pulled back and folded his arms again but stepped toward Drew. "How you find her? Go to every bar in Saigon? She too old now. Maybe back in village with kids like other bar girls. Maybe grandmother now. Maybe dead."

"Are the other men in here looking for their bar girls?" Drew asked.

"No, they come back. Tourists now with friends and family," the barman answered.

"If you can't help me, is there someone else?" Drew pressed.

"You serious? You really want to find her?" The bartender's eyes weren't as tired as they had been a few minutes ago when Drew sat down. The eyes had cleared or maybe it was because the old man's eyelids seemed to have gotten life back and the eyes were open wider. The eyes studied Drew. "How many places you drink tonight?"

"This is number four," Drew answered.

The old man looked at Drew for a good half minute saying nothing then he leaned back in on the bar. "We call it 'Orphan Bar', not real name. You go there. Maybe, there's a chance. Okay? Not tonight. Tomorrow."

"Okay, but where is it? Here, show me on this map." Drew pulled out the folded map and placed it on the bar. The old man studied the map and placed an X on it. Drew looked and noticed it was only several blocks away. He started to fold it when the man reached out and took the map.

"This," the bartender pointed to a street on the map just a couple of blocks away. "Tu Do Street. Now, Dong Khoi. After Americans leave, no more Tu Do Street."

"Thank you," Drew said smiling. "Tomorrow," he said, waving the folded map then putting it away. Drew lingered and finished his beer. He stood and put 50,000 dong on the bar before he left.

It was one-thirty when he started back toward his hotel. He was smiling as he walked back to the hotel. As far as he was concerned, the night had been a success. As he walked the mostly deserted streets, he guessed that he might have consumed two beers during the night, not so much that he wasn't aware of his surroundings. He didn't know whether to feel safe or be on his toes in a city where things used to explode without warning. What he did remember is that on the few occasions when he was in downtown Saigon during the war, he was usually too drunk to care about safety or anything else. With the information the bartender had given him, he felt wide awake and fully aware of everything occurring around him.

Just after two in the morning, he had marched back to the hotel, showered off the sweat and was back in bed. His right forearm rested on his forehead. The last thought he had before he surrendered to sleep was that the next night's foray could yield the results he hoped for.

* * * * *

The clock-radio brought Aaron Foster out of his slumber at eight. It took several tries before he was able to press the button to turn off the music. He sat up squinting despite the little morning light that framed the drawn drapes. Wearing just his boxer shorts, he pulled the drapes wide open and looked out from his tenth-floor room.

Aaron stood in the sunlight drenched room. There was a pre-arranged nine o'clock pick-up for him and his uncle. Before getting himself ready, he walked over to the connecting door. There wasn't a sound in his uncle's room. He knocked on the door to prompt a response. Nothing. Aaron shrugged and went into the bathroom.

He dressed in lightweight long pants and a lightweight short-sleeved shirt. Back out by the window, he stood looking out at the surrounding area while spreading suntan lotion on his face, neck, arms, and hands. The pre-arranged pick-up was for a day-long tour of the Mekong Delta.

He grabbed a towel from the bathroom, rolled it up and stuffed it into a backpack. He had a liter bottle of water in the side pocket of the backpack and slung it over his shoulder. The last thing he picked up was a wide-brimmed khaki-colored boonie hat on the bed. Aaron wanted to be in the lobby well before the driver and guide arrived.

He went to the door between the adjoining rooms. He knocked harder. "Uncle Drew, you up? Ready to go?" Aaron put his ear to the door and heard nothing but waited before knocking again. He hadn't heard any footsteps, but heard the door being unlocked and opened.

"Sorry. I didn't sleep well and forgot to turn on the alarm," Drew explained.

"Driver's here in about 20 minutes."

"You go," Drew said. He stood for a moment looking up slightly at Aaron. "Remember, I've been here before. When you get back, we'll have dinner and find a place for a couple of drinks."

Aaron wasn't going to argue. "Are you okay?" Aaron worried. Drew opened up at times and talked about his time in Vietnam with his nephew. But Drew could also clam up for extended periods of time and be distant.

"I'm fine," Drew insisted. "I'll take a walk around, get my bearings and see if I can locate some familiar spots. You, go and enjoy the scenery and make sure you drink plenty of water."

"Alright, I'll see you later this afternoon," Aaron said then closed the door and headed for the lobby.

Drew locked the door. He flopped onto the bed and fell asleep.

The sounds of scooters, engines revving, and beeping from the street and a room that had slowly warmed because of the midday heat brought Drew back to life. Up on his feet, the first thing he did was adjust the temperature setting to get the a/c running. He knew that wasn't the smartest thing to do if he was going to go out in the midday heat, but he wanted a few minutes of comfort while he dressed.

After he put on his knee length black shorts and a thin white pullover shirt, he pulled his belt tight to the last belt hole. Once he committed to this trip, he went on a weight loss program and dropped twenty-five pounds from his five-foot nine-inch frame. That didn't mean he was lean. He could still stand to lose another twenty, but he knew that carrying the extra weight and getting around on foot in this country could be physically draining.

His cargo style shorts had enough pockets to hold a bottle of water. Drew was ready to take another exploratory walk around town. He wanted to retrace some of the route from the night before to see what it was like during the day, and he wanted to familiarize himself with his destination for the night.

Drew left the comfort of the hotel, stepping out into the bright sun and heat of the day. It was a wide boulevard, and the buildings around didn't cast any shade onto the sidewalk. Within minutes Drew felt perspiration dampen his body. The street was busy and the sidewalk full of people. Two boys, maybe eight or ten years old jogged toward him and blocked his progress.

"Postcards?" both boys offered as they reached into bags hanging over their shoulders. They both let the postcard packs cascade down from their hands.

Drew tried to ignore them and walk past, but they got in step with him. One boy on each side trying to convince him to buy something. Drew didn't want to be rude, but he didn't need the hassle. "No postcards, nothing, okay?" Drew tried to beg off and kept walking. The two boys stayed with him, chattering until reaching the corner where Drew turned toward the Opera House.

The boys turned away to find another foreign target. Drew slowed to look at his map as he walked. He stopped at the next corner looking at the front of the Opera House. Looking to his left and right, he smiled and shook his head. Except that he was standing there, he wouldn't have believed that the street that was once lined with bars and GIs was completely transformed into modern buildings, stores, and hotels. What he remembered as Tu Do Street was swept clean and renamed as he was told the night before. The thought that hit him was that it looked respectable. He lingered at the corner for a minute then crossed the street and went on to the streets behind the Opera House.

Drew was struck by all the coffee shops, business office buildings, eateries and the usual collection of businesses found in any central business district of a big city. Older buildings from his time in Vietnam were still around, but few in number and dwarfed by the modern glass and concrete buildings. Drew found it difficult to locate the bars he'd visited the night before as some businesses were shuttered. He wondered if they stayed that way during the day.

Drew ducked down a dozen alleys before finding what he guessed was the last place he visited the night before. He went to the door, but found it locked. He walked to a window facing the alley, cupped his hands and looked in, but couldn't make out anything inside the darkened interior.

According to the X on his map, he was two streets away from what the bartender called the "Orphan Bar". As Drew walked, the wide boulevards where his hotel and the Opera House were located gave way to regular two-way two-lane traffic streets and smaller businesses still housed in narrow older buildings three to five stories high. Maybe here things hadn't changed as much as he thought.

Drew's pace slowed. Now, he wished he had a map with more detail than the hotel's street map. He could see lots of small structures behind the buildings that fronted the main streets. Comparing the mark on his map to the street and buildings he was walking past, he knew that he'd never find the exact location. The signs and windows advertised and invited passers-by to get massages, have drinks, enjoy the local coffee shops, and eat fast food.

Though not as run down as many of the places he remembered, Drew felt like he was seeing a cleaned-up version of the past. Drew's inability to speak or read Vietnamese wasn't a problem as most of the signage was in English as well as Vietnamese. In some of the doorways, there were young men or women, depending on the type of business, trying to lure him in.

Every open establishment was an opportunity to ask for help, but Drew kept walking past them. He'd been wandering the streets for an hour when he decided that he was on an impossible mission on his own. There were more than enough places to stop and ask the question he needed answered, but knew he had to be strategic. He eliminated the eateries and coffee shops immediately as he believed they lacked staff who might know about the kind of late-night bar he wanted to find. The massage parlors were possibilities, but he believed another bar would be the best choice.

Drew's pace picked up. He dodged the crowd of people moving slower. A few doors ahead, he saw a man leaning on a doorframe. He liked that the man didn't appear to be too young. Entering the bar, it was well lit as the afternoon sun filled the place through two large windows on either side of the door. The bar had a dozen stools and several tables along the wall opposite the bar. The place was simple and clean. The shelves behind the bar were well-stocked and the bartender had help with one woman working the tables. There were a couple of foreigners as well as several locals sitting at tables.

Seeing no one else at the bar, Drew settled onto a bar stool and gave the bartender a nod. The bartender was short, but muscular. His slick black hair was combed straight back.

"What would you like?" The bartender spoke slowly and deliberately.

Drew instantly remembered the "cheap American" comment from the evening before. "If you have draught beer, let me try one," Drew answered.

As the glass was placed on the bar, Drew pulled out his map. "Maybe you can help me," Drew said. When he saw the bartender turning to give him his attention, Drew put the map on the bar.

Drew put his finger by the X that marked the location of the bar he was looking for.

"What is the name?" the bartender asked.

"I don't know the real name. Someone told me it's called the 'Orphan Bar'."

The bartender rubbed his chin. He looked at the map. "Hmm, maybe around here, but I don't know." He waved the woman over to look at the map and told her what Drew had said.

"Yes, maybe I know," she said. She looked up at Drew. "You GI, yes?"

"Yes." Looking at her, Drew guessed she was in her forties or fifties. Her black hair parted in the middle and combed straight down the sides and back.

The bartender and woman started talking to each other. Drew was left sitting and listening to the incomprehensible sounds of the local language.

The bartender slid the map toward him, circled a small area, flipped it over and began to draw on the blank back side of the map then slid it back toward Drew. "She think it is this way. Not open now. You go tonight. Maybe after nine. Okay?" the bartender explained.

Drew smiled. "Okay." He gave the bartender and the woman a thumbs up. He flipped back and forth to look at both sides of the map. The lines drawn were details of the street fronting the bar and a few alleys or walkways off the main street within the block. He was in the right block of buildings, but there were walkways and alleys that created a maze. He guessed that between where he was sitting and the end of the block, there were a couple of easy-to-miss walkways between buildings that would lead to his destination.

Drew finished his beer. Before leaving, he waved the bartender over. "Thank you for your help. When I go out the door, I turn this way, yes?" Drew stood by the bar stool facing the door and pointing to his left. The bartender confirmed what Drew said. Drew put cash on the bar and left.

He turned down a narrow walkway about a minute after leaving the bar. His eyes inspecting the walls on both sides. He walked slowly past a couple of doors that had padlocks on them. The windows opening out to the walkway didn't hint of any life inside. He reached a dead-end and walked back to the busy street. He stood and studied the hand drawn lines on the back of the map then looked up across the street. No, he was convinced he was on the correct side of the street. He passed a massage parlor and a small noodle shop then saw another break between buildings. Drew guessed that if he put both arms out, he'd touch the buildings on each side of the walkway.

Standing and looking down the walkway, it looked like it dead-ended. No windows or doors opened onto the walkway from the two buildings that fronted the main street. He marched down the walkway. Fifty feet off the street, a single level wooden structure with tin roofing blocked straight access and forced Drew to decide whether to go left or right. The side facing the walkway had no signage, doors, or windows. Drew went left following stone blocks that led him to the opposite side of the structure from where he'd started. He was standing on the front side of the structure that was as plain as the back side except for two windows on either side of double-wooden doors. A secure steel bar across the double doors and padlock made it clear that it wasn't open. Drew did a slow three-sixty turn. Several other old wooden structures were lost in this inner courtyard area surrounded by all the businesses that fronted the main streets of the block. This courtyard wasn't like those he'd seen in the United States. Coming back around to look at the secure door, there was no way to be sure that he had found the right place. He stepped back and inspected the door and windows. The only thing he could read was a sign on two windows reading simply "THE BAR".

Drew backed away from the door and did another rotation, concentrating on the other structures in the courtyard. He saw another walkway leading to the main street on the opposite side of the block from where he'd started. He followed the alleyway out onto the busy street then turned and looked back to THE BAR.

From the street, THE BAR was non-descript. He wondered if he'd be able to find it at night. He made a mental note of the businesses on either side of the alleyway from the street and the buildings across the street. He wished he had something to write with so he could put it on his hand-drawn map. Turning back toward the alleyway, he saw the faded paint colors on the wall of one of the buildings facing the alleyway about ten feet into the alleyway. The graffiti looked like it was supposed to represent a fisherman and his small canoe-like boat. Drew was sure he could remember the graffiti.

Drew glanced at his watch. His recon mission had taken a good chunk of the afternoon. He started his trek back to the hotel hoping that what he'd found was the right place. The only way to confirm it would be with a return visit after dark.

* * * * *

Drew flipped through the pages of a tourist magazine while sitting in the hotel lobby waiting for Aaron. He enjoyed looking at the pictures of the local countryside and the modern districts of Saigon that had been completely transformed since his tour of duty.

"Well?" Aaron said, standing over his uncle.

Drew hadn't paid any attention to the people wandering around the lobby. "What the hell did you do?" Drew said, looking up at his nephew from his seated position. "You had a full head of hair at dinner."

Aaron ran both hands over his newly shaved scalp. "Yeah, well, when I got to my room and thought about the day. Or, specifically, the heat and all that sweat running down my face and my hair wet and dripping, I just went at it and the next thing I knew, I had a shaved head."

"The heat got to your head all right. More like into your head," Drew commented. "While you were shaving your head, did you forget your face? You're starting to grow glitter on your face."

Aaron laughed. "I've noticed that, too. After I shaved my head, I realized that all this sweating irritated my skin so I decided a short beard might offset the shaved head.

Drew shook his head. "One thing's for sure, you'll shock anyone who knows you when you get home with this new look."

"Now what? Stay here or are you going to show me the town," Aaron asked. "Let's go."

Out on the street, Drew looked at the scribbled notes he had written on the back of the map after his afternoon walk. They were in no hurry. Drew estimated a six-block walk at a leisure pace would get them back to The Bar around the time suggested by the bartender and woman earlier in the day.

The two men walked side-by-side the first few blocks. Many of the businesses around their hotel were closed for the day. But the farther away from the hotel they walked, the more crowded the streets became.

"Lots of people out tonight," Aaron commented.

"Yeah, lots of younger people like your age or younger," Drew said.

"Not as young as I used to be. I can't stay out late and still pop out of bed these days."

"I've lost count. You're in your mid-thirties now, right."

"Thirty-six this year. I'm entering my pre-middle age stage," Aaron said.

"What the hell is pre-middle age stage?"

"It's when I'm supposed to start thinking about taking things seriously, but I'm not there yet," Aaron bantered.

Drew chuckled. "Well, being back here, I can tell you one thing to always remember. Enjoy life. Make sure there are moments every day that you enjoy because there is nothing guaranteed about tomorrow. Back then, still being alive to wake up each morning was a gift."

They walked without saying anything for a block. Without a word, Drew stepped off the sidewalk and crossed the street with Aaron trailing a couple of paces behind.

"Let me know when you're going to do that. Crossing streets around here can be deadly."

"Sorry," Drew said. He focused on every illuminated sign, light, and door he approached, hoping not to miss the gap between buildings leading to his destination. It looked different in the dark than earlier in daylight. Drew slowed, studying both sides of the street.

"Keep your eyes peeled for a walkway, an alleyway, or any gap between buildings," Drew advised. "Oh, and if you notice some graffiti, tell me."

"Coming up on our left," Aaron responded.

Drew took a few more steps and found himself looking straight down a narrow walkway. The buildings and businesses fronting the main street blocked all the lights from the interior courtyard. Drew stared at the sides of the buildings along the alleyway, hoping to see the graffiti. The lighting wasn't bright enough to see the faded paint on the wall. The Bar had a string of alternating green, blue, red, and yellow Christmas lights drooped along its front, facing the walkway into the courtyard.

When Drew and Aaron reached the internal courtyard, it opened to The Bar and a smaller bar about half the size of The Bar and a noodle shop with five or six people standing at a counter.

"Is this your special place?" Aaron asked.

"Maybe. Let's find out." Drew took a step forward with Aaron following.

"We passed a lot of places to get a drink so this better be special," Aaron said. Drew said nothing.

A dark wood interior greeted them when they stepped into the bar. Sconces along the front and left side wall provided perimeter lighting to an interior about fifteen feet deep and twice as wide. The bar ran the length of the opposite side. Tables filled the main area of the bar.

"A little strange, isn't it?" Drew said over his shoulder.

"Not what I expected," Aaron said only loud enough for his uncle to hear.

The ten bar stools were half occupied. Drew and Aaron took two at the end nearest the door.

"Half the people in here are old guys like you," Aaron said to his uncle. "And the other half look like," Aaron hesitated, considering how to describe what he saw. "The other half look like they could be the adult kids of the old guys."

"Except that they aren't mingling," Drew added.

Aaron looked at the crowd of people again. His uncle had spotted it immediately. It wasn't surprising that the younger folks didn't mingle with the older crowd. Aaron didn't think anything of it.

Aaron was just about to ask Drew a question when the bartender got his attention.

"Gentlemen. Haven't seen you in here before. Just arrived in country?" the long-haired, bearded bartender asked with a smile.

"Arrived yesterday or it might've been the evening before. The time change has me confused," Drew answered.

"Your first time back?"

"Yeah," Drew confirmed.

"Different, isn't it. I came back a few years ago. Life was too up and down for me in the States. In my head, I was here every day, so I decided to come back and stay for a while," the bartender added. "As long as I keep my head down, behave, and keep this place humming along, I'm tolerated. Down to business, what'll it be?"

"Two draught beers," Drew answered.

Aaron's eyes followed the bartender walking away then leaned toward his uncle. "What the hell are we doing here?" Aaron turned his head to take another look at the others in the bar. "It's kind of a dead place. The atmosphere here is not giving me the impression it's going to be hopping anytime soon."

"Probably not," Drew agreed. "I have an ulterior motive for coming here," Drew said. He paused to let the bartender place the beers in front of them.

"What's your name," Drew asked the bartender.

"The locals call me Harry. They picked the name for me because of my long hair and beard. Now, I tell everyone that's my name. As long as I stay here, my real name doesn't matter. You need something while you're in here, just call me Harry."

"Harry, is this place ever referred to as the 'Orphan Bar'?"

Harry looked around the bar for a second then his gaze settled on Drew. "Yeah. Every night, I get a few guys who come in here with a guilt complex looking for that bar girl they hooked up with and they wonder if there's a kid running around who looks like them. The flip side is I've got Vietnamese thirty-somethings coming in here angry. The kids get treated badly because of their American blood. They look different, easy to stand out and get the worst end of the stick. They come in here angry and wonder if their long-lost daddy might come through the door. Then, there's that reality that the guys who come in here never find who they're looking for and the mixed-race kids never find their daddies and stay angry, get drunk in here and continue with their shitty lives.

"As long as they don't get too crazy and too destructive, I let them vent and have their momentary tantrums because they need some place to go, some place that allows them to release that pent up anger and frustration."

Aaron looked over his shoulder. His eyes roving from table to table as he listened to Harry.

"Uncle Drew, we're here for a reason. Out with it," Aaron said. He thought he could guess but wanted to hear it from his uncle now that Harry had provided the background.

Drew looked at his nephew then turned back to Harry. "Does the person in the photo look familiar?" Drew asked as he put two photos on the bar.

Harry studied the photographs. "Lan," Harry called out to one of the two women serving customers at the tables.

Lan walked to the bar. She stood sideways facing Drew while leaning against the empty bar stool behind her. Her silvery ponytail hanging several inches below her narrow shoulders belied her age. She wore a red polo shirt and black pants. A black half apron tied at the waist seemed to wrap around her like a short skirt over the pants.

Drew watched Lan as she took the photographs from the bar counter. She stared at the photographs, one in each hand. She pursed her lips, and her eyes alternated from one photo to the other.

Holding the photo of Drew and the young woman, Lan extended her arm toward Drew and held the photo a few inches from Drew's face. "You, very young," she said smiling. "Now, not very young," she chuckled. The three men laughed. She put the photo of Drew and the young woman on the bar counter but held the photo of the young woman. "I go look. You wait." Lan walked away and disappeared through a doorway on the back wall.

"What does that mean," Drew said, turning back to Harry.

"Wait means wait. To me, all those teen-age bar girls look the same after seeing so many. We have guys come in here almost every night with photos just like the one you have. Lan, she looks at those photos and sees things I don't." Out of the corner of his eye, Harry saw Lan standing just inside the back doorway pointing and gesturing to send Drew.

"She might have something," Harry said, nodding toward the back.

Drew saw Lan waving him to her. Drew pushed himself off the stool and marched in her direction. Aaron followed. Several men sitting at tables in the bar noticed the two men heading to the back wall and doorway.

Lan escorted Drew and Aaron past a closed door and into a back room. It was too small for any office furniture and too big to be a closet. Drew took one step into the room and froze in his tracks. Aaron stood in the open doorway and looked over Drew's shoulder.

Both men were looking at a wall—ceiling to floor and corner-to-corner--of photographs similar to Drew's. The few color photos popped out for attention compared to the hundreds or thousands of fading black and whites. The two side walls weren't filled but had hundreds more photographs.

"Come," Lan prodded.

Drew stood stiffly as if in a trance staring at the wall of photographs.

Aaron leaned closer to Drew's ear. "Uncle Drew, you can go in." Aaron patted Drew's shoulder to signal him to move. As the two men entered the room, Lan bent down and about a foot above the floor and near one of the corners, she pointed to a copy of the same photo Drew had brought.

Drew squatted down and Aaron was bent over. Both studied the photo on the wall. Both looked at Lan and nodded in agreement that it was the same photo.

"Now what?" Aaron asked.

"I don't know," Drew responded.

Aaron straightened, stepped back, and eyed the wall. "It's obvious you thought about this a lot even though you didn't tell me anything. You must have some idea about what you want to do next."

"Not really. It was like a fantasy thing. I didn't really think we'd find her," Drew said.

Aaron needed to be careful what he said next. "Okay, just to be clear, all that's happened is that we found the same photograph. We haven't found her. We don't know how long the picture has been here or who left it."

"Help me up," Drew said.

Aaron held out his hand and pulled Drew up. "We need to talk about this," Aaron said.

Drew stood but looked down at the photo and the photo-covered wall. He looked at Lan, took a hand and squeezed it. "Thank you."

Aaron and Drew walked out of the room of photos. Instead of heading for the bar stools, Aaron guided Drew to a table.

"Did someone have a party scheduled here tonight?" Drew said without expecting an answer. "I guess a quiet conversation might not be so easy."

Aaron spotted the only table available in the back corner, farthest from the bar. The decibel level had risen. The tables and chairs were rearranged. A large group of over a dozen biracial adults took over the center of the available floor space. All but two bar stools were occupied but would probably be taken as soon as Aaron and Drew's drinks were moved.

"How long were we back there?" Drew asked.

Aaron saw a clock behind Harry at the bar. "Ten minutes max."

Lan brought their glasses to the table. "You okay?" she asked as she looked down at Drew. She saw him nod and smile in response.

Lan went back to the bar. "Big shock," Lan said to Harry.

"They come back probably thinking that it's the right thing to do, but then they don't really expect anything will happen. What did he say when you pointed to the photo?"

"Nothing. Just very surprised. He said thank you."

Harry looked into the far corner and saw Aaron and Drew sitting and eyeing the crowd. "Did you check the back of the photo?"

"Yes. Phone number."

"Well, we have that wall for a reason," Harry said.

* * * * *

Phan Nhu Linh sat cross-legged on the floor of her cozy one-room apartment. Her cell phone buzzed, interrupting her concentration on a Chinese textbook. Before answering, she looked at the time on the phone. 10:25. Late for a call on a work night, she thought.

"Hello," she said hesitantly.

"I'm calling from The Bar; some people call it the 'Orphan Bar'." Linh heard a woman's voice saying.

Lan waited through a long silence then added, "did you leave a photograph at a bar with a phone number?"

Linh closed her eyes, thinking about what the woman was saying. "Yes, maybe a year ago. Why?"

"You should come to the bar."

"You mean now?" Linh asked.

"Now. An American brought the same picture. He's still here. Do you speak English?"

"Some," Linh answered.

"When you come, go to the bar. Talk to Harry the bartender." Lan hung up.

Linh kept the phone to her ear after Lan disconnected. Slowly, she lowered her arm, and her phone rested in her lap. She stood up. She needed to change out of her tank top and shorts. She grabbed a white button-down shirt and jeans. She slithered into the jeans, but before putting on the shirt, she stood in her jeans and bra wondering if she should go to the bar alone. No. She needed someone to be with her. She punched in a number, spoke to a friend for less than a minute then put on the shirt, buttoned it, and tied the excess shirt tail into a knot at the waist.

On the street, she waved down a motorcycle taxi and hopped on for the quick ride. She gave the driver directions. This time of night, scooters and motorcycles owned the streets more so than during the day. Like every other local, she felt comfortable with the driver's weaving between other bikes, his quick acceleration and sudden braking, and the leans into the turns. She owned a scooter but hadn't given any thought to using it on this night.

Less than ten minutes after hopping on the bike, she was handing over the fare. She stood at the corner of the main street and alleyway that would lead to The Bar. She stood at the corner watching bikes and scooters zipping by for a few minutes until one slowed to let Mai, a work colleague, climb off her ride.

The two young women headed down the alleyway. "You've been here before?" Mai asked, almost jogging to keep up with the taller Linh.

"Just a couple of times over a few years."

A few steps from the door, Linh was barely moving. Mai breathed deeply, catching her breath and grateful that Linh slowed down before they entered.

Aaron and Drew were on their third round of drinks. Drew wasn't chatty.

"Are we drinking in celebration or is it something else," Aaron wondered.

"When she pointed to the picture, I felt this warm, tingly feeling go through my body. Happy. Right now, I'm numb," Drew said. "I don't know what to think."

Drew watched Aaron stand and walk toward the restroom. His focus moved to the group of young men and women who had taken over the prime area of the floor space. A couple of the older American men, looking to be in their fifties like Drew, had joined them. Drew heard the young adults mixing their conversation of Vietnamese among themselves with passable English with the two American men.

Beyond the throng, Drew saw the door open and two more women entering The Bar. Perhaps they were late arrivals joining the throng a few feet away.

Aaron dropped back into his chair. "Glad to see you smiling."

"The group over there is entertaining," Drew said. "Worth sticking around and watching the interaction."

"Besides, we've got no plans for tomorrow," Aaron added.

Aaron saw two women enter and go to the bar. The taller woman could easily fit in with the large group. Her shoulder-length hair wasn't black, but brown. Her facial features, especially her eyes and nose, made her look less than completely Vietnamese, making Aaron think about Kellie Liang, the Chinese American woman who was a good friend and former girlfriend who he'd lived with several years ago. The taller woman who had just entered wasn't quite as petite as many of the younger Vietnamese women and was four or five inches taller than her friend. The shorter woman had a rounder face.

Unlike the petite young women and girls, these two were not schoolgirls. Aaron guessed they were anywhere between twenty-five and forty in age.

"Somebody got your attention?" Drew asked as his eyes followed Aaron's to the bar.

"Just happened to notice those two come in."

Drew shrugged. "More your age than mine. A lot younger than the gal in my picture who's probably in her fifties now."

"How old was she when you hooked up with her?" Aaron asked as he kept his focus on the two women at the bar.

Drew cocked his head slightly to one side. "You know, I'm embarrassed to say that I don't recall ever asking her so I can't tell you how old she'd be."

With Mai at her side, Linh stood at the bar watching a lone bearded, long-haired man working the customers sitting at the bar.

Harry saw them enter and already guessed at who one of the women might be. He walked to the end of the bar closest to the door and leaned in over the bar counter.

"Harry?" Linh asked.

"Yes. Did you get a call from Lan?"

"Yes."

"Just look in the mirror behind me," Harry instructed. "Don't turn around, but in the mirror, way back in the corner, there are two men at the table, and one has a shaved head. Do you see them?"

Linh looked at the mirror, her eyes roving for several seconds. Several people in the group occupying the middle of the bar's floor space were up and moving around, making it hard for Linh to see the two men. She located the table with the head-shaven young man. "I see them."

"The older guy has the same picture," Harry explained as he put the photo from the back wall onto the bar counter. "He has another picture of her and him together." Harry watched Linh.

Mai had climbed up and sat on the high bar stool as she had trouble seeing the table in the back while standing. Once on the stool, she was able to lift herself higher.

"Who is the younger man?" Linh asked.

"I heard the younger man refer to the older man as his uncle." Harry assumed that the woman in the photo was Linh's mother. "If I'm right, that means the younger man might be your cousin," Harry said.

Linh and Mai looked at each other and chatted for a moment. Other than a word or two, Harry listened without understanding.

"How are they?" Linh asked.

Harry didn't know what to make of the question and waved Lan over to the bar. Harry stepped back while the three women talked.

"I tell Linh and Mai that the older man was surprised, shocked to find the photo. I said he is looking for the woman in the photograph," Lan explained to Harry.

"Do you want me to take you to him?" Harry asked.

"No. We will have a drink then we leave. After we leave, you can give him the phone number. Tell him to call and we make a date to meet," Linh suggested.

Aaron watched Harry and the two women at the bar. He sat back and folded his arms when Lan joined the conversation.

"I wonder what's going on up there," Aaron said, prompting Drew to look toward the bar.

"You can get a better idea if you go up and introduce yourself to them," Drew half-joked.

"I don't speak their language."

"Aaron, it's a bar," Drew said. "Everybody speaks everyone else's language. You should know that by now. Just how innocent and naïve are you? I thought you were a world traveler?"

Aaron understood what his uncle was saying, but the objective of his uncle's trip to this bar changed the usual rules. This wasn't just a night out for drinks and fun.

"Don't worry, they speak more of our language than we do theirs, guaranteed," Drew said. "If you go up to them, they'll know why you're there."

"Not tonight. It's all about you, that photo and anything else you're willing to share."

Aaron ignored the noisy large group a few feet away and kept his eyes on the two women at the bar. Harry had put drinks in front of the two women then went back to checking on the others sitting at the bar.

"Still curious?" Drew asked.

"It seems something interesting is going on but maybe it's my imagination." Aaron's gut feeling told him that whatever the interaction between those women, Harry, and Lan, it had something to do with Drew's photograph. His uncle had his wartime experiences, but Aaron had his own Asia experiences and as he sat back and absorbed the sounds and sights of the bar's atmosphere, the thought that the night held more unexpected moments gnawed at him.

Lan picked up empty glasses and bottles from the large group and replaced them with fresh drinks. As she made her way around the tables and bodies, she looked up and saw Drew waving his arm.

"Can you bring us two more and the check?" Drew asked. Lan nodded, heading back toward the bar, careful to avoid getting bumped by the constant movement of the large group as they kept changing places with one another.

Lan returned several minutes later with two beers and placed a piece of paper on the table.

Aaron picked up the check and calculated the bill. "You're a cheap date, Uncle Drew."

"And I tried to add some excitement for free," Drew said as he picked up the other piece of paper Lan had left on the table. He saw what he assumed to be a phone number. A few words were scribbled on it. "Call this number." A name was written on the paper. Drew handed it to Aaron.

Both men looked up at the bar where the two women had been standing, but they were gone. Neither of them had seen the women leave.

"Let's pay up and go," Drew suggested. He and Aaron took a long last mouth full then headed toward the exit.

Drew and Aaron paused at the bar to put enough dong down to pay and held up the other piece of paper till Harry noticed.

"It's on you," Harry said.

Drew looked around the bar, saw Lan and nodded. "Thanks," he said to Harry. He and Aaron walked out into a dark courtyard and headed down the unlit alleyway.

* * * * *

The hotel lobby wasn't well lit at the late hour when Drew and Aaron entered from their night out. "I need to stop at reception," Drew said. "If you want to go up, I'll see you in the morning."

No one was behind the counter. Drew tapped the bell and waited before seeing a groggy looking young man appear through a door. Drew put the scrap paper up for the young man to see. "This name, what is the family name?" Drew asked.

"Phan is family name," the young man answered.

"Thanks," Drew said and headed for the elevator. Despite the alcohol, Drew wasn't ready to sleep. He sat and rewrote the number and name on the small pad of paper by the phone in his room. Pulling out his cell phone, he set the alarm. He wanted to be up at the beginning of the workday.

After showering, Drew was in bed and still wide awake. What now, he wondered. Make the call and ask . . . what? The air conditioning was doing its work but sweat beaded on Drew's forehead and rolled down the sides of his head, dampening his hair. He played out a make-believe conversation in his head but got as far as saying who he was to Phan Linh and stopped. His eyes stared toward the dark ceiling above. He sat up and swung his legs around. *What was her name?* Drew felt his pulsing heart at the realization that he didn't know the bar girl's real name, her Vietnamese name. She and all the other bar girls had adopted an easy American name for the GIs. He tilted his head back slightly at the thought that he didn't know her name and he didn't know how old she was.

Drew walked over to the adjoining door. He needed to talk and raised his arm to knock but stopped himself in mid-motion. This was his problem to work out, not Aaron's. Drew grabbed a washcloth from the bathroom to wipe the sweat from his brow and returned to the bed, piling the pillows under his head. He drifted off to sleep.

Contact

The internal alarm clock went off and Drew rolled off the bed and onto his feet. He looked at the clock on the bedside table and the time on his phone. 7:20. The phone was set to go off in forty minutes. He turned off the phone's alarm, deciding not to take a chance of laying down and dozing off.

After dressing, Drew knocked on the adjoining room door. "Are you up in there?"

"Yeah, yeah, give me a few minutes," Aaron called out.

Ten minutes passed before Drew heard knocking on his room door from the corridor.

"What's the plan this morning," Aaron asked, standing in the corridor.

"How about a light breakfast and coffee then I want to make that call," Drew said.

In the hotel restaurant, Aaron kept his eyes on his uncle. With Drew's forearms resting on the table, Aaron felt the vibration through the table of Drew's leg nervously pumping up and down. "You seem to be worked up this morning," Aaron commented.

"I didn't sleep well. I have no clue what I'm going to say when she answers the phone."

"Maybe you'll get lucky, and she won't answer, and you'll get a machine," Aaron said.

"I'm not sure that's any better. It just delays the inevitable," Drew said. "I can't take sitting here anymore. I'm going up and doing this."

The two men signed their checks and headed up to Drew's room. Drew looked at the piece of paper by the room's landline phone with printed instructions on how to make local calls. He stared at the long phone number and pressed the buttons. He sat on the side of the bed. His heart was racing. Aaron took the chair by the window. The drapes were pulled open, and the morning sun radiated heat through the window.

Drew pressed the phone's receiver to his ear as he listened to the ringing tone. The phone was answered in Vietnamese after the third ring. Drew hesitated after hearing the Vietnamese.

"Hello, Ms. Phan?" Drew said hesitantly. A few seconds of silence followed.

"Yes, I am Phan Linh."

"You speak English?"

"I speak a little English. If you talk slow, I hope I understand," Linh said.

"My name is Drew Foster. The Bar gave me your phone number. My picture and your picture are the same," Drew started, hoping that he was speaking slow enough for her to understand.

"Yes, I know. I see you at The Bar, but I went home. I have to work very soon. We meet, yes?"

"Yes, I would like to meet you. When do you want to meet?"

Phan Linh wanted to control the meeting. Meeting during her lunch break meant there was a limited amount of time, and she could dictate the location near work. She gave Drew the name of a café and address. "You tell taxi to take you to café. I meet you at twelve o'clock, okay?"

"Yes, okay. Thank you." Drew hung up and let out a deep sigh.

"It sounded like a good call from where I'm sitting," Aaron said. "You've survived a lot worse. This is just your nerves. Now that you've planned to meet, I'm going to go catch up on a couple of things."

"Let's meet around eleven and we can ride over to this café," Drew proposed.

"I wasn't sure you wanted me along for this."

"I confess. This is the reason why I wanted you to come along. On the outside chance that this or something like this might happen, I wanted some support," Drew said.

Aaron shrugged. "Sure. We'll go together." Aaron unlocked the connecting door and went into his room. He opened his laptop but stared out the window. He thought his uncle wanted to revisit some of the areas where he'd spent time during the war. Aaron had read about and seen news reports about veterans returning to Vietnam and having some difficult emotions to deal with on these return trips. That's what Aaron thought this trip was about. It never entered his mind that his uncle's trip was more about searching for his long-lost girlfriend and finding out that he might have a child. This was beyond anything Aaron could have imagined and the idea that he was discovering the existence of a cousin seemed far-fetched. He shook his head as if that would remove these thoughts. He sat down and turned his attention to his laptop.

The downside of being in an older hotel was its slow internet connections. He had dozens of emails waiting to be read. His eyes scanned the names of people sending messages. He clicked his computer mouse, ignoring emails then stopped at Kellie Liang.

He leaned in after opening Kellie's message. Seeing Meilin's name caused him to sit back. After Kellie's disappearance in Hong Kong, Meilin had led him and his former customs colleague, a retired customs attaché, to a location where she thought Kellie might be held. Instead of Kellie, they found one of the two men who had attacked Aaron in his hotel room. Meilin questioned the young man and unexpectedly struck him in the throat when he refused to cooperate, stunning Aaron and the others. She gained everybody's respect that evening.

He thought about how that trip and 9/11 combined to make him rethink his career path. He thought he'd be happy as a lawyer and had transitioned from training to be a customs law enforcement agent to being a lawyer with the agency. But seeing what was going on in Hong Kong and China then being in Washington when the Pentagon was hit on 9/11, he took the opportunity of a government reorganization to move into intel work with the Department of Homeland Security.

The combination of his brief time training as a Customs agent and legal education made him an attractive candidate to move from his legal job at Customs to the intel and analytical position. He enjoyed the change to the new position. He didn't spend all day every day reading and researching in legal case books and treatises or reading court decisions. The variety of the work made each day interesting, and it was easier to break away and get back in physical shape. His career path had more options for upward mobility.

Aaron read the message a second time. Why would meeting up with Meilin cause Kellie to need reassurance? Kellie's career was on an upward trajectory with her nomination. He recognized that they were on very different paths after their Hong Kong trip. Events like her father's legal woes caused problems in their relationship. The fact that she was reaching out to him now meant she wanted to talk.

Aaron glanced at his watch. It was 8:45 in the evening in Washington. Following the hotel printed instructions, he used the hotel phone.

"Hello," Kellie answered on the third ring.

It was a low drawn out, tired greeting. "Kellie, it's Aaron. You sound tired."

"Aaron, it's nice to hear your voice. Thanks for calling. The last few days have been long. I feel like getting under the covers and not coming back out for a while," Kellie said.

"I'm sure the combined pressure of work and the nomination process are tremendous."

"If that was all it was, it wouldn't be so bad, but there's more going on than I could ever have imagined," Kellie added. "Oh, it just hit me that you're out of the country. Where are you?" She heard Aaron chuckle at the question.

"I'm in Vietnam with my uncle. It's his first time back here since the war. I found out last night that he had a very specific reason for this trip but didn't tell me. I've had a few twists thrown at me, too. He finally says he came back to find his old girlfriend. I didn't know what to say but kept thinking nothing good can come out of this search."

Kellie sat up straighter on her sofa when she heard Aaron mention Vietnam. That washed away some of the fatigue she'd been feeling. "How long are you going to be there?"

"I requested a two-week vacation to be with my uncle. He wasn't sure how he'd react to being back here and wanted someone to travel with him for support," Aaron explained. "We've only been here a few days, so I'll probably use up the whole time before getting back to work. But I didn't call to talk about my trip. What else is going on with you? You mentioned Meilin being in town."

"She's been seen at the Chinese Embassy, and we got together for dinner. She's expanding her company's business activities, but there've been strange things happening that may or may not be connected," Kellie said.

"Kellie, nothing you just said tells me anything," Aaron said in prodding Kellie.

"Meilin told me that she's looking to expand into Vietnam. And, within days of that bit of information, I found out that a government employee tried to give a Chinese Embassy staffer confidential government information. But what tops it all is finding out that the FBI uncovered surveillance on me by the Chinese. How's that for some tidbits of what's going on," Kellie said.

"I can understand you being watched by the FBI or other government agencies since you are up for a sensitive position, but why the Chinese?"

"Whatever the FBI says is the explanation for that will make no sense. I haven't been in contact with anyone at the Chinese Embassy and my communications with Meilin are minimal at best," Kellie said.

"What kind of confidential information was the Chinese trying to get from the government employee," Aaron asked.

"I spoke to a journalist who wrote the article about it, and I've dug a little more and found out it was related to dredging operations or technology about dredging. If I put this together with what Meilin said about Vietnam, some of this makes no sense because Vietnam can't handle the big container ships for exports. They don't have deep-water ports."

Aaron tried to digest the information and provide a plausible explanation for the things that were happening in Kellie's life but couldn't on the spot. "I have no magical insight I can share. I've never given any thought to the kind of thing you just explained about dredging, ports, and confidential information. I can tell you that from what I've seen in this city during the first couple of days, there's an energy and vitality that are contagious. It's easy to see why companies would come to Vietnam. But these quick observations of this place do nothing to help you."

"I wasn't expecting you to solve anything. But Meilin's unexpected visit caused me to think back to what we went through in Hong Kong and how we survived that. I can't talk about that with anyone else."

Aaron wasn't sure what to say for a moment. "What if I give you a call every couple of days while I'm here and we'll meet up when I'm back in D.C.?"

"I'd appreciate that."

"If that craziness in Hong Kong didn't overwhelm you, then this is nothing compared to that," Aaron said.

"I'm keeping my eyes and ears open when I'm out," Kellie said. "I'll talk to you in a couple of days, right?" Kellie asked.

"Absolutely." Aaron heard Kellie disconnect the call. After he placed the receiver in its cradle, he went into the bathroom, looked in the mirror and laughed. *Forgot to tell her I shaved my head.*

* * * * *

The windows of the cab were rolled down. There was no air conditioning. Even when the cab was moving and the air stirred in the cab, there was no respite from the midday heat and humidity. Along one of the busy main streets of the city, every block they passed was jammed with grocery stores, eateries, pharmacies, schools and whatever else a city might have.

When Drew and Aaron climbed out of their cab, the backs of their shirts were wet. Drew put his Yankees hat on to protect his scalp given his thinning hair. Both men wore a pair of aviator sunglasses.

"Shaving my head may have been a mistake," Aaron said.

"Why's that?"

"At least the hair I did have slowed the flow of sweat rolling down my neck and face," Aaron answered.

Drew looked at his nephew and chuckled, seeing the sweat beads rolling off Aaron's scalp to his neck, ears, and close-cut beard.

"It grows back." Drew looked around for the café along the congested and noisy main street. "We have a few minutes to find this place." Drew walked along trying to find numbers on the establishments they went by and hoped they were on the right side of the street. Drew held up the piece of paper that had the name and address of the café written on it. "See if you can spot it across the street," Drew suggested.

Aaron tapped Drew on the shoulder and pointed. "Over there." They stepped to the curb to cross the street but stopped for a moment to see if crossing at this location was the same as other streets they'd observed. They stepped out onto the street and put an arm out as if that would stop the motorbikes and vehicles.

"Just keep moving at a steady pace," Drew said.

"But it's two-way traffic," Aaron responded uneasily.

They waded into the traffic lanes of oncoming two and four-wheeled vehicles. Aaron was half a step behind his uncle, trying not to look at what was coming at him. His uncle never turned his head to either side as they crossed the street with drivers honking and beeping at them from one side of the street to the other.

Stepping onto the curb on the opposite side, Aaron took a deep breath, bending forward with a hand on each knee. "Let's not do that again. I didn't think I was going to make it across."

Drew laughed. "You wouldn't have been killed, maimed, maybe."

"You're enjoying this," Aaron noticed.

"Hey, it's life. I'm here, I survived here before. Don't worry, I'll get you back in one piece," Drew said, grinning.

The two men entered the small café. The midday crowd was boisterous and left little choice for seating. A young hostess approached. Drew put up three fingers.

They stopped at a table amid the crowd. "Okay?" the young woman asked.

Drew looked around but saw that there wasn't a better table for conversation. "Okay. Thank you."

Several ceiling fans did nothing more than move the hot air.

"Hope we can spot her when she arrives," Aaron said.

"She spots us," Drew corrected. He kept his Yankees cap on. "Between my hat and your shaved head, she'll notice us."

Without a word, a waitress walked by and put down menus.

Although Drew sat in a chair facing the entrance, there were several occupied tables and people milling around the entrance. He knew that he had no idea what Phan Linh looked like.

"If that was her in the bar last night, would you recognize her?" Drew asked.

Aaron turned his head toward the entrance. "Honestly, I doubt it. The lighting wasn't that good, and except for a couple of times she looked toward us for a few seconds, she had her back to us most of the time. Other than being several inches taller than the other girl and having long hair, I wouldn't recognize her even if she was standing right here," Aaron answered.

Drew turned to get the waitress's attention and Aaron looked at the one-page menu with attempts at English descriptions.

"Hello," Phan Linh said softly, causing both men's heads to snap up to look at her. Linh's long hair was pulled tight to the back and dangled down to her mid-back. Her arms and face had a year-round tan complexion. Her round eyes and slightly more pronounced hips hinted at her mixed-race origins. She dressed comfortably for work in a thin short-sleeved white blouse and black slacks.

Drew half stood and motioned her to sit. "Thank you for coming," he said. "What is the correct way to call you?" he asked, settling back in his chair.

"You call me Linh. Phan is my family name. You are?" Her eyes went to both men.

"I'm Drew Foster and this is Aaron Foster, my nephew," Drew said. "Is the woman in the picture at the bar your mother," Drew said a bit rushed.

"Yes."

Drew waited, expecting her to say more, but she didn't.

"Does she live in the city?" Drew saw the smile disappear from Linh's face.

"She died. Doctors said cancer," Linh said without emotion.

"I'm very sorry to hear that," Drew offered. He looked over at Aaron who sat stiffly looking and listening to the conversation. "Linh, what year were you born?"

"August 1970. I'm thirty-five this year."

"You and Aaron are about the same age," Drew said.

Linh looked at Aaron for a moment, smiling.

"Do you have brothers, sisters, other family?"

"I have uncles, aunts, cousins, but no brothers or sisters. Just me. After the war, we're not close with other people. It was hard for her. She didn't have much education so only bad jobs and not much money," she tried to explain.

"But you speak English well. You went to school," Drew guessed.

"I didn't have many friends. I had time to study myself," Linh said.

"How is your job?" Aaron said, joining the conversation.

"Easy job. I'm like a clerk. I deliver papers and documents to offices in the building. It's boring, but a clean job," Linh said.

"Do you work for a big company?" Aaron continued.

"No, it's a government office called the Maritime Administration of Vietnam. That's how they say it in English."

"It sounds like a good place to work," Aaron noted. Behind his smiling reaction, his conversation with Kellie popped into his thoughts and Kellie's remark about Vietnam and deep-water ports. What would the Maritime Administration have to do with plans about developing those ports?

Aaron lost a few minutes of Drew and Linh's conversation while he was lost in his thoughts. He came out of his reverie to hear Linh apologize for having to get back to work.

"I apologize that we didn't allow you to have lunch," Drew said.

"It's okay. I don't need more food, I need to diet," Linh said patting her flat midsection having no hint of needing to diet.

"May I call you later and we can have dinner?" Drew asked.

"Yes, okay." As Linh stood to leave, Drew and Aaron stood and watched her depart.

"Baby steps," Drew said as they sat down, and he got the waitress's attention. "No need for us to forego lunch."

"A lot there for you to take in," Aaron said.

"Yeah. I didn't know what to say when she said her mother was dead. This country was in chaos and people were being treated like shit after Saigon fell in 1975," Drew said.

"What is your best-case scenario now that you've had a conversation with her?"

"Best case is I get her to move to the U.S.," Drew answered.

"Just how will you manage that? She isn't a kid. She's an adult with a life here. You didn't ask if she's in a relationship. For all we know, she might be divorced with children or something."

"You said best-case. Besides, you're a lawyer, you can help me figure it out."

"Not my area of expertise," Aaron said shaking his head. His thoughts had turned to where Linh worked and whether she had information that could help Kellie. "I don't know what you plan for the rest of the day, but I need to follow-up on an email I saw this morning."

"No problem," Drew said. "I'm a big boy. I'll find something to occupy my time."

Returning to the hotel, Drew and Aaron retreated to their rooms. Aaron didn't know what Drew would do for the remainder of the afternoon, but Aaron retrieved his laptop from his locked computer bag, logged in and began searching.

Aaron's internet search frustrated him. Searches took him to websites in Vietnamese without any English translation available. He searched the U.S. Embassy in Hanoi's website wondering if the embassy provided any commercial and development information to U.S. businesses looking for investment opportunities in Vietnam.

Aaron sat back and rubbed his eyes after an hour and a half of scouring the internet for anything useful. There were tidbits of information about the Maritime Administration and its role in seeking out potential partners to create deepwater seaports. Reading the limited amount of information he found, Vietnam confronted two challenges to a speedy increase in its trade with the U.S. and other major importers of its goods: investment money and investment in the technology to construct in a short period of time the deepwater seaports it didn't have.

Aaron checked the time. The afternoon was slipping away as it approached four o'clock. He did one last internet search and wrote down an address. He couldn't waste time. He secured his laptop in his bag and grabbed a plain white baseball cap. In the hotel lobby, Aaron pulled out 20,000 dong, offering it to a bellman to help get him a ride to the address. The bellman stepped out onto the sidewalk, waving, and getting the attention of a young man in shorts and tank top shirt.

The young man pulled up on a motorbike and listened as the bellman explained where to take the American. The bellman took the extra helmet the driver had and held it out for Aaron.

"No," Aaron said, reluctant to get on the bike. "I want a taxi."

The bellman pointed to his watch. "Too much time. This is faster."

Aaron glared at the bellman as he straddled the bike's seat. Aaron felt around for somewhere to grab and hold. The bellman stepped toward him, grabbed Aaron's wrist, and moved it toward the driver's waist.

"More safe," the bellman said. When the bellman saw Aaron lean forward to reach around the driver, he nodded to the driver.

The bike lurched forward, causing Aaron to tighten his hold on the driver's midsection. The driver weaved through traffic, joining other cyclists at every intersection, and swarming around four-wheeled vehicles. The way the cyclist accelerated and slowed between intersections and steered the motorbike, Aaron's body was in constant motion thrust forward and backward. He was on the same streets as earlier in the day when he and Drew went to lunch and realized that the bellman knew what he was talking about as the streets were much more congested. Looking behind him at one intersection, he calculated that they were several blocks farther ahead of any cars and taxis heading in the same direction. Aaron didn't dare loosen his embrace of the cyclist steering the motorbike.

Aaron saw them pass the café from earlier in the day. According to the map he'd studied earlier, he was only a few blocks away from the Maritime Administration building. Aaron tapped the driver's shoulder and pointed to the curb after noticing the painted crosswalk on the pavement. Pulling over, Aaron climbed off the bike and handed the driver the agreed fare.

A large group of pedestrians were gathered at the crosswalk. Aaron jogged toward them, joining them as they crossed the street. Despite the traffic, he wanted to have a straight-on view of the building's main exit from across the multi-lane avenue. The distance would also prevent Linh from spotting him. He assumed that people would be leaving their offices around five o'clock, but he hadn't checked to learn what the normal office work hours were.

Approaching a spot that was directly across from the Maritime Administration, he noticed a clump of trees near a corner that could provide some shade giving way to a row of storefronts. Aaron decided that he'd rather be standing under the trees and in the shade rather than on the sidewalk and more exposed to the sun.

Aaron checked his watch. If the workday ended at four-thirty, he would know in a few minutes. He waited ten minutes and decided that his wait would continue. The stream of people on both sides of the avenue was becoming more crowded as people seemed to be shoulder to shoulder as they passed Aaron. Luckily, Aaron was taller than most of the people walking and rushing by him. Anyone looking for someone sticking out of the crowd would've spotted Aaron easily. His height and the white hat staying in the same spot for an extended period would've been obvious.

When it got closer to five o'clock, Aaron had moved out from under the trees and closer to a storefront, but Aaron moved a few feet away from the entrance of the business he was in front of when an employee came to the door and stared. Aaron alternated his weight from one foot to the other and wished he'd picked up a magazine from the hotel to pass the time. The loud engine of a diesel-powered bus attracted his attention as it stopped fifty feet away. Aaron watched as a large group of waiting passengers pressed themselves into the crowded vehicle. It spewed plumes of black exhaust as it started moving.

The minutes passed. Aaron concentrated on the building across the street. An increasing number of small groups of people began to exist. It was 5:10 when he spotted Linh walking out with another woman several inches shorter. He thought it might be the same woman who was at The Bar but couldn't be sure. They slowed a couple of paces after exiting, talking then parted ways as the shorter woman left Linh behind. Aaron watched Linh looking around then saw her wave to someone. He stayed in his spot.

A man strode toward her, gave her a peck on the cheek. He wore blue jeans and a light blue buttoned-down shirt with his sleeves rolled up. Aaron couldn't see his face, but he had a full head of thick black hair. The two were only inches apart talking. Aaron watched as Linh was nodding at him, smiling. The man's hand brushed along her arm as she stepped away from him. She waved back and the two went in opposite directions.

The man began walking along the avenue in the direction where Aaron and Drew had met with Linh. Without fully understanding why, Aaron decided he needed to know more about this man, who was he and what was his relationship with Linh. Uncle Drew deserved to have all the facts before doing anything. He removed his cap and put the bill of it in his back pocket, thinking that the white hat made him stand out more than a shaved head. His eyes darted back and forth from the man and the people obstructing his path forward.

He needed to get on the other side of the wide street to decrease the chance of losing sight of the man in blue. He saw a crowd of people ahead crossing the street, Aaron began speed walking. When he reached the designated crossing, he was surrounded by people waiting to cross. He looked over the heads of most around him, seeing the man in blue getting farther away.

As soon as people stepped into the street, Aaron jogged around the group and kept jogging after reaching the opposite side of the avenue. There were too many people to break into a full run. He kept jogging. His sunglasses slid down his nose from all the perspiration on his head and face. He bumped into several people who stepped in front of him, hearing sounds that may have been curses he didn't understand. "Sorry," he said as he passed.

He was into the third block of his pursuit when he saw his target turn down a side street at a corner where a gas station was located. Aaron took a chance and sprinted in the lane of oncoming traffic, darting back onto the sidewalk when a pack of two-wheeled vehicles hugging the curb raced toward him. On the sidewalk, he turned sideways to slide by slower pedestrians.

Reaching the corner by the gas station, he turned and saw the man in blue. The two-lane wide side street seemed deserted in comparison to the wide avenue he'd just left. There was no sidewalk. A few six to ten story recently constructed buildings were interspersed with older wooden structures. There were numerous narrow walkways and alleyways between the narrow buildings.

Aaron guessed he'd walked a hundred yards down the side street when he saw the man in blue enter one of the more modern buildings. With the man inside, Aaron jogged down the street to the building, climbing the few steps up to the glass entry door that opened automatically. He stepped into the well-lit lobby. A desk was off to the side, but no one was sitting there. Mercifully, the air felt ten degrees cooler. He wiped the sweat from his head and face. Looking around, he spotted a building directory and walked over to look at it.

When an elevator chimed, he didn't turn away from the directory, not wanting his face to be seen. He heard at least two people talking and exiting behind him, their shoes echoing off the black marble floor. He heard a third person's steps behind him. They sounded different. He glanced over his shoulder for a second and saw a security guard sitting behind the desk.

The building directory listed businesses on floors two through six. Nothing was listed for the higher floors. He saw a mix of languages: Vietnamese, English and what he guessed was Chinese. Seeing a listing for the fourth floor, he couldn't help but stare at it.

He saw the acronym CODE and ChiTran Overseas Development Enterprise. CODE meant nothing to him, but ChiTran Overseas Development Enterprise jumped out at him. Could this be the same ChiTran that was controlled by Meilin? Kellie said Meilin wanted to grow ChiTran and mentioned Vietnam. Was there an easy way to find out? Did that mean that the man in blue is Chinese or a local working for ChiTran? He knew that linking the man in blue to CODE or ChiTran was crazy since he knew nothing about him and saw nothing to suggest such a link.

Aaron turned and left the building. On the street, he counted the height of the building, wanting to remember it. He looked up and down the street. From the avenue, there was only one other ten-story building on that side of the street. Retracing his path back to the wide avenue, he looked for other landmarks but was left with the gas station on the corner as the landmark to remember.

Standing at the corner of the avenue and side street, Aaron put the cap on his head and started walking, hoping he could find his way back to the hotel. Despite being an experienced traveler, he'd forgotten to get a hotel business card with its address printed to show to any driver. He marched in the direction of the hotel lost in thought. He hoped that his uncle would make a dinner arrangement with Linh as soon as possible. He'd have a few questions of his own. A call to Kellie was a priority. Kellie needed to know what he had just seen. Did this have anything to do with Kellie's comment about the Chinese trying to get information from a government employee?

The walk gave Aaron time to formulate questions and understand the possible links that might exist even if those links were without any evidentiary basis. It also gave him time to realize that he saw nothing good about any of the thoughts thrashing around in his head. He was going to be walking a fine line with his uncle if he started asking Linh questions.

An hour into his brisk walk, Aaron was drenched in sweat. He hadn't made any turns and didn't recognize anything. He stopped in front of an elegant old building. Aaron looked around to stop someone and ask if he was near Notre Dame Cathedral. He chanced stopping a young woman whose age he couldn't guess. She pointed in the direction he needed to go.

He walked another half an hour, stopping twice for directions before recognizing the streets around his hotel. Entering the lobby, Aaron thought of two things: a shower and an email to Kellie.

The door to his room closed harder and louder than he wanted, hoping to avoid his uncle for a bit longer. He wasn't surprised when he heard a knock on the adjoining room door.

"Where the hell have you been," Drew asked, looking at Aaron standing shirtless in the room.

"I got lost," Aaron said truthfully. "I had no way of telling anyone the address to the hotel so I couldn't get a cab. I walked."

Drew laughed. "You got your exercise for the day."

"I need a shower and a few minutes on my computer."

"Take all the time you want. I'll be down in the bar," Drew said and closed the door.

Aaron stood under the shower head with cool water running over his body for a few minutes, then dried and sat at his computer with a towel wrapped around his waist.

"Kellie, I met my uncle's possible daughter. She works for Vietnam's Maritime Administration in Ho Chi Minh City. Now, for the interesting part of the day, I found an office here that goes by CODE, stands for ChiTran Overseas Development Enterprise. By any chance is this connected to Meilin? While I'm not sure he works there, I'm suspicious that someone who might work for CODE is very friendly with my uncle's possible daughter, but I need to find a way to confirm. Talk very soon. Aaron". Aaron sat back, reread the message then hit send. He hoped Kellie would read it before he called her after he and Drew returned from wherever they were headed for dinner.

Aaron and Drew wandered down the street from their hotel in the direction of the Saigon River. Neither had a specific place in mind.

"I don't really feel like I've ever been here before," Drew said. "There's nothing in the city that would hint at the kind of place this was when I was here during the war."

"Did you really spend time getting to know the city back then?"

"Not as much as I should have. I spent most of my time doing what young guys do," Drew answered.

A long city block from the river, they cut across one block and saw several small restaurants.

"What do you think?" Drew asked.

"Pick one and we'll take our chances that we'll feel fine in the morning."

The two sat at a card table on vinyl covered padded chairs. The small restaurant was basic and had a dozen tables. Neon colored lights flashed on signs outside while the inside was lit brightly. A girl that looked to be high school age came to the table and took away the plastic menus, replacing them with paper menus in English.

"Duck," Aaron said and saw his uncle squint. "I mean I'm having duck."

Drew nodded. "I'll do the same."

"Now that you've met Linh, do you have a timeline for what comes next?" Aaron asked after they ordered. "I can't stay here indefinitely. I have a job to get back to."

"Lots of thoughts are scrambled. If there's the possibility that Linh is my daughter, I'd like to do whatever it takes to confirm it. Until that question is answered, I don't have solid next steps."

"That makes sense. The next time we or you meet with her, you have to find out if she wants an answer to that question," Aaron said.

"Yeah, I know. Let's think this through. Why would she have left the picture at the Orphan Bar if she didn't want to know? Doesn't that indicate some desire to find out?"

"I agree with you," Aaron said. "But, like you, she left that photo expecting nothing to ever happen. You were both doing this with no expectation of anything coming of it."

"There's a lot of truth to that."

"We're past that. Both of you came forward. The photos match. It's time to put up or shut up or, in this case, either both of you take the next step of confirming that she's your daughter or one of you decides to walk away," Aaron said.

Drew took a big gulp of a beer that had been set in front of him. "There's a big difference between imagining what could or might happen and reality," Drew said. "Until now, this was stuff in my head bouncing around without anything needing to be decided. It seems a bit crazy now that I need to face up to it."

Aaron sipped his beer, looking over the rim of his glass. He could see Drew's internal struggles from the pressed lips and slight slump of his uncle's shoulders across the table.

They ate, talking sparingly. Aaron saw Drew looking around the restaurant, out the window, anywhere to avoid a lot of eye contact.

"I'll call her first thing in the morning and hope we can arrange something for tomorrow evening," Drew said. "You're right. Tough decisions need to be made but they can't be made until I have a straightforward conversation with her."

"I hope that's possible. Her limited English could make the conversation difficult to have," Aaron commented.

"One way or the other, we'll get there," Drew said.

* * * * *

Aaron had hoped to be calling Kellie earlier in her day, but after his late return to the hotel and dinner out left him calling Kellie well into her morning. He found the main number to call Senator Burke's office, hoping that if he asked to speak to Kellie, she would be in the office.

"Sorry, but Ms. Liang is meeting with the senator," Trish said.

"I'm calling from Vietnam. The time difference makes it important that I talk to her before I go to bed and delay this conversation another eight or nine hours," Aaron explained, hoping that the receptionist would understand.

"Hold on. I'll see what I can do." Trish got up and tapped on the Senator's office door. She opened the door a couple of inches. Kellie and Senator Burke were looking back at her.

"Sorry, but Ms. Liang has a caller from Vietnam. He says it's important."

"Take it," Senator Burke said to Kellie.

Kellie sprang out of the chair and crossed the reception area to her desk. "Aaron, what's going on?"

"That's a good question and one I hope to explore and find out more. I assume you saw my message about CODE and ChiTran."

"I did. It makes sense that ChiTran has an office in Vietnam if the plan is to expand, but the part that still doesn't make sense is expanding in a country with limited capacity to send goods to foreign markets. But if I tie that to what I told you earlier about the Chinese Embassy trying to access dredging technology information then it starts to come together," Kellie said. "How did you manage to come across this information?"

"This may sound crazy, but I saw my uncle's possible daughter, her name is Phan Linh, meet up with a guy just as she was leaving work. They parted ways and, out of curiosity, I followed him. When he went into a building, I went in, looked at the directory and saw the name. I have to believe that the ChiTran Overseas Development Enterprise is the same ChiTran we were dealing with in Hong Kong and China. That leads us to Meilin.

"I think my uncle will ask Phan Linh to do what's necessary to prove or disprove his paternity. While he's busy with that, I'll see what I can find out about CODE. I'm limited in what I'll be able to do for you. Time is a factor," Aaron said.

"Aaron, be careful. Remember, you're there on vacation. You're not part of the embassy or consulate staff. You aren't there on official business."

"I'm very aware of that. If needed, I hope your boss might be able to intervene and save my ass."

"I hope you don't get into a situation where I need to ask him for that kind of help. Things are already dicey for me," Kellie said. "Maybe I can leverage the information you've given me."

"How," Aaron wanted to know.

"I need to work on an answer to that."

"I'll keep you informed about anything I find out. Meanwhile, maybe you can use your new FBI contacts to help," Aaron suggested.

"To say I have FBI contacts is stretching the truth. Aaron, thanks. You don't know how much I appreciate this," Kellie said.

"Anything I can do for you, just tell me."

Aaron pressed the button in the phone's cradle to disconnect the call. He did that instead of saying good-bye. He sat back and closed his eyes.

* * * * *

With her elbows on her desk, Kellie rested her head in the palms of her hands. Good or bad, nothing was going to happen unless she initiated something, but what?

"Are you alright?"

Kellie turned to see Senator Burke standing at her cubicle.

"I'm fine," Kellie answered.

"I'm not convinced that you're fine, but I'll accept the answer. I know there's a lot going on and the last few days have put more stress on you than usual. If there is anything I can do, just tell me," Senator Burke offered.

"There is a possibility that a friend might need your help," Kellie confessed.

"I hope the friend isn't a Chinese friend."

"No, he's a Homeland Security employee who's in Vietnam," Kellie said. "Sometimes things are unforeseeable, unpredictable. I don't know if he'll need help, but it's a 'just in case' situation."

Senator Burke eyed Kellie for a moment, wishing she would tell him more. "Make sure that if he needs my help, he asks for it before it gets so bad that there's nothing I can do."

"I will," Kellie answered.

Kellie nodded and watched the Senator turn and head back toward his office. She waited a minute, giving the Senator time to return to his office. She looked around and saw that most of the cubicles around her were empty.

Kellie pressed the numbers on her cell phone for Agent Kearns.

"Agent Kearns, its Kellie Liang from Senator Burke's office. Have a minute?" It was silent on Kearns's end longer than she expected.

"Yes. I'm good, go ahead," he prompted.

"There's a very strong possibility that the woman whose name I gave you, Meilin Moy, has established an office in Vietnam. The funny thing is that for someone who oversees a major export-driven group of companies having an office in a country that doesn't have any deep-water seaports, at the moment, seems strange."

"Wait a moment. How did you get the info about the office in Vietnam," Kearns interrupted.

"Can we get to that later?"

"If you insist," Kearns agreed.

"What if we create a situation that forces Ms. Moy to have to divulge more information than we have now? What if she confirmed our suspicions about the Chinese Embassy's attempts to get confidential information?"

"You have something in mind, correct?"

"Yes, I do," Kellie answered.

"We should meet and discuss whatever is on your mind in person, not over the phone," Kearns advised.

"Union Station is a crowded place. It's easy to blend into a crowd, not be noticed," Kellie said.

"On the flip side, it can be too noisy, and we might have to talk a lot louder than we want to," Kearns countered.

"You're the pro, you choose a place."

"I'll pick you up at the corner of your building, Constitution and First. Should I bring along someone from Justice?" Kearns wondered.

"I'm not sure. Is your car bugged?"

Kearns laughed. "It sounds like we should talk without any lawyers for now."

Kellie told Kearns how to spot her at the corner. They agreed on a time, and she clicked off.

At eleven-forty, Kellie left the office to get to the corner and meet Kearns. Kearns pulled up in a dark blue Malibu. Seeing a tall thin woman with short black hair and black-framed glasses, he rolled down the window. "Ms. Liang?"

Kellie bent down, "Agent Kearns, I presume."

Kellie slid into the passenger seat. Kellie stayed with her long-time habit of wearing what Aaron considered to be her ugly, black-framed glasses. She thought it sent a signal to everyone that she was all business.

"You've now entered my private office," Kearns started.

It made Kellie chuckle, and she relaxed a little.

"You've come up with a plan of sorts," Kearns asked.

"I'm not sure if it's a plan or musings," Kellie responded. "What I have in mind is creating the illusion that a person is in a lot of trouble to get her to confirm things or to provide information we don't have."

"Who's the victim?"

"Meilin Moy," Kellie said. "To do what I have in mind, we don't have much time. She may only be in town for another couple of days. If it's going to happen, I need to arrange another dinner or lunch to do this. But I need something from you if you have it or if your Justice Department contact has it."

"And what would that be?"

"Print outs of the confidential patent information that were the grounds for the prosecution of the patent examiner," Kellie answered.

Kearns drove down Pennsylvania Avenue, taking a left turn onto 14th Street, heading toward the National Mall. "What else, if anything?"

"You'd have to have a couple of your people there undercover."

"I can arrange for a couple of people to be there. Do I need a way of quietly taking Ms. Moy into custody?"

"That would probably be good to do," Kellie answered.

"I'll ask the Justice Department lawyer to get us the documents," Kearns said. "When do you want to try and do this?"

"Let's try for tomorrow at lunch or dinner. I'll contact Ms. Moy this afternoon, then let you know. Will I have the documents this afternoon?" Kellie asked.

"I'll see what I can do and give you a call. Oh, it would be helpful if you arranged this event for dinner," Kearns said. He was already driving on Independence Avenue toward Capitol Hill. "You haven't answered a question I asked earlier," Kearns said.

Kellie looked at him blankly.

"How did you get the info about Moy having an office in Vietnam?"

"Someone I know, a friend, is in Vietnam. I didn't know he was there until he returned my call. After finding out that I was being watched by the Chinese, I needed to talk to someone, you know, a sympathetic ear. He happened to stumble across something that points to Meilin's company having opened an office in Ho Chi Minh City."

"He happened to stumble across something like that. I'm having trouble accepting that explanation, but I'll let you get away with it for now" Kearns allowed.

Reaching Capitol Hill, Kearns turned left and drove by the Library of Congress and the Supreme Court building. Approaching the traffic light, he pulled over, letting Kellie out.

"Nice meeting you. I'll be in touch later," Kearns said.

"Thanks for the private meeting," Kellie said, exiting the car.

Just after four in the afternoon, an envelope addressed to Kellie Liang was hand delivered to Senator Burke's office. Kellie pulled out the documents and read the note. "Ms. Liang, the documents requested through Agent Kearns. Call if you need to discuss. V. Walters". A phone number was handwritten on the note. Kellie called the number.

"Victoria Walters, can I help you?"

"Ms. Walters. I'm Kellie Liang. I received the documents and wanted to thank you for getting them here so quickly."

"Agent Kearns said it was beyond urgent, like yesterday urgent. Have you had time to review them? Do you have any questions?"

"I've just glanced over them. Frankly, I don't need to have any detailed understanding of the content," Kellie said.

"That's interesting to know. There's a lot of technical and legal descriptions in the documents that most people wouldn't understand. There's an art to writing patents and describing inventions."

"I do appreciate that, but for my purposes, having them is more important than understanding them," Kellie clarified.

Victoria knew there was something afoot that Agent Kearns didn't want to explain when he had asked her to provide the documents to Kellie. Listening to Kellie, Victoria was convinced that neither Agent Kearns nor Kellie Liang wanted her to know something.

"I want to emphasize something. Now that I've gotten the impression that you and Agent Kearns are doing or will do something, it's much easier to keep you out of trouble if I know what you're planning than to try and fix something after the fact if the line is crossed. You might get so far across the line that I can't help you," Victoria said.

"Ms. Walters, I appreciate that. The other side of the coin is that I don't want to get you into hot water by putting you in a position of saying you knew what we are planning to do," Kellie responded.

"I hope you two know what you're doing. You have my number if you need it."

"Thank you," Kellie said as she clicked off. With the documents in her possession, Kellie sent an email to Meilin, arranging her next and possibly her last dinner with Meilin.

Contingencies

Aaron tossed and turned most of the night after talking to Kellie. He slept for an hour here and there and gave up when he saw the first glimpse of dawn around the edges of the pulled curtain. Aaron opened the curtains, inviting in the morning light and opened his laptop. He searched the internet and found the location of the U.S. consulate. Not that far from the hotel, it was within a reasonable walking distance, he concluded. It was too early to call and expect to talk to the person he wanted to speak to.

Aaron went down to the hotel restaurant for coffee. It was something to do to kill time. He picked up an English language newspaper. He ate nothing but consumed a pot of coffee as he caught up on global news. Checking his watch, he decided that he'd spent enough time in the lobby restaurant and went back to the room. He called the consulate, asking to be connected to the Homeland Security Investigations attaché, telling the receptionist that he worked for Homeland Security.

The receptionist put Aaron on hold. He stood by the small desk in the room, looking down onto rush-hour street traffic. The sounds of the beeps and honks from the street echoed between the buildings on both sides of the street.

"Bruce Hoover, can I help you?"

The voice over the phone startled Aaron for a moment. "Mr. Hoover, my name is Aaron Foster. I work in DHS's Intel office in DC. I'm sure you're busy, but I'd like to pop in for ten or fifteen minutes to talk to you."

"Are you here on official business? I never saw any communication from DC about anyone here officially," Bruce Hoover said.

"No, I'm taking some vacation days to travel with my uncle. He's a Vietnam War vet," Aaron explained.

"Is this just a courtesy pop in or something else?"

"It's a little more than a courtesy stop. There may be a developing situation from an intel perspective," Aaron said.

"Are you sure that I'm the right person to talk to? Is this more appropriate for the Langley types?" Bruce Hoover asked.

"What if I explain it to you when we meet and you can judge whether it's in your bailiwick or someone else's," Aaron replied.

"Fair enough. I don't have anything requiring me to be out of the office today so what time should I expect you?"

Aaron checked his watch. "Let's say in an hour, around ten?"

"See you then," Bruce Hoover said. "I'll call the guards and make sure they have your name. If you have your government passport and DHS ID, bring them."

Before leaving the hotel, Aaron trimmed his unshaven face to make it look like he was growing a beard. He walked the several blocks along the busy streets of the central business district. Walking and perspiring were no worse or better than being in a taxi without air conditioning. He felt safer walking than on the back of a motorcycle cab.

Arriving at the consulate, the guards put him through security procedures of emptying all his pockets and walking through a metal detector. He was prepared. His pockets had only what was necessary. He presented his work identification and his government passport. Entering the main consulate building, he waited for someone to escort him.

"Mr. Foster?"

Aaron turned toward the voice calling his name. Aaron shook the hand of a stocky man a couple of inches shorter than himself. Hoover's reddish-brown hair was cut military style. He was dressed comfortably in khaki dress slacks and a short sleeve button down shirt. As Hoover led Aaron to his office, Aaron noticed that Hoover had broad shoulders for a man of his height.

While the hallway was comfortable, Aaron felt the much cooler air of Hoover's office.

"I keep the a/c cranked up when I'm here," Bruce Hoover said. "There's no such thing as getting used to the heat and humidity here.

You've got to accept that when you're out doing anything, it'll be uncomfortable and miserable. Every time I think about those grunts in the jungles during the war, I'm amazed they could function wearing those fatigues and carrying that load all the time."

"My uncle was with a support unit, so he wasn't constantly trudging around in the bush," Aaron said.

"We have a lot of vets starting to travel back. It's good for some, but not all of them," Bruce Hoover said.

"How long have you been with DHS," Hoover asked.

"I started out with Customs when we were still part of the Treasury Department then made a change when the reorganization occurred and Customs was moved to DHS," Aaron said. "I was on the legal side of things but got a bit bored with that."

"The reorganization is still having its negative side effects. I was in the Office of Investigations with Customs and then we became Immigration and Customs Enforcement within DHS. Integrating investigators from other agencies hasn't gone as smoothly as everyone wanted. People from different agencies and different mindsets on investigative priorities cause some turf battles and clashes among the personnel. It'll sort itself out eventually. I guess when some of us older guys retire and don't bring the culture of our former offices to work with us, it'll be better," Hoover elaborated. "But you're not here to talk about all of that."

"Reorgs are always difficult, but this was a big one and it's not surprising there are still some problems. Hopefully, those problems aren't affecting you. I'm not sure where to start so let me plunge into why I wanted to meet," Aaron began. "A friend of mine is a nominee for a political job at the State Department dealing with Chinese issues. I've had a couple of conversations with her in the past few days and she informed me that a government employee was arrested for trying to give the Chinese confidential information."

"And how does that have anything to do with me or anyone in this consulate? What's your friend's name?" Bruce asked.

"Kellie Liang. I'm sure her name will pop up if you do an online search. As a criminal investigator, you probably don't believe in coincidences. I know I don't," Aaron said and paused. He saw Bruce smile. "Between the attempted hand-off of confidential information to the Chinese and a meeting between Kellie Liang and a Chinese CEO visiting DC, China's interest in Vietnam has popped up. The other thing that makes all this more interesting is that the company that the Chinese CEO oversees has an office here that goes by the acronym CODE. That's the ChiTran Overseas Development Enterprise. In China, it goes by ChiTran. ChiTran is a group of companies involved in the manufacture and movement of goods. I know for a fact that they've been caught exporting substandard and dangerous goods to the U.S. An importer was prosecuted for trying to paper over the imports of the illegal products."

"And we're discussing this because you want me to do something?" Bruce asked.

"I doubt there's anything to do at this point," Aaron said.

"At the moment, Vietnam isn't sending that much to the U.S."

"And that's the point. The confidential information that was attempted to be given to the Chinese has to do with technology that could be used to accelerate Vietnam's deep-water seaport capabilities for larger container ships and maybe Chinese naval vessels," Aaron explained.

"I'm not sure that getting into any of that is in my job description. There's nothing to investigate from my perspective. There're definite Chinese business interests here and they're growing. There's a line between me investigating criminal activity that has a connection to the U.S. and any spook related spying and espionage. If I cross that line, I'm in trouble," Bruce responded.

The two men looked at each other. Bruce had been casually leaning back in his chair. Now, he slowly leaned forward. Aaron saw his eyes narrow a bit as if a thought or a question was forming.

"How did you find out about CODE having an office here? Was it this friend that told you about the office here?"

Aaron took a deep breath. "No. It was another one of those coincidences that we don't believe in."

"Try me."

"As I told you, I'm here with my uncle. We've met a woman who may be his daughter. She works at the Maritime Administration. I went to wait for her and talk to her yesterday, but she met up with this guy at the end of the day. Concerned he could present a problem to my uncle's hopes of his daughter moving to the U.S., I decided to follow him and that led me to the building where CODE has its office," Aaron explained.

Bruce closed his eyes for a moment. "You followed this guy. Is he Chinese?"

"Don't know. He could be either Chinese or Vietnamese."

"Did this guy that you followed go to the CODE office?"

"I don't know. I just got into the building he entered, looked at the building directory and saw the name of the company," Aaron said.

"Okay, we have, I'm sorry, you have some big gaps in information. You don't know if this guy you followed even works for CODE and you don't know his nationality."

"But it is interesting that he's hooked up with someone working at the Maritime Administration, right?"

"It's a pretty big leap to get to the conclusions you'd like to reach. The dots aren't connected yet. I'd advise you to think carefully about what you're doing. You stick out like a sore thumb here and tailing anyone could get you into a lot of trouble, the kind we might not be able to get you out of," Bruce cautioned.

Aaron knew that Bruce Hoover was right. The Chinese engaging in illegal activity in the U.S. had nothing to do with what they do Vietnam.

"I don't have any intention to get myself in trouble here."

"That's good to know. We're still working on this relationship with the Vietnamese. Everybody's trying to figure out the boundaries, including me," Bruce added.

"I'll let you get on with the day. I think I've used up my allotted time," Aaron said, standing and moving toward the door.

"It's not a problem. I can appreciate that there are lots of competing commercial interests involved here. I don't get involved on the military side. That's still a sensitive area and can open wounds that we don't want to reopen," Bruce said. "If you do come across something you think I should know, here's my card and direct line number. Good meeting you," Bruce said. He stopped at his office door and watched Aaron head toward the lobby.

Aaron exited the consulate to the blazing late morning sun and tropical temperatures. He found a shaded spot on the sidewalk and watched the people milling around the entrance. The congested flow of traffic was constant. Four and two-wheeled cabs veered to the curb, dropping people off at the consulate.

Aaron turned to make his way back to the hotel. He made an immediate about-face hearing his name called.

"Hey, Aaron!" Drew shouted with his hands cupped around his mouth, having just gotten out of a cab. "What are you doing here?"

"I made a courtesy visit on the DHS agent posted here," Aaron said. "You never know when a good job opportunity might become available. I wanted to know what it was like to work abroad for the agency." Aaron was no stranger to some of the activities of customs attachés. His brief time in Hong Kong gave him a glimpse into that world dealing with criminals and things that might need to be done quietly. The work wasn't always by the book.

"Not a bad idea," Drew said.

"What are you doing here?"

"I tried to talk with someone here yesterday while you were out playing. I was told I needed to make an appointment so that's what I did," Drew said. "I'm back today to get some information."

"About what?"

"This thing with Linh, it got me to thinking that if we confirm that she's my daughter, would she be considered an American citizen. I want to talk to someone who can tell me something about that. And, if she is considered an American citizen she could move to the U.S.," Drew answered.

"That would be a big change for her. She's not a kid anymore. She seems to have a life here," Aaron said without divulging what he had seen the day before.

"But maybe her life could be better in the States. I want to know what this person has to say before we meet with Linh again. That reminds me, we're meeting her for dinner this evening. I did press her a bit by explaining that you have a limited amount of time before you need to go back to work," Drew said.

"I'm guessing that I can't accompany you."

Drew shrugged. "It won't hurt to try and get you in."

Aaron followed Drew back to the Consulate's entry area.

"We have an eleven o'clock meeting," Drew said. He and Aaron provided their identification.

"Weren't you just here?" the guard asked, looking at Aaron.

"Yes. I was meeting with the DHS attaché, Mr. Hoover, but I have another meeting that my uncle arranged."

"Okay, once you two get through security, someone will come get you."

Aaron repeated the security procedure and waited for his uncle. They were met by an unusually tall, slender young Vietnamese man and led to an office.

Aaron and Drew entered a room with a table. Both men saw a woman whose age couldn't be guessed. To them, the woman of average height with shoulder length black hair, warm and inviting smile and sparkling brown eyes could be between twenty-five and forty years old.

Janice Doan stood at the table as Drew and Aaron entered. "Gentlemen, please come in and have a seat." She had no local accent. Janice Doan maintained her inviting smile as the two men sat down. She watched for any reaction when she said anything for the first time. In this job, most of her visitors expected her English to be heavily accented. Her father's connections with Americans meant they were able to escape as Saigon fell in 1975. She had few memories of Vietnam. She grew up in southern California.

"I'm Janice Doan. One of you left a very brief message about possibly identifying a daughter here," Janice began.

"I did," Drew said. Drew explained the evening at the Orphan Bar.

"It sounds like a genuine effort to connect. Luckily for you and her, there are immigration laws aimed at helping people like Ms. Phan. You seem to be willing to establish your parentage of her."

"I'll do what I need to do. If you can tell me what to do and how to go about it, that would mean a lot to me," Drew said.

"There are applications that need to be filled out," Janice Doan explained.

"Whatever we have to do, I'll do."

"I suppose that having met you, she definitely wants to settle in the U.S.," Janice said.

Aaron and Drew looked at each other.

"I need to raise that specific question with her," Drew said.

"I see. It can be difficult for people to leave here and readjust in the U.S. In her case, it could be very hard to integrate into society.

Her age, lack of skills, and the language can work against her. It's easier for children to adjust than for adults," Janice cautioned.

"I wanted to find out how easy or how hard it might be to get her the proper papers if she wanted to move to the U.S.," Drew added.

"I strongly suggest that you find out if she's willing to do what we'll require to relocate to the U.S. If she doesn't want to do this, but you persuade her to do it, this may not turn out as good for her as you imagine," Janice warned. "Talk to her and if she wants to relocate, contact me," Janice said, giving both men her business card.

"We appreciate the information," Aaron said. As they left Janice Doan's office and headed to the street, Aaron worried that his uncle wanted Linh to relocate to the U.S. more than she might want it. In addition to his uncle's questions about her desire to live in the U.S., Aaron needed to find a way to participate in the conversation but get answers to questions that he needed answered about the mystery man he saw her with and whether that man worked for CODE.

* * * * *

"What time is dinner with Linh?" Aaron asked.

"She suggested we meet at seven-thirty. Something about wanting time after work to do a couple of things."

"I called the guy I met with this morning at the consulate. You know, to talk about what his work is like. It's research. He agreed to meet for a drink after work. What if I meet you back here at the hotel at seven and we go to dinner," Aaron said.

"Yeah, sure," Drew said.

Aaron wasted away the afternoon in his room looking online for any information about ChiTran in China and CODE. There was nothing specific. He skimmed dozens of articles about China's export driven economy. He decided to see what might pop up about China's military activities, finding articles about several conflicting claims over islands with countries in the region. He found ChiTran's website, but it was in Chinese. There was nothing new to add to what he already knew.

Aaron grabbed his sunglasses and a generic black baseball style cap and left his room. In the lobby he went to the reception desk and took two hotel business cards with him. Aaron took a deep breath and knew that he would have to get on the back of a motorbike. The late afternoon dictated his mode of transport because of the clogged streets. At the end of the twenty-minute ride, he found his spot across the street from the Maritime Administration building. Aaron felt only slightly guilty about the lie he told his uncle.

Ten minutes after taking up his position on the sidewalk, Aaron saw a black-haired man wearing jeans and a white button-down shirt with rolled up sleeves strolling toward the Maritime Administration building. He watched the man stay on the sidewalk instead of turning and taking the walkway to the door of the building. Aaron's target walked until he crossed the front of the building and was passing the stores fronting the street. The man stopped and turned to watch the Maritime building entrance, but out of direct sight from any of the windows of the building. Aaron suspected that his man in blue from the day before was back and waiting for Linh. Five minutes later, Aaron's suspicions were confirmed when Linh exited the building. The man started walking toward Linh. They held hands walking away together.

Aaron stayed across the street from Linh and her mystery man until reaching a crosswalk and joining dozens of people to cross. Linh and her friend moved casually. Aaron noticed that their slow pace annoyed people who were in a hurry getting around them. Aaron, taking up the slower pace to maintain his distance, felt the arms and shoulders of pedestrians brushing by him. As people rushed past Linh and her friend, Aaron dropped his head to look at the ground when he saw Linh, or her friend turn their heads to check on the pedestrians behind them.

Two blocks from the Maritime Administration building, Aaron saw them entering a coffee shop. Aaron slowed and moved closer to the curb, not taking a chance of being seen. As he neared the coffee shop, its large glass front allowed him to see into the shop before he was directly in front of it. He took a couple of quick glances into the shop as he walked past. The reflection from the sidewalk and street prevented him from seeing what he wanted to see. He waited a couple of minutes before walking back past the shop. The second pass was as futile as the first. The shop was filled with people who blended in together. This hadn't been a complete waste of time. Now, he knew that Linh had something going on with this guy.

A block away from the coffee shop Aaron looked around to spot any motorcycle drivers at the intersection. Not seeing what he was looking for, he walked in the direction of the gas station he'd seen the previous day. He saw two motorcycle drivers sitting on their bikes smoking. Aaron pulled out a handful of dong equal to several dollars and walked toward the two motorcycle drivers. As Aaron approached, he caught a helmet tossed to him.

"Where go?" the driver asked.

Aaron held out the hotel card with the printed address. The driver slid his helmet on, and Aaron did the same.

* * * * *

"Are we dressed appropriately for dinner in this place," Aaron asked as they entered a hotel lobby across the street from the city's Opera House. Aaron had changed his shirt for dinner. He didn't think Linh, or her friend had spotted him, but there was no harm in wearing something different as a precaution. He left his hat in his room.

"We're not going to the fine dining restaurant. I picked it more for ease of location," Drew said.

Phan Linh saw the two American men standing off to the side of the lobby when she entered. They were in conversation, noticing her only when she was just a couple of steps away.

"Linh, good to see you again," Drew said, unsure whether to shake her hand or give her a hug.

Linh smiled but didn't put out a hand or lean in toward either man.

"Well then, let's get a table," Drew said, sounding unsure of himself. He led the way as Linh and Aaron followed. Drew chose the hotel because of its familiarity to him. Its fame during the war was because of its popularity with the foreign press covering the war. There was little about the hotel and restaurant to give it a local feel. Only the staff working in the restaurant seemed to be Vietnamese. Linh looked around at the people sitting at tables and guessed that she might be the only local person dining there.

"Linh, you said that your mother died, and your uncles and aunts are not close family," Drew started. He saw Linh nod, indicating he was correctly repeating what she had told him. "Did you take that picture to the bar to find your father?"

"It's a dream to find the father," Linh answered. "My mother gave me the picture. She told me my father is American. That's why I don't look like other Vietnamese people."

"What if we took a blood test to find out if I'm your father?" Drew asked.

"I dreamed about finding my father. I'm scared to find out if you're my father," Linh said.

Linh's use of the word "scared" made Drew anxious. He glanced at Aaron who sat expressionless. "Are you scared to find out if I'm your father or are you nervous about how you find out if I'm your father," Drew probed, hoping that she would understand the difference.

Linh tilted her head slightly. Her eyes narrowed and she looked away as if searching for the answer to Drew's distinction between the words. "I think nervous, not scared," she said after pondering the question.

"If the test tells us that I'm your father, would you want to live in the U.S.?" Drew asked.

"My whole life I think about living in the United States, but my English is bad and no friends there. I have a job and friends here."

"Do you have a boyfriend or relationship with anyone?" Aaron asked.

"I have a Chinese boyfriend. Vietnamese men don't want people like me," Linh said.

Drew and Aaron looked at each other for a second. Drew understood that Linh lived as an outcast because of her foreign father. Aaron heard her confirm his suspicion.

"How long have you had your Chinese boyfriend?" Aaron asked casually.

"I think six months. He came to Vietnam nine months ago. He travels to China every month for three or four days," Linh explained.

"Six months is a long time. You have a serious relationship with him. Maybe he'll ask you to marry him," Drew suggested with a smile.

Linh laughed. "No, my Chinese is very bad. He speaks a little Vietnamese, and I speak a little Chinese. I don't know how long he will stay in Vietnam. He works hard. His company wants to make things in Vietnam."

Aaron mentally recorded everything Linh said about her Chinese boyfriend. What he heard was consistent with the actions Kellie had described. It all fit except that nothing Linh said would be cause for him, or anyone else, to do anything.

They ordered meals. They each had a couple of beers with dinner. Drew talked about visiting bars on Tu Do Street when he was younger. He talked about meeting Linh's mother and that they had spent a year seeing each other regularly until he left Vietnam in the early months of 1970 without knowing that Linh's mother was pregnant.

Drew circled back to the subject of the evening. "I would like to arrange the test so both of us know the answer to the question if you're my daughter. I'll find out if the test can be done here and I'll pay for it."

"Yes, I will take the test," Linh said softly.

Drew wished he had something other than beer to drink to celebrate this evening. He drank what was left in his glass. "It has been a very nice evening."

"Yes. I enjoy very much. Thank you," Linh said.

Aaron got up from the table. "I'm going to step out and get some air." If there was anything else his uncle wanted to say to Linh, he'd give him some privacy.

"I'll be out after I take care of the bill," Drew said.

Aaron was outside of the restaurant in the lobby. He turned around hearing the soft footsteps and Linh trailing him. "Big changes for you," Aaron commented.

"Maybe," Linh said tilting her head slightly with a thoughtful look on her face.

* * * * *

Aaron slid a note under Drew's door telling his uncle that he was meeting with his DHS attaché contact first thing in the morning. Aaron wore sneakers with his jeans and a thin sky blue short-sleeve shirt and his generic ball cap. Out on the street, he put his sunglasses on though they weren't needed. The early morning sun cast long shadows as a few scooters and motorcycles whizzed by him. A bellman stepped out and stood next to him.

"Taxi?" Aaron said.

The bellman looked up and down the street, shrugging. He pointed to his watch. "Early," the young bellman said.

Aaron walked a couple of blocks toward the hotel where they had dined the night before, realizing that it was bigger, busier, and catered to more foreigners than his hotel. Getting a taxi there would be easier. Although it was early, taxis were lined up along the street in front of the hotel he was approaching.

Aaron tapped the passenger side window, startling the dozing driver. Aaron pulled a map out of his jean pocket and pointed to the X he'd marked on it.

"Okay, okay," the driver said, sitting up and turning the ignition.

After spending time getting to and from the Maritime Administration from the back of a motorcycle, Aaron relaxed in the back of a regular cab as it navigated the streets now familiar to him. Without the swarming scooters and motorcycles obstructing the view through the windshield, Aaron saw the gas station on the corner coming up. He sat forward and pointed to the corner.

Aaron dropped seventy thousand dong on the front seat and slid out. He walked down the side street toward the building where CODE was located. Most of the early morning foot traffic was headed in the opposite direction toward the main avenue.

Aaron alternated his visual attention between the pedestrians and the building's entrance. To his eyes, he saw only locals. He saw two young men exit the building that was his destination. He took the few steps up and entered the building. Aaron pressed the elevator button and stepped in when the doors opened. He pressed four and felt the slight jolt of the elevator starting its ascent.

The back doors of the elevator opened. Aaron stepped out into a narrow area about five feet in depth. A wall with double glass doors ran the full width of the building that was no more than twenty-five feet wide. At the double glass doors, Aaron tried the handle and found it locked. He noticed that the far end of the office space was brighter than the main area he was looking into and saw that there were no windows on either side of the office space.

Aaron took a step back and looked at the signage on the glass door and the brass plaque on the wall. They were in Chinese and Vietnamese, leaving Aaron feeling illiterate. Aaron returned to the ground floor and exited the building. He strolled along the street looking for a place to get coffee that provided a seat giving him a view of the building entrance. Walking down the street, he wondered how he could find out what was on the upper floors of the building.

Aaron entered a coffee shop that had a line of early morning customers. He took a seat giving him a direct view of the building entrance and waited till the line got shorter before getting himself anything. In the few minutes that he watched the entrance of his building of interest, he thought it was strange that there seemed to be one-way traffic of people leaving the building and hardly anyone entering. Glancing at the line of people waiting to order, he concluded that the morning commuting hour was still building to its peak time.

Aaron was getting up to join the line when he suspected he saw his mystery man descending the few steps of the building. Having followed the man, but never close enough to see his face clearly, Aaron trusted his instincts as he saw the man's gait. Wearing jeans and the blue shirt again, Aaron left the coffee shop and took up a pace to follow the man heading toward the main avenue where Aaron had gotten out of the cab. Aaron trotted to close the gap between them when he approached the corner. The stream of people on the sidewalk forced Aaron to get closer, staying only ten feet behind.

The morning sun had them walking in and out of the shadows of buildings. Aaron wiped his shaved scalp. His pulse rate increased immediately. He felt naked in the morning crowd of commuters. In a sea of people with black hair, narrower shoulders and generally shorter stature, Aaron was identifiable and noticeable. He slowed and the gap between the two men doubled.

The man was walking the same route he'd taken when Aaron first followed him, except in the opposite direction. As Aaron maintained his distance, he saw the Maritime Administration building a hundred yards ahead. If he stayed on the same side of the avenue as the Maritime building, the thought of Linh popped into his head.

Aaron divided his focus between the man twenty paces ahead and the storefronts coming up. He saw two small, older men cranking long metal pole-like handles unrolling awnings in front of their stores. An older woman carried baskets of fruit and vegetables out of one of the stores, placing them just outside the door to the store. Aaron slowed, allowing the gap to widen.

Aaron moved closer to the storefronts as he walked, fully into the shadows cast by them. Aaron's target walked past the pathway leading to the Maritime Building entrance. Aaron worried that the man would keep going, but as he'd hoped, the man stopped on the far side like he had the previous day and waited. Aaron stood, hands behind his back and looking down at the fruit and vegetables. He glanced to the side repeatedly.

Aaron smiled and nodded at the old Vietnamese woman with hunched shoulders still bringing baskets of fruit and vegetables out. She and the old man ignored Aaron except to wave a hand or point when they wanted to put things down where Aaron stood. He moved from one side of the storefront to the other.

With a glance to the side, he saw Linh arriving from the opposite side of the Maritime building. She stopped and momentarily held the hand of the mystery man who Aaron was convinced was her Chinese boyfriend. Aaron watched as they stood together talking. They were together for two minutes at most. Linh squeezed the man's hand and walked toward the building. The boyfriend began walking in Aaron's direction. Aaron stepped inside the store. It was small and didn't give him any cover from the wide glass front and open doorway. He walked into the store as far as he could. A cooler with cold drinks was near the counter and the cash register. Aaron bent over the cooler. He pulled a bottle of cola out and took more time than he needed to feel around for money in his pocket. Hoping that the boyfriend had passed the shop, Aaron put thirty thousand dong on the counter. The old man started to get Aaron's change. Aaron waved him off. The old man smiled, exposing a few missing teeth.

Before stepping out, Aaron looked both ways from the doorway. Seeing the boyfriend past the store, Aaron twisted off the cap of his drink and took a big gulp. He stepped out, feeling sure about where the man was heading. The boyfriend was half a block ahead and turned at the corner when he reached the gas station. Seeing him turn, Aaron picked up his pace. Aaron turned the corner and saw the man about to climb the steps and enter his building.

When Aaron entered the small lobby, the boyfriend was gone. Aaron walked over to the elevator and pressed eight. It didn't light up. An older Vietnamese man holding a box looked up at him.

"No," the man said. He pointed to the phone on the wall.

Aaron wandered toward the phone, looked at the list printed next to it, making no sense of whatever was written. He thought it strange that he was able to get to the fourth floor, but not the higher levels. He walked back and pressed four. The button lit up and he rode up to the fourth floor. He got out and looked through the double glass doors. He saw a man and two women moving around in the office. The man wasn't dressed like the boyfriend and at a glance seemed too young. Aaron decided to leave. He rode the elevator down.

Walking back to the main avenue, he couldn't think of any way to get into CODE's office and find out anything that might connect to what Kellie or Meilin was doing. Finding a way to get information from Linh was the only way.

* * * * *

Returning to the hotel, Aaron found Drew in a frustrated and foul mood. "Did you really think you would just be able to whisk her away from here," Aaron said. "A couple of days ago, you thought it was just a fantasy to think you'd find your girlfriend. Now you find you may have a daughter but somehow believe you can take her to the U.S. almost immediately."

Drew paced in his room, looking at Aaron.

"What did Ms. Doan tell you this morning when you called?"

"The process to prove that Linh is my daughter needs an expert in bureaucracy and I'm not that person. I'm guessing you're not either," Drew said.

"Is that the only way?"

"Ms. Doan said something about being able to get her an immigrant visa. Some law got passed to make it easier for people like Linh to get a visa and get to the States."

"What's the problem with that? You can work on the other after she gets to the States, right? Besides, I'm not convinced she wants to go to the States," Aaron said.

"But she said she'd take the test. Now, she doesn't have to if Doan has it right."

"Just be prepared. Once she's faced with having to make the choice of staying or going, she might disappoint you."

"I'm not thinking about this the way you are," Drew conceded. "I'm assuming that there's no real choice to make. Life here is brutal for someone like Linh. I'm not saying it would be a breeze in the States, but I can help her."

Competing thoughts were going through Aaron's mind as he watched his uncle sit on the end of the bed, looking out the window. Aaron wanted Drew to be realistic about what Linh might decide. Realizing that his vacation time in Vietnam was limited, his mind searched for ways to get information from Linh that might help Kellie. "What if I have a talk with Linh. We're close to the same age," Aaron offered. "Maybe she'll say something to me that she wouldn't say to you."

Drew walked to the window. "Yeah, why not." Drew handed Aaron the piece of paper with Linh's phone number. "The sooner the better."

Aaron didn't hesitate to take the number and call Linh. It was already well into the morning workday, and he wanted to give her a chance to decide when she was willing to meet.

* * * * *

At work Linh counted the document folders in a cart ready for delivery. She needed one more copy. She went to the copy room. Two of the three copy machines were in use and someone at each watching the machine feed documents. She strode down a hallway pushing the cart filled with document folders but stopped in a large coat room. Seeing no one inside, she took one folder and placed it in her large handbag, zipped it closed and left. Her cell phone buzzed and vibrated in her pocket. She ignored the phone, pushing the cart into a conference room and placing folders around the table. She flipped open each folder, making sure the correct cover sheet was the first document in each.

Linh left the conference room and pushed the empty cart back into a copy room where three copy machines, two fax machines and a computer were located. Three others were in the room as they stood and waited for the machines to spit out documents.

Linh went down the hall and into a storage room. She was alone. She looked at the unknown number of the missed call. She returned the call.

Aaron surrendered to the lawyer in him and searched the internet and found legal websites about immigration laws providing ways for Linh and others to enter the States. His eyes darted to the phone at the sound of the ring.

"Hello."

Linh hesitated. "Sorry," she said.

"Linh? This is Aaron. I tried to call you," Aaron said. He explained that he called because he wanted to meet with her alone.

"You meet me by my office. A small restaurant with a picture of a pig on the window," Linh said. She gave Aaron the name and described the small restaurant just a few doors down from the Maritime Administration.

Aaron closed his laptop and was on his way. He didn't want to waste time by being late and having Linh waiting for him. He rode on the back of a motorcycle taxi down the now familiar streets toward the Maritime Administration, paying and jumping off directly in front of the building.

Hoping he had written down everything correctly, he walked past three small restaurants then saw a pinkish pig painted on the window and entered. The restaurant was three-quarters full as the lunchtime crowd was beginning to fill the local eateries. A long vinyl covered bench ran the length of one side of the restaurant. Aaron took a space at the far end of the bench that had a table for two.

He placed his generic black baseball cap on the bench and wiped his scalp with the handkerchief from his back pocket. A young girl who looked like she should be in school brought a menu and Aaron indicated two. She left a second one on the table.

Aaron watched the flow of pedestrians out on the sidewalk. The traffic noise drowned out the low volume music playing in the restaurant. He stood up and waved when he saw Linh stepping in through the doorway. She wore jeans and a pink polo-style shirt. Her long hair was pulled back as it had been the other times he'd seen her.

"Thank you for coming," Aaron began.

"I have little time."

"I won't waste your time. I want both you and my uncle to be happy. If you go to the States, but you are not happy there, it will not be good for you. You decide for yourself what is best. If you are not sure what you want to do, then it's okay to go to the consulate, give them your immigration forms and wait. You do not have to take any blood test, but I think you and my uncle should talk to the Americans at the consulate," Aaron explained.

Sitting away from the restaurant entrance and concentrating on Linh, Aaron had no reason to notice the two men entering together and finding a table tucked away in the corner between the service counter and front window. Even if Aaron had seen them enter, they blended in with the local crowd. Only if Aaron's ears could pick up the differences between Vietnamese and Chinese would he have known that one of the men was Chinese and the other Vietnamese.

The Vietnamese young man sat with his back to everyone in the restaurant. The Chinese man leaned to the side toward the front window to see Linh's back. She partially obstructed his view, but he saw enough of the American's face and shaved head. The American stood out like a bright neon sign blinking in a dark alley.

"I'm nervous about moving," Linh said, using the word Drew had used when asking her how she felt. "Here, it's comfortable for me. But if I go to the States, I have a chance and maybe you and Mr. Drew will help."

Aaron debated the direction of the conversation. "I understand that for people like you with a Vietnamese mother and American father, living in Vietnam is difficult. But you are comfortable. How are you lucky to be so comfortable?" Aaron asked.

"My job is good. I have a small apartment by myself, and I can have extra money. My friends, they share apartments," she answered.

"The government pays you well?"

"The government pay is not so well, but I have extra job," Linh said.

"You have to work two jobs for your apartment?"

"It's not really two jobs because both jobs are at the same time," she said. "My English is not very good. Difficult to explain to you."

"What are the different things you do for the two jobs?"

"One job, I just deliver things to people in the building. Other job, people tell me to look for things, so I read some things and tell people if I find the information," Linh explained.

Aaron was leaning forward; he stared directly at Linh as she described her jobs. The description of the second job interested him. "Which job pays you more money, the first job or second job?"

Linh smiled. "Second job is more money."

"Why is it more money?"

"More difficult for me because I need to find documents, read documents, and sometimes copy the documents. It's more fun."

"It's good to have a job that is interesting. You won't be bored all day. What kind of things do you look for?"

"Mostly, I don't understand even when it is Vietnamese. It's about Vietnam making oceans deeper for big ships. Vietnam needs help from Americans, Chinese, Japanese and other people to make the ocean deeper. We need money and help," Linh said.

It was good that Linh couldn't see or feel Aaron's pulse rate tick up at what she'd said.

"If you are doing two jobs in the building, you have different bosses in the same building. Do they get upset with you sometimes?"

Linh bit the inside of her cheek and sat back. No one ever asked about her work. Her work was trivial, meaningless, but Aaron asked questions. Was he genuinely interested? It made sense that he'd ask about her life here if she needed to make a choice between staying or leaving.

Linh decided to keep her answer to the last question simple. "Two jobs, two bosses, no trouble." In truth, it was two jobs, two bosses. One supervisor was her official boss at the Maritime Administration. The other "boss" had nothing to do with the Vietnamese Maritime Administration. She had called her other boss about this lunch, and he was interested in seeing the American.

The Chinese man was hunched over his bowl of noodles, his left forearm resting on the table and chopsticks in his right hand. His eyes kept looking up and across the restaurant seeing the American listening to whatever Linh might be saying. When he finished his bowl of noodles, he threw cash on the table. "Here's money for you to pay. Follow the American with the shaved head when he leaves," he said in poor Vietnamese. He left. His seat was taken by the man he left behind.

"You have plenty of time to think about this. I know it is a shock, a surprise for you. It was a shock for Uncle Drew. I think he's still in shock meeting you. While he hoped, he wasn't sure he'd be able to find your mother and never expected that he might have a child in Vietnam," Aaron said. "I'll make sure that Uncle Drew lets you know when to meet at the consulate."

Linh checked the time. "I have to go back to work."

"I understand. You call me anytime at the hotel." Aaron remembered that he had a hotel business card and handed it over. He watched Linh get up and leave the restaurant.

Aaron waited for the young waitress to return with his change, pocketing some and leaving a tip then exited the restaurant and its thinning lunch crowd. Looking around, he decided he'd make the long walk back to the hotel.

The young Vietnamese man sitting in the corner stayed seated, watching Aaron exit. Once Aaron had started in a direction, the man got up and exited. He took his time getting out onto the street and strolled along the street. Aaron was half a block ahead, but that didn't bother the young local man who kept Aaron easily in sight. Even with the cap on, Aaron was easy to follow being the rare foreigner wandering down the street and taller than most of those on foot.

Twenty minutes into the walk, the Vietnamese young man's button-down white shirt was damp from perspiration and sweat ran down the sides of his face and forehead. Wearing jeans, the man felt the heat on his legs from the early afternoon sun. Ahead, Aaron's pace remained steady. Another twenty minutes of walking and the young man swore at his boss for telling him to follow the foreigner. He was an office worker. He reviewed documents. He accompanied his boss to meetings, but he wasn't whatever this was. He had a simple task to find out where the American was staying.

Drew sat on a lobby sofa by the window farthest from the hotel entrance. He perused a tourist magazine. He dismissed all the tours having to do with the war but considered visiting villages in the countryside and in the Mekong Delta area. Drew looked up and out the window in time to see Aaron on the sidewalk heading for the entrance.

Seeing Aaron about to take the steps into the lobby, Drew saw an Asian man come to a stop on the sidewalk. Drew watched the man on the sidewalk and noticed his eyes seeming to follow Aaron into the building then pulling out his phone. Drew saw Aaron entering the lobby then looked through the window. On the sidewalk, the man's eyes followed Aaron, oblivious to Drew's attention on him.

Drew got up to meet Aaron.

"How was it?" Drew asked.

"I think it was a good idea for me to talk to Linh," Aaron said.

"You can tell me about that in a minute. Anything else of interest to tell me?"

Aaron drew back a little. "No, just my meeting with Linh."

"You were followed back to the hotel by some guy. You probably didn't notice him," Drew offered.

"Followed? Why would someone be following me? Who would be following me?"

"Good questions with no answers. Any reason at all why someone's following you?"

"No. There was no reason for me to think that someone would be following me. Why are you so sure about this?"

"Because of where I was sitting, I saw the guy stop on the sidewalk when you came in and watched him eyeing you as you came inside. He then pulled out his phone and called someone while still watching you," Drew explained.

Out the lobby windows, Aaron saw the flow of people. "There's only one way anyone could know where I was and then follow me," Aaron started. "Linh must've told someone she was meeting me and that someone arranged for me to be followed."

Drew tilted his head back and inhaled deeply, not wanting to believe what Aaron had just said. "Why would she do something like that?"

"I need to piece this together with some things Linh told me," Aaron said. "Things may be more complicated than we think."

"Unfortunately, what I just saw forces me to agree with you," Drew conceded. "You want to huddle over a beer in the lobby bar?"

Aaron looked around the lobby where people were sitting and wandering around the reception desk. "I'd rather we go upstairs to the room. There's no way to know who anyone is and whether there's anyone else keeping an eye on us or, specifically, me," Aaron answered.

"Now don't get paranoid on me," Drew said.

"Neither one of us is hard to follow. We don't melt into a crowd here and that means anyone interested in what we're doing can keep his or her distance without ever being detected."

"I can't disagree with that. But there isn't anything we're doing that should interest anyone or is there something you're not telling me," Drew prodded.

"Let's go upstairs," Aaron suggested.

Before Aaron joined his uncle in the adjoining room, he splashed cold water on his face, stealing a few minutes to be alone and think through the last couple of hours. He wiped his face dry. Through the connecting door, Aaron carried a chair into Drew's room. Drew had the thermostat at a comfortable sixty-eight degrees, feeling the air flowing through the vent. Drew uncapped two beers.

"Do you think she doesn't want to live in the States?"

"Not that simple," Aaron said as he put his chair by the desk, but away from the bright sunlight.

Drew said nothing and waited for Aaron to continue.

Aaron leaned forward, elbows on knees and both hands around the bottle of beer. "She's conflicted. She knows what she has here, and she knows she's better off than most who are in a similar situation. Even though she's an outcast of sorts, she's doing well. If she has the chance to move to the States and she does, she has no idea what she'll have there."

"But I'll help her," Drew said.

"Help how? Aren't you still waiting to get concrete confirmation that she's your daughter before you commit to the kind of help she'll need? What happens if she gets that immigrant visa that Ms. Doan told us about and she gets to the States then you find out she's not your daughter? What then?"

Drew looked at Aaron, listening, sucking in his upper lip. "I'm working under the assumption that she is my daughter. Why else leave the photo at the bar? Why leave a phone number to be contacted and why agree to meet me?"

"Because she just wants to know something about who she is," Aaron responded. "Sometimes it's as simple as that and nothing more."

Drew took a big swig of beer. "Let's move on to you being followed. What're you thinking?"

"The other day, Kellie and I spoke about some things going on back in D.C. and then something Linh said today made my mind snap back to my conversation with Kellie. Linh says she has two jobs. One of those jobs is not an official government job. The non-government job pays better than her government job because she's asked to look at documents and sometimes copy documents. What does that start to sound like to you?"

Drew turned his head and looked out the window. He didn't want to look at Aaron eye-to-eye. He looked back at his nephew. "I know what that starts to sound like, but what does that job have to do with you being followed?"

"I don't know. And we don't know why Linh would make a call to someone that she's having lunch with me. What's even more troubling is that knowing that she's meeting me caused them to follow me. Why?" Aaron added.

"Okay, give. There's something tumbling around in your head."

"Linh's boyfriend is Chinese. While I have no proof, I'm convinced that the Chinese boyfriend works for a Chinese company. This same company's CEO is in D.C. rubbing elbows with Chinese Embassy officials. The FBI knows about Chinese information collection, technology information and that seems to be the same kind of information Linh looks for at the office to give to her non-government boss. I think her non-government boss is her Chinese boyfriend." Aaron didn't say why he had confidence in his belief that the boyfriend worked for the Chinese company he had in mind, hoping his uncle didn't ask.

"Let's say I buy your theory that her Chinese boyfriend is also her other boss. That doesn't explain why he or they would follow you does it?"

Aaron sat back. His shoulders slumped. "No. She knows nothing about me other than you and I are related. She doesn't know who I work for or what I do."

"If she's doing what I think you're describing, she's in deep do-do if she's caught."

"I'd say so," Aaron agreed.

"I wonder if she's given any thought to her fate if she screws up," Drew thought aloud.

Exposure

Yao Jun stared down onto the street below. His small apartment on the tenth floor was a nice benefit as the head man for CODE in Vietnam. Meilin chose Yao Jun to be her point person in Vietnam because he was in his mid-thirties, youthful looking, educated at university in southern China concentrating on international business and still single. Without the extra burdens of a family, Meilin saw him as someone who could devote all his energy to his job responsibilities. He had the slightest hitch in his step from a knee injury playing soccer but was otherwise above average height and still lean. Realizing that many in Vietnam still had negative sentiments toward the Chinese, he promised Meilin that he'd study Vietnamese so he could work with officials effectively.

Yao Jun had met Phan Nhu Linh at a bar just days after arriving in Ho Chi Minh City. New to the country and city, two beers had given him the courage to walk over to Linh's table where she sat with a friend. Jun's eyes saw someone who looked different. Her eyes, her cheeks, her not quite black sheen of hair attracted him. Linh and her friend laughed at his failed attempt to speak Vietnamese and invited him to join them. With a combination of limited English and bad Vietnamese, that first evening was fun. For a month after he introduced himself to Linh and Mai, three of them would go out together until Jun invited Linh to lunches and dinners for two. When he learned where Linh worked, it was perfect.

It was thirty minutes before his staff would leave for the day, but Jun left his fourth-floor office, taking the elevator up to his apartment. He and Linh had spent little time together the past few days because of her dinner and lunches with the Americans. Limited to seeing her briefly before or after work, he waited for her to arrive.

He had nothing special planned except that they'd finally have time together. He read emails from China and checked to see if Meilin had sent him anything while waiting for Linh to arrive. His body jerked at the sound of the buzzer announcing that someone wanted to take the elevator to the tenth floor. He went and pressed a button by his apartment door. As a security precaution, visitors had thirty seconds from the time he pressed his button to get in the elevator and press the floor number.

Linh was the only person who had visited Jun's apartment. Jun had no one he considered to be strictly social friends. Everyone he knew in Vietnam, including Linh, had something to do with the business he was there to do.

Linh stepped out of the elevator and into a narrow lobby area. There were two doors for the adjoining apartments. She'd been here before. Jun often left the door cracked open once she buzzed for the elevator.

Linh pushed the door open and entered. The apartment had no formal entry. She had entered the living room of the apartment. A small kitchenette was situated along a wall facing the entry. All the rooms of the apartment opened to a single corridor.

Jun gave her a hug. "I've missed you," Jun said in his improving Vietnamese.

"I've missed you as well," Linh answered in Cantonese.

"Drink?"

"Cold juice," Linh answered in Vietnamese. She lowered herself onto a sofa while Jun got himself a cold beer and her juice.

Their conversations were a mix of Vietnamese and Chinese with an occasional word or two of English, although Jun had no formal English knowledge.

"Thank you for telling me about your lunch meeting," Jun began, he sat on the sofa, turned slightly toward Linh. "What did he have to say?"

"He and Mr. Drew, the older man, talk about me moving to the States. I can probably get a visa to travel there. They say there are special rules for people like me. The rules make it easier to get the visa," Linh explained.

"After you are in the United States, what happens," Jun asked, masking his concerns with a smile.

"I'm not sure. There are tests to find out if I'm Mr. Drew's daughter. If he is my father, maybe he will take care of me."

"What if the tests say he isn't your father? Did your mother ever say anything that makes you think there are different people who could be your father?" Jun needed to tread carefully, but he wanted to plant seeds of doubt.

"She didn't talk about it very much. She gave me the picture that I left at the bar," Linh said.

"Was that all you talked about today?"

"Aaron, the man you saw, asked me about my job. He's like you because other people don't ask many questions about what I do."

"What do you mean," Jun said, cocking his head.

"He wanted to know if my job lets me have a good life in Vietnam. I think he's worried that if I choose the United States, maybe it won't be a good life for me. He wants me to think what is good for me," Linh explained. "I told him that my situation is good because I live alone and don't need a roommate. He said the government must pay me well and I told him I have two jobs that make it possible for me to have my own apartment."

Jun's brow furrowed. "What did you tell him about your jobs?"

Linh saw the changed look. "I told him about my regular job and my other job."

"Then he asked you more questions, didn't he?"

"Yes," Linh answered barely above a whisper.

"What did you tell him?"

"I described what I did about reading and copying documents. But I never said who asked me to do this or why. I never used names," Linh said.

"Does he know about us?"

"I said I have a Chinese boyfriend."

Jun popped up from the sofa, his left hand on his hip and the other on his forehead. He paced in front of the sofa. "Do you know anything about the man you had lunch with? What kind of job he has?"

"We never talked about that. He's traveling with his uncle who might be my father." Linh stood and blocked Jun, forcing him to stop pacing.

Jun stared at Linh. "You cannot talk about me, my company or what you do for me with anyone," he said with a raised voice. Pointing at her, he said, "I thought you understood this."

Linh slapped his pointing hand away. "I understand. I told you that your name and the name of your business was never mentioned," Linh said in Vietnamese, not caring whether Jun understood every word. "No one points a finger at me. No one puts a finger in my face. Do you understand me?" Linh's voice rose with anger. Her chest rose and fell with each breath.

She turned, walked over to pick up her bag and stepped toward the door.

Jun, a step behind her, reached out and grabbed her left forearm. Linh swung her other arm. The free hand with the bag hit Jun on the side of his face. He let go of the arm.

"I'm sorry," he said.

"I'm not." Linh walked out, slamming the door behind her, and waited for the elevator.

The apartment door opened. "Please, come back in," Jun said standing in the doorway, giving Linh space. When the elevator door opened, Linh stepped in and kept her back to Jun still standing in the doorway.

Out on the street, Linh reached into her bag and felt for her phone. A quick glance and she pressed a couple of buttons to auto-dial her friend Mai. "Meet me at the usual place," Linh said and clicked off.

She wanted to be rid of the oversized handbag she was carrying. She flagged a motorcycle taxi for the short ride to her apartment. She stopped long enough to switch out a few items from her large bag to something smaller. With her keys and money in a smaller bag, Linh used the long strap to place it over her head and shoulder and across her body. She slid a helmet onto her head and headed off on her scooter.

* * * * *

Jun sat on the sofa with his head in the palms of his hands. He wondered if his reaction had created an unnecessary problem. He and Linh had never argued before. He was surprised at his own reaction to what she had said, but her reaction didn't just surprise him, it scared him. At least he had apologized, but she left in anger, and he had no idea how she dealt with her anger.

Jun needed to repair whatever damage had been done. At least temporarily, Jun needed Linh to continue her document surveillance work. If she remained angry and stopped, he'd cut off her funds. But could he afford to stop the payments to her before he found someone else to take over? He didn't know anyone else at the Maritime Administration he could approach. Or, he thought, he did know others, but they were much higher up in the organization and might not be receptive to doing what he needed done. Even if he did find someone, it would cost a lot more than the price he paid for Linh's services. If he failed, what would he tell Meilin?

He sat mulling over his relationship with Linh. There was no emotional or romantic spark or intensity between them. He admitted it was a relationship of mutual convenience and as much about how it helped his business objectives as it was anything else. Being honest with himself, Linh's access to information was the most important thing to him.

Jun changed into a comfortable pair of jeans, sneakers, and a pewter color linen shirt. He wandered up to the corner where his side street intersected the main avenue and hailed a motorcycle taxi. He gave the driver an address by the Saigon River. He knew that Linh's favorite places were within a couple of square blocks by the riverfront.

Near the riverfront, the more comfortable evening invited people to sit outside to eat and drink. Jun started at a familiar corner bar. He ducked in and looked around. He recognized a young woman and approached. "Have you seen Phan Nhu Linh," he asked in Vietnamese. He left after she shook her head.

The sky's sunset glow had faded, and Jun was walking along streets lit up by the lights from cafes, bars, restaurants, and surrounding buildings. He was searching the second block of possible bars and restaurants when he saw Linh and Mai.

"He's here," Mai said, seeing Jun enter through wide open doors.

"What? You mean Jun?"

"Yes. He's here and he's seen me. He's coming," Mai whispered.

Linh didn't turn to look. "We're too predictable. We should look for new places," Linh said, then took a sip of beer from her glass.

Jun walked up to the table, resting his hands on an unoccupied chair. "May I join you?" He looked at both women, but they looked at each other rather than looking at him. Jun pulled out the chair and sat. Mai's reaction to his presence convinced him that she knew what had happened earlier between him and Linh.

"Why are you here?" Linh asked.

"I want you to know I'm sorry."

"I heard you at the apartment," Linh responded.

Jun saw Linh's hands on the table. He reached out to pat the hand closest to him, but his arm stopped, and he pulled it back, placing both hands in his lap.

Mai looked across the table at Linh smiling. Linh's reaction to Jun impressed Mai. Since Jun sat down, Linh had kept her eyes on Mai.

"Aren't we still friends?" Jun asked.

"Things are different now," Linh said flatly. There was no emotion in her words. Her eyes never looked toward Jun.

"I don't understand what you mean. It was a mistake for me to come and find you. I should have left you to calm down this evening and enjoy it with Mai by yourself. We should talk tomorrow. Maybe something is different, but not everything." Jun hoped Linh understood what he meant then stood up to leave. "It's my fault that you had a bad evening." He dug into his pocket and dropped several fifty-thousand dong currency notes on the table and left.

Both women watched him leave. Linh had not looked at Jun while he was at the table, but now turned her head as he exited. "We have a new plan. We can stay here longer," Linh said. She spread the currency on the table to see what Jun had left. She slid two fifty thousand dong bills toward Mai, took two for herself and left two on the table. "We can have more drinks and some food."

Jun walked out and away from the bar. He eyed two places across the street. He decided to go across the street and down a couple of doors where he'd have a drink and some food while keeping his attention on the bar across the street. Settling in and ordering a drink and dinner, he called one of his junior associates who he knew had a motorcycle. He hoped the employee would arrive before Mai and Linh left the bar. He bet that they'd stay and spend some of the money he left them.

Twenty minutes after the call, he saw his young associate guiding his motorcycle down the street and weaving around a few cars and other scooters and motorbikes. Jun walked toward the curb to get the young man's attention then returned to his table on the sidewalk.

The young man removed his helmet, running his hands through a thick mop of damp black hair. He wore black knee-length shorts and a matching black polo shirt. The shirt hung loosely over the young man's narrow shoulders.

"Have a seat. I'll order some snacks. What do you want to drink?" Jun asked in Vietnamese.

"Cola. No alcohol," the young man said, nodding toward his motorbike.

The two men sat for over an hour with little conversation. Jun's limited Vietnamese and the young man's non-existent Cantonese and limited English made conversation difficult. With a few words and hand gestures, Jun succeeded in communicating to the young man who said "understand" several times. The young man would follow Linh when she left the bar across the street.

It was getting late. There were far fewer people wandering the streets. The bars and restaurants were emptying when Jun saw Linh and Mai at the doorway, he tapped the young man on the forearm. "Follow the taller woman," Jun instructed.

The young man got on his motorbike and put on his helmet. He sat and waited, watching Linh, the taller woman, give the other woman a squeeze on the shoulders. He watched Linh walk slowly to a row of parked motorbikes and scooters. The young man looked back at Jun for a second. Jun nodded. The young man watched Linh settle onto the red scooter's seat, putting on a helmet. He saw her check her cross-body bag. He didn't start the bike's engine until Linh had pushed her scooter into the street and started her engine.

The late hour left the streets less crowded. Linh was driving slower than usual and slower than others on the streets. Her outstretched arms felt locked at the elbows. She kept a tight grip on the handles. Her eyes moved from the street ahead, the other motorists around her and the cars and cycles behind her even though there weren't that many around. At an intersection, she slowed for the red light and stayed at the back of a bunched group of scooters and motorcycles. In the mirror, she saw a single headlight several feet behind her.

When the light turned green, she maintained her position behind the bigger group. She checked her rearview mirror and saw the headlight still behind her. Her mind focused on the group ahead and the single headlight behind. She didn't know what was going on, but it made her fearful and sobered her. She saw a red light at the intersection ahead and decelerated. Once stopped, she reached into her bag for her stick. Again, the one bike stayed behind her when she stopped. When the light changed, she guided her scooter close to the curb and looked at the speedometer.

She was going only twenty-five kilometers per hour as the bunched group she had been following accelerated through the intersection. She looked into the rearview mirror and saw the bike behind her catching up, but still going slow and about to pass her. Linh slowed to fifteen kilometers an hour and glanced over at the bike's operator. She was sure it wasn't Jun. She concentrated on the taillight of the bike that had been behind her. It was not accelerating to join the bigger group of bikes and scooters.

Like her, the bike veered closer to the curb, hugging it as it continued. The traffic had thinned out and there were no groups of bikes or scooters on the street. Linh moved several feet into the traffic lane and accelerated to over fifty kilometers an hour. She passed the motorbike she'd been watching and looked into her mirror to see that whoever it was had picked up speed and got in behind her.

Whoever this was, she was going to get rid of him, Linh thought. Maybe some guy saw her come out of the bar and thought she'd had too much to drink and would be an easy mark. She accelerated, saw the headlights behind her getting closer as the driver wanted to close the gap that she'd created. Linh steered her scooter farther toward the left, leaving space between her and the curb. She wanted the bike behind to come up on her right side. Linh braked. She felt her body being forced forward but gripped the handles. Her leg muscles kept her steady on the seat. Her right hand had her security stick, preventing her from gripping the handle as tight as she'd like.

She saw the mystery rider slowing but not decelerating as fast as she had. He was doing what she hoped. He steered to come up on her right side and would pass her. Linh's right hand let go of the handle. She felt for the release button on her expandable baton and pressed it. The full length of the baton and her arm length forced her to get close to the mystery rider. She accelerated and steered to match his speed. When she was only a few feet to the side of the mystery rider, Linh thrust her arm out, baton in hand, making contact.

She accelerated, looked into the rearview mirror, and saw the bike's headlight moving from side to side before the driver lost control and the bike hit the pavement. With a few other bikes and cars on the road, she turned off the main avenue at the next side street. She hoped no one would be able to explain why the motorbike driver lost control. At night, using a black baton, Linh thought no one would have seen it even if they saw her arm reach out toward the motorbike.

Linh waited fifteen minutes along the side street before returning to the main avenue. Looking down the street, a small crowd had gathered around the bike on the ground and whoever the driver was. She turned and drove in the opposite direction toward her apartment.

At the sight of the crash, two men stopped and moved the bike off the street. The driver's legs were bleeding. On his back in the traffic lane, he grimaced in pain and rolled from side to side holding one leg with his hands. One knee had skin scraped off from contact with the pavement. His right forearm was covered in blood. Someone retrieved his cell phone from the street and put it next to him on the ground. The sound of a siren blared in the distance and got louder.

As the emergency medical team picked up the accident victim, the CODE employee and the witnesses to his injuries knew that this would be an unexplained and unresolved street accident like thousands of others in a city where two-wheeled vehicles reign.

Linh steered her scooter among the few on the street and kept her speed steady with a few others. She checked her mirrors to look behind her. After several more traffic signals, she relaxed, confident that there was no one following her. She arrived at her apartment building, pushing her scooter into a narrow spot where it would be lost among the other parked scooters and motorbikes.

In her three hundred square-foot apartment, Linh stepped around a few books and papers on the floor. She showered. She put on a pair of shorts and a tee shirt. She used a towel to press the excess water from her long hair. Looking around at the few pieces of furniture, she smiled. She liked her small private living space. Had she angered Jun enough for him to find another person to do what she was doing for him? She needed the money if she wanted to continue having her private apartment.

Linh sat on her single bed and thought through the evening. She and Mai had enjoyed their evening with drinks and food, but the argument and the ride home consumed Linh's thoughts. She needed to repair her relationship with Jun if she wanted to continue having her comfortable lifestyle. She wondered how long the extra task and lifestyle would last. Would she have to accept Mr. Drew's offer?

Linh shook her head and dismissed what had happened on the way home. Whoever was following her had nothing but bad intentions as far as she was concerned. Whatever happened to him, she had no regrets for doing what she had done. Her self-defense action didn't prevent Linh from falling asleep within minutes of her head sinking into her pillow.

* * * * *

Jun set his alarm to be up earlier than usual. He never received a call from his young associate before going to bed. Maybe the young man didn't understand that he was supposed to call and tell Jun that the woman he was following got home safely. Without him reporting in, Jun got up and decided he'd see for himself. Meeting Linh as she arrived for work would let him know that she made it home and it was a chance to gauge her attitude toward him.

It was still an hour before Linh would arrive at the Maritime building. Jun made hot water for tea and went to his laptop. A message from his boss traveling in the States caught his attention. He read the note informing him that the Chinese Embassy is working on information collection that would be provided as soon as it became available. Without specifics, there was nothing more to do. The note ratcheted up the importance of gauging Linh's morning outlook.

Jun joined the morning crowd on the streets and walked toward the Maritime Administration. He gave himself plenty of time. He found a coffee shop a couple of doors down from the Maritime building and stood inside the shop's door sipping tea and hoping he'd see Linh walk by as she walked to the Maritime building. After ten minutes of sipping, standing, and waiting, he saw Linh approaching with her usual large bag dangling from her shoulder and wearing sunglasses. He stepped out onto the sidewalk and forced a smile.

"Good morning," Jun said as Linh was within a couple of steps.

Linh turned her head. Seeing Jun, she removed her sunglasses and put them in her bag. "Good morning. Why are you here?"

"I wanted to be sure that you are okay this morning."

"I'm fine," she said as she looked at Jun, something she didn't do when he found her in the bar the previous evening. She tried to keep any anger out of her tone toward him.

"I don't want to delay you. I hope we can continue working together and still be good friends. I'm sorry I got upset yesterday."

"I will continue working for now," Linh said, sending Jun a signal, but one that he might not understand. "I have to go."

Jun watched Linh disappear into the building. He strode back to his building. Her words didn't reassure him about being able to work together for much longer. He had no way of knowing if she would be as eager as before to get him the information he wanted. Recruiting a replacement would take time. The weeks or months it might take is time he didn't have.

Jun went straight to the office. His employees were already at their desks except for Bui Chau, the young woman who acted as his secretary and interpreter. She helped Jun communicate with his six other employees. Her shoulder length straight black hair parted in the center was cut short and around her ears, making her face look long and narrow. She was constantly pushing up her glasses. Jun stopped just a couple of steps into the open office space when he saw her marching toward him.

"Vinh's not coming to work today," Chau said in Cantonese.

Jun said nothing. He wondered if something happened after Vinh got on his motorbike and followed Linh. He hoped his lack of response would prod her to say more.

"He's in hospital because he had a motorbike accident last night."

"How bad is it?"

"His mother says both legs are injured. One kneecap is damaged badly. She didn't say how long he'll be in the hospital," Chau said.

"Please give me the information where he is, and I'll go visit him." Jun retreated to his small office in the back and sat staring out the window high in the wall opposite his desk. Thinking through the last twenty-four hours, Jun told himself to concentrate on CODE's two main missions. He let his staff build relationships with local manufacturers as sources for future ChiTran growth. He took charge of the contacts with people he cultivated to collect information relating to Vietnam's technology needs for port expansion. CODE's government directed mission was to get those port activities progressing as fast as possible and exploit Vietnam's manufacturing base before the Americans, Japanese and others had traction in the market.

Sitting alone, Jun questioned whether Vinh had had an accident on his bike or something else happened. The only way to find out what happened to Vinh was to talk to him at the hospital. After what happened at his apartment with Linh earlier in the evening, Jun wondered if Linh could be the cause of Vinh's accident. With that thought, Jun sprang forward in his chair. She'd have to be alert enough to notice someone following her at night. It wasn't so late that they were the only two on the street. If Linh had been that attentive, why wouldn't she have gone straight home? Why take the risk of doing something to another driver? If Linh caused Vinh to lose control of his bike and crash, it was the second time in the evening that she resorted to violence after hitting Jun with her bag.

Without knowing what really happened to Vinh, Jun's suspicions about Linh made his pulse quicken. Until yesterday, she'd never displayed anything but a calm and controlled personality.

Jun stepped out into the open office. "Chau, do you have the hospital information?"

"Should I go with you?"

"Okay, yes, let's go." Jun decided he might need someone to help him navigate the ways of a Vietnamese hospital.

With Chau accompanying him, they took a regular taxi. The large high-rise hospital building wasn't far from the bar where Jun had met Linh and Mai the previous evening. He let Chau do the talking.

"Maybe Vinh can't talk today," Chau said. "He had operation and lots of medicine."

"Can we try. I just want to see him for a few minutes," Jun said.

Chau spoke to a nurse. "We try, but he slept all night after the operation."

Chau got a room number. She and Jun walked the corridor. They stopped at Vinh's room. He shared it with three other patients. An older woman sat next to his bed. Chau went in to speak to her and returned to Jun waiting in the corridor.

"Vinh's mother," Chau said.

"You can explain that we will take care of the hospital bills," Jun said. "If he needs special treatment, the office will take care of it."

"Government will take care of it," Chau said. "Let's go in."

Chau and Jun walked in and stood by the bed on the opposite side of where Vinh's mother sat.

"Mother says Vinh woke up a couple of times to drink water. He talked for a few minutes and went back to sleep," Chau translated.

Jun saw Vinh's arms above the sheets that covered him. Medical dressing covered both forearms. A few spots of blood had seeped through and were visible.

Jun looked at where Vinh's legs were under the sheet and saw a bulge on one leg. "What about his legs? Have the doctors said anything about them?" Jun asked. He waited for the exchange between Chau and Vinh's mother.

"He has bad damage to one knee. Both legs have lots of cuts and scrapes. They must clean them," Chau translated.

Despite their low volume conversation, it roused Vinh from his sleep. His eyelids opened slightly. He blinked several times before being able to open his eyes fully. He tried to talk, but his dry throat prevented it. He pointed and his mother helped him with water.

Without turning his head, Vinh's eyes moved among his three visitors. "I talk to Mr. Yao," Vinh said in a whisper.

Jun stepped around Chau to be closer to Vinh. He leaned down and turned his head so he could hear whatever Vinh wanted to say.

"The woman pushed me with stick or something. I crashed," Vinh whispered in Vietnamese, hoping that Jun understood.

Jun straightened up. He saw the two women looking and expecting him to tell them what Vinh had said. Speaking through Chau, Jun said, "he says he's sorry he won't be able to work for a long time," Jun lied. Chau translated Jun's Cantonese into Vietnamese for Vinh's mother. He looked down at Vinh who smiled back at him.

Jun and Chau stayed a few minutes longer before departing. They rode back to the office without talking. Jun stared out the taxi window, worried that there was an unpredictable side to Linh that could spell trouble for him. He couldn't let her unpredictable nature threaten his work.

Family

Kellie sat on the loveseat in her living room. Her hand holding a glass of tea quivered. It was almost time to leave to meet Meilin. Meilin had agreed to Kellie's suggested seven o'clock dinner, but Kellie called, apologizing that work delayed her and pushed the time back an hour. Kellie and Agent Kearns had agreed in advance to use the false excuse to push dinner back to eight o'clock.

The more time Kellie had to wait, the more she felt the tightness in her stomach and chest. At seven thirty, she stood up, took a deep breath, and left her apartment to hail a cab. Kearns had approved of her choice of restaurant location. It was on the corner of intersecting one-way streets. Kellie's cab driver steered the taxi onto N Street and headed west a few blocks along the one-way street. She got out where it intersected 21st Street, a one-way street headed south.

The restaurant occupied part of the ground floor of an office building on the corner. Kearns advised Kellie to ask for a table away from the entrance. The entry door faced 21st Street. She chatted with the hostess for less than a minute then followed her toward a wall of wine bottles that separated the dining area from the kitchen. The hostess took her to a corner table for two next to the wall of wines and the long, wide windows looking out to N Street.

"Where's the powder room?" Kellie asked. The hostess pointed to a hallway behind a long curtain used to separate part of the dining room from the kitchen. This night, Kellie didn't have a small purse. She needed something large enough for a document folder. She placed her bag on the floor between her feet and the low wall next to the table.

Kellie fixed her gaze on the entrance. The digital display on her cell phone read 7:53 when she saw Meilin enter. At the hostess stand, Meilin stood behind several people waiting to be taken to their tables. Kellie saw the small bag with a short gold chain over Meilin's left shoulder. Kellie turned her head, looking out the window and dialed Agent Kearns.

"This isn't going to work," Kellie said softly. "Meilin has nothing for me to put them in."

"I was afraid this might happen," Kearns responded. "It's okay."

"How is it okay," Kellie said, turning her head and seeing that Meilin was about to be led to the table.

"I'm paid to have plans B and C, if necessary," Kearns said.

"Gotta go," Kellie said and disconnected.

Kearns and his team had eyes on the restaurant. After Meilin entered the restaurant, two women arrived for their reservation to dine. He didn't tell Kellie that he had arranged for two sets of eyes on her and Meilin during dinner. He knew Kellie couldn't call and tell him how the evening was going. One of the two women was an agent on his team and the other was a Justice Department lawyer. His two-person undercover team was instructed to report every thirty minutes or sooner if the need arose.

Kellie's panicked call with the information that she wouldn't be able to do what had been planned didn't surprise Kearns. He had a gut feeling all evening that something like this would be more likely to happen.

Kearns sat in a car on N Street with a direct line of sight on the restaurant. Agents Olvera and Adams were parked on 21st Street. "Olvera, I need you and Adams to pop up to the hotel and do your thing," Kearns instructed. "You have the file, the documents, right?"

"In my lap," Olvera answered.

"I'll be up there in a little while. If you run into a problem, let me know."

Agent Adams made the short drive to Meilin's hotel. They parked by the main hotel lobby entrance. Adams placed a generic "Law Enforcement" placard on the dashboard to dissuade anyone from having the car towed away.

Adams and Olvera entered the well-lit lobby and headed straight for the reception counter. Adams had a slight height advantage, giving him a look of being leaner than Olvera. In their suits, their ties and shirts couldn't hide the appearance of two men who took strength training seriously.

"Is your manager around," Olvera asked before the man behind the reception counter could say anything. Next to Olvera, Agent Adams displayed his FBI identification.

"I'll be right back," the man behind the counter said and disappeared through a door.

"It always gets their attention," Adams said.

The young man returned, followed by a dark suited manager whose paunch and bags under the eyes indicated that the evening shift hours weren't kind to him. The manager would be well-advised to just accept that he was bald and give up the comb-over.

"Is there a problem I can help you with," the manager offered.

"There isn't a problem yet. That's why we're here," Olvera said. "If we could sit somewhere and I'll explain how we can avoid any problems."

The manager guided them to a sofa and chairs in the lobby away from the few scattered guests sitting in the lobby.

"You have a Chinese guest by the name of Ms. Moy. She has close contacts at the Chinese Embassy and there are, shall we say, issues with her activities. We know she's out having dinner, and we would like to deliver some documents to her. This way, she isn't seen with us, you know, just in case she's being watched by anyone from the embassy. They won't suspect that she's talking to us," Olvera explained with a slight smile.

The manager listened and nodded then glanced over at Adams who was also smiling.

"I can have someone from my staff take it up," the manager offered.

"Let me clarify, we need to personally make sure it gets to her room and that no one else handles or looks at the material we have for her. She's very important to us because of her contacts with the Chinese Embassy. Are you getting what I'm saying?" Olvera put the folder on the coffee table and tapped it lightly with his index finger.

The manager looked down at the plain unmarked folder then up at the two agents.

Olvera and Adams hoped the manager had the impression that Meilin Moy was working for them but didn't care what he thought as long as he gave them what they needed.

"I'll get a key card for her room and escort you up," the manager said.

"Sir, if you could provide us with a keycard in its small folder with her room number written on it, that will be more than enough. Besides, we have an arrangement about where exactly she's to find this material. We don't need an escort," Adams said.

The manager stood up. "I'll be back in a moment with the key card."

"He's got something to talk about from his shift this evening," Adams commented.

"No, we don't want him talking to anyone about this conversation. Before we go up, we need to take him aside and make sure he understands that he keeps his mouth shut about our visit," Olvera said.

The sound of rapid footsteps got louder, both agents looked over their shoulders to see the manager returning. Olvera and Adams stood and turned to face the manager.

"Ms. Moy's room is on the eighth floor. I've written the room number on the key card folder. Anything else, gentlemen?"

"Yes. Can we have your business card," Olvera asked. He watched the manager reach into his outer suit jacket pocket and offer a card to both men.

"Mr. Jenkins, just one last thing. I'm sure what we've asked of you is very unusual and out of the norm. We must ask that you not discuss this with anyone. I know that you and the man at reception are aware that two FBI agents have come to the hotel this evening, but beyond that, you are not to talk about why we came, who we came to see and what we came to do. If any of this gets out, we know who to come back to. Are we clear about that," Olvera said as dryly and seriously as possible.

"Yes, I'm clear. If the receptionist asks, what should I say?"

"Tell him we wanted to know if you'd give us great rates if we placed special foreign visitors here for an extended period of time," Adams answered.

"What if he doesn't believe me?"

"You walk away. You don't make up anything else," Olvera advised. "We need to go. Thanks for your help."

Olvera and Adams made their way to the elevator bank and the eighth floor. They saw no one in the corridor as they approached Meilin's room. Olvera opened the door slowly. Adams, standing beside him looked at the floor and door frame to see if Moy had left anything giving her indicators of someone entering her room. The room was dark, and they entered and closed the door.

The bathroom door was several feet inside the room and Olvera reached in and flipped on the bathroom light. It cast enough light into the room to prevent them from tripping over anything. Adams went and turned on a bedside lamp. They looked around the room.

"She's neat," Olvera said.

Adams checked the closet and saw a dress, blouses, slacks, and a jacket hanging. He patted down the hanging garments. Something was in the jacket pocket. He pulled out a long, narrow folder fit neatly in an inside pocket.

"She's got plans to leave very soon," Adams said.

"Where's she headed?"

Adams saw the tickets and itinerary. "Here to the west coast to catch a flight to Bangkok then on to Vietnam."

"Better her than me. Hope she's at least in business class for all those hours," Olvera commented.

Two pieces of luggage, neither one bigger than carry-on size, were upright by the wall opposite the bed. The desk had a closed laptop computer and a thin folder.

Olvera flipped open the folder on the desk and saw nothing but Chinese writing. He went back to the bathroom and checked the counter and looked at Meilin's toiletries.

"She travels light," Adams commented, shaking his head. "I don't think I've ever seen a woman's bathroom this . . . neat and uncluttered. Basically, there's no make-up stuff on the counter," Adams announced. He walked out of the bathroom and into the main room, pulled out the desk chair and sat.

"Let me give Kearns a call." Olvera wandered across the room, plopped into the chair between the bed and exterior wall and dialed Kearns. "We're in her room. Nothing much here," Olvera reported.

"They're an hour into their reservation. I'm guessing they'll be there for a while yet. I'll head up and meet you. Give me a room number and see you after I check in with Jamison," Kearns said.

Kearns punched in Vera's number. "Hey, how are things going inside?"

"Food is great, the wine is zesty, and Ms. Liang is playing the part," Vera said.

"Liang knows we're onto Plan B, but she doesn't know what Plan B is. I didn't run through possible contingencies with her," Kearns said.

"Do I need to find a way to communicate with her?"

"Only if an opportunity arises naturally, yeah," Kearns advised. "How's your dinner companion doing?"

Vera looked across the table at her newest acquaintance, Victoria Walters. "She's enjoying dinner," Vera said, giving Victoria a wink.

"If you need me, call. I'm heading up to the hotel. Enjoy the rest of dinner."

Agent Vera Jamison had the plumb assignment for the evening. A nice restaurant where the meal wasn't rushed, and she could enjoy the plate of butternut squash ravioli and whatever wine the waiter had decided to pair with it. She was surprised when Kearns made the last-minute change to let Victoria Walters take Adams's place as a dinner companion.

"How did you manage to talk Kearns into this," Vera asked.

Victoria smiled. "Something about wanting to keep him and the team out of trouble. Ms. Liang wasn't receptive to my offer of assistance, so I called Agent Kearns. He appreciated my take on things and decided it was better to keep counsel on his good side in case things go sideways. Of course, now that the original plan is out the window, I'm just having a nice dinner out with a new friend," Victoria said. "Where's Plan B taking place?"

"Ms. Moy will have a welcoming committee at the hotel," Vera answered as she looked over at Kellie and Meilin's table.

"I'll be back in a few," Vera said, seeing Kellie rise and walk toward the powder room. She didn't know if there was space for two women or if she'd have to wait outside the door, but she didn't need much time. Vera opened the door and was happily surprised to see the size of the women's restroom. She stood by the longer than expected sink counter and waited.

"Ms. Liang," Vera said as soon as Kellie came out of the stall.

Kellie stopped and stared at the stranger who knew her name waiting for her.

"I'm agent Vera Jamison," Vera flashed her credentials and put them back in her pocket. "I'll make this quick. Just continue going about your dinner. When you two finish dinner, you let her go back to the hotel and you go home or wherever. We'll take care of things. Agent Kearns has the backup plan already in effect."

Kellie nodded, stepping to the sink to wash her hands before returning to the table. Vera waited another minute before heading back to her table.

"How'd it go," Victoria asked as Vera lowered herself into her chair.

"Fine I suppose. She listened, nodded, and went back to her table."

Victoria and Vera looked across the restaurant at the two women. Meilin's back was to them. Kellie looked like an attentive listener. They wished they could hear the conversation, not aware of the fact that Kellie and Meilin were speaking Cantonese most of the time, keeping their conversation from being overheard and understood.

Kellie and Meilin's table was cleared. Kellie ordered coffee to end the dinner. It was her way of signaling Agent Jamison that the evening was nearing its end.

Vera Jamison pulled out her phone and called Kearns when she saw the coffee delivered to Kellie's table. When Kellie took her first sip, they made eye contact for an instant. "They're having coffee, so I think you'll be having company soon," Jamison said.

"Thanks for the heads-up."

"Wait, wait!" Jamison tried to keep Kearns on the line without attracting attention. "Something just hit me. Do we know if her English is good enough for you to talk to her?" For several seconds, she got no response. Across the table, she saw Victoria leaning in over the table.

"Dammit, no, I don't know. What are they speaking at the table," Kearns asked.

"Too far away to tell."

"We need to know the answer to your question. Liang will know. Find a way to get an answer to that question," Keans instructed. "If Liang's answer isn't what we want to hear, we need a Plan C for communication. I promised her that Ms. Moy wouldn't know she's involved so you need to work something out with Liang."

Vera Jamison shook her head.

"Good thing you thought of that," Victoria said, leaning back into her chair and finishing off the last of the wine in her glass.

"We should've thought of that earlier. Another last-minute glitch that could be a problem."

"I can't believe that these two have met up, spent this much time together and spoke only in Chinese," Victoria said.

"I admit that I don't know as much as I should about Ms. Liang. We know she's picked for a job at State and her bio says she speaks Chinese, but she grew up here. How good can her Chinese be? Lots of us took Spanish or French in school, but can't use it," Jamison said.

Jamison, not seeing their waiter, waved the hostess over. "I need this to get done right away," she said, giving her credit card to the hostess.

Kellie signed the credit card bill and closed the folder. "We may not have another chance to do this," she said in Cantonese.

"Probably not. Tomorrow, my day is filled with meetings at the embassy then I leave the day after," Meilin explained.

"The west coast," Kellie remembered, and Meilin nodded.

Kellie and Meilin headed for the door. They veered left between the narrow spaces created by tables, chairs, and other diners. It forced Kellie to walk behind Meilin. Kellie looked to the right at Agent Jamison's table and saw her with a young African-American woman.

Victoria watched Kellie and Meilin. They were about to be behind Agent Jamison who would have to twist around in her chair to see them. When Kellie looked over at their table, Victoria made eye contact, tilted her head toward the outside and used her eyes to send Kellie a signal.

"What do you think," Jamison asked.

"We'll know in a few minutes," Victoria said. She and Jamison looked out, watched Kellie embrace Meilin before Meilin slid into the backseat of a dark sedan. It wasn't a taxi. Kellie stood, her back to the restaurant and turning slightly as if watching the sedan make the turn onto N Street.

It was Agent Jamison's decision to wait a full minute before they went outside.

"Ms. Liang, glad you got the message," Jamison said.

"Subtle, but effective," Kellie said, looking at Victoria.

Victoria smiled, standing between two women who towered over her. "We spoke on the phone earlier. I'm Victoria Walters."

"The person trying to keep me out of trouble? Nice to meet you face-to-face," Kellie said extending her hand.

"I'd love to stand around and chat, but we might have a problem," Jamison said. "How well does Ms. Moy speak English? We're about to ask her a lot of questions and we don't know if she'll understand what she's being asked."

"She's far from fluent in English. My Chinese is better than her English. Is that going to be a problem?"

"Victoria, don't take offense to this, but I think it would be best if you weren't around for the rest of the evening," Jamison said. "I know you're here to keep us on the straight and narrow, but sometimes there are twists and turns along the way. We'll take care of Ms. Moy."

Victoria looked up at the two women. "I know when I'm not wanted. I want a report in the morning." She walked closer to the curb and flagged a cab.

"Come on, I'm parked across the street, we need to get to the hotel," Jamison said as she marched to her car with Kellie following. Once they were in the car and about to turn onto Connecticut Avenue, Jamison called Kearns. "How do you want to do this?"

"Two phones. You have Olvera's number so call back on his phone and stay on the line so that Ms. Liang can hear everything going on in here. I'm assuming she has a phone so if she needs to contact one of us, call my number and tell me if we need to reword a question for Ms. Moy to understand," Kearns instructed.

Jamison pulled over to disconnect and dial Olvera. "Make sure you have the volume up so we can hear," Jamison advised.

"Will do," Olvera answered. "We're going to go silent in here until she arrives so there will be an extended period of nothing. Mute your end so nothing comes through on our end," Olvera said.

"I should've asked. You do have your phone with you, right?"

"It's in here," Kellie said, patting her bag. "What happens when we get there? I don't want Meilin to see me."

"She won't. We can stay in the car and listen in on the conversation from here," Jamison replied.

"Sorry that it didn't work out the way we wanted at the restaurant," Kellie said.

"Just as well. We had to get her somewhere regardless to question her. This way, she left the restaurant, her driver, assuming he's from the embassy, took her back to the hotel without a hitch and left. As far as the driver's concerned all is well with Ms. Moy. She'll go to her room without suspecting that anything is going to happen," Jamison explained. "Do you have Kearns's number? If not, let me have your phone and I'll add it so we're ready to go in case we need to call him."

Kellie handed over her phone.

Olvera, Adams, and Kearns waited in the dark. Olvera gave up the chair he had sat in earlier and took the matching stool and placed it next to the desk and sat. Kearns sat in the chair that Olvera vacated in the corner with a hand gripping the floor lamp so that he could flip the switch. Adams moved into the bathroom and stood leaning against the sink counter. The desk chair was waiting to be occupied.

After exiting the embassy car, Meilin strode through the lobby, not noticing the Chinese security officer dressed in a suit and loosened tie appearing to read a magazine, but there to ensure she made it back to the hotel safely. Arriving at the eighth floor, she wandered down the empty corridor. It was a bit past ten. Her thoughts were divided between regret at not being able to see her cousin again for an indefinite period and impatience to pack and leave the States.

She located the key card in her purse and pressed it against the flat electronic reader on the door, heard it unlock and turned the doorknob. She pushed the door open wide, using light from the corridor to help find the light switch on the wall.

Meilin's right hand went to the light switch as her left shoved the door closed. She turned and froze.

"Who are you?"

"We want to talk," Agent Olvera said. "Please have a seat." Olvera rotated the desk's swivel chair, inviting Meilin to sit.

Meilin took a step. Her head snapped to the left when she saw another man standing in the bathroom. She saw his arms folded, not threatening to grab her or reach out to her. She let the purse strap slide off her shoulder. The purse dropped to the floor. She wanted nothing to restrain her movement if she sensed a higher threat level from the three men.

"I want to know who you are."

Adams knew he was the closest one to Meilin. "Ms. Moy, I'm going to reach into my pocket and get my identification," Adams said. Watching her let the purse go to the floor and seeing her hands ball into fists suggested to Adams that she was expecting them to physically handle her, and she was going to resist. Once in his hand, he held out his FBI credentials in his outstretched hand, making no effort to step closer to Meilin than he had to for her to see it or take it out of his hand.

Meilin took the identification from Adams's hand and examined it as if she was considering whether it was legitimate.

From Agent Jamison's car, Jamison and Kellie saw an Asian man through the glass in a wrinkled suit heading for the door and getting into a dark sedan.

"I wonder if Ms. Moy has her own security detail," Jamison said. "I guess he or they think she's tucked away safely for the night."

Kellie strained to hear what was going on in the room through the cell phone. Olvera's phone was too far from where Meilin and Adams were standing to hear anything well.

"Are you sure I shouldn't go up and help?" Kellie asked.

"I'm sure. Absolutely not," Jamison said. "This is just the start, there's a long way to go this evening. We do not want her to see you. You're here only because we might need you to help word our questions and understand her answers."

After a full minute, Meilin reached out and returned Adams's credentials. As she squatted to pick up her purse, she kept her eyes on the two men sitting in the room. She stood up and walked to the swivel chair. She saw Kearns's hand on the floor lamp that he switched on as she reached the swivel chair.

While she was inspecting Adams' identification, Kearns and Olvera had pulled theirs out to let her examine them.

Meilin reached the chair. She sat on its edge so that her feet touched the floor. She swiveled the chair slightly so that she could keep Adams in view to her left. Olvera and Kearns were in front of her and the desk to her right.

"We have some questions for you, Ms. Moy," Olvera started.

Kearns got up and repositioned himself on the corner of the bed. He sat within a couple of feet of Meilin. Adams had moved into the main portion of the room, positioning himself between Meilin and the door.

Olvera opened a folder. An eight-by-ten color photo was the first item. "Can you confirm that this is you," he said, pointing to a woman walking with two men. Meilin nodded in confirmation.

"Who are the two men?"

"Young man is Xiong Zimo and other man is Zhou Shan."

"What does Mr. Zimo . . ."

"No, Mr. Xiong, not Mr. Zimo," Meilin corrected.

"What does Mr. Xiong do at the embassy?" Olvera asked.

"Many things. I don't work at the embassy. I don't work for government," Meilin answered.

"What about Mr. Zhou," Olvera asked, hoping he got the order of names right.

"Mr. Zhou work for China Customs and now with Mr. Xiong, same office at embassy."

Olvera flipped through more enlarged photographs of Meilin with Xiong and Zhou. "You know these two men very well. Why did you meet with them?"

"I know Mr. Zhou in China. He tells me I should meet Mr. Xiong. Mr. Xiong knows business and trade. My business is making products and trade with United States," Meilin answered.

Kearns pulled out gloves, put them on and went to one of the bedside tables. He pulled out papers from a drawer and placed them on the desk.

Speaking slowly, deliberately as he placed papers on the desk, he asked. "Why do you have these documents?"

Meilin leaned toward the desk and stared at the English language documents. "Not mine," Meilin said.

"Why are they in your room?"

"Not mine," she insisted. "Maybe you put there," Meilin said, pointing at the drawer.

"No, maybe Mr. Xiong gave them to you. We know that Mr. Xiong wanted these documents. Why would he give copies of these documents to you," Kearns asked.

Meilin looked at each man for second and smiled. "Mr. Xiong smart. If he want to give me documents like this, not a copy like this. He send documents by email. Not like this."

Kearns returned the smile. "Okay. Mr. Xiong does send you documents like this by email, yes?"

Meilin's smile disappeared. She tried to say in English what she was thinking in Chinese, but it wasn't coming out right.

Kearns stood up just inches in front of Meilin and paged through the patent documents. The gloves helped flip the pages. "There are lots of descriptions, and drawings on these pages. Why do you have them? Why do you need them?"

"I want to call embassy."

"No calls tonight," Kearns said.

"No more talk," Meilin responded.

"Fine," Kearns said. "We'll stay here all night. We don't want you to be alone."

Meilin's eyes made another round looking at each of the men. She believed Kearns when he said they would stay all night.

"I can order coffee or tea from room service. Don't worry, we'll pay for it," Kearns added.

"Tea please," Meilin answered.

Kearns gave Olvera a nod and Olvera picked up the phone and ordered tea and coffee for the room. Meilin got up from the edge of the chair and went to the bed and sat, her back against the headboard and knees up with her arms wrapped around her knees. Kearns moved and sat in the vacated swivel chair. No one spoke.

"Sounds like we might be here a while," Jamison said in the car. "What do you think she's going to do?"

"In a test of wills, don't bet against Meilin Moy," Kellie answered. "She didn't get to the top of ChiTran by being a pushover. Just the contrary, she's a fighter. Kearns needs to let her know what he wants and what she gets out of giving him something useful. Otherwise, we could still be sitting here tomorrow night."

"You think she's that hard-headed?"

"No, not hard-headed," Kellie said. "She's considering what tactics to use and what strategies are needed in this situation. If we were in China, she'd know how to play this, but she's in a foreign country, confronted by foreign law enforcement and foreign rules. I'd say her silence is time for her to try and figure this out."

"Should we call Kearns and tell him what you just said," Jamison wondered.

"We could, but I need to warn you that what I said is just my impression. I can't read her mind. Remember, we're very distant cousins. Until she arrived in town, I hadn't seen her in years and only occasionally exchanged emails."

Prodded by Jamison, Kellie used her phone to call Kearns. He went into the bathroom to hear what Kellie had to say.

"We'll let her play the silent game for a while. I expect we're going to be here for a fair amount of the night," Kearns said before cutting off.

Kearns was right. He and his two colleagues drained their coffees, and he ordered another pot from room service. Meilin's cup of tea sat on the bedside table untouched. She rested her forehead on her raised knees. The only sounds in the room were the sipping of coffee and ceramic cups replaced on their saucers or the desk. The three men sat or stood.

Meilin knew that the police in China not only bent rules, but often ignored them completely. In a situation where someone is legitimately found with sensitive information, the suspect might be taken to some unknown location and physically abused. Meilin had read the stories about Guantanamo. She didn't know how far the Americans were willing to go in a situation like this. She wondered how the Americans were going to treat her knowing that she had done nothing terror related. But the question flying around in her head was if they would keep her confined for espionage based on those papers.

Her eyes closed, she mindfully explored options. What could she ask for? Could she make a call? But to whom? She didn't want the embassy involved because that would strengthen the FBI's belief about her involvement. Call her cousin? That could jeopardize her cousin's future position in the State Department and upset officials in the Chinese Government holding out hope of having a future high-level contact in the American Government.

Meilin wondered what she could give them. As a corporate executive, she was a tool of the Chinese Government like others in her position. What could she say that was not giving away Chinese Government plans? How could she drop hints and let the imagination of her listeners reach their own conclusions? If the Chinese Embassy didn't know she was questioned, it was unlikely that the Americans would tell them. A mental wrestling match was going on in her head. She wanted to keep her intruders occupied for a bit longer but needed some sleep before her embassy meetings.

Meilin's head snapped up when the toilet seat slammed down. She blinked several times, getting used to the lighting again.

"Sorry," Olvera said, looking at everyone in the room.

Meilin turned her wrist. It was almost one in the morning. She picked up her tea, knowing it was cold. "Need hot tea," she said. No one moved for several seconds.

"I'll call," Kearns said. Twenty minutes passed before a knock on the door interrupted the silence.

"Xie, xie," Meilin said. The three men shrugged.

In the car, Kellie translated. "She said thank you." Kellie and Jamison sat up straighter. Kellie had slouched in the seat after the first half an hour of dead air and Jamison had rested her head against the driver's side window. After more than two hours of nothing, they hoped something might happen.

"Where do you get this paper," Meilin asked nodding toward the documents Kearns had shown her.

"There, in the drawer," Kearns said pointing to the bedside.

"No, you lie. You bring the paper. Show me again."

Olvera handed Meilin the documents. He, Kearns, and Adams watched Meilin as she looked at them.

Meilin concentrated on the portion of the first page under the "Abstract" heading. She tried to read and understand it. She read the words but didn't understand the context as they were used in the document. She flipped through the pictures or drawings. She saw a section about the invention's background and stared at the text.

"I don't understand this English," she said.

Kearns looked at Olvera and Adams. He knew that his team had the same problems when they first encountered the documents.

"What did you and Mr. Xiong talk about at the embassy and at lunch?' Kearns asked. He was willing to let her know that they had seen her with him at both places.

"China and United States, we are competitors," Meilin said. "Right now, you are winning, and we are chasing you. We want to catch up."

"Is the information in these documents helping you catch up?" Kearns asked.

"Not yet. I don't understand these," she said nodding in the direction of the documents.

"Does Mr. Xiong or someone at the embassy understand them and they help you understand them?" Kearns followed up.

"Sometimes, yes," Meilin conceded.

"How do these documents help you," Kearns asked point blank.

"They help China. We want trade like Americans. We help poor countries with trade. We need ports in poor countries for big ships."

"Are the big ships Chinese container ships and Chinese navy ships?"

Meilin shrugged. "I don't know about Chinese navy."

"Can these big ships use Vietnam's ports?"

"No. Maybe in three or four years," Meilin answered.

"Is that why these documents are important?"

Meilin looked around the room. The questions hemmed her into answering only one way. "Yes. China helps Vietnam with ports."

"You have a plane ticket to go to Vietnam. Is Vietnam important to your business?"

Meilin straightened her legs and folded her arms. The only way to know about those tickets is if they searched the room and her clothes.

Kellie leaned in toward the phone as she heard Kearns's question. Meilin said she was traveling to the west coast. She said nothing about any immediate plans to go to Vietnam.

"We want business in Vietnam. We want cheap workers. China workers cost more. But it takes time. We talk to many Vietnamese government and businesspeople," Meilin explained.

"How does Mr. Xiong get these documents?" Kearns asked.

Meilin shrugged. "I don't know. I work in China. I live in China."

Kearns looked at Olvera and Adams. Kearns got up and the three men huddled.

"What do you guys think?" Kearns asked.

"I think she's telling us the truth or something very close to it. The embassy isn't going to tell her all the details of their operations and how they get the info. It's one thing to pass info on to those who can use it to promote China's bottom-line objective, but someone like her doesn't need to know the details. I don't think our embassy guys would share those details if we thought about it that way," Adams offered.

"Makes sense," Olvera agreed. "She gets the info and uses it to advantage."

"She's told us more than I expected to get" Kearns admitted. "China is looking to expand port facilities in different countries. Once they do that, these ports can be used for trade or military purposes. I can't believe that Xiong is the only person at the embassy working to get tech info for port construction. That's something to discuss later. I don't think we'll get much more from her so let's call it quits here."

The three men broke their huddle. Adams and Olvera drifted toward the door.

"Get some sleep, Ms. Moy. Sorry to keep you up so late," Kearns said without sincerity. He followed his colleagues out the door.

Hearing the door close, Meilin jumped off the bed, running to the door and turning the deadbolt. She walked back to the desk and saw that they had left the photos, documents, and key card behind. She went to the closet and checked every pocket, suspecting that they might have placed something in her clothing. Finding nothing unusual, she threw her luggage onto the bed, opened them, and went through her clothes and every zippered compartment of the luggage. Nothing unexpected. She showered and hoped she'd be able to sleep for a few hours.

Jamison flashed her headlights when she saw the three agents exiting the hotel. Adams and Olvera continued walking to their car. Kearns wandered over and leaned down on the passenger side window.

"That was fun," Jamison said sarcastically.

"How are you guys doing," Kearns said looking across to Jamison then to Kellie sitting in the passenger seat.

"A bit sleepy, but fine," Kellie said.

"Ms. Liang, there's a lot there if we read between the lines," Kearns said. "I'm going to try and get a couple of hours of sleep. We'll take a stab at summarizing this and get it to the people who need to know," Kearns said.

"Remember to send Ms. Walters something," Kellie reminded him. "I do have a question. Did you or the other agents see where Meilin is flying to in Vietnam?"

Kearns, leaning on the car door with extended arms, looked at the ground. "I think it's Ho Chi Minh City but can't swear to it. I'll ask the other two in the morning and try to confirm." Kearns straightened, tapped the car door, and walked to his car.

"I'll take you home," Jamison said to Kellie. With the streets deserted and traffic lights blinking at most intersections, Jamison got Kellie to her apartment in less than ten minutes. It was closing in on three in the morning, but Kellie was still awake and thinking about Meilin traveling to Vietnam.

Kellie wanted to shower and get more comfortable, but her mind was racing. She sat down at her corner desk, fingers poised over the keyboard to send Aaron an email when she changed her mind. She got up and grabbed her cell phone. Her two thumbs worked the phone's keypad. She listened and waited longer than usual.

"Hello?"

"Aaron? It's Kellie."

Aaron looked at his watch before saying anything. "What the hell are you doing up and calling at this hour? What's wrong?"

"Nothing's wrong, but I have learned something that you need to know," Kellie started.

"Go on," Aaron urged.

"Meilin will be in Ho Chi Minh City in a couple of days. This is all tied up with what we talked about. You should be careful since she'll recognize you," Kellie warned.

Aaron laughed. "I doubt she'll recognize me."

"You haven't changed that much since we were in Hong Kong, and you spent enough time with her that she won't forget what you look like."

"I haven't told you, but I do look a lot different. I'm growing a beard, and I've shaved my head."

"You're kidding," Kellie said.

"Not kidding and not worried about Meilin. I'll be careful. Besides, my time here is getting short so the chances of us running into each other are slim."

"You've been warned," Kellie said.

"I appreciate this. We'll catch up when I'm back in town," Aaron said.

"Okay. It's late, well, really early and I want to get a little sleep," Kellie said before cutting the connection.

Aaron put his phone away in his pocket and looked at the time again. Calling and telling him that Meilin would be in Vietnam in a couple of days was something she could've put in an email. Why the call in the middle of the night? Something happened to trigger such a spontaneous call. It hit him now, but a few minutes too late. There was more that he needed to know. The travel time required for Meilin to get to Vietnam bought him time, but not enough to exercise the caution he would normally undertake.

* * * * *

Kearns rubbed his eyes. They were red from a lack of sleep and too much time looking at a computer screen. A few of his colleagues were beginning to wander into the office for a new day's work. His two hours pecking a keyboard ended with a three-page summary about him and his team's late night, early morning work. While tapping those keys and playing back Meilin Moy's responses in his head, he kept hearing something Victoria Walters said when they first met.

Meilin's statements about helping poor countries and their trade prospects along with Victoria Walters's suggestion that they needed to think about national security differently collided in his head. He decided his summary needed to include a bolded and underlined statement reflecting his impressions. He suggested to his superiors that China collected information, sharing it with Chinese commercial enterprises and their corporate executives, using Chinese companies as the front for engaging foreign governments. He believed that China planned a network of dual-purpose deep-water ports to compete commercially and militarily.

By the time Olvera, Adams, and Jamison arrived Kearns was ready for them to read the summary and suggest changes. They saw nothing worth changing. It was finished and off his desk. One thing he knew about the document was that someone was going to slap some level of classification on it. What level of classification, he couldn't begin to imagine. Kearns wondered about its uses. The other thing he was concerned about was how widely it would be distributed despite a classification stamped on the document. This was a city where the classification of documents meant nothing to some.

Kearns knew that his summary contained a bit of speculation on his part. The hints to military and security issues would convince some readers to restrict the summary's distribution and provoke others to disseminate it widely.

* * * * *

Meilin tossed and turned for the few hours her body was under the blankets. She didn't consider her time in bed as sleep. When the clock alarm sounded, her hand knocked the teacup and saucer off the bedside table. The teacup hit the carpeted floor but didn't break. She opened her eyes and hit the button to turn off the alarm. The few remaining drops of tea were all that marked the spot where the teacup landed.

Wearing loose-fitting pajamas, she got up, kicking the teacup out of her way and went to the window. She pulled the drapes open, wanting to flood the room with morning sunlight. Instead, she saw a grey sky and rain. In the bathroom, she looked in the mirror. She found her small container of eyedrops, tilted her head back and hoped the drops would give her tired red eyes a more restful look. She was mentally consumed with her morning meetings at the embassy and hoping that she wouldn't slip up. She didn't want anyone to know about her overnight visitors.

Meilin dressed in her usual black slacks, a matching black jacket, and sky-blue button-down blouse. She dug into her luggage and decided on shoes that would give her a couple of inches of elevation. After the indignity she experienced overnight, she wanted to have some feeling of being in charge and the shoes she chose helped.

Arriving at the Chinese Embassy, a young man greeted Meilin and escorted her to her meeting with the embassy's second highest ranking official, the Deputy Chief of Mission. The Deputy had a conference room adjoining his office. When Meilin entered, she saw three men waiting, Xiong Zimo, Zhou Shan and a third man she didn't recognize.

"I'm Zheng Puyi," a tall, lean man with shiny jet-black hair said as he approached Meilin. His square jaw, rimless glasses, and expensive looking haircut projected an image of a Chinese jetsetter to Meilin. "I'm in charge of the economic and commercial section. Sorry I haven't met you earlier," Zheng said.

The Deputy, shorter and more squat man compared to Zheng Puyi, walked into the conference room as Meilin and Zheng stood several feet inside the conference room door.

"Please take a seat," the Deputy urged. The Deputy didn't spend time on pleasantries. He plunged into the topic of the meeting.

"Ms. Moy, I hope you've found our communications helpful. Mr. Zheng's staff explores all possibilities of useful information collection and distribution to you and others," the Deputy said. "I am alerting you to a short period when the flow might not be what you have become accustomed to," the Deputy continued and looked to Mr. Zheng.

"You have a long working relationship with Mr. Zhou from his customs days in Guangzhou and he will continue to identify ways the Americans might tighten controls on China origin goods, making it more urgent that you and other Chinese companies successfully expand operations outside of China," Zheng began.

"Some of Mr. Xiong's work involves indirect ways of helping Chinese commercial expansion. Your company, ChiTran, is an integral part of China's commercial expansion and other companies are doing the same elsewhere. For the next few weeks, we will not be as active in providing information. We are reassessing our resources and how to use them better," Zheng explained. He nodded to Xiong Zimo.

"The Embassy staff is working with our security officers about how we are engaging the Americans in a special program that targets the type of information useful to you," Xiong said, looking across the conference table at Meilin. "The summer months are difficult and there's a natural slowdown in getting the desired information for you," Xiong added.

The Deputy instructed Xiong to provide general statements, no details about the staff's information collection initiative at local law schools, identifying part-time American students who have access to the information China sought. No one wanted Meilin or those like her to have all the details. It protected the government's corporate contacts from being able to provide specifics as to source of information and how it was acquired.

Zhou Shan had nothing to say. The Deputy wanted him in the room only as a familiar face for Meilin.

"What can you report to us," the Deputy asked.

"CODE has a contact in the Vietnamese Maritime Administration. The information you are providing is useful when trying to persuade Vietnam to stop waiting for the Americans and others to start their port expansion projects," Meilin reported. "Financial incentives and construction assistance are on the table when we talk to the Vietnamese. I'm traveling there tomorrow and will evaluate our contacts and see if we need to place more pressure on them. I'll find out what else we need from you and our European colleagues.

"Is there any timeline from Beijing about getting our land and sea networks tied together? The longer it takes, the more financially strained some of us will become," Meilin noted. She didn't want to say outright that it was diverting ChiTran's monetary resources to act as the government's overseas development office and recruit people in Vietnam's government to be the eyes and ears for Beijing. ChiTran had a legitimate business interest in Vietnam, but it came at the cost of creating CODE diverting finances as an entity in Vietnam.

"Beijing wants to have a combined land and sea network of countries that we can rely on for trade and resources. Every country of interest needs money to develop, and we want to underwrite their development projects, gain access to their land-based transport hubs, railway hubs, and seaports. By helping to build the infrastructure we can have future control of maintaining and expanding their infrastructure. There's no definite timeline because each country has unique needs. For you, Ms. Moy, it depends on how quickly you can get officials in Vietnam to accept our proposals and approve our projects," the Deputy explained.

"My Vietnam office identified the need to up the numbers. Japan is ahead of us in providing monetary assistance. I need to give the Vietnamese a figure of hundreds of millions of dollars. Who can tell me how high we can go with the investment?" Meilin pressed.

"I can't give you a figure at this moment. We'll inform Beijing that you are on the way to Vietnam, and you must have it by the time you land," the Deputy offered.

Meilin fumed but hid her displeasure that someone as high up as the Deputy couldn't provide her with more. The Deputy spoke for the government. He had thrown the burden onto her shoulders to keep doing the government's bidding without giving her the details she needed to close the deal. If she needed to get her business up and running in Vietnam to generate revenues, she needed to find a way to use the information her government was providing and get the Vietnamese to move more quickly. Meilin and her team on the ground would need to adopt subtle aggression as a way forward, whatever that entailed. Sitting among the embassy staff, no specific tactics were clear in her mind.

"Are we agreed on the immediate task?" the Deputy asked.

Meilin had been looking at him but lost in her own thoughts. "I'm sorry, could you repeat that?"

"Will the information you have been given and will be given sufficient for you and your people to press the Vietnamese?"

"It'll have to do for now, won't it," Meilin responded curtly. She wasn't happy at all and wondered how she could move things from a different angle by going straight to people in Beijing. But doing that could create other problems by making enemies of people she might need.

"Good. I'll contact Beijing immediately about your travel and needs. Please keep Beijing apprised of the situation. It'll get to us," the Deputy said, rising and leaving the room, followed by Mr. Zheng and Xiong Zimo.

"It wasn't what you wanted, was it," Zhou Shan said, still seated in the chair.

"I'm not the government. I'm siphoning off funds from our China company profits to do the government's bidding in Vietnam. I can't do that for years, but that is what it will require," Meilin said.

"Some of our activities have been compromised. That's why the flow of information will be less than what you've been used to," Shan said. "That's all I will say."

Meilin nodded but said nothing. Zhou Shan's last comment made the encounter with the FBI agents in her room make more sense. The Americans found the information leak and who was collecting information in the embassy. That explained why the agents asked about Xiong Zimo and Zhou Shan. But how much did they really know? Meilin was grateful that they didn't press harder and that her government was discriminating on its disclosure of the plan to her.

"That helps me understand some things," Meilin responded. She wasn't about to say that it explained her sleepless night spending time with the FBI. "What the Deputy had to say makes my trip to Vietnam tomorrow much more important."

"It was good to see you," Shan said. "I would ask about lunch, but we've got a day of security briefings that I must attend."

Zhou Shan escorted Meilin down. He unexpectedly gave her a quick hug before she exited.

Meilin stood just outside the door. The rain had stopped, the clouds had broken up and the sun was shining. A sunny spring afternoon seemed likely, but it wasn't making her feel better. She was already thinking about landing in Ho Chi Minh City and implementing a subtly aggressive strategy if she could have one form in her mind. She didn't have years to wait for Vietnam's potential to become reality. That would bleed profits from her mainland-based operations. She needed to find a way for more government funds to flow through to CODE. She wondered if a quiet approach to someone in China's navy would stem the decrease in profits if the Chinese navy would be happy to see better deep-water capacity in Vietnam. The problem with that was Vietnam's likely reaction to any thought of a Chinese naval presence even if it was just a port of call. Navigating all these commercial, political, and military issues required a full-time person. The last thing Meilin wanted to do was increase expenses, knowing it wasn't realistic.

* * * * *

After Kellie's call, Aaron's imagination shifted into overdrive. The ingredients in his mental bowl were the bits of information Kellie provided during their calls and assumptions he reached after talking to Linh. He checked the time and dashed over to his luggage, found the single pair of dress slacks he'd brought and a white dress shirt, putting them on along with decent shoes.

He ran to the elevator. He rushed through the lobby and waved to a hotel bellman. "Motorbike taxi," Aaron said. He jumped on the bike just as it rolled to a stop. The bellman told the driver where to go.

The driver forced his way between other cyclists, beeping his horn and urging everyone in front of him to move out of the way. Aaron's ab muscles were getting a workout with the acceleration and deceleration between traffic signals. Aaron didn't know what the bellman had said, but it was working. Aaron kept his knees against the bike to protect them. They whizzed by other bikes by inches.

As the driver raced by the gas station Aaron recognized, he was just a minute away from his destination. The driver earned his fare and tip on this ride. Aaron gave the driver double the fare and Aaron saw the broken tooth smile cross the driver's face.

Aaron marched toward the entrance to the Maritime Administration building. Waiting outside for Linh was not an option. He couldn't risk the possibility of her boyfriend coming to greet her. Pushing the door open, he pulled out his passport and his government identification.

A few steps inside the building, he saw several uniformed young men.

"Do you speak English?"

"I do, a little," one of the men said.

"I would like to see Ms. Phan Nhu Linh," Aaron said, hoping they understood his pronunciation.

The young man professing to speak some English walked away. Aaron watched him looking through a notebook. Picking up the phone, he spoke to someone and returned. "You wait."

"Thank you," Aaron said and walked over to a wooden bench along the wall on the opposite side of the doors. He checked the time. It was nearing that time when he had seen Linh's boyfriend show up to meet her. He looked through the glass door to see if the boyfriend would show up.

Linh descended the staircase at one end of the building and walked down the corridor to the center of the ground floor where the main entrance was located. She stopped ten feet away when she saw Aaron. "Mr. Aaron, why are you here?"

Aaron twisted around at the sound of his name. "I'm sorry to come, but we need to talk. It's very important."

"We talk already," Linh said, taking only a couple of steps toward him. Aaron showing up unannounced caused her to think about what she'd said to him at lunch the previous day and her encounters with Jun and the motorcyclist.

Aaron saw the uniformed security officers several feet away out of the corner of his eye. He wondered if this looked as awkward to them as it felt to him. He was acting on the spur of the moment with no detailed plan. Unlike some people, he wasn't the best at winging it.

Linh closed the gap between them to five feet and stopped. Her eyes shifted for just a second, looking over Aaron's shoulder.

Aaron glanced over his shoulder and saw the boyfriend through the glass window. He looked at Linh. "We should go. Is there another door? I don't want him to see us," Aaron said. Aaron looked to his right and saw that two of the security officers had taken steps closer sensing that Linh was uncomfortable.

"Come," Linh said. She turned and headed back down the long corridor toward the staircase at one far end of the building. She led Aaron through a set of doors into the stairwell. "You wait five minutes."

Linh ran up the steps. It was the end of her workday and she wanted to switch out of the shoes she wore at work to something more comfortable.

"What's wrong," Mai asked, seeing Linh kicking off her shoes.

"One of the Americans is here. Jun is out in the front waiting for me. I can't meet Jun now. I need to leave the back way."

"Do you want me to tell Jun anything," Mai asked.

"Tell him I must work longer today. Tell him that you will call me and have me call him later," Linh instructed.

"I'll tell him," Mai said and left.

Linh took a deep breath. Running into Mai, she had left Aaron waiting longer than five minutes. She rushed down the stairs, seeing Aaron leaning against the wall. They walked around the stairway and exited through a back door. They entered an alleyway behind the building and snaked around small, single-story old huts and buildings, some having tin roofs.

Aaron followed Linh. As they made their way down narrow paths, it reminded him of the Orphan Bar's location tucked away behind and amid lots of other main buildings that fronted the main streets. The buildings fronting the main streets projected a sense of newer, modern buildings that hid decades old, rundown buildings and shacks. Linh stopped and looked around.

"Is something wrong?" Aaron asked.

"Lost," Linh said.

"Where are you taking us?"

"My apartment."

"No, now isn't a good time to go there. We need to go to my hotel," Aaron said. "Let's get to the main street."

Linh didn't object.

Aaron wasn't concerned. Yes, lost among the buildings and on this one block, but once out onto a main avenue, they'd leave it to a taxi driver to get them back to his hotel. They meandered down narrow pathways for twenty more minutes. They wandered down several walkways that led to a door, turned around, retracing steps only to go down other walkways that dead-ended at other doors.

When Linh and Aaron exited the maze, they stood on the sidewalk, looked at each other and laughed. "Taxi?" Aaron said.

Linh stepped toward the curb. Several taxis passed her by before one stopped, and they ducked into it. Aaron held out the hotel's business card.

"Okay, okay," the driver said, put the vehicle in gear and joined the rush hour flow.

Aaron felt his shirt clinging to his skin. He pulled his shirt from his skin. The cab's four windows were rolled down. Between traffic signals when the taxi moved, the air flowing in through the windows cooled him down.

"Are you okay? Your face is all red," Linh commented.

"I'm fine, just hot." Aaron thought about the next two or three decisions he had to make. His uncle wasn't going to like them.

The taxi driver navigated the congested streets. When they got out of the cab at the hotel, an hour had passed since exiting the back of the Maritime Administration. Entering the lobby, Linh walked along side Aaron. The eyes of the hotel staff who'd gotten used to seeing Aaron and Drew followed the two to the elevator.

Aaron led Linh to his tenth-floor room. As he stepped into the room ahead of Linh, he was glad he hadn't left the room in too much of a mess. His jeans were thrown over a piece of luggage resting on the room's luggage rack, and he'd thrown the covers up on the bed. The desk had his laptop and a few pieces of paper strewn on it.

Aaron knocked on the door to the adjoining room. "Uncle Drew, are you decent in there? If so, open the door. We have a guest." Aaron waited a moment then turned around and saw that Linh had stopped several feet inside the room's entrance and stood by the closet door.

Drew opened the door and looked at Aaron for a moment then noticed Linh standing farther back. "This is a surprise."

"We need to talk about new arrangements," Aaron said. Aaron stepped aside, extending his arm out toward Drew's room as an invitation to Linh to join them.

The three conferred around a small table in Drew's room. Drew sat at the foot of the bed while Linh and Aaron found chairs.

"Linh, when you called your boyfriend about our lunch, he told someone to follow me back to this hotel. He knows what I look like, and he knows I am staying at this hotel."

"I don't know people follow you," Linh said.

"I believe you," Aaron said. "You said he's Chinese and he's your other boss. He gives you money for information. Is that right?"

Linh nodded.

"Your boyfriend's boss from China is coming here in a day or two. Your boyfriend will tell her about me and you. I don't want them to know my hotel," Aaron explained. He looked over at Drew. "That's why we need to move."

"Does this put Linh in an awkward or dangerous situation?" Drew asked.

"I don't know," Aaron said.

"Me and my boyfriend have a fight," Linh interjected.

"Why?" Drew asked.

"I told Mr. Aaron about my other job, not government job. He's mad at me," Linh added.

"Did he hit you?" Aaron asked.

"No. He try to grab my arm, so I hit him with my big bag." She saw both men look at each other and chuckle. "I leave his apartment and drink with my friend Mai. But maybe there's other trouble." She studied the two men. "I make motorcycle crash."

"We don't understand. What do you mean that you made a motorcycle crash?" Drew asked.

"I'm going home on my scooter. A man follows me on motorbike. I slow down, he slow down. I go fast, he go fast. Then, I go fast and slow down quickly. He is next to me, and I use my stick and push him." Linh used her hands to show what she meant. Her left hand representing her movements and the right hand being her pursuer. Aaron and Drew understood.

"What stick are you talking about?" Aaron asked.

Linh reached into her large purse, pulled out the retractable baton, held it out to her side and pressed a button. The baton snapped open to its full length.

"That'll do the trick," Drew said.

"How bad was he hurt?" Aaron asked.

"I don't know. I ride away," Linh answered. "Now I think Jun ask him to follow me like he follow you," Linh added.

"We've still got days arranged for this place," Drew said.

"It's up to you, but Linh's boyfriend knows I'm here. I can't take a chance of running into him or his boss who I met in Hong Kong. This Chinese boyfriend's boss is Kellie's distant cousin," Aaron explained. "I don't know if Linh is in danger, but she has created an awkward situation. At some point, if her boss put someone up to following her, he's going to find out how this guy crashed his bike. Something triggered in his head to have her followed and we don't know why. That's where things get awkward at the very least and potentially dangerous for Linh," Aaron added.

Drew sat on the edge of the bed. His eyes fixed on his nephew. "Do you think it's safe for Linh to go home?" Drew asked, wanting Aaron's assessment.

"I can't say for certain, but she's probably safe for now," Aaron said.

"I go home. It's okay. I call Jun. He's waiting for me to call," Linh said. "If I don't call, he's mad at me."

"Linh, do you have a passport?" Drew asked.

"Yes. I have old passport."

"Is it still good? Can you use it to leave Vietnam?" Drew asked. "When you go home, you check and call me or Aaron and tell us."

"Okay. I'll check. I should go home," Linh said.

"Do you want one of us to go with you," Drew asked.

"No. I go home myself."

"Linh, I want to get a visa for you to go to the United States. We can talk to people at the consulate and get help to arrange that," Drew said.

"We talk about it later," Linh responded. She stood up, forcing Drew and Aaron to accept her decision that she was going home.

She walked past Aaron to the door. Drew slid off the end of the bed to follow Linh.

"No, you stay. I go now by myself."

The two men watched Linh leave.

"If you're going to commit to Linh's move to the States you need to move faster," Aaron said.

"Yeah, I'm getting that message. Our presence is causing some headaches for her. We're complicating her life in ways we or I didn't intend to," Drew said.

"I think all we've done is accelerate the time when she was going to be confronted with a decision because everything I was assuming seems to be playing out. She's now working for the Chinese and funneling info to them. She's had a fight with her Chinese boyfriend who is the contact, and he put a tail on me and her. What's going to make this worse is the presence of Meilin in a couple of days. She's no one to mess with," Aaron explained.

"You make it sound like she's some monster boss," Drew said.

"No, not a monster boss. She's focused and intense when it comes to business. When it comes to physical threats, she's into martial arts. To look at her, you'd never think she could lift ten pounds, but I witnessed a split second of her use of those skills. She is lightning fast and it's the art of surprise that she uses," Aaron said. "As a woman, she got to the top of ChiTran because she can think on her feet as well as plan and implement."

"Make sure I'm not left alone with her," Drew said.

"One way to avoid either of us being in her presence is to move to another hotel. I'd like to find a place between here and the Maritime Administration in case we need a room for Linh. We can make it convenient for her to get back and forth if it comes to that," Aaron suggested. "I'm going to see what I can find online. In the meantime, you should find out what you need to do and how long things will take if you're going to get that visa for Linh," Aaron suggested.

Aaron calculated that they had twenty-four to thirty-six hours to move to a new location. He went to his room and started searching online.

Linh took a motorcycle taxi to her apartment. Cars, buses, scooters, and motorcycles competed for space on the streets. Streetlamps, store front lights and vehicle headlights took over providing illumination outside. When she entered her apartment, Linh walked to the sink and splashed water over her face to remove the sweat and diesel fumes and other pollutants from her face. She grabbed a bottle of water from her small fridge and plopped down into a chair.

She compared her feelings now to those of the night she got the call from Lan. That night and into the next day she was on a cloud. She was excited and fearful of meeting an American who might be her father and wondered what it would be like to live in America. She allowed herself to think about a new world and new beginning. The last day and a half changed her thoughts about leaving. It was no longer about wanting to leave but about being forced to leave. Her relationship with Jun had changed. She didn't know how much longer she would have her second job and the money she earned from it. Without that money, her life would slide in the wrong direction. She didn't want to be poor and living in the city. She didn't want to return to village life.

Linh got up and found her locked box of important documents. She opened the box and found her passport at the bottom. It looked as if it had been issued yesterday. She checked the dates and saw that it had a year left before it expired. Linh called and gave Drew whatever information he needed.

"Linh, in the morning I'll find out everything I must do to get you a visa. As far as I'm concerned, you are already part of my family," Drew said.

"Okay, thank you," was all Linh could think to say before disconnecting.

Linh dreaded making the call to Jun but had no choice. He answered on the third ring.

"How are you?" he asked.

"Very tired. I just got home," Linh said truthfully.

"We must talk. Tomorrow I can make the time, but after that, I will be very busy and it will be difficult to find time to meet," Jun explained.

Linh thought about pressing him with questions after what Aaron had said about Jun's boss from China arriving, but she decided that it was better that she had that information without letting him know what she knew. "Tomorrow, I'll meet you after work. Bye."

Linh stared at the phone. Jun didn't mention the evening before and the accident or anything about his boss coming except his reference to being too busy after tomorrow. Linh looked around her compact apartment. She got up and busied herself by creating a few short stacks of clothing, books, and other belongings that she couldn't do without in case she needed to leave with little time to gather her things.

As she moved around her apartment creating the small piles of essential belongings, anger brewed inside her. As a biracial person, she was already treated like a second-class citizen in her own country. Now, her thoughts went to things Aaron and Jun had said to her over the past couple of days. Between what Aaron said and what Jun didn't say, she wondered if one or both were manipulating her. She wasn't just tired of the way people treated her, she wanted, needed to take more control of her life.

* * * * *

"What are you doing?" Drew asked.

"I'm taking my stuff over to the new hotel I've booked," Aaron said.

"You said we had some time."

"I found a place that's closer to Linh's job. It's cheaper than here, not as luxurious, but stretches our money in case we need to stay longer than expected. And her boyfriend won't know where we are."

"I was hoping to spend at least one more night here before packing up."

"Uncle Drew, if you want to stay here another night, that's fine. I'll give you the details of where I'm going to be, and you can move over there anytime you want. Linh's boyfriend doesn't know what you look like. As for me, I don't need to go out and become an 'accident' victim, if you know what I mean," Aaron said, using air quotes. "If this guy can get someone to follow me and Linh, we have no idea when we're being followed or by whom. The more you're seen with me, the more likely we're both going to be watched."

"I understand why you're doing this now. I'll join you over there tomorrow. Given what you're saying about this other place, I'll enjoy a good night's sleep here and be up early to call Ms. Doan at the consulate. I need details about moving things along for Linh's visa application," Drew said.

Aaron pulled two pieces of wheeled luggage and had his computer bag draped over his shoulder. In the lobby, he scanned the people and faces but had no idea how he'd spot anyone interested in him and wanting to follow his movements. After paying for his room, including the night he wasn't spending there, the bellman flagged a cab to take him to his new hotel.

Approaching his new hotel, the exterior of the hotel building appeared fresh and new compared to the hotel he'd left, but the lobby was small and dimly lit. He turned down assistance with his luggage and squeezed into an elevator that reminded him of small elevators in Europe. It went straight to the sixth floor. The corridor's orange-brown carpeting was worn in the center from all the foot traffic.

This hotel still used keys, not key cards. He entered a room that smelled musty, and a hint of cigarette smoke wafted in the air. He dismissed the thought of asking for another room as he guessed all of them had a cigarette odor. Hitting the lights, he saw what he'd expect from a budget hotel. A small, plain desk, no drawers, a straight back unpadded wooden chair, and thin curtains. Looking at the bed, it dipped slightly in the center. Aaron chuckled as he thought about what his uncle's reaction would be when he moved to the new hotel. Aaron adjusted the thermostat, grateful that the air conditioning worked. He sank into the single bed when he sat on it. After a few minutes, he got up. As the room cooled, he opened his luggage, hung a couple of shirts in the small closet, put his computer bag on the desk, and placed his toiletries in the bathroom. While busying himself, his thoughts about Meilin's impending arrival and whether that created a threat to Linh's safety consumed him.

Aaron was crossing the room but stopped and looked around the room. There was nothing in the room to distract him from his thoughts. A window of time existed before Meilin arrived. He couldn't allow it to close without taking some risks. Aaron looked at the printed instructions by the phone and dialed Linh's number.

"Linh, I'm sorry to call you this late," Aaron said when she answered. It wasn't that late, but he assumed she didn't expect to hear from him again so soon.

"Not late," Linh said.

"I have questions about your work for your Chinese boyfriend."

Linh was silent upon hearing why Aaron called. "What questions?"

It was Aaron's turn to hesitate. He was on a hotel phone. In his mind, he believed that someone or anyone could be listening. "I don't want to ask my questions on the phone. I want to ask you in person, face-to-face."

"Tonight, now?"

"Yes, if that's possible for you. There might be things I should do before your boyfriend's boss from China arrives," Aaron said.

There was no way Linh wanted Aaron or Drew to know where she lived. She thought about someplace to meet. "We meet at bar with pictures," Linh suggested.

Aaron thought for a moment. He wasn't sure he could find the bar, having been there only one time and at night. "Can you tell me the address and I'll write it down and meet you." He found a piece of paper in his computer bag and Linh gave him the information. She agreed to meet him on the main avenue, and they'd walk to The Bar together.

Thirty minutes later, Aaron swung his leg off the motorcycle cab, paid the fare and met Linh. They walked down the unlit narrow pathway leading to the string of lights hanging in front of The Bar and entered.

"Harry, how are you," Aaron said as he and Linh walked in and toward a table.

"Good to see you again. Everything good?"

"All's going well," Aaron said as he and Linh sat in the half empty establishment.

Lan walked over smiling, happy to see the pair together. Lan and Linh spoke in Vietnamese for minute, both smiling and chuckling about something that Aaron didn't understand. Neither woman translated.

With Lan walking away, Linh's smile disappeared. "What questions?"

"It's about your work for the boyfriend. Do you keep copies of the information you give to Jun?"

"No. I keep nothing."

"How do you know what to copy?"

"Jun tells me what kind of information he wants to see and if I see documents with information, I make copies."

"When you give him copies, is it a computer disk or paper copies," Aaron asked.

"Mostly paper copies. We have copy room at work. If I see something that is close to what Jun told me, I make the copy. But I can't look at everything. It takes too much time and other people use the same copy room. I need to be careful," Linh said.

"Have you ever given him information on a computer disk or other type of computer memory device like a small memory stick?"

"No, never. I don't have a chance to use the computer for this. I only give him paper," Linh answered.

"Does Jun keep the documents in his apartment or in the office?"

Linh shrugged. "Usually, I give to him at his apartment or when we are out. Maybe he uses it in his office."

"Do you go to his office sometimes? Do you have keys for his apartment or office?"

"I go to office if nobody is there. Just me and Jun. I don't have keys," Linh said. Linh spotted Lan coming over with drinks and didn't say anything more until Lan had stepped away from the table. "Why?"

"I'd like to see the kind of information in the documents," Aaron said.

"In Vietnamese, how will you understand?"

"You can help me, or I can find other people to translate the documents," Aaron said. He was thinking that if Jun and the Chinese were so interested in certain information that Linh obtained for them then he might be able to persuade someone at the consulate to look at the documents and see what the Chinese were after and whether the information was linked to what Kellie had divulged.

Linh looked at her watch. "Do you have lots of dong?"

Aaron checked his wallet and pocket. "I have lots of dong. How much do you need?" Aaron asked.

"Maybe we need hundred dollars American, and you buy good whiskey," Linh said. "We have to go."

"When?"

"Now. We drink fast and go."

They downed most of their drinks in minutes and Aaron pulled out dong. Linh popped up and was several steps toward the door when Aaron caught up with her after throwing down money to cover their drinks. Outside, he jogged to catch up to her. Linh looked up and down the main avenue. She hailed a taxi.

"We find store and you buy nice whiskey," Linh said, seeing Aaron nod in agreement. They passed the gas station that was on the corner of the main avenue and side street that led down to Jun's office and apartment. Linh instructed the driver to stop, and they both slid out of the cab. Linh surveyed what was still open and saw a small shop across the street. "You go there," she pointed.

Aaron was no connoisseur of hard liquor but saw a bottle with a nice shape and attractive label and pointed. A narrow shouldered middle-aged man with a paunch put the bottle on the glass countertop, turned the bottle for Aaron to see the price tag. Aaron put four hundred thousand dong, about twenty-five dollars, on the counter. He didn't wait for change. He saw Linh waiting across the street.

The side street had no streetlamps. Apartments and a few shops and bars provided streaks of light onto the narrow street.

"I need dong and whiskey," Linh said, stopping at the structure next to Jun's office and apartment building. She watched Aaron dig into his pocket for his wallet. He held out half million dong notes. She took four notes and the bottle of whiskey.

"You wait," Linh said. "If I go to the elevator, you come inside. You tell guard you are lost."

"Does he speak any English?"

"No, but you take time, make him try to help you when I'm upstairs," Linh explained.

"Don't let him use the telephone, you stop him," Linh instructed.

Aaron understood. She relied on him to buy her time, and he couldn't let this guy make a call to anyone. He stepped closer to the building as Linh took the front steps two at a time and entered the lobby. Aaron approached the building so he could see the full width of it. He stayed on the street. He saw Linh at a desk where a middle-aged man in uniform sat. Aaron watched the two chatting. Linh smiled as she spoke. She put the bottle of liquor on the desk in front of the man.

As he watched, Linh moved to the side of the desk, and she put one leg over the corner and sat on the desk. It left no doubt in Aaron's mind that this was not the first time that the security guard had seen Linh in the building. The security guard reached down then placed two cups on the desk and opened the bottle.

Aaron stepped back into the shadows and watched the interaction through the glass front of the building. The attention Linh was showering on the security guard made him oblivious to the rest of the world around him. He downed the whiskey he'd poured for himself while Linh barely let it touch her lips. Aaron checked the time. He wasn't sure why she had said they had to hurry as she was taking her time. After the security guard gulped another cup of whiskey, Linh leaned in close to the guard as if whispering in his ear. He reacted with a broad smile. Aaron saw Linh's closed left hand reaching down toward the man's lap. He never looked down. She straightened up but remained sitting on the corner of the desk.

The security guard looked around in case someone was watching. He didn't see Aaron outside still in the shadows. The guard opened the desk's middle drawer an inch or two and reached in for the key ring. He handed the keys to Linh. He poured more for himself and just the slightest splash for Linh, not noticing that she'd barely consumed any. Several minutes passed before Linh got up and went to the elevators.

Aaron saw Linh disappear into an elevator and watched the security guard. With Linh gone, the guard looked down into his lap and picked up the dong notes. Aaron saw him spreading them out in his one hand like playing cards. A wide smile spread across his face, and he poured more whiskey into his cup. Aaron wanted to wait as long as possible before entering the building. He hoped that with as much whiskey as this guy had drunk, he'd never think about making a call to anyone.

Fifteen minutes after Linh had taken the elevator, Aaron climbed the steps and entered the building. He drifted toward the security guard's desk. The man's cheeks were red from the alcohol. The security guard said something in Vietnamese. Aaron stopped a foot in front of the desk. The security guard pushed himself out of his chair, tilting his head back slightly, his eyelids only half open. He folded his arms.

"I'm lost," Aaron said. "Do you speak English?"

The security guard shook his head and started speaking and pointed to the door.

"I'm lost," Aaron repeated loudly. "Café? Beer?" When Aaron saw the bottle of whiskey on the desk, he pointed at the bottle then himself.

"No, no," the security guard said, coming around the desk, he used both hands to push the bigger foreigner toward the door.

Aaron used his body weight to lean naturally against the shorter guard's hands and arms, resisting without getting physical. Aaron heard a non-stop stream of Vietnamese from the guard. Without doing anything more than allowing his body weight to resist the guard's efforts, he saw beads of sweat on the guard's forehead.

Both men froze when the elevator chimed. The guard dropped his arms to his sides and Aaron stood erect. Linh took a step out, stopped, eyed both. She held a folder to her chest and walked toward the security guard, speaking in Vietnamese.

Linh saw the guard looking at her then turned his attention back to Aaron. She pressed the folder to her chest with her left forearm. With the guard's attention focused on Aaron, Linh removed a key and put it in her pocket.

"He says you leave, go," Linh said, looking at Aaron. She turned back to the security guard and held out the key ring. He took the keys and retreated toward the desk.

Aaron exited and disappeared into the shadows of the neighboring building where he stopped and waited for Linh.

Linh took a few minutes to chat with the security guard. She wanted to make sure he didn't think that she and the foreigner were together. Linh saw that her cup of whiskey was still on the desk. After the guard returned to his chair, she went over and downed the cup he'd poured for her. Confident that the guard was none the wiser, she gave him a big smile, a pat on the hand and left.

"What did you find," Aaron asked when she caught up with him.

"Copies I gave to Jun. All in Vietnamese. I cannot explain in English," Linh said. "You need to find translator."

They walked up to the main avenue together, but parted ways as each flagged a ride. Aaron rode back to his shabby hotel room thinking about how he could wrangle some assistance from Attaché Hoover at the consulate. He'd get up and make a call first thing in the morning.

Linh rested her head on the back of the taxi's seat. She knew that Drew was committed to doing something for her, having traveled back to Vietnam to find his long-lost love, but finding a possible daughter instead. As for Aaron, she hadn't been sure about him. Each conversation with him alone had centered on work. Getting the documents for him, she believed that Aaron would feel like he owed her something. She didn't know what or if she'd need anything from Aaron but felt assured that he'd feel obligated to her after the evening's venture into Jun's office.

* * * * *

It wasn't yet midnight, but the hotel lobby was deserted except for a couple of people milling around the dimly lit lobby. Aaron looked around the lobby and saw no one behind the reception desk.

Aaron walked over to the reception counter. "Hello?" Aaron said loudly hoping someone would be within hearing distance. He waited. He pressed a bell on the reception counter, hoping someone would hear it.

A young man with sleeves rolled up and a loosened tie appeared through a doorway. He wiped his mouth with the back of his hand.

"Speak English," Aaron said and saw the young man nod. "Do you have a fax machine? I want to send a fax."

"You give to me, and I send it," the young man said.

"Okay. I'll come back in half an hour," Aaron said, pointing to his watch. He needed time to get Kellie's fax number.

In his room, Aaron's fingers danced over his keyboard, sending Kellie his request for a fax number without telling her what he would send. He asked her to call him as soon as she received it regardless of the time. Within ten minutes of his emailed request, he was rushing back to the lobby with a fax number. He didn't write a note on the cover sheet other than asking Kellie to call.

Because of the number of pages being transmitted, Aaron stood at the reception desk for twenty minutes before the young man returned with his documents. With the pages now sent to Kellie, Aaron sat on the bed, his back against the headboard and tilting his head against the wall. He felt his shoulders relax and slump. Whatever energy he'd relied on during the evening, it was draining out of him. He wished his phone would ring.

Aaron's head snapped forward when his phone buzzed and rang. He'd dozed off. "Hey, hope you got the documents," Aaron said, assuming it was Kellie.

"Yes, thanks. I can't read any of it. Do you have any idea what it might be? Where and how did you get it? Or is it better if I don't know?"

"I can explain the where and how I got it the next time we see each other. Now that we have this, I thought it would be good if we both got them translated. You have people in D.C. who might be able to get it done and I'll see whether the consulate can translate it. The documents are from the Maritime Administration but were given to Meilin's people here who have an interest in whatever these documents cover. Once they're translated, we'll have a better idea why Meilin's CODE office is here and what it's up to," Aaron said.

"I've done a bit of research and this whole thing is consistent with what China's doing and using the face of the private sector to gain control and access of foreign ports. I've been reading about how a Chinese company has a stake in the Port of Los Angeles. Lots of money being thrown around," Kellie said.

"Money buys influence anywhere and everywhere. Combine money with other resources and it's hard for people to resist an offer," Aaron said.

"After we know what's in the documents, we'll compare and discuss what's next," Aaron suggested.

"Agreed. Thanks, and get some sleep," Kellie said. "Aaron, sorry I've dragged you into this, but appreciate what you're doing. I hope this doesn't cause you or your uncle any trouble. And please be careful."

"All for a good cause," Aaron said. "You can thank me in person."

"I will," Kellie said and cut the connection.

Aaron ran his hand over his shaved scalp, forgetting for a moment that there was no hair to run his fingers through. Based on what Linh had said, he couldn't rely on Linh to read and understand the documents if what the documents contained met his suspicions. Though not ready to sleep, he'd try to force himself to sleep and be up early for another trip to the consulate.

Connections

"I've got something we need to have translated," Kellie said to Agent Kearns. "We should find out if what I've received reflects what's in the patent documents that were intended for the Chinese."

"I'm not sure I'm following you," Kearns answered. "What do you have? Is it reliable?"

"We won't know what these documents say until someone who reads Vietnamese can tell us," Kellie said. "We know that Meilin Moy is traveling to Vietnam. She has an office there. My contact tells me that these documents are from Vietnam's Maritime agency and were copied and provided to Ms. Moy's office, all unofficial, under the table activity. Ms. Moy's office seems to have someone getting inside info for them."

"What are we really looking at here," Kearns wondered aloud. "Should we be reaching out to the intel guys?"

"We'll know more about that once we have these documents translated. Do you have a way of getting that done quickly?"

Kearns was drawing a blank.

Kellie broke the silence. "This needs to get done asap. I want to avoid as much bureaucracy as possible. If we go through official channels requesting translation work, this could take days or weeks."

"That's why I'm drawing a blank," Kearns said. "If we don't go through official channels and use the proper translation services, we run the risk of everyone questioning the quality or accuracy of the translation. We could find ourselves in a catch-22 situation. Do you know any staffers on the Hill who could do it? Someone like yourself since you seem to be fluent in Chinese."

"That's the problem. I can speak it, but I'm horrible at reading and writing. Even if I could think of someone, we could have that problem," Kellie explained. "I have an idea. I'll call you back and let you know if it pans out. In the meantime, you can ask around on your end."

Kellie hung up and tapped the keys on her computer, creating a list of phone numbers. She developed a script for the calls she was about to make.

On her cell phone, Kellie keyed in the first phone number. "Hello," she said. "It's been a while since I've been at your restaurant. I'm wondering if there's anyone there who can help me with Vietnamese."

"Just a moment," a woman said, surrendering the phone to someone else.

"Can I help you," a male voice asked.

"Maybe. I have some papers in Vietnamese and hoped there might be someone there who could help me understand what the document says," Kellie said.

"This is a restaurant, not a translation service."

Kellie heard the line go dead. Undeterred, she went to the next number on her list. Again, she apologized that she hadn't been to the restaurant recently then asked for the help she needed.

"I wish I could help you, but I don't read Vietnamese well," a woman said.

"Do you know someone who might be able to help?" Kellie asked. She waited while the woman looked up a number and name.

Kellie hoped the third time would be a charm. She dialed the number given to her and explained to the man on the other end where she'd gotten the number.

"I'm not sure I can help you. I grew up here and went to school here. My Vietnamese is very limited," the man explained.

"There's no one who works at your restaurant who could look at what I have and give me some idea about what they say," Kellie pressed.

"Well, wait a minute. My father's retired. He worked here for a while. He came here from Vietnam. He's in his sixties now, but he could probably help."

"I'm willing to pay him for the trouble," Kellie offered.

"Give me your phone number and I promise to give you a call back. He's usually at home so I'll ask him right away."

"Thank you very much," Kellie said, giving him her cell phone number. She debated giving Kearns a call and decided against it. He might not think her approach was the way to go and would try to dissuade her.

Kellie didn't have long to wait before her cell phone buzzed. The exchange was brief. Mr. Duong gave her an address to a specific Vietnamese eatery in Falls Church, Virginia. She had a choice between a subway and a long taxi ride from Capitol Hill. Before leaving, Kellie pulled up a map on her computer and studied it.

After the subway ride out, Kellie got a taxi to Eden Center in Falls Church. She'd never been there. As the driver pulled into the parking area, the signs in Vietnamese struck her as if she'd been transported to a different country. It was like entering Chinatown with Chinese writing and décor. It was similar here, except it was Vietnamese. The restaurants and shops catered to the large number of Vietnamese in the area.

Kellie's taxi driver was familiar with the area and pulled up in front of the address she had given him. She entered what looked like a bakery and coffee shop. The glass display at the far end attracted her attention. It was filled with a variety of sweets. Two women stood behind the glass display case and the cash register. The seating area wasn't large, but several tables were along the front wall of glass and the side walls. Kellie had walked far enough into the shop that she had to look behind her to see the man she was meeting.

Mr. Duong sat wearing a baseball style cap that had "Saigon" stitched on it. Not knowing what Kellie looked like, Mr. Duong had told Kellie he'd be wearing the hat. He knew that the woman he was meeting had a Chinese name, but didn't connect her to the tall, Asian looking woman entering the bakery.

Kellie walked over to Mr. Duong who stood up at the table once he noticed Kellie heading toward him. He placed the hat on the table. She was several inches taller than the slightly built older man. He had a thin patch of white hair. His tanned and etched face made him appear older than a man in his sixties..

"Mr. Duong, thank you so much for meeting me," Kellie said. "Did the person who called you tell you why I needed your help?"

"He said you need me to look at papers in Vietnamese." Duong's English sounded good though tinged with a heavy accent. "Do you want coffee or tea while I look at the papers?"

Kellie looked toward the counter. "Just tea, thank you."

Duong looked toward the display counter and spoke in Vietnamese. "They know me here," he said. "What kind of work do you do?" he asked.

Kellie kept her answer simple. "I work on Capitol Hill. If I use normal procedures to have a document like this translated, it could take weeks. I wanted to find a faster way of understanding what these documents say," Kellie said.

"I understand. When you work for the government, it's sometimes better to find other solutions than normal procedures," Duong said with a knowing smile.

"If it's not too intrusive, may I ask what you did before you came to the United States," Kellie asked. She saw Duong's fixed smile and his eyes on her. His chest rose as he inhaled. Kellie thought they were engaging in a game of measured responses.

"I was a government official in Saigon. But I spent more time with the Americans than I did with my own people. It was dangerous for me and my family to stay. I had American friends who helped us leave. Because of my work I became proficient in translating," he answered.

Kellie nodded while he spoke and understood. Neither of them would engage in pursuing greater details of the other's work. She dug the documents out of her leather briefcase and placed them on the table. She had a small notepad to write on for herself.

"You need all this translated? It's too much to do here," Duong said.

"Oh, no, no. I hope that if you look at the first few pages, you might be able to tell me what these documents are about," Kellie clarified.

Kellie watched Duong's facial expressions change as he looked at the first page. His brow tensed; his lips pursed.

"These are government documents. How did you get them?"

"A friend faxed them to me," Kellie said.

Duong took a pair of thick lensed glasses from his shirt pocket. He read the Maritime Administration documents. He said nothing.

His left hand went to his chin repeatedly as he read. He wasn't skimming the text. He was absorbing it.

Kellie sat, alternately sipping her tea, looking out the window and watching Duong slightly bent over the table reading. For a man who said there was too much to translate, she felt like he was going to read every page before he stopped to say anything. She rejected the thought of interrupting him while he appeared consumed by the documents. She watched as he flipped back and forth between pages he was reading and those he'd already read. Kellie told herself not to fidget while she sat and waited. She didn't want to distract Duong.

Kellie gazed out onto the parking lot.

"Okay," Duong said, pushing himself against the back of the chair. He saw Kellie's head turn toward him in surprise. "Very interesting and very difficult. Even in Vietnamese, maybe I don't understand some of this well. Am I in trouble for looking at this?"

"No, why would you be in trouble for looking at this?"

"I have seen many American government documents and things like this are usually classified," Duong said. He looked out at the parking lot, wishing he had chosen a different place to sit rather than by the window. When she first arrived, he was confident she'd come alone. After reading several pages of the document, he wondered if she really was alone or if someone might be keeping tabs on her.

"This isn't classified because no one else has seen them and no one knows what they say. And no one knows that you've seen these documents. I'm the only person who knows that you've looked at them," Kellie assured him. "I don't need to tell anyone that you've seen them," Kellie explained.

"Vietnam is different now, not like when I left," Duong began. "This government needs money and help to develop, create jobs. This document says the Maritime Administration will recommend accepting help from China because Chinese will give very good financial terms for ports, but this means China will have control of the ports or maybe parts of the ports like terminals at the ports. Chinese companies will get preference to expand and construct port facilities. The document mentions that Maritime Administration will help Chinese companies get patents for new dredging technology and other technologies for this type of work. This will help the Chinese construct deep water ports faster and allow trade to increase in less time."

"Is there anything specific in the documents about the technology China will use to construct these ports?"

"I don't understand the question," Duong said.

"The Chinese may be stealing the technology information and will use it to improve their construction capabilities, and they will use it as part of the offer of assistance to Vietnam and other governments," Kellie said.

Duong chuckled. "They will never say they steal information, not in this document. They say that Vietnam must help protect the technology by giving Chinese companies patents then Chinese will use the new technology and give Vietnam loans to proceed with port construction and making the ports deeper for bigger ships. Chinese will operate the ports and make money from shipping companies and others involved in trade."

Kellie wasn't a patent lawyer, but her gut was telling her that the Chinese, including Meilin's Vietnamese office, CODE, might use the stolen information to get patents in Vietnam. What she wasn't sure of was if that happened, how financially damaging it would be for American and other foreign companies. The financial impact might be in the hundreds of millions or possibly billions of dollars over time.

"Thank you for looking at these documents. I appreciate your help." Kellie reached into her briefcase and retrieved an envelope from an inside pocket of the briefcase. "This is for your troubles," she said. She placed a plain white envelope on the table.

"Thank you. I'm happy I could help. You must be careful about these things. Chinese are good businesspeople. They have their ways, not like the American way," Duong said. He nodded as Kellie got up and left.

Duong stayed seated, watching the tall Asian looking woman step out onto the sidewalk and make a call on her cell phone. The longer he observed her, the more he thought about the documents and how she might have obtained them. He hoped that by looking at them, he hadn't exposed himself to any legal or other problems. Duong pulled out his wallet and removed a faded black and white photo of him with a tall American. Both wore uniforms. *Colonel,*

I hope this won't force me to ask you for help, Duong thought as he looked up and saw that the woman was gone.

Kellie wasn't a stranger to how some Chinese played the game. She knew that some played by different rules. This felt different. There was nothing that felt physically threatening about what the Chinese were doing. But she could envision waking up one day years down the road and realizing that what she was seeing now could mean direct confrontations later that are physically threatening.

Riding the subway back to the office, something Duong said stuck in Kellie's mind. It nagged her. She was missing something if the Chinese were stealing information and asking the Maritime Administration for its help in getting patents in Vietnam. Her thoughts bounced back and forth between the journalist Quarles and Victoria Walters, the Justice Department lawyer, as people who might shed more light on this.

Back at her desk in the Dirksen Senate Building, Kellie found her call with Quarles frustrating and useless. Although he'd reported on Lucas Moore's arraignment and the charges against Moore, he couldn't answer the questions that troubled her.

Kellie took a deep breath as if that erased her frustration with the Quarles call and pressed the digits.

"Victoria Walters, who's calling?"

"Victoria, it's Kellie Liang. Hoping that you can enlighten me about patents." Kellie heard a sigh from the other end.

"Maybe. That's not my strong suit," Victoria answered.

"This Lucas Moore case involving patent files attempted to be given to the Chinese, what happens if the Chinese or a Chinese company takes that info and files it as if it's theirs in Vietnam?" Kellie asked.

"I can't be completely sure because we are different than a lot of countries around the world. Here, our system is a first to invent system and other countries give priority to a company or person who files the patent application first, not necessarily the first to invent," Victoria said.

"Theoretically, that means that if Moore gave the Chinese a patent file and some Chinese company took the info and made it look like it was their filing in Vietnam, it's possible that a Chinese company would get the patent," Kellie hypothesized.

"Yeah. It would put the real inventor or owner in a bind. It could mean the loss of a lot of future income and lost investment already made for all the research done, prototype testing, refining the technology, and such before the company puts things together to file the patent. All that investment could be lost as to that market where the Chinese file the patent. Of course, any Chinese company stealing the file would still have to develop the product covered by the patent and see if it can replicate it and have the invention function as intended. The benefit for the thief is that the patent must provide a detailed explanation or description of the invention. This can save the enterprise stealing and copying the invention tons of investment money at the front end. If a company is already involved in the industry related to the new patent, it's probably familiar with existing technology and can figure out what the invention will do to improve on what already exists," Victoria explained.

"Then there are concrete benefits to stealing the information," Kellie concluded.

"Absolutely. The financial benefits can be enormous. It could create an administrative and economic nightmare for the company inventing the technology by being shut out of a national market like Vietnam."

"This is very helpful, Victoria. Thank you." Kellie ended the call. Kellie sat back. Her mind was reeling. What if there were a handful of other Lucas Moores providing the Chinese with information from patent files? How much new technology information could be flowing out of the patent office? Other than raising the question with the director at the recent hearing, was anyone focused on this?

* * * * *

Senator Earnest Layton limped along the third-floor corridor in the Dirksen Senate Office Building. With the day's hearings done and most of the constituent visits finished for the day, the corridors were easy to walk. The jacket of his navy-blue suit no longer buttoned. People nodded as they walked by the recognizable fifth-term Oklahoma senator. A horse-riding accident a few years earlier had left him with a limp. The injury had also contributed to a lack of physical activity and increasing girth.

Layton's secretary had called ahead to make sure that his young colleague was still in his office and would wait for his visit. When Layton entered Senator Burke's suite of offices, he saw lots of heads looking downward at keyboards and computer screens.

"Senator Layton," Trish said, standing and leading him to Burke's office. "He's expecting you."

Layton nodded, smiled, and walked past Trish. He saw Senator Burke coming around from behind the desk and gesturing for him to sit on the leather sofa.

"To what do I owe this honor of a personal visit?"

"Don't get too excited," Senator Layton cautioned. "My longevity in this town lends itself to finding out things before everyone else knows. If you recall that recent hearing with the newly confirmed director of the patent office, you raised questions about information confidentiality and security."

"I put those questions to the director, but it was Ms. Liang on my staff who flagged the issue and recommended that we raise them," Burke explained.

"There may be more to that than meets the eye," Layton teased. "There's a classified memo or report floating around at the FBI about lax security at the patent office and its people being prime targets of the Chinese. I didn't get all the details, but the FBI has learned more within the last twenty-four hours."

"We did make a point of that during the hearing with the new director. We warned him that we'd summon him back to the committee and have him tell us what he's doing about this," Burke reminded Layton.

"What about Ms. Liang? What does she know? Does she have contacts that can shed more light on this?"

"We haven't discussed it," Burke said. He wasn't going to say anything about the FBI visiting him at home or their interest in talking to her.

"Her familial background lends itself to being a target. Aren't you concerned about that," Layton suggested.

"There is absolutely nothing, no evidence to cause me any concern. In fact, I would say it's just the opposite. She's been keen to get me to raise the questions we need answers to at these hearings. While our colleagues are consumed by Afghanistan and Iraq, she's been pressing me to make sure that we don't forget that there is intense competition and possible economic threats from the other side of the world," Burke insisted. "Earnest, don't get cold feet about her nomination. She's a lot more valuable to us than a lot of the appointees we've confirmed in this town." Burke used Senator Layton's first name to emphasize his point.

"I want you to understand that things are going to happen. My gut tells me the FBI won't sit around and wait. There are a few good cowboys over there who might stir the pot," Layton said.

"Then the problem is within the agencies they're looking at rather than here in my office. Why would Ms. Liang know more than the FBI? Did this anonymous person tell you that Ms. Liang knows something or did something," Burke countered.

Senator Layton used both hands to push himself up from the sofa. "Nathan, you have a bright future here. There's power to be had along with that future. There's nothing wrong with playing it safe," Layton advised.

"This has nothing to do with playing it safe," Burke responded. "I'm not willing to cling to old biases and stereotypes."

The two men stared at each other for several seconds. "I best be on my way," Layton said and limped toward the door.

Burke put a hand on the open door. "Thanks for stopping by."

Senator Burke stood in his office doorway and watched the older man leave. Once Layton was gone, Burke wandered across the office reception area toward Kellie's cubicle. "Come over to my office," he said to Kellie, sitting and looking up at him.

"Just had a visit from Senator Layton. He got an unofficial call from a source at the FBI about more to come about the info leaks from the patent office. Have you been in touch with them?" Burke asked.

Kellie didn't want to divulge anything about the overnight operation and her role in it. "As you know, I've spoken to Agent Kearns. He hasn't told me anything more about the leak at the patent office," Kellie said.

"Okay. Let me know if there're new developments on that front. I don't want to be the last to know if something's going to blow up and I should've known," Burke requested. "It's been a long day, go home."

"Wait," she said as Burke began to turn away. "My DHS friend who's in Vietnam right now did some digging around and faxed me some documents. What I've been able to learn is that our resourceful patent examiner may have provided information that's being used by the Chinese to get patents in Vietnam and using the technology information to persuade the Vietnamese to allow them to construct and expand ports and have control over those facilities."

Senator Burke wiped his forehead. "This sounds like a complicated chess match and right now, it sounds to me like we're losing more pieces than they are. We need to lean on the FBI and get them to investigate this patent angle."

Kellie left Burke's office, went to her cubicle, gathered up her purse, a few documents and made her way toward Union Station and her apartment. The short walk in the cool evening breeze was refreshing, but the idle walk allowed her thoughts to roam. Her mind raised Aaron's image and how Meilin's arrival in Vietnam might affect him. She then wondered what else Senator Layton knew about the FBI's activities and if that included the overnight visit to Meilin's hotel room. The more Kellie thought about Aaron, Meilin, and the FBI, the more she realized that she had no control over anything. She felt almost as helpless as she had when she'd been abducted and taken across the border to China without any documentation or any way to communicate with anyone.

She couldn't make decisions and instruct others to do anything. But could she use the information she had to prod others?

* * * * *

Senator Burke sat in his office with Kellie's latest bit of information churning in his head. It was late in the day and Trish was gone. He found the Senate directory and dialed Senator Layton's office.

The phone rang and rang, finally picked up by a young staffer. "Is the Senator still in," Burke asked. "If he is, can you tell him that Senator Burke would like five minutes of his time." Burke heard the receiver being placed on a hard surface and waited.

"He's in and said he'll wait for you, but he has to leave in thirty minutes."

"Okay, I'm on my way." Burke grabbed his suit jacket, putting it on as he exited his suite of offices. He strode down the hall and took the stairway up one floor. Out of breath, he marched down the corridor to Senator Layton's office and saw a young man at the reception desk.

"He's waiting for you," the young man said. He got up and left once Senator Burke entered Senator Layton's office.

"What's prompted this," Layton asked.

"I spoke to Ms. Liang after you left. I don't need to know who your FBI source is, but I'd advise you to call your source and have the appropriate law enforcement agencies conduct an operation at the Patent Office," Burke suggested.

"What do you know now that you didn't know half an hour ago?"

"Ms. Liang has a friend who is vacationing in Vietnam. Her friend works for Homeland Security. After she told him what was happening here, he decided to take it upon himself to discreetly sniff around. Long story short, it looks like the confidential patent information is being used by the Chinese to file their own patents, shut out the real owners, and use financial incentives to gain control of Vietnam's future port facilities," Burke explained.

"You didn't know this when I met with you just a while ago? Why was your Ms. Liang withholding this information from you," Layton asked.

"If she was withholding information, she wouldn't have told me anything about this. In fact, she volunteered the information without my asking. I thought you'd want to know this. I thought you could get your high-placed FBI source to act on it," Burke said. "You do know that Vietnam is halfway around the world from here, right? Information doesn't flow at our convenience. If you can overlook your bias against Ms. Liang for a moment and consider the implications of what's being uncovered, maybe you can tell your source that she's spoken with Agent Kearns."

"I'll pass it on. Thanks," Layton said.

Burke looked down on Layton sitting behind his desk and realized his meeting was finished. Burke wasn't in a rush as he walked back to his office. He shook his head slightly thinking that Layton's position of power allowed the older man to hang on to outdated prejudices but also benefit from the contributions of those he didn't respect.

Alone in his office, Layton picked up the phone and called his FBI source. "This is urgent. Based on that China info you related and other input I've received, you need to find a way to impress that patent office director. The consequences of lax security over there are bigger than we thought. A written note or phone call won't do. I hope you get my drift."

"It's too late to get something done today," the source responded.

"You've got all evening and all night to coordinate things," Layton suggested.

"Kearns's team has been working on this so they're up to speed. I'll start with him."

Movement

aron's informative morning call stirred Bruce Hoover's interest, but he believed that Aaron misled him by saying he'd avoid risky activities. Although Hoover had a Vietnamese national working for him, he doubted the young man who drove him around and acted as a translator would be able to read the documents Aaron was bringing.

Before Aaron's arrival, Hoover made calls to several offices in the consulate.

Hoover heard voices. He went and stood in the doorway of his office and saw Aaron following an escort to his office. Aaron's shoulders seemed to be drooping. "You look a bit haggard," Hoover said, seeing Aaron's bloodshot eyes.

"Didn't sleep well. I switched hotels a couple of nights ago when I found out someone followed me," Aaron said. Aaron placed a folder on Bruce Hoover's desk. "Those are the pages I brought for you." Aaron looked over his left shoulder and noticed for the first time that a woman was sitting in Hoover's office. When Aaron walked in and sat down, Hoover had been blocking his view of part of the office.

"What's the matter," Hoover asked, seeing Aaron close his eyes and his head tilt slightly toward the ceiling.

Seeing the woman and making the comment about being followed hit him simultaneously. "Nothing," Aaron said, thinking that he needed to be more alert. He thought it strange that Hoover didn't introduce her and decided not to ask.

Hoover lifted the folder in his outstretched hand waiting for the woman to take it from him. "She's going to take a look at them and tell us what she thinks is in these pages. While she's looking at them, I have some questions," Hoover said.

"For the moment, I'll run with the assumptions you're making," Hoover started. "The person who provided these papers works at the Maritime Administration, but who makes the decisions or recommendations within that office? Someone in a position of influence makes the decision or recommendation to do what you say the Chinese want to do. All you've done is find a person who has access to the documents and can get you the copies.

"Here's the way I think this is happening," Hoover continued. "The person pushing the China agenda has found a way to influence a senior Maritime Administration person to move things forward. In order to keep tabs on how the Maritime Administration officials are leaning on the China proposal, our China guy needs to see the memos and other documents being passed around within the agency having anything to do with China's proposal to provide loans, construct ports and terminals. Having constant access to the internal memos and documents allows the Chinese to stay on top of whatever is going on inside the agency, but what we don't know is who within the Maritime Administration may be in China's pocket. That bit of information is important and is worth getting."

"Maybe something in those documents," Aaron said, nodding toward the woman behind him, "will provide us with a name. The other way to get that name is for me to ask that question."

"No, you're getting too wrapped up in this," Hoover warned. "You had lunch with someone, you were followed back to your hotel and didn't notice. You don't have the training to protect yourself. And equally important, if you keep this up you run the risk of creating a diplomatic problem for us."

"I'm keeping my distance."

"I get that, but what if they decide to close that gap and get too close and try to do something? They might force you to do something you shouldn't," Hoover responded.

"Excuse me," the woman interrupted.

Aaron stood slightly and turned his chair.

"I read the first five pages. The local administrator of the Maritime Administration recommends that the Minister of Transport in Hanoi act quickly to approve CODE's proposal for port infrastructure projects in Ho Chi Minh City and in Vung Tau. China promises to use latest technology to accelerate pace of construction, based on Vietnam's acceptance of loan conditions, timelines, and granting of patents. The references to patents are included in these documents. China will provide loans for the project and can be paid back by giving CODE and other Chinese construction companies percentage of any charges for use of the ports by shipping companies, exporters, and other logistics companies. This is very good for China and Vietnam," the woman said.

Turning to Hoover, "there you have it," Aaron said. "This is not good for us in so many ways."

"Can you write up a paragraph or two summarizing what you've just read and told us?" Hoover asked the woman. She nodded, picked up the documents and left Hoover's office.

"Yeah, your earlier scenario without the documents was not encouraging. Hearing her summary was worse than I expected. Do we have evidence that the patents the Chinese are referring to are based on info stolen in the U.S.?" Hoover asked.

"I think I can get that verified," Aaron responded. "I'll send that question back to D.C. and hope for a quick turnaround."

"This isn't in my job description, on the other hand, I can't ignore it now that I'm aware of it. I'll have to find out who the appropriate person is to take this on. Will you be okay if I mention your name?"

"If disclosing my name is going to get me in trouble, try not to identify me. But if you need to identify me so that I can help then I'm good with that," Aaron said.

"Why don't you stick around. I want to start asking around. Maybe we can put a few heads together and find a way to postpone or derail this thing," Hoover mused.

"Be mindful of the fact that CODE's big boss is probably landing here no later than tomorrow, if not today. She's probably coming to meet with people to move this thing along," Aaron added. "While you're wandering the halls, get me a computer to use so I can send that email for verification about the patent info."

Hoover logged into his computer and let Aaron take his seat. "Have at it."

Aaron's fingers tapped the keys, sending Kellie an email explaining that he needed verification that the Chinese patent documents were based on stolen information. After transmitting the note, he sent a second email from his phone to allay any concerns she might have in receiving the first note from an unknown person. Now, she'd know that he was disclosing a lot of information to his Vietnam-based Homeland Security colleague.

* * * * *

Kellie's laptop pinged her. Sitting down to read the incoming email, the laptop sounded again. After reading both of Aaron's notes, she squeezed her head between the palms of her hands, elbows resting on her small corner desk.

After reading Aaron's emails, Kellie decided to call Kearns. "Any progress on a translation," Kellie asked.

"I'm running into the kind of bureaucracy I was afraid of by asking for translation support," Kearns replied. "And I'm getting pulled in different directions because of that report I wrote up after the Ms. Moy meeting."

"Why? What's going on?"

"There are well-placed people who want to shake things up over at the patent office. With thousands of employees, it's hard to figure out how to go about doing that, but I think we've finally got that figured out. No need for you to be concerned about any of that," Kearns replied.

"It's not pressure, but I received a message from the consulate in Ho Chi Minh City," Kellie said, pausing for effect. "They would like us to tell them that the document we have in Vietnamese is a translation of the Chinese patents to be filed in Vietnam based on stolen patent information from the United States. And they'd like it yesterday."

"Damn it, how are we going to do that? It could take days or weeks before we can arrange that."

Kellie closed her eyes tight, wishing she had an alternative option, but she didn't. "I'm going to propose something that you'll think is crazy. If you're willing to go along with it, maybe we can get this done this evening."

"Right now, I have nothing so let me hear your idea."

"It's unofficial, but it might be as good as anything official. Given all the Vietnamese in the area, there must be someone who can read this stuff and tell us what we have. Lots of well-educated Vietnamese had to leave their country, came here and are in the area."

"I don't hate the idea, but this is sensitive and technical stuff," Kearns said.

"At the moment, it isn't classified stuff so we're in the clear from that angle," Kellie said.

"Where do you even begin?"

"I'll call around to a few establishments and hope for the best. Are you up for a field trip this evening if I get lucky?" Kellie asked.

"My job is 24/7. If that's what it takes, you've got my number."

After Kearns clicked off, Kellie went to her briefcase, having dropped Duong's phone number into it. She took a deep breath and called.

"Mr. Duong? It's Kellie Liang. Sorry to call so late, but I wanted to thank you for your help earlier," Kellie said.

"Not a problem. I hope I helped. It's not easy to find someone who can do this kind of work. Maybe I should have a new part-time job doing this," he said.

"Maybe you should," Kellie agreed. She had hoped for a better opening from Mr. Duong. She couldn't wait. "Could you give me just a little more of your time? I'd be your first client."

"You mean you need me to look at more documents?"

"Yes. In fact, I need you to look at a few more pages of the documents I brought earlier today," Kellie said.

"Oh, I see. We could meet again tomorrow at the same place."

"I'm being pressured. Is there any way to do this tonight," Kellie said and waited as she heard no response for what seemed like minutes.

"Oh, tonight. I see."

"I promise this shouldn't take too long. I'm asking you to look for something very specific," Kellie added.

"Okay," Duong agreed, provided an address, and ended the call.

Kellie jotted down Duong's address before he hung up. She then coordinated a pickup by Kearns. Kellie had two sets of documents for Duong to compare. The document in Vietnamese and the one Victoria Walters had provided.

Kellie gave Kearns the address and he steered them onto I-66, heading west of the downtown area. "You surprised me when you called. I thought it'd take a lot longer to find someone who could do this," Kearns remarked.

"I have friends in low places," Kellie joked, hoping to ward off his questions.

"It's as if you already had someone lined up. There I was thinking you'd be lucky to find anyone if you spent all day tomorrow."

"I'm resourceful," Kellie said.

"Okay. You're not going to tell me."

"Nothing to tell," Kellie said.

Kearns exited the highway and drove into a neighborhood of small brick homes. There were many with noticeable additions. There were no "McMansions" on the streets he was navigating.

Kellie strained her eyes to see the house numbers, relying on porch lights to provide any illumination where the house numbers were attached.

"We're close. Should be on your side," Kellie said.

Kearns pulled into a driveway. There was no garage. The red-brick house seemed small compared to the new-builds in the region. Kellie walked up the half-dozen concrete steps leading to the front door and pressed the doorbell. Kearns stood behind her.

When the door opened, Kellie saw that Duong stood eye-to-eye with her although he stood a few inches higher than her inside the house. "Mr. Duong, this is FBI Agent Kearns," she said as she turned so that she didn't block Duong's line of sight.

Agent Kearns held out his FBI credentials.

"You told me there was no trouble if I looked at the documents," Duong said, irritated that Kellie was accompanied by an FBI agent. She had said nothing when she called that she'd be accompanied by anyone.

"Mr. Duong, you're not in any trouble. Ms. Liang and I are working together, and it will speed things up if we both hear what you have to say. I promise you that everything is fine. Ms. Liang is a witness to my assurances to you," Kearns said.

Duong retreated slowly from the doorway and waved them into the house. Stepping in, Kellie and Agent Kearns stood in the small living room where a sofa and two recliners created an L-shaped sitting area.

Duong led them to a small dining room where a table for four was set up with little room for anyone to walk if all four chairs were occupied. Duong gestured for Kellie and Kearns to take seats away from the doorway they'd come through as Duong went into the kitchen and brought them glasses of water then sat.

Kellie had removed the documents while they waited for Duong.

"Mr. Duong, as I explained when I called, we have these documents in Vietnamese," Kellie said, placing a hand on one pile of documents. "The documents in this other folder are in English." Kellie had a red tab indicating the pages she needed Duong to compare. "Can you tell us if any of the pages in Vietnamese look like they are the same as these that are in English?"

As Duong listened to Kellie, he never heard her say that the two of them had met earlier and sensed that the FBI agent didn't know about the afternoon meeting. Duong excused himself and left the table.

"Are you sure about this?" Kearns whispered.

"I haven't heard you propose anything. Do you have any better ideas?"

Duong returned wearing his glasses. "Now I can see," he said. He slid the two piles of documents toward him. He studied six pages of the English language documents. It took time. "Not easy to read and understand. It's very technical," Duong said. He flipped over the first four pages of Vietnamese then focused on the fifth page where he seemed to be stumped by his native language.

"I'm sorry, but even Vietnamese is technical. I must read it carefully," Duong said.

Kellie had a pocket-sized notepad on the table. The fingers of her right hand twirled a pen as if it was a miniature baton.

"Okay," Duong said after forty-five minutes. He leaned against the back of his chair, took off his glasses and rubbed his eyes. "I don't understand everything because the writing is strange to me. I'm not familiar with some of the technical words, but my opinion is that the Vietnamese document and these pages in English that you want me to compare appear to be the same. That is what I think."

Kellie and Kearns looked at each other hearing Duong confirm what they suspected.

"Mr. Duong, you've done us a great favor," Kearns said. "I want to repeat that you are not in any trouble. In fact, I am grateful that you were willing to help us this evening." Kearns gave Duong his card. "If you ever think there's anything I can do to help you, please give me a call."

As Kellie gathered up the documents and replaced them in their respective folders, she pulled out an envelope with a check she'd prepared earlier. "I wish you success in your new part-time translation business," she said as she handed the envelope to Duong.

"Too old for a new business," Duong said.

Duong trailed his two guests to the door. After they pulled out of his driveway, he picked up the envelope and business cards, turned off all the lights downstairs and climbed the steps. In his bedroom facing the rear of the house, Duong turned on a bedside lamp and sat on the side of the bed. From the bedside table's drawer, he pulled out an address book. He punched in a number and waited.

"Colonel?"

"Captain Duong. This is a surprise." It was a familiar gravelly voice of an older man. "Are you in trouble?"

"I don't know, that's why I'm calling. An FBI agent and woman just left. They asked me to translate some documents."

"Who's the woman," the Colonel asked.

"She works for a senator. I looked her up after I met her this afternoon. She gave me her business card. She's supposed to become a high-level person at the State Department," Duong said. He read the details from Kellie's and Kearns's business cards.

"Are the documents you looked at classified?"

"They told me the documents aren't classified, but I'm worried that I could be in trouble," Doung said.

"Leave it with me. I'll double check and make sure that there aren't any problems."

"Thank you," Doung said and ended the call.

Looking down at the envelope on the bed, he opened it and saw the check for five hundred dollars. Duong smiled and shrugged. Staring at the check, he wondered just how much his help had really been worth. The afternoon and evening had been profitable given the amount of time he'd spent reading the documents. Making seven hundred tax-free dollars for the day, he guessed he shouldn't talk to anyone about what he'd read in the afternoon and evening.

"That was helpful," Kellie said as she rode with Kearns.

"In more ways than one," Kearns responded. "Mr. Duong's assessment helps both of us. You can get back to your DHS guy and I have more to go on when we confront the patent office."

"What's that all about," Kellie asked.

"I'm going to play my FBI card and tell you that I can't divulge things yet. You'll find out soon," Kearns said.

Driving back into D.C., Kearns dropped Kellie off in front of her apartment. As she turned in the seat and exited the car, Kearns pressed the button to roll down the passenger window. "You've met with him before haven't you," Kearns guessed.

"What makes you say that?"

"This evening was arranged too quickly. You don't just find some guy that fast. It takes a little hunting and digging."

Kellie was bent down slightly to look through the passenger window. "I'm playing my Capitol Hill card."

Kearns laughed. "Send me a summary note about Duong's comments on the documents. I need to have something for the file."

"It'll be in your inbox before you're home. Later," Kellie said, turning and heading into her building.

After feeling the warm April evening air during the few moments walking from the car to the building, she pulled a window open once in the apartment. Kellie changed into a tee-shirt and jogging shorts. She opted for her love seat, sat cross-legged, and placed her laptop on her lap. A short note to Aaron took priority over the summary Kearns wanted.

Kellie made sure that her note to Aaron explained that she had an unofficial translation that was done by a native Vietnamese individual whose name she wasn't willing to disclose. She assured Aaron that the Vietnamese document that included the proposed Chinese patent file was based on a patent application filed in the U.S. and that the translator believed that the Chinese information was based on the stolen information because of the dates of the documents involved. Kellie's summary to Kearns differed slightly from her note to Aaron.

It had been a good day even though her bank account took a big hit, she thought. She decided to do something she rarely did by herself. She uncorked a chilled bottle of white Bordeaux and poured herself a glass.

* * * * *

After receiving the written summary of the Vietnamese documents Aaron had brought, Bruce Hoover worked the phones and walked the halls in the consulate to gather a team of people. He distributed copies of the summary. A couple of people scratched their heads wondering what the big deal was while a couple of others picked up their phones and called people at the U.S. Embassy in Hanoi. Hoover wasn't sure whether to sketch out a plan of action or let someone with a higher pay grade make the call about next steps.

Hoover saw Aaron still sitting where he'd left his visitor hours earlier. "You seem to be comfortable behind my desk. We seem to have a bit of confusion about what to do with the information we've uncovered. So, right now, I'd be happy to let you take over."

"It gets better," Aaron said.

"Meaning what," Hoover prompted with a slightly alarmed look.

"Meaning while you consulted others, I received an email from the States. According to my D.C. contact, the Vietnamese document I sent includes the patent info stolen from U.S. patent applications recently. She had her translator compare the language of the patent application to the Vietnamese document."

"I think the question is what's next for us?"

Hoover took the guest's chair in his office. He and Aaron looked at each other.

"I'm going to suggest something, but we'll need the CG to do something quickly," Aaron said.

"I don't tell the Consul General what to do or how quickly to do it. He's the boss in this building," Hoover reminded Aaron.

"Get ten minutes of his time, explain what we've uncovered and suggest that he go see the Administrator at the Maritime Administration. While he's there, he could drop as many hints as possible that we need to maintain an open line of communication for our mutual commercial interests. You might ask the CG to throw in something about our Deputy Chief of Mission at the embassy having an upcoming meeting with the head of Vietnam's intellectual property office about Vietnam meeting its obligations under the bilateral agreement," Aaron suggested.

"Do we know if the DCM has a meeting scheduled?"

"No, but you could propose to the CG that he make a call to the embassy and ask the DCM to do that as part of our strategy," Aaron answered. "Look, this is soft pressure. It's a way to deliver a message to the Maritime Administration that we're on to what the Chinese are doing. Another option is for the CG to insist on a meeting and lay this all out on the table. It's the CG's choice."

"Maybe both of us should meet with him," Hoover proposed.

"Look at me. I'm not dressed to meet with the CG."

"You know the job comes first. I think he can overlook your fashion choice for the day," Hoover answered. Hoover mentally rearranged his next steps. Instead of meeting with staff members he'd identified as having an interest in the China-Vietnam antics that had been uncovered, he called the CG's office and said he needed to speak to the CG on an urgent development.

"We're getting squeezed in between the CG's return from his lunch meeting and the beginning of his afternoon agenda. I'm going to let you do the talking. You're more familiar with what's been going on here and back home," Hoover said.

"How much time do we have before the CG's back in the building," Aaron asked.

"Just over an hour. Use the time to prep what you're going to say and, remember, we'll only get a few minutes of the CG's time," Hoover advised.

"Maybe I can run back to the hotel, change and come back."

"Forget about your fucking clothes and focus!"

Aaron glared at Hoover for a moment. "You're right." Aaron sat in the corner of Hoover's office where the woman had been reading documents earlier. He grabbed a piece of paper and started writing the bullet points to cover for the CG meeting.

Hoover's office a/c was on high, but it didn't stop Aaron from feeling sweat rolling down from his scalp and down the side of his face. Aaron's head snapped toward Hoover's desk at the sound of the ringing phone. He watched as Hoover answered and nodded a couple of times.

"Just a slight change in schedule in our favor," Hoover said as he hung up. "The CG's secretary said to get to the office in about ten minutes. We're going to get a few extra minutes of his time. Get your thoughts together."

Aaron looked down at his three sheets of paper where he had scribbled, lined out what he'd written and rewritten his bullet points. He should be better at this, he thought. He folded one of the sheets lengthwise and wrote on the blank side of the paper.

"I hope you're not going to read to the CG," Hoover said.

"No. I just need to get things in order," Aaron replied.

Hoover walked to the office door and gave Aaron a nod to get moving.

Aaron followed Hoover to the CG's office. The outer office where the secretary sat was large enough to accommodate several people who might have to wait for the CG.

"He should be here in about five," the secretary said, her eyes lingering over Aaron as they stood waiting. "Take a seat."

When the Consul General walked in, his suit jacket was draped over his forearm and his necktie was loose. "Follow me, gentlemen," the CG ordered. The CG's office was huge with a small conference table, desk, leather sofa and chairs. He hung his jacket on a hook behind his office door and rolled up the sleeves of his white shirt.

Aaron and Bruce Hoover followed the tall, thin man into his office. Aaron thought the CG might've been a basketball player in his younger days. The CG was six-four or six-five in height, very lean and had salt and pepper hair.

Aaron and Bruce Hoover stood in front of the CG's desk. "Take a seat," the CG said, sitting on the edge of his chair behind the desk and the fingers of his hands interlaced on his desk.

"Aaron Foster is with DHS in D.C. Although he's here on vacation, he came across something that we think you should be aware of. We're hoping you might intervene in some way," Hoover began.

"Okay, Mr. Foster. You're on. Tell me what I need to know and what your suggested plan of action is," the CG said.

Hoping to grab the CG's attention right away, Aaron started with the patent examiner's arrest for the attempted hand-off of confidential information to the Chinese. Aaron explained that the Chinese had given the Maritime Administration documents in Vietnamese that were based on the stolen patent files and the information from the U.S. patent office. Aaron summarized how he believed the Chinese were proposing to use the documents. Aaron raised the point of Meilin Moy, the top executive of ChiTran and CODE, being en route to Vietnam.

"How do we know about the timing of a possible meeting between Moy and the Maritime Administration," the CG asked.

"I got that information from my D.C. contact," Aaron said.

"I'd like to know who you are getting all this from," the CG said.

"She's a staffer to a senator."

"Who is she? She's a staffer but is she reliable? How junior or senior is she on this senator's staff? All staffers are not created equal as with so many things."

Aaron knew he wasn't going to be able to withhold the name. "Kellie Liang, someone I've known for many years and very reliable. She's also a nominee for a position at the State Department."

The CG's chair swiveled as Aaron mentioned Kellie's name. His eyes narrowed as he looked at his computer screen. "Here it is. The name sounded familiar as soon as you said it. We may be a long way from D.C., but I still keep up with what's going on within my own agency and definitely so with names of people who I might be working with in the future," the CG commented. "Her bio is very impressive. Okay, so what do we do about this mess? We can't just barge into a Vietnamese government office. We don't have a lot of time to send a message that we know what they are up to. I'm also concerned that we might show too much of our hand. They'll want to know how we know so much."

"If I may," Aaron started, "that last point about how we know so much gets complicated but there have been too many coincidences. This is going to take a few minutes," Aaron said, mindful of the CG's time.

"Don't worry about the clock, this is important enough to make others wait," the CG said.

Aaron gave the CG an abbreviated version of his trip with his uncle, the search for the bargirl and discovery of Linh and learning that she worked for the Maritime Administration. Aaron added the fact that Linh's boyfriend worked at CODE.

"This sounds more like a novel of some kind," the CG said, sitting back comfortably in his chair. The CG was almost chuckling as he looked at Aaron and Hoover and mulled over everything he'd heard.

"I'll get my secretary to nail down a meeting with the administrator over at Maritime. We'll make it clear that we want it tomorrow, but no later than the day after. As for your uncle's possible daughter and what she's done to help you, she could be in a precarious situation. Let me talk to Ms. Doan and see what we can do about her and a visa. Aaron, I want you to accompany me to the meeting at Maritime as soon as that's scheduled. Be sure my secretary has your phone number or some other way to reach you," the CG said. "Okay, mission accomplished, thanks for keeping my job interesting, gentlemen." The CG stood up, signaling to Aaron and Hoover that they were finished.

"Very interesting man," Aaron said as he and Hoover walked back to Hoover's office.

* * * * *

Aaron parted with Hoover after the CG's meeting, knowing that Hoover would brief others in the consulate. Aaron taxied back to the hotel. Drew sat waiting in the lobby with his outstretched legs crossed at the ankles.

"I wasn't sure I'd see you here," Aaron said. "Hope you haven't been waiting too long."

"Show me your room," Drew insisted. "I haven't checked out of the other place yet. I'm not giving up the room over there until I know what I'm moving to and right now, I'm not impressed with what I've seen." Drew surveyed the small lobby with its old furniture covered by worn fabrics and discolored vinyl flooring.

"Then there's no need to see my room," Aaron said.

"That bad?"

"Could be worse," Aaron remarked.

"Yeah, it could be a sleeping bag on the ground without a mosquito net. Now that we've settled that, what's going on with Linh?"

"About that, there's been a little development," Aaron started. He looked around and noted that there was no one else in the lobby and took a seat next to his uncle. "She's an operator. She figured out a way to get some documents for me from her Chinese boyfriend's office. With that in hand, I've been working with the consulate here and folks back in D.C. As far as you're concerned, you should be pleased that the CG appreciates what Linh did and he's aware that it might put her in a tight spot. He's willing to ask Ms. Doan to get things moving on the visa front. You should check in with Ms. Doan and see what you and Linh need to do."

"What did Linh do?" Drew asked.

Aaron described Linh's flirting with the security guard and how a little cash and alcohol played a part in getting keys to the boyfriend's office. "I didn't go into all those details with the CG, but he understands that she had a hand in all of this and he's showing his appreciation by asking Ms. Doan to look into helping her."

"The better question is whether she's in any kind of danger by staying here," Drew wondered. "What about you? Are you now working, vacationing, what?"

"Until I get on a plane, most of my time is probably going to be working. It's either being in contact with Kellie or working with Hoover here," Aaron answered. "You should be hearing from Ms. Doan. If you don't, give her a call and get things going. We might find ourselves in a time crunch."

"Does that mean I'm biding my time in the hotel room?"

"I'd stick around the hotel. Let the staff know where you are in case Ms. Doan calls, or the hotel can help you get a cheap pre-paid phone with a local number for the rest of your trip. Once you have it, make sure Linh, Ms. Doan and I have the number," Aaron suggested.

"What's next for you as you play secret agent," Drew asked.

Almost on cue, Aaron's phone vibrated, and he reached to answer it. The call lasted less than a minute. "I've got an appointment with the CG tomorrow afternoon. We have some time this afternoon, this evening and in the morning. We should get a hold of Linh and tell her some of what's going on," Aaron said. "Come to think of it, let's go out and I'll help you get that pre-paid phone. No sense in waiting and then we'll call Linh."

A young man behind the reception counter gave Aaron and Drew directions. They found a small street-front stall where a young man sat on a stool surrounded by hundreds of cell phones and accessories. Using a few words of English and a lot of pointing and hand gestures, they left the young man with a pre-paid phone after twenty minutes. The enterprising young man made a call using the phone to show Drew that it was powered up and ready to use. Drew put the scrap paper with his new phone number in his slim wallet.

"What next?" Drew asked.

"Let's find a place to sit and call Linh."

Over the next two hours, Drew called Linh's number half a dozen times. She never answered. "We have no clue where her apartment is do we?"

"She's never given us an address. We've always met somewhere," Aaron answered.

"What do you think?"

"Hard to know what's going on. She could've met up with the boyfriend, gone out with friends from work, gone shopping, who knows," Aaron said.

Linh left work at the usual time among the crowd of co-workers through the main front doors when she didn't see Jun. She hoped that he'd gotten the message that things were not as they were a few days ago. Having cut off contact with him, she still glanced into folders and kept track of what Jun might want but didn't make copies of anything.

All day, she tried to understand why Aaron had so much interest in the documents that Jun wanted her to copy. Every time she looked at them, she gave up because nothing she read made sense to her. She kept telling herself that she wasn't smart enough to understand them, but she decided that if someone else found the documents in Jun's possession they would think of her, and it could create problems for her. She would probably lose her job.

Then she saw him in the Maritime building meeting with the highest officials regularly. To Linh, Jun's working relationship with the senior officers had become too cozy, too fast. She couldn't think of any foreigner having the kind of open-door access that Jun had with the most senior people especially since he had only been in Vietnam for several months.

As she walked out into the late day heat, Linh reached into her pants pocket and felt the two loose keys to Jun's office. It reminded her that she had a task for later in the evening. After hooking up with Mai for a casual light dinner and a drink, she feigned yawns and an exaggerated effort to keep her eyes open. As far as Mai was concerned, Linh was headed home.

Linh detoured away from the route to her apartment once she was out of Mai's sight. She hailed a motorcycle taxi, hopped on, and gave directions. She secured her shoulder bag onto her lap with the shoulder strap crossing her body. She stopped the driver on the main avenue where it intersected with the side street to Jun's office building and apartment. It had been dark for a couple of hours. It was nearing nine o'clock. She hoped it was late enough that the foot traffic through the building would be minimal.

The building's lobby lights lit up the concrete steps leading up to the entrance door. The familiar security guard was on duty and once he saw her, she was greeted by a wide smile, causing the man's eyes to appear closed. The collar of the guard's khaki colored uniform was stained with sweat. Linh approached the desk, and she saw the security guard lean to his right and heard a drawer open. He raised the bottle she'd brought for him that was still half full.

Linh sat on the corner of the desk as she had before and let her shoulder bag hang at her side. She sipped the cup of whiskey that he poured. She chatted for several minutes.

"You want to go up?"

"Yes. I'll need the keys again," Linh said, surprised that he asked without prompting.

In the elevator, Linh put Jun's office key back on the keyring and kept the extra key in her pocket. She stepped out of the elevator and into the dimly lit area outside the doors to Jun's offices. Once inside, she locked the door. She stood in the dark for a minute to allow her vision to adjust. As her eyes saw the faint outlines of the chairs and desks, she walked to Jun's office in the rear of the space. In his office, a flickering light source outside helped Linh avoid walking into a coffee table and a floor lamp.

Linh pushed the office door closed but didn't let it latch. She flipped on a floor lamp and looked around. The pile of document folders on the desk caught her eye. Her eyes roamed the rest of the office and saw a bookcase also piled with document folders. The document folders on Jun's desk were labeled in Chinese. She spread the three two-inch thick folders across the desk, hoping that the documents themselves would be in Vietnamese.

Inside the first folder, stapled pages in Vietnamese were separated from the Chinese pages. She identified the Vietnamese pages as copies she'd made for Jun. She pulled the Vietnamese documents out of the folder. She did the same with the other two folders. Finding a waste basket, she piled the Vietnamese language documents on the floor next to the waste basket and knelt on the floor. She felt inside her shoulder bag and pulled out a lighter and plastic bags. She took the first stapled batch of papers on the floor, flicked the lighter on and let the flame consume the paper, dropping the ashes into the waste basket.

The elevator chimed. Linh dropped the burning papers, stomping out the flames and jumped up to turn off the floor lamp. She went to Jun's office door and pulled it open, peeking around the door frame.

The security guard stepped out of the elevator. He walked to the door and pulled it. Linh watched him put his face to the glass, cupping his hands around his face to make out what was going on inside the darkened office. Linh knew that he expected to see her there. After another minute passed, he re-entered the elevator and left. Linh checked her watch. She'd been in Jun's office for thirty minutes and the guard had given her his key ring. She needed more time, but she worried that he'd go down and call Jun.

Linh worked with the light from the lighter. She finished burning all the documents she'd had in her pile, wishing she could look through more files but decided she shouldn't push her luck. She grabbed the plastic bags, doubled them, and dumped the ashes from the waste basket into the plastic bags. She tied the bags and put them in her shoulder bag and zipped it. In the dark, she stacked the document folders on Jun's desk and placed the pile where they'd been before she moved them.

There was nothing she could do about the odor or the ashes she'd stomped on and ground into the flooring. Without an open window, anyone would know that something had been burning. One look at the floor and the search would be on for what was put to flame.

She'd been in the office longer than she intended but convinced herself that it couldn't be helped. She let herself out of the office, relocked the office door, and pressed the button for the elevator.

"Where have you been? You have all my keys," the security guard said as soon as he saw Linh exit the elevator.

"I'm so sorry, but while I was in Mr. Yao's office, I saw something I needed to talk to him about and went to see him. I should've brought the keys back sooner. I'm very sorry," Linh said, hoping that the guard wouldn't call Jun to confirm her story.

"Okay, but I can't keep giving you the keys."

"Maybe you can have an extra made for me," Linh said smiling.

"I'm not allowed to do that," the guard replied.

"I'm joking," Linh said. "Goodnight." Walking up the side street, she was near the intersection and saw a trash bin. She dropped the bagged ashes of the documents.

Linh walked. The more distance she put between her and Jun's office the more she knew that those burned documents burned the bridge between her and Jun. She wouldn't be able to afford her apartment. Her days of living what she believed to be her life of luxury were done. There were two choices. She could return to the days of scrimping for everything she needed while sharing living spaces with others or do whatever Drew Foster said she had to do to get that visa.

Jolt

It was Agent Kearns's first visit to the Patent Office's new headquarters building in Alexandria, Virginia. Entering the building, he craned his neck to gawk at the ground to ceiling glass atrium of the new building. Being a government guy, he thought it was a monument to wasted space. For a building built to accommodate a government agency, it projected questionable decision-making by failing to maximize workspace in his opinion.

Kearns didn't know who was stirring the pot, but his summary about the night with Meilin Moy had attracted attention. As he walked toward a security desk, he realized that whoever was behind what he was there to do was irrelevant. The instructions came from above and he was there to follow through with his team. Agents Olvera, Jamison, and Adams were in tow. They wore their FBI vests over light shirts and tactical pants along with their firearms. Kearns was told that coordination had occurred between the FBI and local law enforcement officers who would be showing up in minutes to help with the afternoon's mission.

After flashing his credentials, the security guards instructed Kearns to wait.

"I was going up to meet with the director," Kearns said.

"No, I've been told that the director will be meeting you here and he'll take you down to the auditorium," a female security guard responded.

Kearns turned away and huddled with his colleagues at the top of a long set of stairs.

"We've got company," Olvera said, causing the agents to reposition themselves into a line to greet the man they assumed was the director.

The director was of average height with neatly combed thin white hair. He was in a dark blue suit, white shirt and had a well-knotted red and blue tie. "Who's in charge?" the director asked when he was within several feet of the group of agents. To the director's side, a man looking to be in his forties, about twenty years younger than the director, stood silent.

Chris Kearns took a half-step forward and extended his right hand. The director stopped and folded his arms. The man accompanying the director dropped his head slightly and directed his eyes to the floor, looking embarrassed when the director refused to shake Kearns's hand.

"Why are you here dressed like you're conducting a raid? I thought this was going to be a low-key thing," the director said. His Texas-tanned face was tense.

Kearns ignored the director's rudeness. "I'm sure you've been informed about our task this afternoon. We consider the task and determine how to prepare for it and what we need to be prepared for to fulfill that task," Kearns explained.

"I don't appreciate late night calls and orders with a short deadline to prepare. My staff was running around and calling all morning to get this done," the director said.

"I'm sorry about that but I had nothing to do with any of that. As you say, people far above us made decisions. I'm here to follow the instructions I've been given, that's all," Kearns replied. "Could you tell me what they were told about this afternoon's meeting," Kearns asked.

"We told them that we were starting an agency-wide personnel security review and that this three o'clock meeting is mandatory. If they don't attend, they would be putting their participation in the agency's tuition assistance program at risk. I wasn't sure who was taking the lead so seeing you and those other agents dressed this way is upsetting," the director said. "These people aren't criminals," the director added.

"Sir, I would remind you that we're here doing this because one of your employees is exactly that, a criminal," Kearns responded.

The director looked over to Curtis Campbell, his chief of staff. "Mr. Campbell will take over for me." The director turned on his heels and walked away.

"Sorry about that," Curtis said. "When you've been the top guy at a large law firm and used to being the one to make other people jump on your command, it's hard to be appointed to a job by the President and find out that there are lots of other people with more power, more connections, and more pull than you. These first few weeks have not been easy for the director."

"He'll learn," Kearns said. "Either he'll figure it out and adapt or he won't be in town very long."

"Moving on, here are copies of the list of names I was told to provide," Curtis said, handing Kearns a small pile of papers.

Kearns took them and glanced at the list that had forty-five names then handed copies to his team and instructed them to distribute them to the uniformed local police officers who arrived and waited just inside the main entrance. Olvera took them over.

"How many entrances are there to the building," Kearns asked.

"I'm not sure. I'll have the security guard help you get your people where you want them," Curtis replied.

Kearns and his team made sure there was a police officer posted at every entry and exit point. The instructions were to allow anyone to enter but check anyone exiting against the list Curtis Campbell had provided. Anyone on the list wouldn't be allowed to exit unless Kearns or one of his team approved it.

Campbell led Kearns and his team down to the auditorium. The back of the building was one level lower than where Kearns and his team had entered. At the bottom of the stairs, a uniformed officer was already standing by the back entrance to the building going out to the street. Kearns eyed the wide-open area they were walking through and decided that they didn't all need to be in the auditorium.

"David, why don't you hang out near the bottom of the steps. Ed, you can take up a spot on the opposite side of the auditorium near the food court area," Kearns instructed. "Vera and I will be inside the auditorium with Curtis."

When they entered, there were people sitting in the auditorium scattered around the room. Kearns went to the front of the auditorium. "I'd appreciate it if you could all take seats up front in the first couple of rows. We'll get your names before we get started," Kearns said.

He asked Vera and Curtis to coax anyone hesitant in moving to the front.

As the number of people waiting in the auditorium approached the number expected, Kearns was struck by the diversity of the small group of men and women as well as their ethnicity. As they moved to the seats in the front, several Asian employees sat next to each other while several women also sat clustered together. A few of the white and African Americans sat next to each other. Just like the shock of finding out that a patent examiner could be targeted by the Chinese, he had never given any thought to the diversity of people who worked at the Patent Office. Honestly, he had never thought about the Patent Office as an area of risk. That was until now.

Outside the auditorium, David Olvera walked around the open area next to the long stairway leading down from the main floor atrium area. He noticed that several people had looked his way longer than normal because of his FBI vest. He'd seen several stopped by the uniformed officer at the door to be checked against the list before exiting.

Olvera noticed a long auburn-haired young man in jeans, rolled up flannel shirt sleeves and a small computer bag over his shoulder give him a darting look as he strode toward the auditorium. Olvera stopped moving and watched. The young man disappeared into the doorway but exited a second later, heading in the opposite direction toward Agent Adams.

Olvera jogged after the young man. "Hey, hold up," Olvera yelled out.

The young man looked over his shoulder at Olvera but didn't stop. He cut through the food court area of counters and racks. He saw another man begin running toward him from a different direction. He ran for an exit and saw a uniformed officer standing in front of the door.

The police officer, seeing the young man running toward him with two agents pursuing, stepped in front of the door. He wore a vest under his uniform and felt confident that even if the young man didn't slow or stop, no harm would be done to him. The officer judged that he outweighed the man coming at him by fifty pounds. He let his right hand rest on his pistol. As the officer prepared to absorb the young man's body colliding into him, the only thought he had was *what the hell is this moron thinking.* The officer widened his stance, took one step forward and lowered his shoulder into the young man's midsection and watched the body crumple to the floor. If he had wanted, the officer could have slammed the man to the floor. Instead, he lifted the man to his feet then shoved him backwards into the arms of Olvera and Adams coming from behind.

"This young man assaulted me," the officer said with a grin. "I was just standing there, and he deliberately ran into me. You two are witnesses."

Olvera and Adams stifled a laugh. "We'll make sure to note that you prevented this man from hurting himself by preventing him from falling after he assaulted you," Olvera said. "Thanks."

Olvera and Adams each had an arm and walked the man to a nearby table and chairs. "I want to see some identification," Olvera demanded.

The young man dug into his back pocket and put a Virginia driver's license on the table.

"I want to see your office ID, too," Olvera said. Once on the table, Olvera compared the two forms of identification.

"Devon Conrad," Olvera read aloud. The names on the agency badge and driver's license matched. "Are you supposed to be in the auditorium?"

Conrad's eyes went back and forth between Adams and Olvera. "Yeah. I got an email from my supervisor and voice message telling me I had to attend."

"Why did you see us and run," Olvera asked.

Conrad's chair squeaked as his left leg pumped nervously under the table and the fingers of his left hand tapped the table. "Saw you guys and the cops at the door and got nervous. I've got some outstanding issues."

"What kind of issues," Adams asked.

"We're about to get started. What's going on out here," Kearns said as he marched toward the table.

"We're hoping Mr. Conrad can explain why he changed his mind about attending the meeting and ran for the exit," Olvera answered. "He's about to explain what outstanding issues he has with the law."

Devon Conrad looked at his three-person audience. "I've skipped out of paying a couple of restaurant checks and I have a handful of parking tickets and a speeding ticket," he said sheepishly.

"And you think the FBI is here because of that?" Kearns said, looking up at the ceiling and shaking his head. "I'm going back into the auditorium. We're locating a couple of people who haven't shown up. And get his butt in there."

"Let's go," Adams instructed. Adams and Olvera walked Devon Conrad into the auditorium and to the front row.

Kearns was at the front of the room and ready. He walked over to Olvera. "Take that guy, Conrad, and do a one-on-one with him. He may be rattled enough to answer any questions. I'll proceed in here as planned," Kearns said.

As Kearns got ready to speak, he saw a security guard escorting the lone absentee into the auditorium. "You can take this seat right up front. This gentleman's leaving," Kearns said and pointed to the chair that Devon Conrad was vacating.

Olvera took Devon Conrad out to the food court area. He led Conrad to a table in the corner. This time of day, the area was nearly deserted. Having a general idea about the program Conrad and the others were participating in, Olvera wanted to get Devon Conrad talking by asking him to describe the program and why he needed to be in the tuition reimbursement program.

Conrad confessed that he incurred a lot of debt in college and couldn't offset it with part-time work. He admitted that he lived beyond his means and put lots of expenses on credit cards.

"Other than skipping out on those restaurant bills and letting those ticket expenses pile up, have you done anything else that's illegal," Olvera asked.

"No. If I had done anything like that before I had this job, I probably wouldn't have been hired," Conrad answered.

"Do you have acquaintances or friends from other countries?"

"No. We have some people who were born abroad who work here or their parents came from abroad," Conrad said.

"How about your classes? Do you have classmates from abroad," Olvera posed.

"Sure. There are some foreign students."

"Are you friends with any of them? Do any of them work for a foreign government?"

"Not friends, but I had one guy who seemed like he wanted to be friends, but it got a bit uncomfortable, so I just kept my distance."

"Explain that a little more," Olvera prompted.

"He'd ask me what I did at work, where I worked, how long I'd worked there and if I had a specialty of any kind. I mean, he didn't ask me all these at once, but whenever he'd see me, it would be one or two questions then talking about nothing at all. Anytime I asked him those questions, he'd clam up. It was like he wanted me to spill my guts, but he kept everything about himself to himself. I thought that was a little too strange."

"Do you know what country he's from and what he did during the day?"

"He was Asian. Could be Chinese, Japanese, Korean. Like I said, I decided that it was all too strange and kept my distance."

"You ever see him with your patent colleagues who were attending classes at the same law school?"

"Yeah. A couple of times I saw him having coffee with Lucas Moore. Between classes or before evening classes started, I'd see them," Conrad offered.

"You do know about Moore's situation, right?"

"I heard. Pretty stupid of him. I admit that I've done some dumb stuff, but what he did was really stupid."

"Lucas Moore was giving that guy, who works for the Chinese Embassy, information," Olvera said. "Have you seen that same Chinese guy getting close to other people at the law school?"

"No. Like I said, I started ignoring the guy. You could talk to a couple of others taking evening courses at the same place. They might know," Conrad said.

Olvera slid a blank piece of paper across the table to Devon Conrad. "Write down your name, emails and all your phone numbers," Olvera instructed. "You'll have to deal with your tickets and skipping out on those food bills on your own. We have no interest in that," Olvera added. "One last thing, here's my card. If you are ever approached by a foreign government person about your work and what you do and questions like that, give me a call. That is something we want to know about. If someone does that, try to get their name and where they work. You're good to go. Get in the auditorium with the rest of your colleagues."

"What about the cop over there?"

Olvera chuckled. "He's good." Olvera sat and watched Conrad walking toward and entering the auditorium. He drifted over to the auditorium doorway and saw Kearns and Jamison talking to two people while all the others were getting checked-off of the list and allowed to leave.

"I don't know what your security protocols are, but you should have a thorough search conducted on their computers and anything else at their workstations," Kearns said to Curtis Campbell after two employees volunteered information about having contact with Xiong Zimo.

"Do we let them go back to work?" Campbell asked.

"I wouldn't let them do anything until everything is checked out. They've agreed to let us look through their backpacks before they leave," Kearns added. "This is a government facility; they use government equipment, and they know that everything is subject to search since they are accessing information provided to them in their official capacity. We need to be sure there haven't been any illegal information transmissions," Kearns explained.

"I'll have our tech people take a look right away," Campbell responded. "Otherwise, are we finished?"

"For today, yeah. You have thousands of people looking at a lot of sensitive information. They need to have it in the backs of their minds that there could be random checks about handling information. You need to warn them about people hoping to gain their trust and get information from them," Kearns said.

"The Lucas Moore case was a wake-up call," Campbell said.

"The implications of that case are still being played out because of the far-reaching effects it's having. It's over for Moore, but we're still working on that case," Kearns added.

"Will you be able to let me know more down the road?"

"If it'll help get your staff to be more careful and sensitive to these issues, sure," Kearns answered. "It's becoming clearer to me that Xiong Zimo from the Chinese Embassy was good at finding his potential targets and we have no way of knowing whether the

Chinese, or other countries, have other people like him doing the same thing," Kearns said.

* * * * *

After walking through the CODE office door, Jun Yao's nose crinkled as he entered. He grabbed the handkerchief in his back pocket and covered his nose and mouth. With morning light streaming through the rear windows in his office, it cast more light into the main workspace. Jun's head swiveled back and forth looking for anything hinting at something burning. There was no smoke anywhere. Nothing was charred in the main work area that his staff occupied during the day.

Jun marched into his personal office and the odor was stronger. He stopped in the doorway but saw nothing out of place on his desk or the table in his office. His eyes went to the floor and saw the leftover black ashes leaving a black-stained spot on the floor. He walked to the back wall of his office and pushed windows open, hoping the air would replace the smokey stench. Sitting down at his desk, he used his legs to wheel his chair toward the discolored floor. He stared at the spot then sat back in his chair. He wheeled it back behind his desk and let his eyes roam the desk's surface from left to right. His pens and calendar were where he expected them to be. The pile of folders on the right corner didn't appear to be touched.

Jun tugged desk drawers. They were still locked. He walked over to the shelves behind the closet's folding doors. Nothing appeared to be moved. Back in his chair at the desk, he slid the pile of folders toward him.

"No! No!"

Chau Bui ran to Jun's office door. "Are you okay?"

Jun's head snapped toward her. He hadn't heard anyone arrive at the office. His head tilted back and rested on the back of his chair.

"I'm sorry. Yes, I'm okay. Please go back to your desk," Jun said noticing that the lights in the main workspace had been turned on.

Chau was slow to turn away, giving Jun a long look before walking away.

Jun searched through the pile of folders. The Vietnamese language documents were missing from several folders. Jun went to

Chau's desk. "Get someone to change the lock on our door. I want it done today," he ordered.

Jun marched out of his office and went straight to the elevator. In the lobby, Jun went straight for the uniformed security officer. "Who worked last night," he said in Chinese, then tried to his best to speak in Vietnamese.

"Not me," the guard said, seeing Jun's reddened face.

Chau, seeing her boss's angry look had followed Jun out of the office, but had to wait for another elevator.

Jun spoke slowly to get every word right but couldn't say everything he wanted the security guard to understand. Frustrated, he switched to Chinese when he saw Chau rushing toward the security desk. She delivered an accurate translation. "You tell the building manager to call us right away. We want whoever worked last night to tell us who had our office key, who went there and then the guard should be fired from his job." When Chau finished, Jun gave Chau a nod and they turned and went back to the elevator before the security guard had any chance to respond.

In Jun's mind there was only one person who would have entered the office and burned those documents. He didn't need this complication just before Meilin was going to arrive. He had no intention of allowing his problems with Linh to surface while Meilin was in Vietnam. The most important task he had was to ensure that Meilin would have a successful meeting at the Maritime Administration.

Delay

Xiong Zimo deplaned at Tokyo's Narita Airport with a backpack slung over his shoulder and pulling a piece of wheeled carry-on luggage. He had two checked bags being transferred to another plane for his flight to Beijing. His eyelids were half closed. Twisting and turning in his narrow coach class seat for nearly fourteen hours from Washington Dulles Airport didn't allow for quality sleep.

Xiong wasn't given any advance warning that he was being transferred home. He was told that he needed more training to learn the subtleties of his work. He wasn't surprised. His close call in the Lucas Moore case didn't sit well with his bosses. He was given hours to pack up then handed a plane ticket. At Dulles Airport, he'd seen Meilin Moy, but because she was on a different flight, he had no chance to talk to her before departing.

Narita's international terminal teemed with travelers waiting for their flights or ending their trips and heading to immigration and customs. The airport was a major hub for flights in both directions across the Pacific Ocean. The time of day never mattered as the terminal was always filled with international travelers trying to find someplace to rest before another long flight.

Xiong wandered toward a screen listing departing flights. His journey began nineteen hours ago. It was late afternoon in Tokyo and in the middle of the night in Washington where he'd started. Finding his next flight on the monitor, Xiong's shoulders drooped when he saw that the flight was delayed with no new departure time listed. He found a single seat and plopped down in the crowd.

Several pairs of airport police officers strolled through the international terminal. With so many people transiting the terminal after long hours on planes, tempers could be short simply from fatigue in a place with limited places to rest. The police officers wore black uniforms with wide white belts and holstered pistols. They randomly stopped and checked passports and boarding passes. They stopped and gestured to people to remove their backpacks, purses and other belongings from seats and put their bags of items on the floor to free up seating.

Xiong Zimo melted into the background. To anyone looking around the terminal, he looked like he could be Japanese, Chinese, Korean or several other nationalities from the region. His eyes were closed when he felt the tap on his foot. Opening his eyes, he saw a pair of uniformed officers standing in front of him. They were young with close cut, short black hair. Physically, they looked like they could be twins with slim waists and slightly wider shoulders and standing at the same height.

"Passport."

Xiong Zimo dug into his jeans pocket and produced his Chinese passport. As he watched the officers examine his passport, he looked at the small metal name tag pinned to one of the officers' uniforms. Xiong didn't speak Japanese and though the written characters were familiar to him, he had to look at the alphabetical spelling of the names.

The officer holding Xiong's passport gave him a head nod. Xiong grabbed his backpack and the handle of his carry-on and followed the officer holding his passport. The second officer trailed him. As he followed, he glanced at the monitor as he passed it in case the status of his flight had changed. There was no departure time listed.

Xiong Zimo was escorted to an elevator and taken two floors down and into an interview room. The two young officers pointed to a chair for Xiong to take. Xiong placed the backpack on the table in front of him and the wheeled piece of luggage next to him. When one of the officers reached for the backpack, Xiong pushed himself out of the chair and grabbed the officer's arm. "No!"

The officer reaching for the backpack tugged it and moved it to the opposite side of the table. The second officer came around, placed both hands on Xiong's shoulders, and shoved him down into the chair. Once the officer let go of his shoulders, he pulled the wheeled piece of luggage toward the opposite wall.

Xiong saw an older officer standing against the wall with his arms folded. His hair was more gray than black, and his face was rounded out by full cheeks. He had slight bags under the eyes.

Getting his breathing under control, Xiong wondered why they had stopped him.

"You speak English," the older officer said.

"Yes," Xiong said and noticed that the older man had been handed Xiong's passport. Xiong didn't turn his head away from the older officer, but out of the corner of his eye, he saw one of the young officers standing at the end of the table rummaging through the backpack's various pockets.

Xiong gambled. He pulled out the Diplomatic Immunity identification card he had and put it on the table.

The older officer stepped forward to examine it. "Do you have one from the Japanese government?" He knew the answer. He glanced over to his young colleague who had three USB memory sticks in the palm of his hand. The older officer nodded and watched the young officer exit.

"What are you doing," Xiong asked.

"We do random checks in case anyone is trafficking in pornographic photographs or have images of children," the officer answered. "You relax. If everything is fine, you'll be allowed to go very soon."

When the older officer exited, Xiong heard the door latch and lock. He was alone in the room, noticing for the first time the mirror on the wall that he was facing. Now, he started to think that this had been pre-planned.

In the adjoining room, Jordan Ueda from the U.S. Embassy in Tokyo stood looking over a young officer's shoulder as the USB memory sticks were checked. Next to them, the older officer was on the phone talking to another officer who was with the ground crew transferring checked luggage from Xiong's flight from Washington to the plane scheduled to take Xiong to Beijing.

Jordan Ueda's attention bounced back and forth between the computer screen and the phone conversation occurring next him.

The young officer sitting at the computer opened document folders and then randomly searched through them.

Ueda spoke and read Japanese but didn't speak or read Chinese. The young officer searching through the files did read Chinese.

"Are there any documents describing technology," Ueda said in Japanese.

"Lots of memos and reports, but nothing related to any technologies," the officer answered.

The older officer hung up. "They did a random search of the checked bags. There was nothing there."

Ueda nodded and continued to stare at the computer monitor. He recognized some of the Chinese characters, but not enough to understand what was written. Jordan Ueda was a third generation Japanese American. Without any pressure from his parents, he searched for opportunities to learn Japanese, including an academic year in Japan during high school and college. Living abroad gave him a taste of another world and he worked toward a career that would give him chances to be in foreign countries. Ueda was in his third foreign post after being in Thailand and the Philippines earlier in his State Department career. He felt at home working in Tokyo for the State Department and hoped he'd be able to extend his stay.

The young officer stayed on a page longer than he had on any other.

"What is it," Ueda asked.

"This one is interesting. He's writing to his superiors about contact with American students. He explains where they work, the type of work and the information that might benefit China if he can develop closer friendships with them," the young officer explained in Japanese.

"When did he write this report," Ueda inquired.

Scrolling to the top of the document, it was dated October 2004. The report was about seven months old. "Does it provide names of the Americans he contacted," Ueda wondered.

"Not in this one," the officer said. He scrolled through more documents, looking at the dates of the different reports and slowed when he saw another report in late January 2005. "This one says he has two very good candidates. He explains to his superior that he'll need to promise some arrangements for them, but the candidates are eager to help."

"Could you print this one out," Ueda said.

After the printer spit out the document, Ueda picked it up from the tray and handed the document to the older officer.

"It's going to take me a long time to go through these documents," the young officer said, looking over his shoulder at Ueda and the older officer.

"I'd appreciate it if you could take that document and try to get the two names," Ueda said to the older officer. "If he finds anything more of interest, he'll bring it into you,"

The older officer nodded and went back to the interview room. He placed the document on the table, stepped back and folded his arms. "I'd like the names of your candidates," the officer said.

Xiong Zimo's lips pressed together, and his nostrils flared. He couldn't deny anything. He had no way out. He could scream his outrage at them, but that wouldn't change anything. Just like in China, these guys had the authority to pull anyone and anything aside for inspection, examination, or an interview. Xiong's tight facial expression relaxed, and he was almost smiling. He wondered why the Japanese were asking about his potential sources of information in the United States.

Xiong's relaxed feeling yielded to another thought, and he couldn't stop the unconscious change he felt as his cheeks flushed slightly, and his brow furrowed. If they confirmed he was recruiting people for information in the States, would he be detained indefinitely? Even if he gave up two names, he wasn't guaranteed anything. His thoughts played tricks on him. Keeping him would prompt his government to file a protest for detaining a diplomat. But the circumstances of talking to him during a flight delay wasn't really a detention. He wondered if the flight delay was a ruse giving them the time to talk to him. There was no way to know if it was a ruse. He bet that if he gave up the names, the Japanese would let him go.

"If I give you two names, then I can go, yes?"

"Please, the two names," the officer repeated.

"The Americans know about one of them already. Lucas Moore. The second name is Oliver Vega."

Jordan Ueda listened and wrote down the names. He'd have them transmitted back to Washington once he returned to the embassy. Next to him, the young officer pored over more documents.

"Make copies of the documents and we can return all this," Ueda suggested.

The officer at the computer inserted each USB memory stick and copied them onto the computer's hard drive before saving them again onto new USB memory sticks that he could give to Ueda to take back to the embassy.

The older officer stepped into the adjoining room. "Do you have what you wanted?" He saw Ueda nod. He took Xiong's USB memory sticks and returned to the interview room, leaving the door open.

"One of my officers will take you back upstairs. I think there's a departure time on the board for your flight to Beijing," the older man said. He placed the memory sticks on the table and watched Xiong scoop them up and put them back into his backpack.

Xiong stood, slung his backpack over his shoulder and grabbed the handle of his carry-on and exited. He didn't say anything or look back as he left.

Back in the adjoining room, the young officer leaned in toward the computer screen reading.

"What's so interesting," Ueda wondered.

"This document instructs the Chinese Embassy to collect any commercially useful technological information from any source that can accelerate China's development of an international network of seaports, airports, and other key hubs to promote trade of raw materials and Chinese goods. Information that can promote and fulfill economic and military objectives are priorities for medium- and long-term interests," the officer read.

The older officer standing and pondering what he'd heard looked at Jordan Ueda. "Before you leave, is there anything you know that you can share about the two names we were given?"

"It's better if I send over something after I'm back at the embassy and gather background information for you. What your young colleague read to us means lots of people in different Japanese government ministries will be interested in any background I might be able to provide. Along with the background information, I'll let you know the different parts of my government that's interested in this," Ueda said. He took the memory sticks, bowed to the older officer, and left the airport.

Xiong sat with hundreds of others waiting for flights. His flight to Beijing was leaving four hours later than originally scheduled. He sat thinking that nothing that happened since landing at Narita seemed random. Maybe he was paranoid, but he believed he was given enough time to deplane, sit and relax, but as soon as those young officers saw him and confirmed his identity, he was going to be interviewed. He thought about how smooth the whole operation had gone, including the explanation of needing to ensure that he didn't possess any illegal material. That was just an excuse to look through everything.

A smile spread across Xiong's face. It was impressive. The Americans and Japanese coordinated and found a way to see what information he had and would divulge. While he was trying to get technological information from his American contacts, they applied technology against him. The Americans had flagged him in some system, followed him from Washington, knew what flight he was on and where he would be connecting to his next flight. Xiong accepted it as a learning opportunity. His next decision was whether he'd tell his superiors in Beijing about the airport interview. Would they know before he arrived in Beijing that he'd been questioned. He had a few more hours to make a final decision.

* * * * *

Back in his office, Jordan Ueda was alone after the trek into central Tokyo from the airport. Most of the embassy staff were gone for the day. Although tempted to call it a day after the round-trip to Narita and the hours spent at the airport, he wanted to check off everything he needed to do as the follow-up to the day's events rather than face it in the morning.

Ueda's email to his supervisor was brief, providing Moore's and Vega's names to be passed on to Washington. He placed the memory sticks and a short memo in an inter-office envelope addressed to his supervisor with a notation that the material needed to be translated from Chinese.

Ueda looked at the memo he had received when instructed to go to the airport. He had hoped it had enough background for his recommendations to the Japanese officer but there wasn't much. The Japanese were asked to conduct a search and look for anything hinting at technology information of any kind that may have originated from sources in the United States.

Ueda wrote a one-page summary that warned of China's commercial intelligence gathering efforts in the United States. His summary referred to attempts to get non-public patent application information, but the Japanese should contact him directly with specific questions that he would respond to after more research. As Ueda proofread what he'd typed, he sat back and rubbed his chin. This sounded too nerdy or academic to believe.

He realized the page said nothing of substance and hoped it wouldn't upset his Japanese contacts too much. As Ueda hit send, he realized that global competition between countries was reaching levels of information theft that he'd never considered. He knew nothing about patents, the process of getting one or the benefits of getting patent information before they became public. He had so much to learn.

Office Visits

The buzzing cell phone bounced around on the wooden surface of the bedside table. Drew rolled onto his side and reached out without looking. "Yeah, hello," he said then cleared his throat.

"Mr. Drew?"

Drew rolled onto his back forcing his eyes open at the sound of Linh's voice. "Is something wrong?"

"Nothing wrong. I have time to go to consulate with you today. Maybe at my lunch time. Okay?"

Drew said nothing for the moment. "Can I call you later? I'll have to check with Ms. Doan, the woman at the consulate. I'll call your cell phone, yes?"

"I wait for you to call," Linh said then clicked off.

Drew sat up on the side of the bed then glanced over at the clock. 7:45. He hadn't gotten any call from Janice Doan after Aaron said she'd be calling. He'd give her a call when it was likely that she'd be in the office. It surprised him that Linh was suddenly calling about the visa. He wondered if her Chinese boyfriend had done something. In the bathroom, he looked in the mirror and shook his head. Since discovering Linh's existence, the events of recent days were not what he'd expected.

Drew made multiple calls in the morning before connecting with Ms. Doan at the consulate who wasn't happy to be told to accommodate Drew's request for the lunchtime meeting with him and Linh. He and Linh went through the usual security before being escorted into the consulate and to Janice Doan's office.

Ms. Doan gave Drew several documents that he and Linh had to fill out before a visa could be issued. "I want to talk to her alone," Janice Doan said. Her way of telling Drew to leave. "Just take a seat out in the hallway. I'll get you when we're done."

The Consul General instructed Janice Doan's office that Linh's visa application should be expedited because of special circumstances. There was no reason given for the special circumstances justifying the expedited treatment. Janice Doan knew that Linh qualified for a visa under special American immigration laws aimed at Vietnamese who were fathered by Americans during the war. Drew Foster's willingness to admit that he was Linh's father eliminated the doubt and Linh's physical appearance as a biracial person allowed her to meet the legal requirements for a visa.

"Have you applied for a visa before," Janice Doan asked in Vietnamese.

Linh shook her head.

"Have you committed any crimes?"

Linh wasn't sure how to answer the question. Her encounter with the motorcycle rider and burning Jun's documents leapt to mind. "You mean like police stopping me on my scooter because my light didn't work," Linh said to buy time.

"No. I mean have you been taken to court and a judge deciding you have broken the law," Janice clarified.

"No, never," Linh said. Understanding that the difference was that she hadn't been caught doing anything.

Janice pursued a line of questions about Linh's mother and other relatives. After hearing Linh's explanation that she and her mother were not welcome in the family and that she had been on her own after her mother died, Janice Doan understood the situation. She was satisfied that Linh's decision to pack up and leave her country of birth was likely her best option.

"You and Mr. Foster bring back those papers and we'll take care of the visa right away," Janice said. She led Linh to the door.

"Everything good?" Drew asked when he saw the door open and Ms. Doan in her office doorway.

"Just get those documents back to me as soon as you can, and we can move forward."

"Good, thanks," Drew said as he and Linh walked to leave the consulate. "After work, you should come to my hotel and we can work on these papers together," Drew suggested.

Linh agreed then hopped on a motorcycle taxi and headed back to work.

* * * *

Aaron's focus had been on documents and the afternoon's task of accompanying the Consul General to a meeting with the Maritime Administration official. He stopped and realized that he should do one more thing. He punched in Kellie's phone number.

"Hello? Aaron?" Kellie said, seeing his number appear on her phone.

"Kellie, this is a very quick update. The CG here wants me to be at a meeting between him and the Administrator of the Maritime Administration. The CG understood the implications of the documents and is on it," Aaron explained.

"Thanks. It's good knowing that what we've done might make some difference," Kellie said. "You don't know how much I appreciate everything you've been doing."

Aaron wasn't sure what to say. "I'll see you very soon. Maybe we'll have something to celebrate. I gotta go," Aaron said and ended the call. He was quick to return his attention to the CG and their meeting at the Maritime Administration.

Linh scurried down the main second floor corridor clutching half a dozen document filled folders to her chest. As she approached the staircase leading up from the main entrance lobby, two men, foreigners, were about to step into her path. Her eyes locked onto Aaron and as she tried to avoid the two men, her grip loosened, spilling two folders filled with papers onto the corridor floor.

"Let me help," Aaron said, bending down to help Linh collect the papers. "Are you alright?"

"Yes, fine, thank you," she said to Aaron then looking up at the taller man who stopped while she and Aaron placed the loose documents into a pile.

"I'm sorry we startled you and caused you to drop these," the Consul General said.

"No, my fault," Linh said. "I'll finish this, you go," she said to Aaron.

Aaron and the CG continued toward a corner office. "That woman is Phan Nhu Linh. She's the one who helped get us the documents we're here to discuss," Aaron said quietly. "I didn't tell her I was coming here for a meeting. I think that seeing me surprised her," Aaron added.

The CG nodded and kept marching down the corridor.

"Mr. Ngo will be with you in moment," the secretary said when Aaron and CG McAlister entered the Administrator's outer office.

CG McAlister stood and looked out the window behind the secretary's desk. Aaron studied the maps of the nearby coastal area and the waterways in and around Ho Chi Minh City.

The sound of Mr. Ngo's office door opening got both men's attention. Aaron saw a bowling ball of a man standing in the doorway. Ngo was a foot shorter than the tall CG and several inches shorter than Aaron. Ngo stepped back to allow his two visitors into his office and shook hands with both.

Ngo invited Aaron and the CG to sit at a round table that accommodated four people instead of the chairs facing his desk. Before sitting, Ngo took the business cards offered by his two guests. "We'll have some tea in a moment," Ngo said in his accented English. When they heard a tap on the office door, Ngo let a woman enter. She joined the three men at the table, taking out a notepad.

"My English not very good," Ngo said. "She can help me understand."

Aaron wiped his brow with a handkerchief. He was wearing a sport jacket over a white shirt and hoped that his undershirt would absorb the perspiration on his body. He noticed that the CG hadn't broken a sweat. When the window unit air conditioner clicked on, Aaron hoped it would drop the temperature by several degrees but suspected the large office tested the unit's capacity to cool a room.

The secretary entered, delivered the tea, and slipped out of the office.

The first few minutes of the meeting started with pleasantries and the CG thanking Ngo for his time. Aaron watched the career diplomat talk with a constant look of a subtle smile on his face.

"Mr. Ngo, we have a mutual interest in Vietnam's economic development and the improvements for Vietnam's ports here in Ho Chi Minh City along the river and at Vung Tau on the coast. As you know, we concluded a bilateral trade agreement a few years ago because we are confident of Vietnam's future growth," the CG began. The CG watched as the interpreter had moved her chair close to Mr. Ngo so she could keep her voice down.

"We're aware that there might be some Chinese interference in our mutual and bilateral efforts." The CG stopped, hoping that this point would have an effect, but Ngo's expression was unchanged, his lower lip taut.

"I've asked the embassy in Hanoi to contact the head of Vietnam's intellectual property office. We have evidence of Chinese attempts to steal American patents and translate them into Chinese and Vietnamese." The CG paused again. "The American concern is that we now believe that the Chinese are using the stolen information to persuade Vietnamese government officials that there should be more cooperation with the Chinese and to give Chinese businesses preferential treatment in your infrastructure and port facilities projects," the CG added.

CG McAlister was careful not to imply that Mr. Ngo was doing anything improper. The CG wanted Mr. Ngo to understand that the Chinese were engaging in a game of deception and that he might be the victim of that deception.

"Has there been any reply from our government offices in Hanoi," Ngo asked through the interpreter.

"It's too soon to say because we just made the inquiry yesterday after obtaining and translating the documents that serve as evidence of what the Chinese are doing."

Ngo nodded slowly as he listened to the interpreter. He had been recommending to his superiors in Hanoi that Vietnam work closer with the Chinese because of their shorter timeline for completing the work necessary for larger ships to serve Ho Chi Minh City. Knowing that he occupied the highest position he would be able to achieve, he was hoping that these projects would be the crowning achievements of his career.

"When you say evidence, where did you get this evidence and how do you know it is linked directly to what we're trying to do," Ngo asked.

"There's a trail of documents. It starts with an attempt by the Chinese to obtain confidential information from an American government employee. We've been able to compare Chinese documents to the American documents. The most convincing documents have been the Chinese documents translated into Vietnamese to make it appear that the Chinese documents are based on original Chinese work, but, in reality, it is the work of non-Chinese companies. Those other companies are developing the technology that the Chinese want to use for the projects in Vietnam. In other words, a Chinese company is trying to sell you on the idea that it will use the latest technology on these projects even though they have no experience with the technology," the CG explained.

Ngo's blood pressure rose. His tanned cheeks turned slightly red. "Do you have information about the Chinese company or those involved in this deception?"

"An investigation is underway in the United States. We need a little more time to identify the specific links in Vietnam," the CG deflected. Neither the CG nor Aaron had any intention to identify CODE as the Chinese entity. "We can't say that the activities of the Chinese enterprise here have broken any Vietnamese laws. We do know that the activities in the United States are illegal, and we've prosecuted one person already."

"Deceiving government officials by lying or by using stolen information then making them look original needs to be punished," Ngo said. His eyes darted around the room as if a distracting thought had interrupted him. "I'll have to confer with my colleagues in Hanoi. Unfortunately, I believe this will slow our decisions on our port projects."

"I should tell you that when I communicated with the embassy, we asked that the information we've given you also be provided to those at your headquarters," the CG said.

"If there are details you can provide in writing, please send them. You can also email them to my secretary," Ngo replied.

"We won't take more of your time," the CG said as he stood and started to drift toward the door with Aaron following his lead.

Mr. Ngo and the interpreter followed. In the outer office, Aaron made sure to get information from the secretary to follow up and send whatever he and the CG thought would be appropriate to provide.

The main second floor corridor was busier than when they arrived with more staff walking up and down the corridor. Aaron and the CG were twenty feet from the top of the stairway when Aaron saw a man and woman reach the second floor and turn in their direction. Aaron's brow instinctively went up in surprise then he swallowed the wrong way and started coughing. He covered his mouth. The cough did what he was trying to avoid. The man and woman looked his way.

"Are you okay," the CG asked.

"I'm fine," Aaron said, turning his head slightly toward the CG and away from the man and woman.

Aaron took a deep breath, knowing that Linh's Chinese boyfriend, Jun, recognized him. It was the woman who concerned him. The short black hair, tiny physique under a loose-fitting white blouse and black pants and heels, he took a quick glance over his shoulder after he and the CG passed them. He never expected to see Meilin Moy here in this building. His heart was racing. Would she recognize him? Did Jun know his name, and would he tell Meilin who he was? As he descended the staircase, he looked back, but they were out of sight. Aaron hoped that his beard and shaved head would give him an appearance that Meilin wouldn't recognize.

"Do you know them," Meilin asked as she and Jun continued down the corridor.

"I don't know them, but I recognized the shorter one," Jun answered. There wasn't time for Jun to explain before entering Ngo's outer office.

Ngo's secretary took them straight into his office where he sat behind his desk. As Meilin entered, she saw the teapot and cups still on the round table, but they weren't for her and Jun. Meilin smiled and extended her hand as Ngo rose from his chair. She hoped her expression didn't change upon seeing the short man's girth. "Mr. Ngo, it's nice to meet you," Meilin said in English.

Ngo gave Jun a nod of familiarity having met with Jun many times, but he was surprised by the woman's tiny stature. Meilin's narrow shoulders and short hair style made her look boyish. A young man entered the office and moved a chair from the table to sit next to Ngo and bridge the Chinese-Vietnamese language barrier.

"We appreciate you finding time to meet with us. Ms. Moy has just traveled from the United States," Jun said.

"Mr. Yao, you are a good friend of this office, and we have developed a good working relationship," Ngo began. "Mr. Yao said this would be a good opportunity for us to discuss how we continue in the future," Ngo said, looking to Meilin. He saw Meilin's fixed smile.

"Our commercial efforts to support Vietnamese development is a joint effort and we believe that we cannot develop as fast as we'd like unless your ports facilitate larger ships," Meilin said.

"Yes, on this last point, we might not be able to move as quickly as Mr. Yao and I thought we could," Ngo said. "The decision-making on choosing CODE to moving things forward on our port construction and improvement projects has met an unexpected obstacle."

After waiting for the interpreter to finish, Jun Yao leaned forward. "I don't understand what you mean."

"The delay is with my headquarters office in Hanoi," Ngo decided to put the blame elsewhere. "The documentation that you've provided is undergoing much more scrutiny than I expected."

Meilin expected to hear good news. This wasn't what Jun said she'd be hearing from the head of the Maritime Administration in Ho Chi Minh City. "Have your colleagues said anything specific about the documents? What's causing them to scrutinize them," Meilin interjected.

"Well, it isn't so specific, but CODE is not a company that itself does the port construction and projects involving dredging and other port projects. There might be concern that our interaction should be more direct with the Chinese company that will do the work," Ngo said. He couldn't reveal to his Chinese visitors that the Americans were behind the delay.

"I've traveled a long distance to come and meet with you. When was this delay brought to your attention," Meilin inquired.

"This is a very recent development. I learned of this after you left the United States. It's so recent that I've been too busy to let Mr.

Yao know about this. I apologize," Ngo said, hoping to keep Jun Yao from the potential wrath of his boss.

Having seen the Americans leaving as they entered, Meilin was suspicious of the timing. She didn't get to the top of ChiTran by being duped easily. She wasn't swallowing the story he was telling. The only thing she believed was that there had been no time to let Jun Yao know about this.

"Can't you explain to the people in Hanoi that CODE is working directly with the companies that will do the work," Jun said.

Meilin didn't hear what Jun said. In her mind, she saw the documents the FBI agents had in her hotel room. She played back their questions. The FBI found her plane ticket. But how would they have made the connection to CODE in such a short time? She was missing something.

"I know that Vietnam attracts a lot of commercial interests from foreign countries. We aren't naïve in this way," Meilin said. "Mr. Yao has worked diligently to identify where we will invest in Vietnamese companies, but we need a better and faster way of getting these products out of Vietnam and to foreign markets. You know that the Americans are our number one competitor, and they will do things to frustrate our efforts," Meilin continued.

Ngo fidgeted with Aaron Foster's business card while listening to Meilin. Ngo wasn't taking the bait. He couldn't disclose anything about his meeting with the Americans.

"Should I travel to Hanoi and meet with your colleagues there," Meilin said as she sat forward on the edge of the chair. She watched Ngo twirling a business card between his fingers.

"There's no need for anything so extreme. Mr. Yao can tell you that we've had very good and cooperative interaction. Going to Hanoi will only make people wonder if there are problems. It might cause them to send people down here to examine things and slow the pace of any decisions on all projects," Ngo explained.

Meilin, while listening, focused on the business card held vertically between Ngo's thumb and forefinger. She saw an embossed gold design in one corner and bold black lettering centered on the card. Her eyes went back and forth between attention to Ngo and the card. Each time she looked at the card, she looked at the printed name.

"I appreciate what you are saying. We do not want to do anything that will add delays to any decisions," Meilin said. "Mr. Yao and I shouldn't take more of your time."

Jun Yao looked at his boss. He thought there was more to discuss. He wanted to question Ngo about ways to overcome whatever the problems might be to get these projects started. He saw Meilin standing in front of her chair. Slowly, he pushed himself to his feet.

A minute later, they were marching down the corridor. "You haven't been keeping me up to date on things," Meilin said just above a whisper.

"Yes, I have. I wasn't aware of any delays until this meeting."

"You've missed things, or you just withheld information from me," Meilin insisted.

Jun never thought to tell Meilin about the motorcycle incident involving Vinh because it had nothing to do with any of this. In the short time since Meilin arrived, the timing wasn't right to say anything about the burned documents, but that was the only thing he could think of that he hadn't mentioned.

Meilin descended the stairway as if she was late for something and Jun was a step behind. She stepped outside the building, took a couple of steps away from the doors before turning on her young associate. Even wearing heels, she was several inches shorter than Jun. She looked up and stared into his eyes. "Have you encountered any Americans during the last two weeks?"

"No."

"Did you recognize either of the two Americans who were leaving when we arrived?"

"I did recognize the one with the shaved head," Jun admitted.

"Why did you recognize him? Who is he? What do you know about him?" Meilin rattled off questions before Jun had a chance to say anything.

"We shouldn't talk here," Jun said, hoping that Meilin would calm down by the time they went somewhere to talk.

"We'll go to your office," Meilin said.

They hailed a cab and were at Jun's office building twenty minutes later. Meilin walked through the workspace nodding at the staff and took a seat in Jun's office.

"Do you smoke," Meilin inquired.

"No," Jun answered. His staff opened windows in Jun's office and ran fans in it to eliminate the smoky odor, but the odor lingered. "We had a little problem, but everything is fine," Jun decided to say.

"Tell me about the American," Meilin instructed.

"I've seen him before," Jun said.

Meilin's glare was steady. She demanded to know more.

"After I arrived here and met Mr. Ngo, everything began to progress well. I wanted to make sure I knew what was going on with him and his senior staff, so I recruited someone to provide me with copies of documents that were related to our interests. If I gave Mr. Ngo documents that would help him make recommendations in our favor, I would get copies of internal documents. It allowed me to monitor how things were moving forward for us," Jun explained.

"Who did you recruit?"

"A woman who works in the copy room and distributes documents in the building. She's low level, but works in the mailroom, copy room, things like that."

"None of this answers my questions about the American," Meilin said. She saw Jun shifting in his chair.

"I saw him having lunch with the woman I recruited," Jun admitted.

"Do you know his name?"

"I have no idea what his name is."

"You recruited someone to pass you information from the Maritime Administration and when you see her with an American you didn't think to find out who he is," Meilin pressed.

"I'm sorry. I didn't think to ask her. I should have done that right away," Jun said.

"Yes, you should have. There's no excuse for such a lapse in judgment. And as for the American, I do know who he is," Meilin said insistently. "I was able to see it on the card Mr. Ngo kept playing with while we met. The woman you recruited and saw having lunch with this American creates a big problem for us and he might be the reason we've run into this delay, which we, meaning ChiTran, CODE, and China cannot afford. This could cost us millions and years of delay."

As Meilin's eyes remained fixed on Jun, she recalled Kaili saying that Aaron Foster was traveling somewhere, but she never said where.

Meilin wasn't surprised that Aaron was with a government agency since he had been with one when she met him in Hong Kong in 1998. The question that bothered her was what his function was now and what did he know. She got up and paced in Jun's office.

"Do you know where this American is staying," Meilin asked.

"I had someone follow him when he finished his lunch. He went back to his hotel," Jun replied.

Meilin nodded. Her thoughts were racing. She needed to sort out all the different information tidbits flying around in her head. Knowing that Aaron is in Vietnam, she assumed that Kaili and Aaron had been in contact. She stopped pacing and tilted her head realizing that she didn't recognize him when she passed the two Americans in the corridor, but he recognized her. She had to make lots of assumptions. Even if Kaili had nothing to do with the FBI's night visit in her room, she might find out about it if she was poised for a high-level job. Meilin decided the documents the FBI had, Aaron's presence in Vietnam, and meeting with Mr. Ngo had to be part of a coordinated plan.

Meilin's ChiTran and CODE gambit in Vietnam was at risk. If she abandoned it without explaining it to the Chinese Government contacts who approved of the move on condition of her greasing some wheels for a greater Chinese presence in Vietnam, her future foreign expansion plans would be refused. A wrong move now would be like stepping on a land mine and causing her efforts to explode in her face. But she needed to do something drastic.

"Do you think that Mr. Ngo suspects you have someone passing information to you," Meilin asked.

"I doubt it. The one thing I've been confident of is that my internal source has been very good at being careful and discreet," Jun said. Meilin's confrontational mood convinced him that it wouldn't do him any good to tell her that Linh was no longer reliable and was now a threat to exposing everything if she hadn't already.

Meilin began pacing again. "We can't confront the Americans and find out how they know things and how much they know. The man who had lunch with your internal source is Aaron Foster. He was at the Maritime Administration today and he is well connected," Meilin said. "There's only one person who can shed light on how much damage has been done," Meilin said.

Termination

"Well, did you convince her," Meilin asked. Meilin gave Jun privacy in his office and spent thirty minutes in the outer office chatting briefly with staff through Chau Bui acting as her interpreter.

"I had to offer her something to agree to meet," Jun said.

"What did you offer her?"

"I told her I'd give her a final payment. But the final payment offer is good only if she picks it up today. At first, she said she didn't care about getting the final payment, but I tripled the amount as a way of convincing her to come," Jun said.

Meilin shrugged. In the big scheme of things, it was less than a hundred fifty dollars. "Where are we meeting?"

"There's an industrial zone several miles west of downtown. I've had Ms. Bui contact one of our potential partners. On-site security guards will be informed of us coming to let us into the area and they'll keep the facility open late so we can use an office there. I told them you were in town for a very short time, and I wanted to take you there so that you could see it," Jun explained.

"Won't they want someone to be there? Won't she be suspicious about this? Wouldn't she think you could do this at your office," Meilin questioned.

"Ms. Bui told them that we're only interested in seeing the location and offices, nothing about any detailed discussion of future cooperation or transactions. You are only interested in the facilities and distance from the city. By going there, you get to see roads and other related infrastructure between the city and the industrial park. As for my source, I've never had her at the office during work hours.

All my meetings with her are after hours. I didn't want any of the staff to know about her or to be able to identify her. She can't take this amount of time off during the day," Jun explained. He decided not to tell Meilin about his midday lunches with Linh.

"You've always met downtown. She's going to be suspicious," Meilin said.

"I told her that I was already out here at meetings during the day. That's why she needs to meet out here. Ms. Bui helped me get easy to describe detailed directions," Jun said.

Meilin forced herself to drown her misgivings with Jun's explanation. "Does she know she's also meeting with me," Meilin asked.

"I didn't say that you'd be there," Jun replied.

"When do we leave?"

"The traffic may be difficult so we should leave as soon as we can," Jun recommended.

Meilin ignored the urge to go to the hotel and change into something more suited for visiting a warehouse and industrial park.

Chau Bui accompanied Jun and Meilin down to the street. Chau gave detailed directions to a taxi driver, including instructions for him to wait to bring them back. Chau offered him double the fare as an incentive not to leave her Chinese bosses stranded.

Linh rushed to her apartment after work to change into jeans and a comfortable Polo shirt. She gathered her long black hair and banded it behind her neck. Searching her small apartment, she opted for a belt bag to hold money, cell phone, and her collapsed baton. As she sat bent over to lace her sneakers, sweat dripped from her forehead. She was nervous. By the time she reached the meeting point, it would be dark. She stopped lacing and sat back.

She didn't want to go alone. She pressed the first few numbers for Mai and stopped. No, Mai didn't know about her "other" job. Instead, she punched in Aaron's cell phone number.

"Are you busy," Linh asked when she heard the connection made.

"Linh?" Aaron answered. "Ahh, no, I'm not busy right now," Aaron said, pushing himself onto his feet from the sunken mattress he'd been sitting on. He walked to the window and looked out into the glow of the setting sun. "What's the matter?"

"I must meet Jun in a strange place. I don't want to go alone," Linh said.

"I can go with you," Aaron offered, forgetting momentarily that Linh didn't know where he was staying. "I changed hotels. I will call you back in two minutes and someone will tell you where to meet me," Aaron explained.

At the front desk, Aaron had a young woman use his phone to call Linh and provide the name and address of the hotel.

"She says she will come now," the young woman said, handing back Aaron's phone.

Aaron drifted to the door and stood outside then wondered if he should've changed clothes. Not knowing where he was going, he worried that the knee length shorts, t-shirt and sandals might not be the best thing to wear, but he didn't want to be in his room when Linh arrived. He checked his watch every few minutes. Twenty minutes after Linh spoke to the woman in the hotel, she arrived on a motorcycle cab.

"We get taxi," Linh said. She led Aaron to a spot on the main avenue where they flagged down a cab. Linh spent several minutes explaining the directions to the driver who kept shaking his head that he wasn't familiar with the area where she and Aaron needed to go. Linh convinced him to call someone, and Linh spoke to someone on the phone who spoke to the driver. She spent ten minutes explaining the directions and negotiating before the driver put the car in gear.

"We pay extra for this," Linh said.

"Are you sure he understands the directions?" Aaron wondered after watching the back and forth.

"I think he pretends. He wants more money for the long drive and traffic," Linh explained.

During the first ten minutes of the stop and go ride, Aaron watched the traffic out the windshield and the fading glow of the evening. Each time he glanced over at Linh, she was looking out the passenger window on her side. Her lower lip was sucked in and the fingers of one hand drummed silently on her thigh.

"You're nervous about this meeting, why," Aaron said.

"I always meet Jun in his apartment or office after work. Never like this. I saw him today at work with woman. She's older. I think his Chinese boss."

Aaron nodded but said nothing about seeing Jun and Meilin pass him in the corridor of her building. Aaron stared out onto the well-lit streets, seeing pedestrians clogging the sidewalks. He checked his watch for no reason. He didn't know how far they were going or where.

"Linh, what did Jun say? Can you tell me exactly what he said when he asked you to meet him," Aaron said.

Despite her limited English, Aaron understood. "Did Jun say he was meeting you alone or are you meeting Jun and his boss?"

"He say nothing about boss," Linh answered.

Aaron wondered if paying Linh was all that this was about or if there was something else. He closed his eyes for a moment. Aaron thought about what he was going to do when they arrived at their destination. Whatever else might happen, he had to be sure Linh was safe.

As they rode, the streets were crowded with trucks, motorbikes, scooters, and cars. The horns beeped without a pause. Aaron wished for earplugs that he didn't have. His mind was occupied by different scenarios that might play out when Linh went to meet Jun. If Meilin was waiting for Linh along with Jun, that would change everything. He wasn't so much afraid of Meilin but was aware of her ability to spring surprises as she did in Hong Kong years ago.

The driver slowed as they drove along a chain link fence. Behind the fenced area was a mix of a construction site and finished buildings. Light poles stood along the perimeter at measured distances. Aaron focused on the area and looked for surveillance cameras along the top of the fencing and light poles. The driver made a left turn but stopped before reaching the small security gate house.

Aaron listened to the brief back and forth between Linh and the driver. The driver pulled up and stopped when the uniformed security guard stepped out. Linh leaned forward toward the open driver's side window. After a brief conversation, the guard raised the horizontal bar.

"What did the guard say," Aaron asked.

"He told our driver to go straight then make a right turn. We will see another car parked at the building," Linh answered.

Aaron's eyes scoured the industrial park. Many of the buildings were large new warehouses. Several deep holes were dug for new construction. He saw skeletal steel beams, girders, and trusses for future buildings. When the cab turned, the cab's headlights and the lights of the industrial park shined on a lone car parked by a finished building. As the cab came to a stop next another parked taxi, Aaron saw a driver sitting and waiting in the car.

"Are you sure this is the right place," Aaron asked.

"Guard told us to come here," Linh said.

"Before you go in, ask the driver in that taxi how many people he brought here," Aaron suggested.

Linh gave Aaron a long look, shrugged and got out of the car and walked over to the other driver. As she walked toward Aaron sitting in the taxi, she saw his window opening.

"He bring two people. A man and woman," Linh said.

Aaron opened his door, but before he got out of the taxi, he showed the driver a pile of Vietnamese dong and had Linh explain to him that he would get all of it if he waited.

"He understands," Linh said.

Aaron followed Linh to a double wide metal door at the corner of the building. A light was on above the door. The new metal door opened without a squeak. They stepped onto a concrete floor in a warehouse area that had some framing for future storage rooms or offices. Centered on the wall opposite of the door by where they were standing, steps led up to a finished second floor office. Light cast from the office down onto the concrete floor indicated that the office had windows on the three interior sides. The window facing Aaron and Linh was covered by a thin curtain.

Bare bulbs emitted light from the center of the open area about half the size of a soccer field. Standing just inside the door, it was dim where Linh and Aaron stood because of the distance from the high-strung lights.

"I'll wait here," Aaron said.

Linh nodded and walked toward the opposite wall where the office was located.

Jun heard something and got up to look out the window. "About time she arrived," Jun said, peeping out the window from one side.

"She's twenty minutes late," Meilin said, sitting by a desk in the large office. Whoever occupied it during the day wanted to be comfortable based on the expensive leather chairs and sofa in the office. In addition to the three windows looking down into the warehouse area, a fourth window looked out and had a window air conditioning unit.

"Is this going to be a production facility," Meilin asked.

Jun watched Linh walking toward the stairs. "No, the plan is to bring the finished product here, sort it, pack it, and move it to the port from here. The production facility is about fifty miles south," Jun replied.

Jun looked away from Linh and toward the door. "I think someone came with her," he said.

"Can you see who it might be," Meilin asked.

"The lighting isn't good enough by the door," Jun said.

"Is it a man, a woman?"

"No way to tell. Whoever it might be looks to have moved into the corner where it's darker," Jun said. "I shouldn't be surprised if someone came with her. This was a strange place to choose to meet."

"Does she have any close friends," Meilin asked.

"She has a close friend from work who she goes out with for drinks and dinner," Jun said. "Maybe it's her."

"I meant friends who are men," Meilin clarified.

"Not that I know of."

Jun went to the door and opened it when he saw that Linh was at the base of the stairs. Light from the office lit up the floor below and the stairway. He glanced toward the entry into the building, but he saw nothing.

Linh saw Jun standing in the doorway at the top of the stairs and saw him extend his arm in a gesture of invitation to enter. She walked past him and saw an older, petite woman sitting in the office and stopped after taking a few steps into the office.

Linh saw the woman's raised eyebrows. A sign of surprise from the woman.

Meilin saw the taller, young woman's full figure and the western influences in her face. For a split second, Meilin thought Linh could be Kaili's sister.

"Please sit," Jun said as he walked past Linh and sat on the leather sofa. He had left the door open.

Linh looked at Jun and back to the woman. She and Jun worked out their communication with both using their limited knowledge of the other's language. Linh wondered whether the woman spoke Vietnamese. "I'm Phan Nhu Linh," Linh said as she focused on the woman.

Meilin looked at Jun. She guessed at what Linh was saying but wanted Jun to confirm.

"Her name is Phan Nhu Linh," Jun said to Meilin in Chinese. All three understood.

"Do you speak any English," Meilin asked. "My name is Moy Meilin."

"My English maybe is better than my Chinese," Linh answered. Knowing that Jun spoke hardly any English, Linh wondered if Meilin was going to translate. After a moment of silence, she concluded that Meilin wasn't going to translate for Jun's benefit.

"You work for Jun. You find important documents for him," Meilin said.

"No more work for Jun and no more friends with Jun," Linh said.

"Why? Did he do something or did something happen at work?"

"At his flat, he got angry, he grabbed at me," Linh answered.

Meilin looked over at Jun and spoke in Cantonese. "She says she was at your flat and you tried to grab her. Is that true?"

Jun sat forward. "It was a misunderstanding. She told me about the lunch she had with the American. He asked her about her work. Instead of just explaining her job for the Maritime Administration, she told him what she does for me, and I got upset. I told her from the beginning that she was never to reveal anything she does for me to anyone." The longer he talked, the louder Jun's voice became.

In the dark corner of the building, Aaron heard the man's voice getting louder. He didn't understand anything being said in Cantonese. He walked toward the stairway. His eyes went back and forth between the open doorway and the window that looked down onto the area that he was crossing. He stood under the stairway and out of sight.

Linh remained standing. Her hands rested on the belt bag at her waist. Jun's raised voice caused her to use her right hand and unzip the belt bag a few inches. Meilin sat with her legs crossed. Meilin was too short for her foot to touch the floor. Meilin's voice was calm.

"But you didn't answer my question. Did you grab this young woman," Meilin asked again in Cantonese.

"I hollered at her. I think that made her mad. She told the American what she did for me without giving him my name or the company's name," Jun explained. "When she tried to leave my flat, I did reach out to stop her, but she flung her bag at me and left my flat."

Meilin stared at Jun. "You made things worse by doing that." She turned back to Linh and reverted to English. "Is that the only time Jun has done something to you?"

Linh acted on her hunch. "I think he made someone follow me that night. It made me scared," she said in English. "I met a friend for dinner and drinks and when I left on my sooter, I saw someone on a motorbike riding behind me for a long distance."

Meilin understood vulnerability. Being the petite woman that she was, she'd had her own problems with men when she was younger and could relate to what Linh was saying. With the recent FBI encounter in her hotel room, Meilin sympathized with Linh's anxiety.

Looking to Jun, Meilin asked, "did you have her followed?"

Jun's eyes moved to Linh. His lips tensed. "Yes. I was worried that she might have had too much to drink. I wanted to be sure she got home safely. I had someone from the office follow her."

Switching between Cantonese and English, Meilin was the only one grasping the full story. She didn't like the impression she was getting from Jun. Hearing Linh's side of the story, Linh's instincts impressed Meilin.

"You got home safely that night, but now things are very tense between the two of you," Meilin summarized.

"There's more," Jun said softly. "Linh felt threatened by the guy following her. He's now in the hospital. He'll have permanent injuries."

Meilin sat forward. Her feet reached the floor. "What did you do," Meilin asked, prompting Linh to explain.

"I tried to speed up to get away, but other motorbike speeds up, too. If I slow down to see what he would do, he slow down to stay behind me. Finally, I sped up and braked suddenly to surprise him, make him come up next to me while we were still moving. I always have something with me for protection. I used my stick to push him over and he crashed onto the street. I keep going."

Aaron strained to hear anything being said above him but couldn't make out anything except the sounds of voices. He wondered how long it could take for Linh to get paid. What could they possibly be talking about, he wondered.

"I like you," Meilin said looking at Linh.

Sensing that Meilin was siding with Linh, "that's not all," Jun interrupted. "She got into the office and burned documents. That was the smell you noticed in my office," Jun said in Cantonese.

Meilin didn't know whether to be angry at Linh or Jun or both. She could understand Linh's anger, but she couldn't justify Jun, her employee, withholding the information except for his fear of making her upset.

"What documents did you burn in Jun's office," Meilin asked.

"I burn just Vietnamese documents. They are copies of documents Mr. Ngo has in his office. I'm afraid. I don't want Jun to show Mr. Ngo and make trouble for me. Chinese documents still in Jun's office. I can't trust Jun," Linh explained. "He keeps many Vietnamese documents still in the office."

Meilin took a deep breath. Could she trust Jun? Or was all this the domino effect from what started in Washington?

"We're cutting ties with Linh. That's why we're here. I'll pay her and we leave," Jun said, tired of Meilin's questions and conversation with Linh that he couldn't understand.

Being able to hear both sides of what was happening between Jun and Linh, Meilin couldn't help but like the young woman's feistiness. Though she liked the strong-willed attitude Linh possessed, Meilin saw it as a detriment, too. Linh acting on impulse was a liability.

Jun sat on the edge of the sofa, straightened his back to be more erect. "Let's pay her and we can all leave," he said as a command rather than a suggestion.

Linh reacted to Jun's abrupt tone by letting her fingers feel the collapsed baton. She looked over at Meilin. The older woman remained still in her chair.

Jun stood up, reached into his inside jacket pocket, and pulled out an envelope. He didn't hold it out for Linh to take. "You don't say anything more to the Americans or Mr. Ngo about your work for me. You don't say anything to anyone, even friends," Jun insisted.

Linh glared at Jun. "What about you? If Mr. Ngo or other people find out, I will lose my job. I will lose everything."

"Mr. Yao will say nothing," Meilin said from her chair.

Jun extended his arm, holding out the envelope for Linh to take. When she reached for it, he didn't let it go immediately then saw that her other hand was in her belt bag. Jun released the envelope.

"You check it," Meilin suggested.

Linh did as Meilin said. She saw the large dong denominations and assumed the right amount was in the envelope. She didn't want to spend time counting it out. She felt an odd trust for the woman.

"Thank you," Linh said, turned and walked out of the office.

Meilin pushed herself out of the chair and went out onto the landing at the top of the steps in time to see Linh reach the bottom of the stairway. In the light below, she saw a man come out from under the stairway to join Linh.

"Hello Aaron Foster," Meilin said. She saw the man with the shaved head and beard look over his shoulder. He said nothing and kept walking with Linh to the exit. Meilin went back into the office. "Can you ask someone to go to the hotel where Mr. Foster is staying right away? I want to know if Linh and Mr. Foster are going there now. If the two of them go there, I want pictures of them," Meilin instructed.

Jun said nothing. He got on his cell phone and made a call.

Linh and Aaron marched across the floor of the warehouse and out to the waiting taxi.

"She know you," Linh asked.

Aaron wasn't sure how to answer. "She guesses that it's me. She's not sure." They slid into the back seat of the waiting taxi. "Tell him to take us back to where he picked us up," Aaron said to Linh. Aaron pulled out his cell phone and called his uncle.

"Uncle Drew. Hope you're not already tucked away in bed."

"No chance. It's still early," Drew answered.

"Meet me at my hotel that's too good for you," Aaron chided. "We need to talk and make certain arrangements asap. Linh is with me."

"Okay, sounds serious."

"It is. We should be there in the next thirty to forty-five minutes," Aaron said. Aaron looked over at Linh in the faint light available from the streetlamps and other vehicles. He saw her nod.

The ride back into the center of the city was faster than the ride out. Linh and Aaron were at the hotel in thirty minutes. There was no sign of Drew in the lobby. Aaron didn't like the idea of them lingering in the lobby and took Linh up to his room.

"Where are you," Aaron said when his uncle answered the phone.

"About five minutes away."

"Come straight up to the room," Aaron instructed, giving his uncle the room number.

Ten minutes later, Aaron heard the knock and let Drew into the small room.

Drew stepped in and stopped after clearing the door. "And you wanted me to check-in to this place?"

"Don't knock it. There's a bed, a private shower and air conditioning," Aaron said. Linh sat on the edge of the bed, avoiding the sunken center.

"Did you notice anything unusual at your hotel before you left," Aaron asked.

"I didn't notice anything," Drew answered. "I had a beer in the lobby lounge. I've gotten to know the bartender. He's friendly."

"Anybody seem to follow you out?"

"Again, not that I noticed. What the hell is going on?"

"Linh got her final payment for her extra work for her Chinese boss. Things are complicated. We're not sure we can trust the Chinese guy from getting her in trouble at the Maritime Administration. What's the timeline for her visa," Aaron asked.

"Only a few days. We've submitted all the documentation. That little push from the CG has helped move things along," Drew said. "What are you not telling me?"

"I'm only telling you things you need to know, nothing more."

"Not a good answer," Drew said.

"The only one I'm giving you," Aaron said, giving his uncle a stern stare. He broke eye contact and looked at Linh. "Linh, you should pack right away. You need to be ready to travel. I want you to stay here at the hotel until you leave for the States. I'll get you a room," Aaron said.

"What about work?"

"You go to work only one or two more days. That's all. Don't worry about work. I can go with you tonight to help pack and bring some things here."

"What are you thinking," Drew asked.

"She stays here at this hotel until that visa issues then the two of you fly to the States," Aaron answered. Aaron stood, hands on hips looking at Linh. "Linh, I changed my decision. Tomorrow, you quit your job. I don't want you to go to work after tomorrow."

"What I say to my boss?"

"Tell him the U.S. consulate contacted you and you are traveling to meet someone who they think is your father. It isn't a big lie, right?"

"What about my apartment?"

"Call and tell them the same thing," Aaron advised. "If someone asks, you tell everyone the same thing. This way, it's easier for you."

Linh sucked in her lips. She wasn't sure that she was ready for her whole world to change this fast.

"I'll try to reach Ms. Doan first thing tomorrow morning and find out about the visas so that I can make some flight reservations," Drew said. "What about you? When are you leaving?"

"Hopefully with you, but I'll wait to see how things work out the next day or two," Aaron said. "Let's get Linh a room."

The three went to the lobby. Aaron wasn't surprised to find rooms available and booked one on the same floor as his. He took the key and handed it over to Linh.

"I'll talk to you in the morning," Drew said, leaving Linh and Aaron to go to Linh's apartment.

Drew detoured on the way back to his hotel by way of The Bar. He sat on a bar stool and Harry served him a beer.

"How's it going," Harry asked.

"It's bat-shit crazy," Drew said.

Harry cocked his head prompting an explanation.

"My nephew and I followed up after the evening when we found that picture on your wall back there. My nephew started digging around and now we're not sure what's really going on with anything coming from that. My nephew seems to be playing some cloak and dagger games. I keep telling him that we should just get home and leave whatever is going on to those who are here. No need to get too involved." Drew didn't want to tell Harry or anyone else the real story.

"I got news for you. This place has turned into a wild place," Harry said, not surprised by what Drew said. "There's a lot of money flowing into this place and a lot of influence to be bought. You just can't get caught or you find yourself in a very unhappy place. Vietnam is attracting lots of attention. You're not the first to come in here and discover the new Vietnam isn't like what you remember."

Drew headed back to the hotel after two beers.

In the hotel lobby, Drew attracted no attention other than from those working at the front desk where he had become a familiar face after his lengthy stay. Chau and the young man who had followed Aaron to the hotel days earlier sat in the lobby trying to look like a couple and waited for Aaron. After a couple of hours and no sight of Aaron, they couldn't believe they had missed his return. Chau and the young man had arrived at the hotel within thirty minutes of Jun's call.

Jun flipped onto his back in bed when his cell phone rang and answered.

"We haven't seen the American," Chau said.

Jun checked the time. It was just past midnight. "Okay. I'll see you at the office in the morning." In Jun's mind, the only other place the American could be is with Linh. He needed to let go of everything connected to Linh. Being able to work under Meilin and staying on her good side was going to take a lot of effort. Allowing thoughts of Linh and the trouble she had caused to distract him could only lead to more problems. Though it was dark in his bedroom, he covered his eyes with his forearm and went to sleep.

* * * * *

"Do you know what to say to your boss," Aaron asked. Aaron was up early the next morning and brought coffee back to the hotel. He and Linh sat in his room sipping the hot brew."

"I say what you told me yesterday. I need to go right away because my American father is here, but he will leave soon," Linh said.

"Yes. After you tell them, you leave, and we'll meet up and come back here."

Linh sat on the only chair in Aaron's room. He saw that although her legs were crossed at the ankles, her left foot and leg bounced.

"Are you okay," Aaron asked.

"Maybe no," Linh answered honestly. "Scared."

"Scared of quitting the job?"

"No, scared of going to the United States."

Aaron nodded. Watching Linh, Aaron realized that Linh needed to be with him or Drew until she got on a plane. He worried that if she was left alone her fears might overwhelm her. Aaron and Linh finished their coffee. "Is it time to go?"

Linh didn't say anything. She stood up to leave and Aaron followed. The retail shops across the street from the Maritime Administration were closed at this hour of the morning. Aaron didn't like the idea of standing and waiting by the shops like he'd done before when they were open, even though the awnings provided some protection from the morning sun. Instead, he walked down toward the corner, stepped off the sidewalk into the shade cast by a few trees.

Aaron leaned against the tree and watched the sidewalks fill with morning foot traffic. He hoped that Linh would get things done quickly and come out. The longer he waited, the higher the volume of vehicle engines, horns, and beeping scooters and motorbikes. An hour into his vigil, he saw Linh on the edge of the sidewalk across the street trying to see where he was.

Aaron jogged out from under the tree and waved. That got Linh's attention. She gestured for him to wait, and she'd navigate the opening in traffic to cross the street. It took several minutes before she joined Aaron. He guided her back to the tree he used as cover from the sun.

"Why come here?"

"Before we go anywhere, I want you to look around and see if you recognize anyone in case Jun sent someone to follow you," Aaron said. He knew he was frightening Linh and probably going overboard but Jun had a history of having people followed so he wanted to be sure. The last thing Aaron needed was for Jun and, more importantly, Meilin to find out where he and Linh were staying.

He watched Linh slowly survey the opposite side of the street.

"I don't know anyone over there," Linh said.

They hailed a taxi and went back to the hotel. Aaron kept looking back through the rear window. It was a sea of motorbikes. Even if someone was following, he'd never be able to identify anyone in the swarm of bikes mixed in with the cars and trucks. He instructed Linh to have them dropped off a couple of blocks from the hotel. They detoured to a coffee shop and Aaron kept an eye on everyone that came in from his seat against a wall. Thirty minutes later, they left.

"You go to the hotel. I'll be there in ten minutes," Aaron said after exiting the coffee shop. He pretended to make a call, standing with his back against the wall of the retail shops but watching anyone leaving the coffee shop. Satisfied that Linh wasn't being followed, he put his phone away and walked to the hotel.

Aaron knocked on Linh's door. "Are you okay," he asked when she opened the door.

"Yes. I'm fine, better than before," Linh answered. "My boss not happy, but he say it's okay. How long I have to live in the hotel?"

"I'll check with the consulate and Uncle Drew. I hope only one or two more days," Aaron replied.

* * * * *

During the brief time he had been in Vietnam, Drew had adopted a morning routine of drinking coffee and reading the available English language newspaper in the hotel lobby before exploring different parts of the city. The routine afforded him a little people watching time in the mornings, enjoying the comings and goings of locals and foreigners in and around the hotel.

He had nothing planned for the day except to wait to hear from Aaron about Linh's trip into the office and to call Ms. Doan at the consulate about Linh's visa as soon as it was business hours.

Drew looked up from the newspaper and saw a woman enter the hotel. He was used to seeing boyishly thin young women around the city, but this woman was not a teen or twenty-something. His eyes followed her to the reception desk. He turned his attention back to the newspaper.

"No, madame, no Aaron Foster," the man at reception said. "But there is a different guest named Foster, not Aaron."

Jun had given Meilin the location of the hotel. She wanted to verify for herself that the man she saw was Aaron. She couldn't be sure. The Aaron she remembered had a full head of hair and no beard but that was seven years ago and by now he could've changed his appearance.

Drew's ears heard the English spoken by the man at the reception desk. By the looks of the woman, he expected the conversation to be in Vietnamese, not English. Since the man behind the reception counter was facing in his direction, it was easier for Drew to hear him. He couldn't hear what the woman was saying. Hearing Aaron's name mentioned, Drew lowered his arms and the newspaper.

Meilin tapped her fingers on the reception counter. "Was Aaron Foster a guest here last week or a few days ago?" She watched and heard the young man tapping the keyboard.

"Checked out," the young man said.

"He has a beard and no hair, right?"

"Yes, that was him. Easy to remember," the young man said. "Not many guests look like that."

Drew dropped his head as if reading the paper in his lap, but his eyes watched the woman conversing at the counter. Drew leaned forward, both forearms resting on his knees and putting the newspaper on the table.

"Thank you," Meilin said. She put sunglasses on and started for the hotel exit.

Drew was on his feet. He wanted to get outside before she got too far ahead and into a taxi. He got out to the corner, and she was gone. He hadn't seen any taxi or car pull up. He looked around and saw the woman on foot and striding down the street. She was already half a block away.

Drew needed to close the distance between them. Foregoing a taxi, Drew decided she wasn't going very far on foot in this humid weather. Two blocks up, she turned right and was walking in the direction of the Opera House. This was familiar territory. She turned left onto what he remembered as Tu Do Street but renamed as Dong

Khoi. A block up the street on the other side of the Opera House, Drew saw a nice-looking older hotel.

Drew followed the woman as they walked by the front of the Opera House and a small parking lot next to it. She turned right off Dong Khoi after the car park. A grand old hotel stood on the corner. It wasn't a modern high-rise, but a structure of only four floors fronting the street. Fearing she might duck into the hotel or a shop along the street, Drew closed the gap to ten feet. The area was congested with tourists and locals. He brushed past several groups strolling along the street.

Drew saw the woman enter the hotel. He followed, entering a lobby of dark woods and tiles contrasted against the light-colored columns and the ornate older colonial style. Coming in from the bright sunlit day, he couldn't slow or stop to allow his vision to adjust. He took a breath and hoped that the hotel employees would assume he was a hotel guest. He saw the woman head down a corridor. She bypassed the elevator for the wide carpeted stairway. Drew needed to follow, but not so close as to arouse suspicion. The stairway wasn't completely carpeted but covered the center portion of the steps and absorbed the sound of Drew's footsteps.

On the third floor of the building, the woman headed down the corridor. Drew followed in the same direction. He slowed his pace. Seeing her stop by a door, he turned toward a room door and put his hands in his pockets, pretending to feel for keys. She disappeared behind the door. Drew walked down toward the door that she had stopped at and looked at the room number.

Drew checked his watch. He wanted to give the woman a few minutes in the room. He wandered down to the opposite end of the corridor. Taking his time walking down the corridor, he admired the woodwork around the doors and ceiling and the rich color and finish on the floor. It was an elegant old building that had been taken care of during and after the war. Reaching the end of the corridor, he started back toward the woman's room. He passed other hotel guests and nodded.

Standing at the door of the woman's room, Drew looked down the hallway in both directions. Noticing the peep hole, he stepped to the side hoping to be out of its visual range. He knocked.

Meilin's body flinched at the sound of the knock. She looked over and saw that the bed was made. The room had been serviced. She wasn't expecting room service. She got up from the room's desk chair and went to the door. On her tiptoes, she looked through the peep hole but saw no one.

"Who is it?"

Drew knew he couldn't fake an accent to sound like a hotel employee. "Aaron Foster."

Meilin took a deep breath. She couldn't remember what Aaron's voice sounded like. It had been too long since she heard his voice. Her mind made an instant safety assessment.

"I'm going to open the door then step back so just wait a moment before coming in," Meilin instructed. Meilin opened the door an inch and walked backwards into the room five feet.

Drew saw the door open then counted to three. "I'm coming in," he said and pushed the door open and entered the room far enough to close the door behind him.

"Who are you?"

"I'm Drew Foster. I'm Aaron's uncle and Linh's father," Drew answered. "Why are you looking for Aaron?"

Meilin stepped backward farther into the room. She needed to keep space between them. "I have to know who is disrupting my business plans here."

As Meilin retreated farther into the room, Drew took several steps and stopped. "I saw you at the hotel this morning asking about Aaron. He's no longer there. He's not here to interfere with your business. He came with me. I came to find Linh," Drew said. "Right now, he's doing whatever he needs to do to protect my daughter, his cousin. I hope that clears things up for you. One last thing, if you or your people do anything to Linh, I'll come looking for whoever is responsible for any harm to her. I hope that's clear."

Meilin said nothing. Her thoughts flashed back to Hong Kong when Kaili had been abducted and taken across the border to southern China. She had just met Kaili and didn't know anything about her other than that Kaili was a distant cousin in trouble and in need of help. Looking at Drew and hearing what he said, she felt that the situation was now reversed. She or Jun was seen as the threat and Linh needed help.

"It's clear. Linh is not connected to me or my company."

"Then I hope I don't see you again," Drew said. He turned and left the room.

Meilin closed the door, making sure it was locked and bolted. She went to her desk. With a deep sigh, she felt relieved. She called Jun. "You make sure that no one from the office, including yourself, makes any contact with Ms. Phan. Is that clear," Meilin ordered.

Drew smiled to himself as he walked back to the hotel. The encounter with the woman at the hotel went better than he expected. His prepaid cell phone buzzed in his pocket. "Yes, hello?"

"Mr. Foster, Janice Doan at the consulate. Ms. Phan's visa has been processed. She can come by at her convenience."

"What if we pop by this afternoon?"

"Yes, that's fine. I don't need to be there. I'll make sure my colleagues are aware," Janice Doan said and cut the connection.

Great, he thought. He hoped that before the end of the day, he'd have plane tickets in hand for him and Linh to start the journey home.

Networks

O liver Vega pulled his long black hair back and tucked the hair behind his ears. He sat on a shaded bench in the green space between the buildings of the Patent Office campus. A cup of coffee was on the bench next to him. He checked his watch. 10:45. In a few minutes, he had to meet his supervisor for a work performance review. None of his colleagues in his group had said anything about being reviewed. It wasn't near the end of the fiscal year, but maybe it could be a mid-year review, he thought.

Vega got up and walked toward his building when he saw his supervisor coming out. Vega saw him wave then gesture to go toward the Madison Building. In the open atrium, Vega waited till his supervisor joined him.

"What's this meeting about," Vega asked.

"I don't have all the details. We'll know in a few minutes," the supervisor replied. He led Vega into the elevator.

"I thought I was just meeting with you," Vega said.

"The director's Chief of Staff, Curtis Campbell, wanted this meeting."

Vega looked at himself in the stainless-steel reflection wearing khaki pants and a George Washington University sweatshirt. Though it wasn't a tight fit, he pulled on the neck of the sweatshirt.

The two men walked to Campbell's office. The supervisor tapped on Campbell's door. When it opened, the supervisor gave a nod, turned, and left.

"Come in," Campbell said to Vega, pointing to a chair.

As he stepped into Campbell's office, Vega's head jerked to the side seeing a man and woman standing in the corner. Vega stared at them as he moved to a chair and sat down.

Campbell closed the door behind him. "I'm going to let the three of you have some privacy," he said and left the office.

Adams took up a position in front of the door and Vera Jamison pulled a chair from the corner, angling it toward Vega and sat down. Both agents let Vega see their FBI credentials.

"We're here to check some information we've received and thought this would be a good place for us to talk," Jamison said, trying to put Vega at ease. "Is it correct that you are a part-time law student?"

Vega nodded.

"You weren't on our list as participating in the agency's tuition program. Is that correct?"

"Yes," Vega said.

"How are you paying for tuition?"

"I'm paying out of my own pocket and have some loans to cover it. Why do you care?"

"Cut to the chase," Adams said.

"Your name was mentioned by Xiong Zimo. He works for the Chinese Government. Do you know him?" Jamison asked.

"I know who he is, but we're not friends or anything. He asked me lots of questions. I didn't want anything to do with him. His approach was awkward because there was nothing subtle about what he wanted. No one with an ounce of sense could mistake what he wanted," Vega explained.

"Does that mean that he asked you to give him information about your work," Jamison asked.

"Never straight out like that, but he was clearly interested to know the details. I thought it was all too weird. He's Chinese, coming to class from work, dressed in a suit all the time and his English was pretty good. It made me uncomfortable. After a couple of initial conversations, I kept my distance," Vega added.

"Did you ever think to report it to anyone," Adams asked.

"Not really."

"Did you see him getting friendly with others who work here," Jamison asked.

"It wasn't something I paid much attention to. I worked all day then went to classes in the evening. I'm too tired to do anything other than concentrate on those two things."

Jamison looked over at Adams.

"Take the rest of the day off," Jamison said. "We've already cleared that with Mr. Campbell. You can go."

Adams moved away from the door to allow Vega to leave. Vega eyed them as he stood up and walked out.

Campbell re-entered his office. "The tech team's already doing a diagnostic to see if there's anything they can find that's suspicious activity and security is checking around his work station."

"He seemed sincere in his responses, so we think he's okay," Jamison said.

"As we've said before, for your sake and the sake of everyone in this agency, it would be a good idea to adopt, implement and enforce stronger security measures. Otherwise, we might not be the only law enforcement agents making regular visits here," Adams cautioned.

"Understood and I agree," Campbell said. "It's not easy in a place like this where so much information comes in as confidential and becomes public in the process. We're all potential targets."

"Given that we've heard from a couple of people we've interviewed that they were approached by Xiong, a good place to start might be an awareness campaign with a hotline to report suspicious contacts," Adams suggested.

* * * * *

Paperwork piled up on FBI Agent Chris Kearns's desk. He didn't have time to go through the stack of folders and work it down. Every time he wrote up something about what he and his team were doing about the Chinese Embassy staff, and anything related to it, he got more requests for details. The people above him were burying him under more paper.

Kearns's cell phone buzzed. He didn't get a chance to say anything. "Ahh, shit, this can't be good," he muttered aloud to himself. He grabbed the suit jacket off the back of his chair.

"Olvera, I've been summoned to HQ. Deal with anything that pops up till I get back," Kearns said as he walked by David Olvera's desk.

"Everything okay," Olvera asked.

"Something's up. I don't know what it is, but everything is not okay, otherwise I wouldn't have gotten the call," Kearns replied as he walked away.

Kearns thought his short trip to Pennsylvania Avenue would take less time than going through building security and trying to find the office of the person who summoned him. He knew it was never good to get asked to see someone several levels above his direct boss. During his short trip to the building, Kearns thought through his actions and those of his team during the past couple of weeks. Most of that time was spent dealing with everything stemming from Xiong Zimo's unsuccessful attempt to get info from Lucas Moore.

Once in the building and on the right floor, Kearns walked slowly to read all titles on the doors along the corridor. Kearns stopped when he saw the sign for the Executive Assistant Director for National Security. Not sure whether to walk in or knock, he knocked lightly and opened the door.

"Here to see the assistant director," Kearns said to the woman sitting behind a desk in the outer office. He stood at the desk while she picked up the phone and announced Kearns's arrival. When she was done, her eyes invited him to take a seat.

Kearns stepped away from the desk but remained standing. A door opened and Kearns saw a man with his necktie loosened and his sleeves rolled up showing muscular forearms. The assistant director wasn't a thin man but wasn't carrying extra weight on a frame of average height. The assistant director looked like a man trying to find the time to fight off the weight gain that comes with a desk job.

"Come in, Kearns."

Chris Kearns walked by the assistant director and stopped several feet past the door. He waited till the assistant director came around and plopped into his chair.

"Take a seat. Wondering why you're here?"

"Yes sir," Kearns answered as he lowered himself in the chair facing the assistant director.

"I've seen several reports originating from your desk recently. I started to think you were writing a book," the assistant director said smiling. "I wasn't paying too much attention to the reports until a couple of days ago. These reports seemed to be all over the place. Scattershot. There's a Vietnamese angle and a Chinese angle to all this. And let's not forget the out of left field Patent and Trademark Office security breach.

"I started asking questions of other people and no one gave me the answers I wanted so I thought I'd go straight to the source. There are a couple of details lacking in these reports. For example, do you have a Chinese linguist on your team or someone who speaks or reads Vietnamese? If not, I'm wondering how you have all this detail about the contents of the documents. No one I've spoken to is aware of any requests for foreign language support, but everything points to having that support."

Chris Kearns filled his lungs with a deep breath. "Our surveillance on the Chinese Embassy and the embassy employee who attempted to get confidential information eventually led us directly to someone who speaks Chinese, and she is unidentified in my reports. She's in a sensitive position here in town and we hoped to protect her from any unwanted attention. In fact, she was being watched by Chinese security and we were able to terminate that surveillance. Her assistance has been critical to our investigation."

"Okay, I appreciate your efforts to protect a source. I'm fine with that explanation for now. That answers the question about the Chinese, but that leaves us with the Vietnamese part of this investigation."

"Once we had the Chinese documents, we needed to find out if the Vietnamese documents were translations of the Chinese or English materials we had," Kearns began.

"Does your unidentified asset also have Vietnamese language skills?"

"No, sir."

"How did you deal with that obstacle?"

Kearns thought about how to describe the situation without sounding like he was throwing Kellie Liang under the bus. "We were trying to find a way to expedite a translation of the documents, so while I looked into the procedures to do that, my asset, as you describe her, went about finding some creative ways of doing that as well."

"Did you know what those creative ways were?"

"Not until she had already engaged someone to do it," Kearns answered. "She reached out to the local Vietnamese community and identified someone who could help."

"Here we are worried that confidential information is being sought by the Chinese and without any concern for divulging that same confidential information we give some schmuck off the street access to that information. Is that a good way to sum up?"

"Technically, sir, none of the documents we shared are classified," Kearns replied.

"But aren't all these documents based on information originally considered at least confidential in nature," the assistant director challenged. "If the foreign language documents had been reviewed properly, are you confident that they would not be classified."

"No, sir. I'm sure that in time somebody would've stamped them with a 'Confidential' classification or higher. But my asset thought of a creative and, shall I say, timely solution to the predicament we were in, and I have to add that her assistance allowed us to interview the Chinese Embassy employee while he was in-transit to China and get another name and person working at the Patent Office to interview. In a perfect world, we would have immediate access to whatever translation services we need, but we don't. In the field, we need to remember that perfect is the enemy of good."

The assistant director leaned back. His chair reclined slightly. "I'm not trying to give you a hard time. I needed to understand more of the details that are missing from your summaries. This particular case is giving me and others heartburn. We know that the level of economic espionage is growing, but seeing this case involving a patent examiner takes this to a different level completely. How the hell do we clamp down on thousands of people working over there and secure all the tech info businesses are submitting?"

"It took my team by surprise, too," Kearns said. "The night we prevented Lucas Moore from giving Xiong the files, we expected that Moore worked for a defense related agency or company. We were all stunned when we found out where he works."

"Tell me about the woman, your asset."

"I'd prefer not to reveal her identity," Kearns said.

"She's not officially with the FBI in any way?"

"No. She works on Capitol Hill and events happened to cause her path to intersect with our investigative path. It all fell into place that she was receptive to helping us because of the Chinese angle and her ability to speak the language. It turned out that a Chinese national who became a person of interest at one point during the investigation was someone she knows."

"Agent Kearns, now you're telling me things you withheld from your reports. Your asset knows a person of interest in this case. How or what is the status on that?"

"We interviewed the person of interest. She was preparing to leave the country. Based on the interview, she did not appear to be directly involved in the matter we were investigating so we had no reason to prevent her departure, and she has now left. But I can say that information she provided in her interview allowed us to connect the dots with some questionable activities in Vietnam that our consulate is following up on," Kearns explained.

The assistant director mulled the information. As big as Washington, D.C., is, it's also a small town in an odd way. The assistant director was no stranger to people working on Capitol Hill. Like a lot of senior government officials, he kept his eyes and ears open to others who might be in sensitive government jobs. The thought that someone who worked on the Hill and spoke Chinese spurred his mind to consider who helped Kearns's team.

"I'm recalling that at the beginning of this, you met with Senator Burke," the assistant director said.

"That's correct."

"He has someone on his staff who's Asian, right?"

"She's Chinese American," Kearns corrected. "Her father's Chinese and her mother is American."

"She's your asset, isn't she?"

"I'll neither confirm nor deny," Kearns said.

Hearing Kearns's response and smiling, the assistant director let his chair return to its upright position. "You have to know that there's a deep background report on her given her nomination."

"I'm aware of it, but that has nothing to do with this investigation," Kearns answered.

"You're right. I think we're done. I appreciate the additional details." The assistant director rose and extended a hand. The two men shook hands and Kearns exited the office.

The assistant director shook his head. He didn't like agents being cowboys but if Kearns had stuck to the standard bureaucratic process, he wouldn't have progressed as fast as he did. If it was Liang who was involved and the one who came up with the unusual idea of seeking out someone in the local Vietnamese community to help, it was creative thinking outside the box. He thought there should be a better position for someone like her where she could put her skills and talent to better use, assuming she was the one working with Kearns.

The assistant director's contact list included lots of government officials with fancy titles. He also had a list of other people who had government and military backgrounds involved in private pursuits to advance either American interests or interests of internationalists concerned with China's economic and military ambitions. The assistant director pulled out his private cell phone and called a man that a small circle of people referred to as the Colonel.

* * * * *

Kellie rode the escalator up at Dupont Circle. She glanced behind her. As the escalator reached ground level, she stepped off the escalator and onto the sidewalk. She surveyed the faces around her, a routine that had become ingrained over recent days. The days were getting longer, and it was still light out as it approached seven in the evening.

Kellie strode briskly, but it wouldn't be enough to prevent someone from following her because of the number of street crossings she had to make to get to her apartment. Anyone good at shadowing someone would've been able to keep her in sight. That didn't stop Kellie from trying to make it as difficult as possible. As she reached her street, she employed another new habit of looking at the cars parked between the corner of her block and where she turned up the steps to enter her building. She looked for anyone sitting in the car.

Two men dressed in dark suits sat in a parked black Cadillac sedan. The car was midway between where Kellie had turned and entered her building and the far end of her block. She didn't see them. Their plan was to give her ten minutes.

Kellie stood barefoot peeking out her window onto the street. She looked down the street in the direction of the cars she didn't pass by on her way to the apartment. There was still enough natural light to let her see the Cadillac. She couldn't see faces because of the angle, but she saw two men.

Kellie pulled her cell phone from her bag and punched in Vera Jamison's number. The benefit of spending hours in a car in the middle of the night with someone was that there was a level of familiarity gained even if most of the time was spent just sitting together without conversation. To Kellie's mind, Vera was approachable.

"Hey, it's Kellie, I need to ask a question. Is the FBI keeping watch on me?"

"Not that I know of, but I really have no idea. Why? What's up," Vera asked.

"A Caddy is parked on the street. From my window, I see two suits sitting in it."

"If you're sure they are Caddies, it's definitely not us. We wouldn't use those in that way. Maybe it's the Chinese resuming their watch," Vera said.

"Don't think so."

"I can come by, check them out," Vera offered.

"If you don't mind, I'd appreciate it," Kellie said.

"It's going to take at least twenty minutes, probably a little longer," Vera said.

"I don't plan on going anywhere," Kellie answered. She gave Vera her apartment address in case Vera had forgotten after that pre-dawn drop-off after the night with Meilin.

Kellie ended the call and walked to the kitchen to see what she had in the refrigerator. A plastic bowl of mixed fruit, yogurt, cheeses, and skim milk made up the scarce choices. Her head swiveled toward the door at the sound of the knock. She closed the refrigerator door, felt for her phone in her front pocket and moved to the door. Through the peephole, she saw two men of equal height in suits.

Kellie stood to the side of the door frame so she'd be out of the way in case the door was forced open. She opened the door only as far as the chain would allow. The two men appeared to be in their late twenties or early thirties, both clean shaved.

"Who are you?"

"Security detail," the blond-haired young man standing closest to the door said. The brown-haired young man in the back said nothing.

Both flashed identification but replaced them in their jacket pockets before Kellie could examine them. All she saw was a blur of images that seemed to have photos and an agency logo.

"We were instructed not to bother you during the day while you were at work. If you could just come with us. We'd appreciate it."

"You've been parked on the street watching and waiting? Is this part of the State Department background check," Kellie asked. Across the landing, she saw the door to Connie's apartment open a few inches.

"Yes, but we don't know anything more other than where we've been told to drive you."

"Give me a couple of minutes to get my things and I'll be with you," Kellie said, closing the door and leaving the two standing on the stairway landing.

The dark-haired young man left his partner and returned to the car. He got in behind the steering wheel and leaned toward the passenger side. He reached for the cell phone signal scrambler in the footwell and turned it on. They wouldn't have to take Kellie's phone from her and raise her suspicions. But she wouldn't be able to call anyone from the car. He got out and stood in front of the car to make a quick call. Seeing his partner and Kellie walking out, he opened the rear passenger door then got in behind the steering wheel.

Kellie still wore the black pants and blue blouse from earlier in the day. She grabbed a dark blue sweater and her small purse with its long shoulder strap.

"How long is this going to take," Kellie asked.

"Hopefully, our travel time will be about forty-five minutes, but that depends on traffic," the driver answered. It was late enough that the rush hour parking restrictions were no longer in place. The driver picked a route to avoid the delays that street parking might cause. He made good time after getting onto Canal Road and the Cabin

John Parkway. Avoiding any time on the beltway, he headed west and through Potomac.

Kellie tried her phone, knowing that Vera Jamison was supposed to be at her apartment, but her phone couldn't get a signal.

"Either of you have a cell phone I could borrow? I can't get a signal, and I was expecting someone to stop by my place. I need to let them know I won't be there."

"Try mine," the blond headed guy in the passenger seat said and handed Kellie his phone knowing that the call wouldn't go through.

"Your phone doesn't work, either. Thanks anyway," Kellie said and handed it back. After going through the village of Potomac, she was in an unfamiliar area. Despite living in the D.C. area for years, exploring this area in the suburbs had never occurred to her. The houses were huge and surrounded by generous land that Kellie could never imagine she could afford. The farther out River Road they went, the more space there was between homes.

They reached a T intersection. Kellie had no idea where she was, and the only natural light was a glow on the horizon that would be gone in minutes. The driver turned left.

"Where are we going," Kellie asked.

"We should be there in ten minutes," the driver replied.

Kellie's pulse quickened. Her breathing was faster and shallower. She hit the button to lower her window, but the windows were locked. "Can you open the window? I'd like some fresh air."

The driver opened the window a couple of inches. Kellie felt a bit calmer, but she started thinking about how she'd been abducted in Hong Kong, taken into China, and stuck there without her passport. She took a deep breath. This was different, but she couldn't help but think back to that event. These two hadn't drugged her. They opened the window for her. They let her keep her phone. Out the window, it was dark. To Kellie, they might as well have been a hundred miles from the city. She saw hardly any lights. The country road was narrow. There were occasional roads turning off the one they were on, but those seemed to be narrower country roads.

She was geographically lost and looked out through the windshield. The driver switched on the high beams allowing Kellie to see the road ahead until it disappeared into the night. The road edge surrendered to a dirt and grassy edge. The car decelerated with the driver letting up on the gas pedal. Kellie looked around but saw nothing. A hundred yards farther and the car turned into a driveway lined with hedges and trees.

A large house appeared as the car proceeded down the paved driveway. The driveway became a circular driveway in front of a massive two-story structure. The ground floor windows that fronted the circular driveway cast enough light that the footlights along the edge of the driveway and along the sides of the steps to the front door weren't needed.

The blond-haired young man got out and opened the door for Kellie. "You can go on in. They're waiting for you."

Kellie said nothing as she took the steps to the door which opened as she reached the last step.

The suited young man who opened and held the door open for her looked to be from the same mold as the two men in the car. Something wasn't right, Kellie thought. These three weren't just drivers and servants. Everything about them screamed *security* to her. They were young, fit, and disciplined in the way they moved. Kellie stepped into a two-story foyer that had a curved staircase leading upstairs where she saw that the lights from the foyer faded to the darkened second floor.

"This way, please," the young man said after closing and locking the door.

Their footsteps echoed off the marble tiled floor. Kellie followed him past the staircase to the backside of what she considered a mansion. He turned and opened a door leading into an expansive room with dark hardwood flooring covered by a large area rug. The inside wall was lined with shelves filled with books that would make a visitor think this was a library, but the exterior wall of glass opened onto a patio area surrounding an in-ground pool.

The furnishings were a mishmash of leather chairs and a couple of matching sofas and a long cherry wood dining table that could seat ten for dining. The far wall held a large flat screen television. Kellie wasn't sure what the room should be used for as she entered.

After the quick visual of the room, she saw eight people sitting and standing around the room. Three women and five men. From their looks, Kellie guessed she was the youngest of the crowd. She stopped and stood five feet into the room with the door closed behind her.

"Ms. Liang, we're very glad to see you," a man sitting at the dining table said as he got up to greet her. Instead of a suit, he wore a sport coat over a black silk shirt and gray slacks.

Kellie nodded. The man approaching her was big. She guessed that he could be six-four and probably a good two-hundred fifty pounds, but not fat. He was wide at the shoulders and everywhere else. She shook his large, thick hand. She thought he could be a bigger and older version of the three young men she'd already encountered.

"You have me at a disadvantage," Kellie said, looking around the room. Everyone was smartly dressed and smiling at her, but no one else got up to greet her. "I'm no longer believing that this has to do with the State Department background investigation."

"You're only partially correct," one of the women said. "This has nothing to do with a background investigation, but it is related to the State Department."

Kellie was listening, expecting the woman to continue, but she didn't. "Excuse me, but who are you? What is this and why am I here?"

"All good questions," the big man answered. "But tonight is not the night for you to get answers to those questions. Our group has studied your file. We're familiar with the paper version of you and your background. We know about your father's import business and the problems it caused you and everything that happened in Hong Kong and China in 1998. To keep it short, let's just say that we know about your professional background and some of the personal obstacles. And we're also impressed by your recent quiet work with the FBI."

Kellie stood, looked around, closed her eyes, and shook her head for a few seconds before looking at the no-name man towering over her. "If all of you know all of this, then what am I doing here," Kellie said with an attitude.

The big man smiled at her then turned to the others in the room. "See, just the kind of reaction we'd expect from her." He turned back to his unhappy visitor. "Call me Colonel. That's all that you'll get this evening. You get no names tonight. If you are a great sketch artist from memory for faces and somehow find us on the internet, you're even better than we believe. What I will tell you is that we are all well-placed in international business. We have global interests. We like predictability, stability, and continuity. We know that being in global business subjects us to some bad actors in the world and, usually, we can deal with that. There are times, however, when some bad actors might require more than the usual measures to be used to bring us back to the kind of stability we and the global economy need for continued success," the Colonel explained.

"And what does any of what you've just said have to do with me," Kellie replied.

"You have special talents and creative problem-solving skills that we like. We're concerned that what you have to offer could be lost or not fully utilized if you are limited to a specific State Department position. There, you have a strict chain of command, a specific portfolio, and the constant turf battles with people more worried about who gets credit for things as opposed to getting things done," the Colonel said.

Kellie listened, trying to decipher what the Colonel was saying. "Is this your way of offering me an alternative to the State Department? If it is, it isn't a very clear job description."

"Dear, we became aware of you very recently and we've only had a very short time to study your file. Knowing what's in the file and now seeing you in person, I like you even more," said a woman with a British accent from where she sat across the room. Her shoulder length blond hair was in that transition mode of becoming lighter with age. "It's too early to provide you with a specific job description. Now that I see you, I see lots of possibilities that will have to be discussed."

Kellie looked at the others. Two of the eight people in the room were Asian. She couldn't know for sure if they were Chinese, Korean, Japanese or from another Asian country. One man might be Latino. The Colonel was obviously an American, but the rest could be American, Canadian, or European.

"I'm not in the job market," Kellie said as her eyes moved from one person to another in the room. "If I'm confirmed for the position at State, I'll be working to create that stability that you value in a part of the world that you're probably concerned about and where you're chasing profits."

"But that's the problem. Your position there would be limited to greater China. We understand that the world is bigger than that. And, chaos erupts unexpectedly in many places," a man's voice said.

Kellie saw the man sitting at the dinner table farther away. He had a slight accent, causing Kellie to peg him as being from Central or South America. The man had a distinct look with a wide forehead and dark eyes that gave way to pronounced cheeks and a narrow chin. His face was triangular.

"Does this group," Kellie waved her left arm around the room, "have a name or a corporate identity?"

"Not relevant to you at this point," the Colonel answered. "This is a preliminary meet and greet. We're just feeling each other out."

"You and your colleagues are doing all of the feeling out. I'm the one being felt, and I don't like how I feel about that. What if I'd like to go back to my apartment?"

"I can summon the two gentlemen who drove you here to take you back. By no means are we holding you captive like you were in China," the Colonel said.

"I'd appreciate that. It wasn't my plan to be out this evening and it's going to be late by the time I get home."

The Colonel nodded. Someone in the room pressed a button to have the car brought around. "I'll accompany you," the Colonel said. He led Kellie out of the room and back to the door. The same Cadillac pulled up and the blond-haired young man opened the rear passenger door for Kellie.

"A pleasure to meet you in person Ms. Liang. Good luck with the confirmation vote that's coming up. I hope this wasn't too much of an inconvenience. One last thing for you to keep in mind. You work for people who have power to some degree. But, frankly, it's perceived power, not real power. This small group here in this room and others who are part of our group have real power. We put tens of millions in the coffers of campaigns that put people in office. Our corporate staff and the lobbyists we pay help write those laws those we put in office believe they thought up and promote as theirs. Our power is real. I hope you'll remember that as you wake up and go to work on the Hill."

Kellie wasn't sure what she should say. "You and your friends provided me with an evening like no other. Thank you." She shook the Colonel's outstretched hand and descended the few steps to the car.

The Colonel stood and watched the car head down the long driveway. He turned and returned to the room where the seven others remained.

"What're your initial thoughts now that you've seen her," the Colonel asked.

"We talked while you were out of the room," the British accented woman said. "It's not unanimous, but five of us are inclined to make the investment. If you're with us, that makes six in her favor."

The Colonel stood in the center of the room, turning to look at his gathered guests. "Well then, I think I need to make a few calls and to insure we have a favorable outcome when the vote for her confirmation occurs.

* * * * *

Vera Jamison knocked on Kellie's apartment door. After waiting what she thought was the appropriate amount of time, she knocked harder.

Connie heard the pounding and opened her door to look across the landing. "She's not there," Connie said.

"What?"

"She's not there. She left a little while ago. Two guys in suits were here and she went with them."

"How long ago was that? She called and asked if I could come over. I'm surprised she'd leave knowing that I was coming."

"No clue," Connie said.

"Thanks. I'll call her later and make sure she's alright." Vera Jamison exited the building. On the sidewalk, she looked up and down the street. She wondered why Kellie didn't call and let her know she wouldn't be there. Vera's instincts as an agent told her that something wasn't right. She got into her car and didn't like the sightline to Kellie's building from her parking spot. She pulled out and drove toward Dupont Circle, making a U-turn before she got to the intersection. She squeezed into a tight spot across the street from Kellie's building with an unobstructed view of the entrance.

Vera's head was back against the headrest. She'd spent the first hour sketching snippets of faces as the streetlamps highlighted features of people walking by. With fewer pedestrians to sketch, Vera listened to music for half an hour. It was after nine. She could see cars approaching from behind by looking into her side mirror without moving her head. She concentrated on makes and models of cars moving by and license plates.

It was approaching ten when Vera saw another car turn onto the street but moving slower than most. She lowered herself in the front seat so that her head wasn't raised, making it appear that the car wasn't occupied. Vera saw that it was a dark Cadillac sedan as it passed her and rolled to a stop about two car lengths ahead of her car. Vera lowered herself but was able to see the New York license plate. She watched a young man get out of the front passenger seat and open the rear door. Vera's patience was rewarded.

After Kellie crossed the street and entered the building, the Cadillac pulled away. Vera stayed in her car and waited till the Cadillac turned and was out of sight before she made a move to get out. Vera jogged across the street, entered the building, and knocked on Kellie's apartment door.

When the door opened, the chain was still latched. "You going to let me in?"

"Sorry," Kellie said, closing the door momentarily to unlatch the chain. "Come in. I'm so sorry. I tried to call you, but I couldn't get a signal from the car. It was so strange."

"What do you mean you couldn't get a signal? You were still around here. There are plenty of towers. Where the hell did you go?"

"We went out to the country somewhere. It seemed like another twenty or thirty minutes after going through Potomac Village. I've never been out the way they went," Kellie explained.

"When did you try to call me?"

"Probably within the first ten or fifteen minutes after I left," Kellie replied.

"They probably had something in the car to prevent you from making calls. Instead of taking your phone and making you suspicious and panicky, they let you keep your phone but had a scrambler or something," Vera said. "What the hell happened?"

"It was strange. These two guys, well dressed, business-like said they waited till I was off work to come get me for another State Department background security related thing."

"Is that the story they told you," Vera said.

Kellie wasn't quick to answer. "Actually, they didn't come out and say any of that. Now that I think about it, I'm the one who made that assumption and asked them if this was about the State Department. They just went along with what I said. I made it easy for them."

"You're fine, right? You're not hurt?"

"No. I'm fine. There was a group of people. They knew who I was. They said they had a file on me and said I would feel too constricted in a job at the State Department. It was like a preliminary job interview, but they never said what the job is or where the job is. Like I said, it was very weird."

"What about names, who these people work for," Vera pressed.

"Yeah, that was another weird thing that added to the mystery. They didn't introduce themselves. No names, no titles, no company names, nothing that could identify them. The main guy who did all the talking said to call him Colonel. That was as close to a name as I got."

Vera hadn't moved from the spot where she stopped and stood after entering Kellie's apartment. "People in this town like to give themselves lofty ranks and titles so whoever this self-named Colonel is might turn out to be something a lot less," Vera said.

"No, I think this guy might be the real thing. On the one hand, he did most of the talking, but it isn't like the others deferred to him as if he was the man in charge. A couple of others who spoke weren't Americans. One woman had a British English accent and one of the men is probably from somewhere in South America. These people are internationalists. He's one of them.

"They're smart. They got me out there at night when there was no way for me to see where this place is located. No names, nothing that I can do to try and identify them. They had a chance to supplement what they know about me on paper with a face-to-face meeting. I'm not sure what they got out of my presence," Kellie added.

"Sit," Kellie said. Kellie poured a glass of wine for them without asking. They sat. "Maybe you can suggest a course I can take to become more like you and your fellow agents," Kellie said with a laugh.

"It's not a good way to live if you're constantly suspecting every new face to be a bad guy," Vera said. "You don't make many friends that way."

"Well, I need to learn to be more perceptive when people try to get close to me. I was too gullible this evening going along with those guys," Kellie said.

"No, not gullible. It was reasonable. You've been under the microscope recently and you'll probably be under it for some time to come. Everything you do, everywhere you go, you're being assessed by someone and the scrutiny at that level can overwhelm you, so you'll have to find an outlet for the stress," Vera advised.

"Sign me up for some rigorous outdoor activities," Kellie said.

"You could sign up to skydive, or go bungee jumping, zip lining or get shot at by paintballs in the woods," Vera suggested with a smile.

Kellie laughed. "Those are some things to think about. I need more diversions from work."

"I can help you find some of that if you want," Vera answered.

"I'd like that. And thanks for coming over this evening and checking up on me. I really appreciate it," Kellie said.

"I'm glad I stuck around. You know your neighbor is discreet and keeps an eye out for you. If it wasn't for her, I would've left. I've got to get going," Vera said, finishing her glass of wine.

"I hope there's no need to tell your colleagues about this evening," Kellie said.

"I've made a mental note of the evening's events. I don't think any crime was committed," Vera replied.

Vera left Kellie's apartment. Because of Kellie's job situation, Vera's plan was to write down those mental notes and get it into a file for herself to keep once she was home.

It was late, but Kellie wasn't in the mood to sleep. She went to her small desk and turned on her computer and checked emails. The list of new incoming emails included one from Aaron that had arrived a few hours earlier, while she was out.

"Kellie, hope to see you within the next several days. Lots happened here. My uncle and I are coming home with his daughter, will explain more about that later. Another angle involving the daughter has to do with her work at the Maritime Administration and working for CODE. No elaboration now, that's for when we speak face-to-face. Saw Meilin, she didn't recognize me, but had her suspicions. The Consul General and I had a meeting at the Maritime Administration. I think we've shut down, for now, CODE/ChiTran/China's efforts to use the stolen information to gain an edge in port developments. Hopefully, the U.S. Embassy in Hanoi will carefully inform D.C. via cable as to some of what has happened. Your clearance level should allow you to see whatever they communicate."

Kellie sat back staring at the email and the hints to so much Aaron didn't want to say in an email. She reread the sentences about the uncle's daughter, Aaron's cousin. She shook her head; the thought of cousins struck her. The irony of it hit her. Meilin, Kellie's distant and illegitimate cousin involved in resolving her Hong Kong abduction situation and now Aaron's newly discovered illegitimate cousin working for the Maritime Administration and CODE.

Kellie realized that Aaron's cousin must have had a hand in putting the brakes on Meilin's Vietnam operation. It made sense to get Aaron's cousin out of the country, she thought. Despite the lack of detail in the email, Kellie knew that Aaron's cousin should be interviewed by people who would want to know what she saw, what she did, and who the players are in Vietnam.

Kellie wasn't sure how to reply. She kept it simple. "Want to see you when you're back. Hope I get to meet your cousin. Lots to talk about. Love, Kellie." She stared at the short note and wondered if she should change how she ended it. She hit send.

Kellie's head sunk into the pillow, deadening the little night sounds from the back of her building. The more she tried not to think about anything and invite sleep, the more the Colonel's voice echoed in her head. She couldn't argue about the point he made about the role of money and the power that money gave to those who controlled how it was doled out. She wondered if the people in the room were using it for her or against her. When sleep arrived, it was fitful.

Predictability

Aaron steered his silver Miata into a no parking zone by the curb and turned on his hazard lights. The late April sun made it feel like summer instead of late spring. After being in Ho Chi Minh City, the D.C. heat didn't bother him. With the top down, he popped out of the car and jogged up the steps and into the building, taking the steps two at a time. He knocked on the door.

He listened as the door was being unlocked. "Hey stranger," he said when the door opened and stepped into the doorway and gave Kellie a hug. He felt her tight embrace before she stepped back.

Kellie laughed. It was her first sight of Aaron since he got home from Vietnam five days earlier. "I don't think the shaved head look suits you and what's going on with your neck?"

"I thought I told you I was growing a beard while I was gone. Anyway, shaving it off wasn't as easy as I thought it would be. It irritated my skin. Enough of that. Are you ready? I'm illegally parked."

Kellie reached out, grabbed a hat. "Let's go."

"You have directions," Aaron said, putting on his sunglasses.

"Sort of," Kellie answered. "We're going house hunting for that place I told you about being taken to."

"We have all day, right?"

"Yeah. Senator Burke wants me to take the day off and try not to think about what's going on. I should know what my fate is by the end of the day," Kellie said.

"I thought this was just a formality at this point," Aaron said as he steered the car around Dupont Circle and got onto Massachusetts Avenue heading northwest.

"Nothing is that easy and the Senator has been hush-hush about things the past several days, which makes me feel somewhat pessimistic. Something has been going on behind the scenes, but he says he's sparing me all the headaches since it's out of my control."

"That being the case we might as well enjoy a sunny day and the ride."

"Where's your uncle and your newly discovered cousin?"

"They're settling in and getting used to living with each other in northern Virginia. My uncle has already arranged a DNA test to confirm that he is Linh's father."

"It seems a bit strange to me that he's taken this on without proof," Kellie said.

Aaron shrugged. "He went through a lot just to travel back to Vietnam, and I didn't realize it until we were there that he had me tagging along for support in case he needed it. I'm not sure that the results really matter to him."

They rode out and through Potomac Village, following the route Kellie had been taken by the two young men. They reached a T intersection.

"Which way?"

"Left," Kellie said. As Aaron made the turn and pressed the accelerator, they drove along farmland and vegetation growing wild. Kellie wasn't surprised by the open land without any houses or businesses. In the sunlight, she saw why there weren't many lights during the night drive out.

Aaron slowed each time a sign indicated he was approaching a road in case Kellie instructed him to turn. She said nothing as they passed one road after another. Aaron pulled his foot off the accelerator, letting the car slow when he saw the road narrow and the cracked and potholed pavement ahead.

"Are you sure this is the way," Aaron said as the uneven and cracked pavement caused them to bob up and down in their seats.

"We're beyond the point where I recognize anything. It was dark and I couldn't see anything. For all I know, the windows may have been tinted and made everything even darker."

"Do you remember the car slowing and bouncing around like this?"

"The car was not a little Miata convertible. It was a luxury sedan so even if we were on this road, it probably would've felt different than this," Kellie replied.

The narrow road wound around large trees and between high mounds of wildly growing bushes. They passed two houses while on the road before it connected to a wider, well-maintained, and lined road.

"Don't get going too fast. I'd like to look for any long driveways if we come up on any," Kellie said.

"Not a problem. There isn't much traffic out here," Aaron answered.

There were a few more dwellings, but most were farmhouses, not the mansions of the kind Kellie hoped to see. "Have you ever driven out here," Kellie asked.

"Nope. I'm just as lost as you are. We're a little more than an hour out of the nation's capital but it feels like we're in Indiana or Kansas or someplace that far away," Aaron said.

"Up ahead, that row of trees," Kellie pointed. "Let's see if it borders a driveway."

Aaron checked the rearview mirror. There was nothing behind him. He slowed to ten miles an hour and looked for a driveway meeting the road. There were three-foot high reflectors on each side of the driveway to help drivers at night. A row of trees on either side of the driveway provided a canopy. Aaron steered the Miata to the edge of the pavement.

"Well, what do you think? Could this be it?"

Kellie stared down the driveway. "Let's keep going. There may be other places that have driveways like this."

Aaron got them back on the road. They passed another property with a long driveway, but the driveway was bordered by a stone wall leading up to a massive two-story home.

"We seem to have entered the land of the monied class," Aaron said.

"Even though these homes have large green spaces between them, they're too close together because it would be easy to see the lights at night."

Aaron drove the country roads for another half an hour.

"Can you find your way back to that first place where we pulled over?"

Aaron got them turned around. Backtracking and hoping that he remembered all the turns, he drove for forty-five minutes before seeing the stone wall bordering a driveway. "We're close. What do you want me to do when we get there?"

"Go back to that one with the trees and drive up to the house," Kellie answered.

Aaron did as he was directed. The tree-lined drive was a quarter mile long and opened onto a circular driveway in front of a two-story mansion. A small compact car was parked off to the side of the concrete steps leading to the enormous front double doors. Aaron stopped in front of the steps.

Kellie got out of the car, using her hand to shade her eyes, she looked up at the large stone structure and started to walk toward the small car.

"Can I help you," a middle-aged woman wearing an apron called out.

"I was just wondering who lives here," Kellie said.

"At the moment, no one lives here," the woman answered.

"Is the place for sale," Aaron hollered out.

"Not that I'm aware. You don't see a sign, do you?"

"No sign," Kellie said. "Does anyone use the house for anything? Is it rented out for special events or something?"

"My employers have a contract for us to come here regularly and maintain the property. That's all I know. I've been coming here for at least six months, and no one has lived here in all that time."

"Okay, thanks," Kellie said and got back in the car.

"Well, now what?"

"Back into the city," Kellie said. "Don't you think that's strange? Nobody lives there, but somebody is paying to make sure it's ready for use. I wonder who owns it. We should try to remember the address."

"I'm having a hard enough time just remembering how we got out here."

The late afternoon traffic around D.C. on a warm April afternoon had a way of drawing people out. It was well before rush hour and Aaron thought he was driving against the heavy flow but the roads leading into the city were busier than he expected.

"How about an early bite to eat before places get crowded," Aaron suggested.

"Sounds good," Kellie said with her head resting on the back of the seat.

Aaron reached across and gave her thigh a squeeze. Kellie's hand gently covered his. They let the music from the radio fill the air. Aaron didn't take the same route back and detoured over toward Bethesda where each block offered multiple choices for a place to dine.

Choosing a French bistro, they took advantage of the Happy Hour prices for both food and wine. Sitting outside, the shaded table was comfortable and tempted them to linger over the wine after the food was consumed.

Kellie resisted looking at her cell phone. It hadn't rung all day. They said no news is good news, but she wasn't convinced in this instance.

* * * * *

"How the hell could this happen and why didn't I know about this!"

Trish looked over her shoulder at the closed door to Senator Burke's office. It was one thing to see him angry about something, but he never reacted by yelling. Two young staffers looked in her direction from their desks. She shrugged.

"This is bullshit, and you know it," Senator Burke said into the phone. "We have the White House, and we have a majority in the Senate. We have a majority on every committee. This should've been an automatic confirmation," Burke wasn't yelling, but the person on the other end knew he was angry.

"Nathan, things like this happen," Senator Layton said, trying to soothe his young colleague.

"Things like this happen because of backroom deals and power plays," Senator Burke said.

"I'm not the chair of the Foreign Relations Committee. I don't control how that committee is run," Layton said.

"No, but you have a lot more influence with the chairman given your tenure and chairmanship of other committees. What deal did you or he make," Burke pressed.

"No deals. There're legitimate concerns about Ms. Liang's background, her commitment, her loyalty, and her experience."

"Bullshit. We confirm lots of people for positions that they have no business filling. Kellie Liang has more experience for this position than most would ever have," Burke hissed. "If her name was Smith and she had the same qualifications, this would've been a slam dunk confirmation. The committee's unfavorable recommendation kills the nomination. And you know that the White House won't fight for her."

"I'm sorry you're so upset. We have to move forward and find someone else," Senator Layton suggested.

Nathan Burke slammed the receiver into the cradle. His own party went against one of their own nominees. The palms of his hands on his desk, Nathan Burke stood leaning over his desk with his head down. He didn't see this defeat coming. He knew there were a few people within the party who opposed the nomination, but that opposition wasn't because of Kellie's experience or competency. It was because some junior senators did what they were told by senior senators. But for the committee to issue an unfavorable recommendation was outrageous.

Burke walked over to the leather sofa and slumped into the corner. He was Kellie's boss, and in a way, her sponsor. He'd have to break the news to her. Then what? He wouldn't blame her if she quit on the spot because of the disappointment. No, it would be because of something much more than that. She was the "go to" person for a lot of senate staffers from both parties when it came to China issues, yet the senators themselves had just stabbed her in the back. How could she give him and his colleagues all her effort and energy when it was clear that they neither respected her nor were they willing to reward her experience and efforts.

Burke shook his head as he recalled an old song. He remembered the lyric *smiling faces show no traces of the evil that lurks within*. In that moment, everything about the song and all it said was so true of the place where he worked by choice.

Sitting on the sofa, Burke's body was limp. He had been assuming that the next step would be confirmation by the full Senate. He had testified in favor of Kellie's nomination, worked to get assurances from the White House that the support was unwavering, and talked to colleagues to remove any doubts. Somehow, either it hadn't been enough or something beyond his control had happened. He was mentally and emotionally exhausted.

Burke thought about how he would explain the negative recommendation to Kellie when he had no explanation. There was no reason given and he had no rationale to give. He looked at the clock above the door. He decided he'd let Kellie have time for dinner before calling and ruining her evening.

* * * * *

After leaving the restaurant, Aaron and Kellie returned to her apartment. Enjoying the warm afternoon and evening air, Kellie had pulled the curtain open, allowing the remaining evening light to filter in and opened a window a few inches for some fresh air. Aaron sat in a chair watching Kellie's fingers work the keyboard at her small corner desk. While at the restaurant, Kellie borrowed a pen and wrote down the address of the mansion they had found. Now, she was trying to find out who owned the place. She searched state and county property records.

"I don't know if this is it, but it looks like the place is owned by a business, not an individual," Kellie said as she stared at the screen. "It's called the Glo-Ex Fund. It's a strange name."

"Maybe you can search the business name and get info about it," Aaron suggested.

Kellie started tapping the keyboard while Aaron sat back and watched her. She said nothing as her search took her from website to website. "I'm going in circles," Kellie said. "The mansion is owned by this Glo-Ex Fund. The Fund is a Delaware corporation, and its address takes me back to the mansion address. They have a designated agent for some corporate correspondences, but nothing that tells me anything about what they do."

"At least you know who owns the place."

"It doesn't really add much," Kellie said. She spent the next several minutes searching on the term "Glo-Ex", coming up with nothing. She sat back frustrated. She turned her head and looked down at the street.

"Oh shit!"

"What's the matter," Aaron asked, getting out of the chair, and moving to the window. He saw the dark sedan stopped on the street below. The door of the rear passenger door was already being closed and Aaron saw a man heading into the apartment building. "Do you know who these guys are?"

"Looks like the same car that I was in when I was taken out to that mansion we saw today. Well, I'm not going anywhere with them this time," Kellie said. The young men who came to the door the other night stayed with the car. Kellie looked closer to the building's entrance and saw just the top of a head disappear through the door. A minute later Kellie heard the chime of her doorbell.

Kellie looked through the peephole and opened the door a few inches and leaned against the wall. She saw Aaron approaching the door and used the hand behind the door to signal him to stop.

"Colonel, this is a surprise," Kellie said through the small opening of the door.

"I'm sorry to come unannounced, but there have been some important developments that I thought you should know right away," the large man said. "May I come in?"

"Actually, I have company." Kellie saw the slight rise of the Colonel's one eyebrow. "Interesting that you'd be surprised that I might have a life."

"No, it isn't that. It makes the conversation I was planning more complicated." The Colonel looked down the stairway and took a deep breath. "Would it be possible to talk for just a few minutes alone?"

Kellie understood that whatever caused the Colonel to come was important enough that he didn't want to leave without saying it. "At the moment, I can't think of anything you have to tell me that you can't say in front of my guest so come in." Kellie pushed the door open and let the Colonel walk past her.

Aaron eyed the large man who made him feel small. Aaron was impressed by the man's broad frame. Aaron guessed he was at least sixty years old, but solid through the shoulders and chest.

Kellie stood with her arms crossed and looked at Aaron. "Aaron, meet the Colonel. I don't know his name." She cocked her head to one side and waited a few seconds. "I guess we're still not on a first name basis, are we?"

Aaron decided to take the plunge. "Aaron Foster. I understand you had Kellie delivered to your place recently."

The Colonel nodded. "Mr. Foster, people call me Colonel. And, yes, people I work with wanted to meet Ms. Liang. But I'm aware that the two of you have been friends for several years."

Aaron confirmed the Colonel's statement by nodding. It confirmed something Kellie had told him. The file on Kellie had a lot of information in it including names of her closest friends or, perhaps, names of people she's had contact with regardless of whether they are close friends or just acquaintances.

The Colonel wasn't surprised by Kellie's less than warm welcome after the evening out in the countryside. "Let me get right to the reason for my dropping by. First, I was sorry to hear that the Senate will not confirm you for the State position that you are more than qualified to fill. It was a very poor decision by many of our elected officials."

Unconsciously, Kellie's eyes widened, and her arms tightened their grip, giving away the fact that the news was a surprise to her.

The Colonel hid his surprise that she hadn't been informed by this time in the evening. "Given this development, which must be extremely disappointing, those of us who met with you want to offer you an opportunity to work for us. Let me start by saying that we looked at what your government salary would've been had you been confirmed, and we would more than triple that amount. Obviously, there would be a generous benefits package to go along with the salary. We were serious when we said we believe that you have skills that are worth more than what the government can pay you."

Listening to the Colonel, Aaron looked at Kellie. She wasn't showing it, but he knew she was crushed by the news of being rejected for the State Department job. She had done so much after her father's criminal case, working to prove to everyone that what he did had nothing to do with her, and she had worked tirelessly for the senator. Under normal circumstances, Aaron knew that money alone wouldn't be enough to influence Kellie, but these weren't normal circumstances and the timing of the Colonel showing up only hours after the Senate action made Aaron suspicious.

"I hope you don't think I'm giving you an answer here, on the spot," Kellie said. "None of you provided me with any information. I don't know your names, the name of your organization, where your offices are, what you or your organization does."

"I appreciate the position you're in. Let's do this. I'll leave you and Mr. Foster. You know that you have a job opportunity waiting for you. Put your questions together and we'll meet in three days and answers will be provided," the Colonel said. He turned toward the door and took a step then turned back toward Kellie and Aaron, "sorry, I almost forgot. We can meet in three days, but that means you'll have to fly to Geneva for the meeting. You'd have to leave the day after tomorrow."

"I'm not paying to fly to Geneva so you can . . ."

"No, no. We'll fly you there. We don't expect you to pay for the trip, the accommodations or anything related to being in Geneva. Flight details for the trip will be provided to you tomorrow," the Colonel said. "I'll even agree to let you bring someone along if that'll make you feel better. We'll cover all expenses for anyone traveling with you."

Kellie gave Aaron a quick glance.

"I hope to see you in three days." The Colonel left the apartment.

Kellie went to the window and watched as the Colonel waited at the curb until the Cadillac pulled up. She saw the familiar young man open the door for the Colonel. She watched the car's taillights as the Cadillac headed toward Dupont Circle.

"Wow. Now that really was strange," Aaron said.

"To him and his group, I doubt it's at all strange. I think they're used to operating that way," Kellie said from the window.

"Normally, I'd say I know what you're going to do, but that news about what happened today throws everything up in the air. I wouldn't blame you for chucking everything and getting on that plane to Geneva."

Kellie plopped down on her sofa, folding her arms, and leaning forward as if she was in pain. "What angers me is to hear it from him. Why didn't Senator Burke call me?"

Just then, Kellie's cell phone buzzed. She picked it up from the coffee table and answered.

"Kellie, sorry it's taken me so long to call you. The day didn't go as we had hoped it would," Senator Burke began. "I've been calling around and making some inquiries about how this happened. I'm sorry to say that there's nothing I can do to reverse this. I hope you know I'm disappointed and angry at my colleagues for what they did to you."

"I had a visit from someone who told me the news," Kellie said flatly.

"What do you mean you had a visit?"

"Some guy who calls himself Colonel. He didn't give a name, but he stopped by and informed me about the results."

"Was he sent by one of my colleagues," Senator Burke asked.

"He didn't mention anything about anyone from the Hill. My nomination made some people curious about who I am and what I've done," Kellie said, debating whether to say anything about the real reason the Colonel broke the news. "I guess once he heard that the nomination was doomed, he wanted me to know that he could provide me with an alternative."

"You mean this guy, whoever he really is, offered you a job?"

"Nothing is firm, but there's a soft offer on the table," Kellie said.

"Kellie, I can't imagine your disappointment, but you know how much I value your work. I hope you'll remain on my staff. While I can't match what your salary would've been, I'll do what I can to make up some of the financial loss resulting from today's stupid decision."

"I appreciate that. Could you give me a few days to think about things," Kellie asked, knowing that if she did get on that plane, she'd need time off.

"Of course. Give me a call in a few days and let me know where things stand," Senator Burke replied. "I'll wait to hear from you."

Kellie ended the call. She looked up at Aaron who had remained still and listening. Kellie sat back and a smile slowly spread across her face.

Aaron knew that look on Kellie's face after years of being friends and something more. He turned and walked to the kitchen. He took a chilled bottle of white Burgundy and filled two glasses. "I'd open Champagne, but you don't have any."

Aaron handed Kellie her glass and they clinked their glasses together. "Here's to Geneva," Aaron said.

"Here's to Geneva," Kellie repeated. "As they say, when one door closes, another opens."

They sat and sipped their wine. "It's going to take a while to finish that bottle. You may as well spend the night," Kellie said.

With every sip, Kellie wondered what might happen after her trip to Geneva.

The End

Books by Timothy Trainer

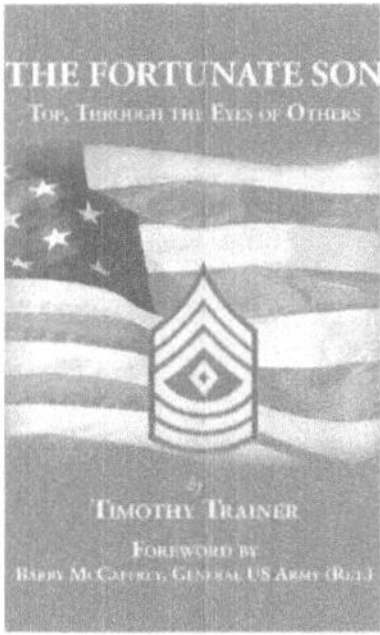

The Fortunate Son recounts the parallel lives of an army brat and a group of Vietnam veterans who intersect decades after the war. The veterans open up to me, the army brat, perhaps in a way they never have with their own families. Why? Through my father, Top, their First Sergeant, we have a common link. Over the years, we've gotten to know each other. They begin to understand the sacrifices of an army family. But, more importantly, they want me to understand how our family's sacrifice and my father's tour of duty in Vietnam with them, in the jungles, gave them confidence to believe they would make it home alive. **ISBN: 978-1-941049-73-0**

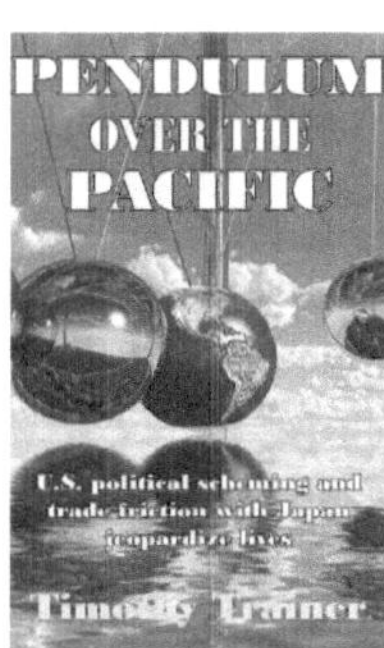

In **Pendulum Over the Pacific**, the President's nephew and advisor goes rogue, teaming with a hawkish U.S. Senator who is scheming to force Japan to lower its trade surplus with the U.S. The senator and nephew see Japan's trade surplus as a threat to the U.S. economy. They decide to manipulate facts and use history to their advantage to force the President to renegotiate an existing U.S.-Japan trade deal. It's the 1980s when Japan was the "bad" trade partner, before China's rise. **ISBN: 978-1-941049-92-1**

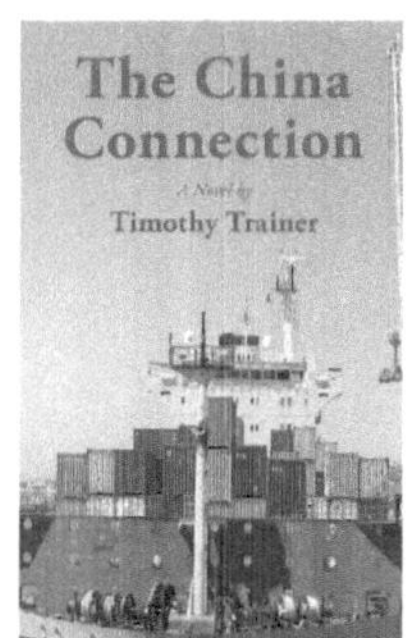

In **The China Connection**, it's a year after Hong Kong's reversion to China. Aaron and Kellie's dual purpose Hong Kong trip for business and pleasure descends into chaos when Kellie fails to deliver the blueprint Chinese entrepreneurs seek in hopes of greater riches in the U.S. market. After a day-long meeting, she awakes the next morning across the border in southern China without her travel documents. Aaron, while waiting for Kellie's return, is attacked in his hotel room. He panics.

Helpless, Aaron enlists the aid of Roger, a retired Customs attaché in Hong Kong. Roger questions the nature of the contents of millions of containers leaving Hong Kong and wonders how he can profit from it. Aaron and Roger cobble together a group of people to rescue Kellie from across the border. This small group of government and non-government people engage in questionable tactics to find Kellie. **ISBN: 978-1-956823-26-4**

About the Author

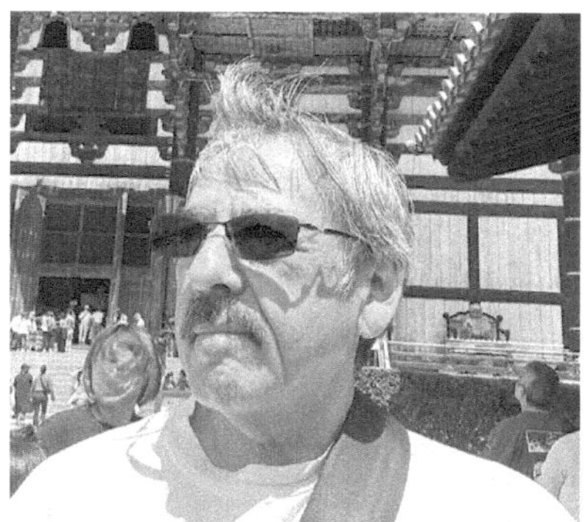 **Timothy Trainer** was born in Tokyo, Japan. An Army brat, he grew up on various Army posts then served a tour of enlistment in the Army. After his service, he earned multiple degrees. His advanced studies included a return to Japan to study in Tokyo for sixteen months.

After earning his law degree, he moved to the Washington, DC, area in 1987. His legal career focused on intellectual property issues with a more specific emphasis on combating international trade in infringing goods. He worked at multiple federal agencies that required extensive travel and consultations with foreign governments. In the private sector, he headed a DC-based trade association resulting in his work with INTERPOL, UN Economic Commission for Europe, and other international organizations. He has testified before congressional committees on several occasions. He was a private-sector advisor with a clearance to the US Department of Commerce from 2000-2020.

Joshua Tree Publishing published three prior books authored by Mr. Trainer. *The Fortunate Son: Top, Through the Eyes of Others* was published in 2017, and the novels, *The China Connection* (2023) and *Pendulum Over the Pacific* (2019). Mr. Trainer has authored numerous professional articles and co-authored a legal treatise for fifteen years. His book, *Potato Chips to Computer Chips: War on Fake Stuff* was published in 2015 by Thomson Reuters.